Reading
Borough Council
Working better with you

Reading Borough Libraries

Email:info@readinglibraries.org.uk
Website: www.readinglibraries.org.uk

Reading 0118 9015950
Battle   0118 9015100
Caversham 0118 9015103
Palmer Park 0118 9015106
Southcote 0118 9015109
Tilehurst 0118 9015112
Whitley 0118 9015115

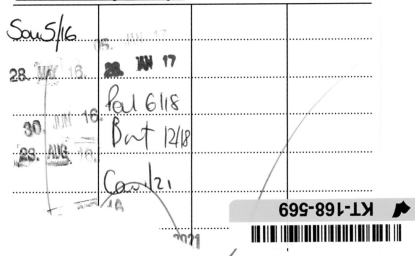

Sou 5/16
05. JAN. 17
28. MAY 16
28. JAN 17
30. JUN 16
Pal 6/18
Bnt 12/18
28. AUG 16
Cav /21
2021

KT-168-569

DEAD
SILENT

MARK ROBERTS was born and raised in Liverpool, and was educated at St Francis Xavier's College. He was a teacher for twenty years before becoming a writer. He is the author of *What She Saw*, which was longlisted for a CWA Gold Dagger.

Also by Mark Roberts

The Sixth Soul

What She Saw

The Eve Clay Thrillers

Blood Mist

Dead Silent

DEAD SILENT

MARK ROBERTS

First published in the UK in 2016 by Head of Zeus, Ltd.

9 7 5 3 1 2 4 6 8

A catalogue record for this book is available from
the British Library.

ISBN (HB): 9781784082925
ISBN (TPB): 9781784082932
ISBN (E): 9781784082918

Typeset by Adrian McLaughlin

For Kath and Ted, John, Deborah and Chris.

Look back over the past with its
changing empires that rise and fall,
and you can foresee the future too.

—MARCUS AURELIUS

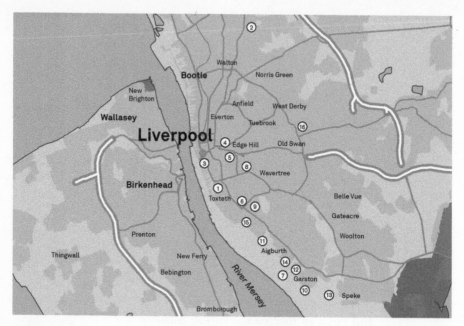

1	Croxteth Rd	5	University of Liverpool	9	Sefton Park	13	Trinity Rd Police Station
2	Aintree Racecourse	6	Ullet Road	10	Old Liverpool Airport	14	Jericho Lane
3	Merseyside Police HQ	7	Otterspool Tip	11	Aigburth Road	15	Lark Lane
4	Royal Liverpool Hospital	8	St Michael's Care Home	12	Cressington Park	16	The Park Hospital

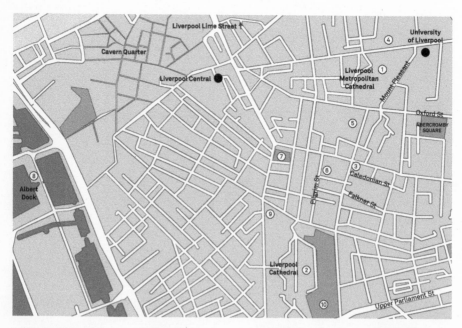

1	Liverpool Metropolitan Cathedral	3	The Philharmonic Pub	6	Pilgrim Street	8	The Albert Dock
		4	Brownlow Hill	7	St Luke Bombed Out Church	9	Upper Duke Street
2	Liverpool Cathedral	5	Hope Street			10	The Garden of St James

Prologue

Thursday, 24th October 1985

'Eve, thank you very much for coming to see me,' gushed Mrs Tripp. She smiled from behind her desk as Eve stood her ground at the door of the office.

Breathless, having run from the garden where she had been playing football with the big lads, Eve said, 'You're welcome, Mrs Tripp.'

The pleasantness of Mrs Tripp's manner caused Eve to look down and perform a simple trick to check she wasn't dreaming. She looked at the black trainers on her feet and told herself, *Squeeze your toes.* She squeezed her toes and confirmed. She was wide awake and it was all real.

'Come and take a seat, child,' encouraged Mrs Tripp, her newly permed hair crowned with an outsized yellow ribbon.

You're too old and fat, thought Eve, *to even try and look like that Madonna one.*

As she walked to the chair across from Mrs Tripp's desk, Eve smiled at the boss of St Michael's Catholic Care Home for Children, her feet firmly on the ground, her eyes locked on to the fat lady's gaze, and sat down.

'I like your Everton kit, Eve.'

She glanced down. Blue socks bunched at the ankles, soil- and grass-stained shins from the sliding tackle she had put in a few minutes earlier, white shorts and blue-and-white top.

'So do I,' said Eve. 'I just wish they weren't sponsored by Hafnia.'

'Why's that, Eve?'

'Hafnia's a canned-meat company. In Denmark. Ham. It's dead sly on the animals.'

'Oh, Eve, how many times have we had this out?' Mrs Tripp chuckled, smiling with her face but not with her eyes. 'You're a growing girl and you need to eat meat as part of a balanced diet.'

'As soon as I'm big enough—'

'Yes, I know! I know...'

Silence descended. Mrs Tripp looked as far into the distance as the four walls of her office would allow. Eve looked out of the window behind Mrs Tripp. In the sky above the River Mersey there were two horizontal red lines, as if a giant had drawn two bloody fingers across the grey autumnal clouds.

'My, how you've grown, Eve. I remember the first time you sat on that very chair across from my desk.'

'So do I.' Eve smiled. *It was bloody awful.* 'You're a very busy woman, Mrs Tripp. All those kids. All them staff. How can I help you?'

Mrs Tripp clapped her hands and laughed too loudly. 'It's not a question of how *you* can help *me*; it's a question of how *we* can help *you*.'

From the corner of the office came a solitary sigh. Eve looked and a tall, thin man with snow-white hair, dressed all in black except for a white dog collar, stepped out of the shadows into the muddy light of the room.

As he walked towards the desk, he closed the cover of a card file bulging with papers, a file Eve recognised as the one *they* kept on *her*. Behind his left ear she saw a thin hand-rolled cigarette. She looked back at his face, his unsmiling eyes fixed on her. She stared back but stood up as the priest advanced slowly, observing, thinking, nodding.

He placed the file down on Mrs Tripp's desk and, with the strangest sensation in her head that she had lived through this exact moment at another point in her life, Eve read the letters of her name in black felt-tip pen: 'EVETTE CLAY'.

'This is Father Anthony Murphy. Father Murphy, this is Evette Clay.'

Father Murphy placed the hand-rolled cigarette between his lips, flicked his thumbnail against the red tip of a match and lit the loose strands of tobacco. He took in a huge lungful of smoke and blew it out in a thin stream.

'Hello, Eve.' His voice rumbled, his speech posher than a TV newsreader.

'Good afternoon, Father Murphy.' She sat down again and Father Murphy remained standing.

'How old are you, Eve?' asked the priest.

'As old as the hills.' She laughed, alone.

'So I gather.'

'Seven and a half, if it's numbers you're after, Father.' She guessed the next question. 'And I've lived here for just over *one* year.'

'Up until when, you lived in St Claire's with Sister Philomena?'

'Yes.' Her exuberance deserted her. 'Did you know Sister Philomena, Father?'

'No.' A strand of hope, a connection, faded. 'Does that disappoint you, Eve?'

'Just because you're a priest, it doesn't mean you know all the nuns in the world. I was just wondering if—'

'Father Murphy isn't just a priest, as if that on its own isn't enough responsibility,' Mrs Tripp railroaded over her. 'He's a fully qualified doctor.'

'Oh!' said Eve, mustering as much enthusiasm as she could.

'I've come to see you, Eve.' Ash dropped on to Mrs Tripp's desk.

But I'm not ill, she thought, yet said nothing.

'It's fair to say, isn't it, Eve, there have been one or two episodes of odd behaviour,' said Mrs Tripp. Eve knew what was coming next. 'When you set off the fire alarm.'

'That was an accident. Jimmy Peace was there. He vouched for me.'

Mrs Tripp turned to Father Murphy. 'She's very popular with all the staff and the children. People make exceptions for her.'

'No they don't, they tell the truth,' said Eve.

'Christmas morning. You refused to get out of bed and open your presents.'

'I was sad because I couldn't stop thinking about Philomena. I did get up by lunchtime. And I'd opened my presents by tea. And then I just did what I do most days. I accepted that she's dead. And just got on with it. What else can I do?' The ball of tears behind her eyes threatened to break, but the voice inside her shouted, *'Don't you dare don't you dare don't you dare!'* And with that, a surge of anger and a beam of light. The memory of the toughest girl she'd ever met in the care system, Natasha Seventeen, and the last piece of advice she'd given her before she left St Michael's: *'Don't act depressed, kid, or they'll cart you off to the funny farm!'*

'Jesus Christ!' said Eve, all the bits and pieces falling into place.

'Eve, blasphemy isn't allowed here!'

'I'm saying my prayers. And I'm asking Jesus to give me strength.'

Eve stood up, turned away from Mrs Tripp and made herself as tall as she could in front of the priest. There was a glimmer of a smile behind the sternness in his eyes.

'Father Murphy, can I ask you a question, please?'

'Of course you can, Eve.'

'Are you one of those head doctors by any chance? What are they called now? Yeah. Are you a shrimp?'

'I believe the expression is *shrink*.' He took a drag on his cigarette, tapped a ball of ash on to the floor. Eve warmed to the man.

'Am I glad you're here, Father Murphy.'

'You are?'

'Yes. You're just the man we need round here.'

'I think it would be a really good idea to talk about the past,' said Mrs Tripp.

'Me too, me too,' said Eve. 'Thank you, Father Murphy.' She sat down across from Mrs Tripp. 'The past. Yes, let's talk about the past.'

She glanced up at Father Murphy, the lower half of his face concealed behind the hand in which he held his cigarette. She recalled a scene from a TV sit-com she had watched.

'Mrs Tripp, tell me about your childhood,' said Eve.

The only things redder than Mrs Tripp's face were the lines in the sky above the River Mersey.

'Go and finish your game of football before it gets dark,' said Father Murphy. 'I've heard about your great loss and I know enough of Sister Philomena to know she'd be completely and utterly proud of the way you are coping at such a tender age. God bless you, Eve. We will meet again. Please know, you will always be in my prayers.'

'Thank you, Father, for understanding.'

He smiled, made the sign of the cross over her head.

The silence in the room behind her as she made her way to the door felt like treacle.

Eve closed the door after herself, checked the corridor. It was empty. She waited.

'You flicked ash on to my desk and my carpet!' complained Mrs Tripp.

'And you have wasted my time,' replied Father Murphy. 'Which is the larger sin? She's perfectly sane in spite of all the things she has had to endure. She's a credit to Sister Philomena, who saved her from the powers of darkness and moulded her into the child she is.'

Silence. As Father Murphy's footsteps approached the door of the office, Eve absorbed his words.

She hurtled down the corridor, running faster than she ever had.

Running. Running. Running like the Devil was at her heels.

Part One
Darkness

The Tower of Babel (2)
by Pieter Bruegel the Elder (1563)

There is no mercy at work in the universe.
The First Born knelt at the foot of his bed, staring at a big shiny picture of a painting in a book resting on the top blanket. Just as he had been ordered to do. He looked at it through the splayed fingers and thumbs of both hands, one digit for every year he had been alive.

The Tower of Babel (2) 1563. He rolled the words around in his head.

P-i-e-t-e-r Br-u-e-g-e-l. He spelled out the painter's name printed underneath the title.

He knew he had to get it right or the voice would be angry with him again. The voice swam inside his head, an awful voice that he was forced to listen to every day, for as long as he could remember.

'There is no mercy at work in the universe. God will never be pleased with man's achievements. Nor will God ever tolerate being outshone by man. *Look at the darkness of the earth from which the tower rises up.*'

The First Born tried humming to drown the noise inside his head but it only caused the voice to rise up louder, stronger, angrier.

'Look at the way the darkness of the earth spills on to the water and engulfs the boats. There is no escape. The people who built the tower cannot be seen because they are hiding in the structure that they have built. Look at the arches of the many, many windows that run along each level of the ascending tower.'

The First Born felt the blood drain from his legs, arms and head. He clutched at the blanket on the bed to stop himself falling sideways on to the floor.

'Speak the truth!' commanded the voice inside his head.

The First Born knew the words he had to speak off by heart. 'God can come down at any moment and punish me for my sins just as he came down and punished the people who built the Tower of Babel. They tried to hide. But there is no hiding place from God.' He felt something thumping inside his chest, the swelling of tears behind his eyes.

And then there were more words that the First Born didn't grasp, a question that the voice asked over and over again.

'Look at the picture. Is this the beginning of babble?'

The First Born looked at the picture, even though it scared him.

'Look at the way the tower reaches into the sky, sending the handiwork of mankind into the skirt of heaven. Look at the way it pierces the clouds. Look at the way the top of the unfinished tower glows red like fire.'

The First Born removed his fingers from the picture and looked again. The clouds at the top seemed like smoke pouring from a burning building. He tried to see people hiding in the blackened windows, to find some sign of human life, but all he saw was darkness. It was so lonely there. He shivered.

'This is what God does to mankind when mankind works together and builds a unified structure. In the eyes of God, this is sin. You are a sinner. And you have shown me you understand that sin has one consequence. Death.'

The First Born closed his eyes and gave the expected reply. 'True Language died. Babble was born.'

The other voice was now calm and even. 'There is no mercy at work in the universe.'

Thursday,
20th December 2018

1

2.38 am

'*He's been slaughtered.*'

The old woman's words rolled around DCI Eve Clay's head as she sprinted from her car to the Sefton Park entrance of Lark Lane, where Scientific Support officers had already sealed off the scene of the crime.

'DCI Clay!' she told the constable running the log at the top of the lane.

'*He's been slaughtered.*' That's what the old woman had apparently said to the witnesses who had discovered her wandering at the junction of Pelham Grove and Lark Lane. But that was all.

The moon hung low in the clear sky. Sharp light fell on the glass façades of the shops and restaurants on either side of Lark Lane and, for a moment, Clay imagined she was running down a locked-in corridor of ice.

Closing in on a group of people under a streetlight, Clay slowed to read the scene. A female constable was crouched on her haunches next to an old woman lying in the recovery position on a pair of padded coats on the pavement. Looming above her, DS Gina Riley was deep in conversation with a couple, a man who looked like he'd been made from rubber tyres, and a beanpole woman. They put Clay in mind of Popeye and Olive Oyl.

'DCI Eve Clay.' She showed her warrant card. 'You're the couple who found her?'

'Yes,' said the man.

The woman looked at Clay with pleading eyes.

'Thank you for helping her. Do you know the old lady's name?'

'No!' They answered in one voice.

'Do you know where she lives?' asked Clay.

'Pelham Grove, I'm pretty sure,' said the woman.

'Which side?'

'I've seen her coming in and out of the even side,' said the man.

'But she didn't appear to be physically injured?'

'Not until she fitted and smacked her head on the pavement.'

Clay stooped to take a closer look at the old woman, at the fresh wound on her forehead. The coats had been carefully laid under her body to stop her temperature from plummeting on contact with the freezing pavement, and the recovery position was neatly executed. She looked up at the witnesses.

'Are you care workers?' They looked at each other as if Clay was a gifted psychic. 'You've made a really good job of this.' She stood up to her full height. 'So, what happened?'

'She was wandering around in the middle of the road. We approached her and she said, *He's been slaughtered.* Then she wandered here, to this spot, had a seizure and hit the deck. We called 999. She stopped fitting after a minute and fifteen. We timed it. When she stopped fitting, we put her in the recovery position.'

'You didn't see anyone else around?' asked Clay.

'No,' said the man, calmly and firmly.

'Take me to where you think she lives,' said Clay.

A police car, siren off, blue light turning, sat outside The Albert on the corner of Lark Lane and Pelham Grove. Clay followed the man and woman into Pelham Grove and took in the whole scene with a 360-degree turn.

DS Karl Stone was getting dressed in a white protective suit at the back of a Scientific Support van.

Facing each other on either side of Pelham Grove, the tall Victorian terrace houses looked eerie in shadows and moonlight.

'Used to be large single dwellings, family homes when families were big,' said Stone. 'Most of the houses are flatted now, mainly student accommodation.'

Clay did a mental date check: the middle of December. 'A witness famine.' She sank deeper into the logic of the time and place, scanned the houses picked out by the Scientific Support van's Night Owl light. 'Looks like she's walked out of her home, away from the scene.' Clay combed the pavement with her torch, but there were no obvious bloodstains.

An ambulance siren drew closer at speed, giving Clay an unpleasant itch under her wrist. *Not much time.*

She dressed quickly in a protective suit. Lights came on in bedrooms as people woke up to the gathering police presence on their doorsteps. Her heart sank. Whatever had happened, it looked like those neighbours who were still in residence had slept through it.

'Who's the *he?* Who's *been slaughtered?* Husband? Brother? Father? Son?' A thought hit her hard. 'The killer's timed this so that the students wouldn't be around.'

As DS Bill Hendricks hurried into Pelham Grove, he called, 'The paramedics are loading her on to a trolley stretcher.'

'DS Riley!' called Clay. 'You go in the ambulance with the old woman. Call me when she comes round.'

'I got it!' Riley shouted back.

'DCI Clay!' The man's voice was loud and urgent. He was facing a house near the centre of the terrace. 'We're pretty certain this is the one.'

Clay hurried along the pavement and up the stone steps. She reached down to the edge of the door and gave it a shove with her gloved fingers.

The door opened a few centimetres. A strange pattern of light emerged within the house.

She turned to the witnesses. 'I think you're right. This is it.'

DS Bill Hendricks and DS Karl Stone were behind her. 'You've given your details to the WPC?' They nodded. 'Thank you for your assistance.'

'We won't breathe a word to anyone about any of this,' said the woman.

'I'd appreciate that,' said Clay. 'Because if there has been a murder, my guess is the killer lives around here.' She registered their astonishment, allowed the uncomfortable notion to sink in. 'You've helped the old lady. Help me with your ongoing silence.'

2

2.42 am

Clay opened the front door a little wider and eyed the door bell covered with two beige sticking plasters in an uneven X. The home of a person or people who did not expect visitors.

The flickering light inside the property grew brighter.

The door of the neighbouring house opened. A middle-aged man, blinking himself awake, asked, 'What's going on?'

'Who lives here, sir?' Clay asked him, holding up her warrant card.

'Professor Leonard Lawson and his daughter Louise.'

'Karl,' she said to Stone, 'talk to this gentleman, please. DS Hendricks, I'd like you to come inside the house with me.'

She looked around, saw DS Terry Mason and his assistant Sergeant Paul Price with two large evidence bags crammed with aluminium stacking plates.

Clay pushed the door open wide.

As the hall came into view, her eyes were drawn to the top of the staircase. A faulty white electrical appliance appeared to be casting out bands of intense light from a room upstairs.

She took in the whole scene. To the right of the staircase, and in the doorways leading into the rooms downstairs, nothing appeared to stand out.

Clay turned her attention back to the light at the top of the stairs.

'OK, Terry, plate up the floor from the front door to the top of the stairs. We're aiming for wherever that light's coming from.'

'He's been slaughtered!'

Within seconds, Mason and Price were at the stairs, three plates down, three steps forward, moving with acrobatic precision. With moth-like compulsion to get directly to the light, Clay was grateful for their speed but also tempted to call, *Go faster, faster, faster!*

She stepped into the hall, followed the Scientific Support officers on to the stairs. She looked up at the light and called, 'Police! Anyone there, call out to me! We're coming up the stairs!'

Light bounced from a bedroom and shadows danced inside the light. Mason and Price were on the upstairs landing, heading towards it.

The dizzy days of Clay's youth flashed through her mind, school discos and rock concerts. 'It's a strobe light!' she said. And the strangeness of such an item in this place made her wonder out loud, 'But why?'

'We'll soon find out,' said Hendricks, at her back.

'Paul?' DC Price looked at DS Mason. 'As soon as we've plated up here, I'll carry on upstairs while you go down and look for a point of entry.'

They were at the bedroom door and Clay was at the top of the stairs.

'OK!' said Clay. 'Stop there! Thank you.'

'Eve!' Stone called from the front door. 'The neighbour told me he's been asleep since ten o'clock last night. Didn't hear or see a thing. Doesn't know jack.'

The father? thought Clay. *He's been slaughtered.*

Her senses flared into life.

'Karl, as soon as DC Price has finished putting the plates downstairs, I want you to start rooting through the house with him and looking for any information you can about the Lawsons.'

Clay turned her attention back to the bedroom door.

Light. Bright, fast-moving, repeating patterns of pure white light poured from the bedroom, swamping the darkness of the rectangular upstairs landing.

At the bedroom door, DS Mason handed her the stepping plates inside an evidence bag.

She looked at him. 'Go and prepare downstairs.'

Deeper inside the house, Clay heard air rattling in the pipes. The screw at her centre turned, clarity increased and she was compelled to get inside the bedroom.

The faintest smell of blood sharpened in her nostrils.

She opened the bedroom door wide enough to place down two plates, sufficient for her to stand inside the room and look at what had happened under the relentless white light of the stroboscope.

She glanced back at Hendricks and caught her own reflection in an oval mirror on the landing wall. The pattern of light transformed her into something other than her normal self. Her tall, thin body hidden by a white protective suit, her black hair concealed by a hood, only her face visible.

Turning back to the bedroom door, Clay heard her own voice – 'Call out if you can hear me?' – even though she knew in her heart there would be no sign of life, that she had arrived at a place made forever different because a killer had called there. The wind whispered 'Murder' as it pushed on the window frame.

She stooped, pressed her little finger to a spot near the bottom of the door and began to open it.

3

2.46 am

Clay looked through the widening gap in the doorway and counted to three as strobe light bombarded the walls and ceiling and darkness drummed inside its stark white rhythm.

She entered the room and her eyes settled on the right-hand corner and the source of the disorientating light. The effect was bizarre.

An old man's naked body appeared to hang upside down in mid-air. His arms stretched straight up to the ceiling. His legs, bent at the knee, feet parallel to his hands, mirrored the arms. The flat of his back was half a metre from the carpet, a human being as a crooked U, defying gravity.

She took out plates from the evidence bag and, advancing towards the corpse, laid them down and stepped on them.

'Come in, Bill. Take a video on your phone as you do so! I want a filmed record of what the killer wanted us to see.'

He stepped in behind her and she felt a crumb of comfort, sensing his tall, physical presence. 'I'm filming!'

'I need to get closer. I need to know what's really going on here.'

As she stepped nearer, Clay made out the shape of a long, thin line above Leonard Lawson's body, a line that came and went under the bullying light. She reached out her right hand and with her index finger touched the solid shape of the line.

It felt like wood. She looked closer, at his wrists and his ankles, and saw that he was tied to a wooden pole by dark, ragged rope.

His head lolled back, thin wisps of long, grey hair dancing in the mean breeze that leaked through the old wooden window frame behind his suspended corpse.

She concentrated on his face and head. His eyes showed just red-streaked white, the irises having rolled to the back of his head. On the left-hand side of his skull there was a vivid mark, where a blunt object had smacked him with force.

Clay looked for the beginning and the end of the pole from which he was hanging. She traced the top of the pole to the corner where two walls met and the bottom to the base of the bed beneath the mattress.

Closing her eyes, she digested the details in her mind and prepared to empty her senses to focus long and hard on the whole picture: Leonard Lawson strung up like a beast, his body staged above a strobe light.

But the shadow-rich cave in her own head was invaded by the patterns of light and dark that had battered her retina. She opened her eyes and looked again.

The light fell with such energy and recklessness that it stripped death from the old man's features. It turned his face into a shifting façade of extreme emotions, almost within the same second. In silence, he laughed hysterically then veered into an ecstasy that morphed into absolute madness.

'What's that?' Clay asked, her skin crawling, noticing another piece of wood that had been shielded by the thick pole from which Leonard Lawson's body was suspended. She angled her head and drove a beam of torchlight on to this other length of wood. Then she crouched on to her haunches and checked his bare back.

'We'll have to turn the strobe off and the main light on.'

She reached down to the electrical socket on the skirting board and plunged the room into virtual darkness. Second-hand streetlight seeped in through a gap in the curtains and Clay used her torch to make it back to the door.

'Jesus! What have you seen, Eve?' Hendricks asked.

'Have a look for yourself. Are you ready?'

Clay turned on the main light and called central switchboard.

'DCI Clay. Pelham Grove off Lark Lane is now a murder scene. I want as many officers as we've got in and around the Sefton Park area.'

4

2.50 am

Stone weighed up the spaces downstairs in the Lawsons' house, noticed that there was no sign of disturbance or violence.

Starting in the hallway, he gained an overview of all the downstairs rooms with the lights on and doors wide open. In the living room at the front of the house, DC Price brushed the door with black fingerprint dust.

Stone moved to the next room. Door open and light on, the room was full of books and dominated by a huge walnut desk on which sat an old Imperial typewriter. Professor Lawson's study.

Next to the study, Stone discovered a small parlour with a three-piece suite and a coffee table; the best furniture so far, from a bygone age when perhaps the Lawsons received visitors.

At the kitchen door, Stone listened. From upstairs, Clay and Hendricks's voices travelled through the fabric of the building and Mason moved around with stealth and speed.

A lightbulb hung from the ceiling, thinly disguised by a brown lightshade. He turned the kitchen light on and off and on again and saw a stove from the 1970s and a 1960s Formica-topped dining table and chairs.

Coldness sailed into Stone's face from the back door as he looked for a point of entry. He counted: sixteen rectangular pieces of glass in the wooden door, each of which appeared whole and untouched. The wind crawled under the door and round the top and side, whispering, hissing.

Stone looked at the door handle, the skeleton key in the mortise lock and the pane of glass closest to it. He clicked his torch on and explored the edges of the pane. Fine flakes of gloss paint littered the ledge, sitting among sand-like grains of glass.

He turned the key in the lock and opened the door, calling, 'Pricey, can you stop what you're doing and come here right now!'

Brush and dust pot in hand, DC Price marched across the kitchen.

'What have you got, Karl?'

'Put your hand by that bottom ledge.' Stone pointed at the glass rectangle nearest the lock. As Price put his brush into the dust pot to free up his right hand, Stone crouched outside the kitchen door. 'Don't move your hand!'

Stone pressed both index fingers into the top corners of the glass rectangle and it moved, slowly at first, then falling easily into Price's hand.

'Neat and tidy. Taken out and put back in its place,' said DS Stone.

Holding the glass by its top two corners, DC Price held it up to the light and examined the surface. 'Not that neat, not that tidy.'

Stone took the glass from Price and saw a set of clear fingerprints. He handed it back and said, 'We need to get this off to be processed against the national fingerprint database right now.'

On his iPhone, Stone opened Messages, Contacts and texted Clay: *Eve, we have a point of entry, the back door of the house leading out from the kitchen. There are clear prints on the glass. If they belong to the killer and he has a record, he might as well have left his name and address.*

He pressed send and watched Price, in the hall, slip the glass into a plastic evidence bag and hand it to a constable at the front door.

Stone walked into the front living room and looked around.

With no pictures on the walls, an old-fashioned green velvet three-piece suite and a basic television set, it felt miserly.

His phone vibrated. 'Clay Msg' with attachment. He opened the text and paused mid-breath. Not quite believing his eyes, he blinked and looked again.

It was a picture of Leonard Lawson, under the ceiling light; dead, naked, hanging upside down like a slaughtered beast, hands and feet tied to the pole.

Price entered the room with his brush and pot of fingerprint dust. 'What's wrong with your face?' he asked.

Stone turned the screen so Price could see it.

'Upstairs, right now?'

Stone nodded. 'I guess we drew the long straws tonight.' He looked at the photo again. 'What's that?' he said out loud, noticing something he'd overlooked in the initial shock.

'What are you looking at?' asked Price.

Stone zoomed in on a single detail around the old man's torso, isolating it, making it bigger. 'I've never seen anything like that before. Have you?'

5

2.54 am

Under the plain ceiling light, Clay took a series of photographs of Leonard Lawson's body, with several close-ups of the spear on which he was impaled. The top end of a narrow dark-brown shaft stuck out from his shoulder. The central section of the shaft was buried inside his chest cavity and the top end with the bloody metal point protruded from the base of his back rib cage.

'Ten to four,' said Clay.

'How do you mean, Eve?' asked Hendricks.

'If the top and the tip of the spear were the hands of a clock...' She drew a large circle in the air, corresponding to the position of the spear. 'It's pointing at ten to four.'

She looked at the point of the spear. Two roughly cut triangular sections of metal, soldered together, and the base of the triangle hammered into the wood on which it sat alongside small tacks.

'It's home-made but well made,' said Clay, her heart sinking, the chance to follow up a massive lead through commercial producers as dead as dust. The shaft itself looked old, an offcut, and could have been plucked from a skip on the street by any passer-by.

The metal point was streaked with lines of Leonard Lawson's blood and a small pool of blood had dripped on to the worn carpet.

'OK,' said Clay to herself. 'The bigger picture.'

She walked to the bedroom door and looked at the room as a whole, in a stable light, from the point of view of someone entering.

She was struck by the unmade double bed, its blankets and sheets bunched up near the foot, a pair of blue pyjamas folded neatly on the pillow. Her pulse quickened as she imagined the old man, stripped bare in his bedroom and knowing he was going to die. She imagined his terror, his confusion, and wondered sadly what his last conscious thought had been.

In the alcove beside the double bed was an old-fashioned dressing table with a trio of mirrors. The right-hand mirror had been closed over to cover half of the larger central mirror, leaving the left-hand mirror free to reflect what it caught in the room.

'Anything?' asked Hendricks.

'Yes,' said Clay. 'The left-hand half of the mirror is reflecting the torso of Leonard Lawson's body, upside down, and the entire spear entering and leaving his body. Go and position yourself so that you can see what shows up in the open left-hand mirror.'

Hendricks moved to the window.

'I can see his head and his arms reaching up.'

Clay moved towards the dressing table and carefully opened the right-hand mirror to the same angle as the left-hand one. She moved to the right. 'I can see his legs suspended from the pole and his feet poking up to the ceiling.' She stepped back. 'Three mirrors on a dressing table and a multitude of ways of seeing one man's death.'

Hendricks explored the space in front of the window.

'What are you looking for?' asked Clay.

He pointed at the dressing table in the alcove. 'It should be here!' He pointed at the window. 'To take full advantage of the light coming in from the window. I think the killer's moved the dressing table.' He looked down at the threadbare carpet. 'But it's so worn, I can't see any indentations from its feet.'

'To reflect his human sculpture,' said Clay. The words lit a fast-burning fuse in her head. *Death as a work of art.*

As Clay walked to the dressing table, she asked, 'What's the word, the name? When a painting's in three linked panels?'

She recalled such an item in the chapel of St Claire's, the place she'd called home from when she was a baby until the age of six. It was golden and decorated with angels. 'Triptych.' She answered her own question with a word buried deep in child-hood memory.

There were four sections in the wooden body of the dressing table. Two long rectangular drawers in the centre and two hinged doors on either side.

She opened the doors and drawers and they were all empty.

'Bill?' She looked at Leonard Lawson. 'Why did he keep his wife's dressing table and none of her personal belongings?'

'Let's talk to his daughter about her mother when she comes round.'

His words prompted Clay to replay events in reverse.

Louise Lawson was in the back of an ambulance with Gina Riley. She had had an epileptic fit on the street as she escaped from the scene of her father's murder. If she suffered from pho-tosensitive epilepsy, it figured that she had been in her father's room at some point and must have seen his body.

'I wonder what state she's going to be in when she does come round,' she said, sadness flooding through her.

In the central mirror, Clay's attention was seized by a discol-ouration on the wall opposite Leonard Lawson's bed. She turned and saw it was a clean rectangle, the grime on the wallpaper around it defining the shape.

'Terry! Bring a tape measure!' she called. She pointed at the space. 'The killer's taken a trophy, a picture.' Terry Mason's foot-steps seemed to echo as he came to the room. 'It's the first thing the old man saw when he woke up in the morning and the last thing he saw at night.' Mason appeared. 'Terry, can you measure the dimensions. Missing picture. But of what?'

6

2.59 am

Clay looked at Leonard Lawson's body, inverted and dehumanised in death, and focused on what it told her about the perpetrator. So much attention to detail. So little blood. Someone who'd clean the toilet with a toothbrush, maybe, beneath a framed cross-stitch on the bathroom wall: 'Cleanliness is next to Godliness'.

'The picture's fifty centimetres wide and thirty-five centimetres deep,' said Mason, heading to the door.

Clay committed this fact to memory and resisted the urge to close Professor Lawson's eyelids and give him back a crumb of dignity.

Clicking on her torch, she shone the light into his face. Leonard Lawson's mouth was partially open, revealing long incisors and canine teeth; all the back teeth were missing. His swollen tongue was trapped between his front teeth. She placed an index finger on his lower lip and pushed down, shining the light inside his mouth.

You bit down on your tongue as he smacked you on the head, she thought, observing the small pool of blood and spit on the floor beneath his mouth.

Somewhere in the house, the steady clicking of a camera resumed. To Clay's ears it had the rhythm of a faulty clock, fast-forwarding through time.

She saw something narrow and white in the professor's mouth cavity and trained the light on it. It ran around the top of his tongue and disappeared down the sides. String.

'Bill, look at this.' She peered at the top of his tongue and made out a knot in the string. 'The killer tied the old man's tongue,' she said. 'I'm pretty certain Leonard Lawson knew his killer.'

'The attention to detail?' asked Hendricks.

She stepped back, looked at the whole scene again. 'And I don't think the killer acted alone.' Now that the initial shock was ebbing, the detail started to amaze her. 'It's too complex. The staging of the body. The strobe light. The use of mirrors.'

Outside, the wind whipped through the street, sent a can rattling along a gutter and filled the house with what sounded like a painful dying breath.

Clay phoned Karl Stone and he picked up immediately.

'Jesus,' said Stone. 'I got the picture. *Who* or *what* are we looking for?'

'You're on the nail, Karl,' replied Clay. 'Dig up an address book, scraps of paper, anything. Look for any contacts of Leonard Lawson's or his daughter's, Louise. *Anything* to report?'

'He stuck the glass pane back into the door at the point of entry.'

A narrative rolled through Clay's mind. *He? They? They came in through the kitchen door, walked up the stairs, entered Professor Lawson's bedroom, killed him, set him up in the corner like a hunted and trapped beast, set up a strobe light, took the only picture from the wall, walked back down the stairs and out of the house. How long? Fifteen, twenty minutes? Most of the work took place post-mortem. If they'd simply killed him, they'd have been in the house less than two minutes.*

She took out her iPhone and took three photos of the wall behind Leonard Lawson's body. She texted the images to Riley, with a message: *Gina, please ask Louise what the picture was in her father's bedroom.*

'What are you thinking, Bill?'

'The words *medieval* and *torture*. Motive. Sex? No. Money? No. It's a revenge killing. This is the work of a highly intelligent and sophisticated monster. Looks to me like they are sending him to hell.'

'We're looking for someone human but uniquely inhuman.' She laughed, suddenly, bitterly and, as quickly, fell silent.

'What's so funny?'

'The way the body's staged, it's going to be a nightmare to move.' As she spoke, she felt lightheaded and hot, as if she'd stepped into the heads of the perpetrators. 'From a forensic point of view. How are we going to get Leonard Lawson's body to Dr Lamb in the mortuary without corrupting the evidence?'

7

3.00 am

The first of her senses to stir in the darkness was hearing. The woman heard the sound of hissing and, in the loop between wakefulness and sleep, imagined a snake winding through the gloom towards her.

Light. In two lines. One vertical, where the curtains hung with the narrowest parting, and one below her bed, at the base of the bedroom door. The door led into the hall of their flat, with the bathroom at the end of it, where the hissing came from, the hissing of jets of water.

The woman pictured the shower head and the lines of red-hot water cascading down his body. She didn't know how her husband stood such fierce heat.

The bedside table held three items. An alarm clock; it was three in the morning. A bottle of sleeping tablets. A novel about a good woman escaping a bad marriage.

Her husband coughed as the hissing jets of water died. She imagined the tropical conditions in the bathroom, the clouds hanging in the air, condensation running down the walls and mirrors, pools forming on the floor.

But her head was muddy with Zolpidem and to challenge him – 'Where have you been while I slept?' – would involve talking and she didn't want to hear his voice.

His footsteps came closer to the bedroom door; her dread increased with every one.

The bathroom she could face in the morning.

Again.

He stopped at the bedroom door and she wondered why he was pausing, this man who never stopped. He switched off the light in the hall; as the door opened, darkness followed him in.

She was already on her side, eyes shut, feigning the breathing of deep sleep.

She felt the fabric of his pyjamas as his form fitted around hers, touching but only by the slightest degree. The dampness of his hair gave off an aroma like wet leaves and the heat pouring from his body created an unpleasant warmth that seeped beneath her skin.

He smelled like his father when he was alive.

But the thing that made her most want to give up the pretence of sleep was his heartbeat. Like a drum played by an overactive child on a mission to drive the adult world insane, his heart banged at his ribs and she could feel it as wave after wave.

'Are you awake?' he asked. 'No.' He answered his own question. 'Working. Working in my shed. Fixing things I don't have time to fix in the day because I am busy fixing other things in the day. You have seen me, have you not?'

Your shed? she thought. *Your precious shed.*

She opened one eye, looked at the clock, prayed for sleep and hoped for morning and to find him quiet beside her, cold where he'd been hot, his heart still where it had been pounding, dead where he had been alive, ready to rot away with his father.

And that is the day when I take a sledgehammer to it and turn it to kindling.

8

3.30 am

From the eighth floor of the Royal Liverpool Hospital, DS Gina Riley looked west, across the lights of the city centre to the Wirral Peninsula and its blanket of snow, heading inland from the North Atlantic.

'Where am I?' asked the elderly lady in the bed.

'Hello, Miss Lawson.' Riley sat on the chair near her head and in her eye line. 'You're in the Royal Hospital. My name is Gina Riley. I'm a police officer with Merseyside Constabulary.' There was a softness in her voice that made her words sound like a lullaby. She began to guide her, step by agonising step, backwards through recent events. 'I came here with you in an ambulance when you were unconscious.' Riley watched as cold recall manifested itself on Miss Lawson's face. 'You had an epileptic seizure on Lark Lane. You hit your head on the pavement—'

Miss Lawson raised her left hand, a woman seemingly sick to death of life, asking for silence with a small gesture. Riley noticed the friendship bracelet on her right wrist, three intertwined strands, gold, blue and green.

Her eyes closed. 'Oh no! No! No, no, no...' Miss Lawson's hands came together and Riley placed a hand across them.

'I'm so sorry, Miss Lawson.'

Her lips moved and a small, almost inaudible sound came out on her breath.

'Speak up, please, Miss Lawson.' Riley pressed her ear closer to Miss Lawson's mouth and listened hard.

'Father?' said Miss Lawson. 'He's been slaughtered? I'm not dreaming?'

'I'm afraid not.'

In spite of the dressed wound to her head and the NHS gown, there was a natural refinement to the woman that said, 'Dignity at all times, dignity at all costs'.

'Is there anyone I can send for, anyone who can come and comfort you?'

'No one. Who? Who can comfort me?' She seemed utterly perplexed, and her eyes filled. Riley imagined the slow-burning horror of her dawning realisation. 'My God. When I woke, I thought, a dream, a bad dream, a nightmare, my father... God, no...' She clapped her hand to her mouth as if to press down a scream rising within her and her eyes widened. Noises sounded in her throat, inarticulate expressions of terror and amazement. Slowly the mounting tension in Miss Lawson's body reached a peak and she wept silent tears, tears that Riley guessed she would shed for the rest of her days.

Louise Lawson turned her face away. Her whole body convulsed with sobs, but the only sounds she made were fractured in-breaths.

She held the friendship bracelet between her thumb and fingertips. 'Why? Why my father?'

'Miss Lawson?' Riley leaned in to her. 'Look at me. Please. I know how dreadful this must be for you, but I need you to look at something for me.' Miss Lawson stared at her as if she had suddenly turned into an unspeakably cruel monster. Riley pushed on. 'Will you look at a picture for me?'

She pulled up the photo gallery on her iPhone and opened the shot of the wall opposite Leonard Lawson's bed.

'Miss Lawson, I want to show you a picture.' She turned the screen towards her and slowly drew the image into her line of vision. 'Can you see the picture?'

'Yes.'

'What is it a picture of?'

'It's... it's... his bedroom... where... the wall opposite his bed... but... it's missing... his picture...'

'The picture on your father's wall, Miss Lawson. It was a picture of your mother?'

'No... no, not Mother. It was the tower...'

'The tower?'

Miss Lawson looked at Riley with pleading eyes. 'Please don't... please... please don't make me relive it... because I can't... think... remember... hope... no hope. The house... Think straight... I... I can't... I keep seeing him... like that... the horrible flashing...' She jabbed a finger into space. 'It's like it's there, right there in front of me.'

'It's not there, Louise. You're safe with me. You're in a state of shock. Your mind's playing tricks on you. Who can I get for you? Louise, do you have a relative? A neighbour? A friend?'

'No one.'

A cold wash of sorrow passed through Riley. She looked at the woman, the decades that had lined her face, and the thought that she was utterly alone in her greatest hour of need made her unbearably sad.

'No one?' she whispered.

'No one.'

Memory seemed to play out across the old lady's exhausted features, rolling through her mind and crunching the muscles of her face into a knot. Riley felt as if she'd contracted a virus from her: the physical weight of Miss Lawson's terror ran through her own body like a red-hot vibration.

'Louise, the person who did this to your father took away his picture of the tower. This is significant. This could help us catch him.'

'I hear. Thank you. I understand. Can we just. Be.' Louise looked at the wall opposite. Riley followed her gaze. Her attention was drawn to the chaos of the wind and the approaching snow outside. 'Babel.'

'The Tower of Babel?' Riley confirmed.

'The Tower of Babel.'

Riley walked into the furthest corner of the room, saw Louise close her eyes, and looked into the sky. The night clouds were pregnant with snow. She called Clay and within a few moments, she connected.

'The missing picture on Leonard Lawson's wall is an Old Testament scene, Book of Genesis. It's the Tower of Babel.'

Clay knew the story well. It was one that Sister Philomena had taught her at an early age. 'Mankind at odds with God, the ensuing wrath of the Almighty and the scattering of people,' she said.

Outside, the snow started falling.

9

3.35 am

Outside Leonard Lawson's house, Clay took out her phone and saw that she had missed a call from her husband, Thomas. And although she didn't have time, she needed to hear his voice, to counterbalance the freak show she was mired in and reassure her, in the fist of night, that there was another side to life. After four rings, he picked up her call.

'Thomas?'

'Hi...' Freshly stirred from sleep, she could tell he was happy to hear from her. 'How's the wandering old woman?'

'Her name's Louise Lawson and her father's Leonard. She's alive and in the Royal. But her father's been murdered...' She felt the smile fall from her face.

'Where are you?' asked Thomas.

'Just off Lark Lane.'

'Not far from home.'

'I don't think I'll make it home to see Philip before he goes to nursery. Doctor, Doctor, I've got a chronic case of RMS.'

'RMS? Slip behind the screen and take off all of your clothes...'

She laughed. 'You're a filthy animal, Doctor, but that's not the only reason I married you.'

'RMS? Hmmm... What symptoms are you displaying?'

'Guilt, regret, feeling rotten because I'm hardly ever home.'

'Rotten Mother Syndrome. You're not a rotten mother.

When you're with Philip, you're there 100 per cent for him. He loves you. He lights up when he sees you, and when you're not here, he talks about you all the time. He's only a small kid, but small kids are very good at working out who loves them and who doesn't. And when you're not with him, you miss him so much it's like physical pain.'

'You're kind.'

'I'm honest.'

'Tell him I love him and if I can't get home I'll phone him before he leaves for nursery.'

'I'll tell him, but he always says the same thing when I do. *I know*.'

The smile returned to her face and the heaviness that clogged her heart lifted a little.

She looked over her shoulder, defensively, saw Karl Stone and was glad he wasn't that near to or looking at her. Stepping away from the house, she asked, 'Are you all right?'

'I'm in bed. I'm talking to you. Wish you were here.'

'Me too.'

There was a tender lull between them. She pictured him in bed, soft lamplight falling on his hair and skin, the smile he shared with her alone, his hands on her body in their bedroom. The exact opposite of the carnage in Leonard Lawson's room.

'Are you praying?' asked Thomas. 'You just said *Jesus*.'

'I was remembering something I've just been drowning in. The old man? I honestly don't think there's a modern precedent for it. I feel like I've been in a medieval dungeon.'

'You're going to be busy then. But keep this plate spinning for us: I'm going to do something really nice for you the next time we're together. If you get a chance, think, what would I really like to happen to me?'

There were other reasons she loved her husband so much. The way he listened attentively but didn't hustle for details. How, in the grip of the worst that people could do to other human beings, he gave her choices in life.

'I'd really like to see Philip before he goes to nursery in the morning.'

As she spoke the words, a part of her couldn't believe that their son was now three years old and had small friends of his own whom she knew by sight but little else – Eleanor and Luke – and a slice of life that didn't involve her.

'I have to tell you, Ms Clay, that you aren't a rotten mother. I want you to get out of my surgery right now and get back to work immediately.'

Every other officer she knew who was married to a civilian caught various shades of hell because of the demands of the job. In over a decade, Thomas hadn't given her a moment of grief. But the sound of other people *working* pulled her guilt lever.

'I've got to go, Thomas.'

'I love you too. Oh, I nearly forgot to mention: we missed a message on the answer machine. It sounded like an old man. He didn't leave a name.'

'What did he want?'

'To talk to you. No name. No number. Said he had something to give you, something from a long time ago.'

A discordant note echoed deep inside her.

'Did you do 1471?'

'Caller withheld.'

Silence. 'I love you.'

She closed the call down. Turning back to the open door of Leonard Lawson's house, all thoughts of home dissolved as she returned inside. She wondered what the killers were doing at that moment.

No one, thought Clay with growing certainty, *could have staged that death alone.* She wondered if and when they'd killed before? And if and when they'd kill again?

Two killers. One murder. No time.

10

3.45 am

Clay identified two rooms of immediate interest in the old man's house. Upstairs, Louise Lawson's bedroom. Downstairs, Leonard Lawson's study.

Although there was no sign of any disturbance in the bedroom, she knew Louise Lawson would never sleep in it again, never even cross the threshold of the house.

She stood in the middle of the bedroom. The dominant image was a picture of a feminised Sacred Heart of Jesus on the wall facing the bed, the closest Louise had come to allowing a male into her room. For a moment, Clay felt the weight of another woman's loneliness, imagining her own self years hence, a widow with no one to hold her at night and a grown-up son who had left home. She chased the notion away.

On the wall above Louise's three-mirrored dressing table, which looked identical to the one in her father's bedroom, was a framed cross-stitch sampler, the writing a neat and elegant linked script.

Silence is Golden

Clay looked around, distracted by a nagging itch. *Have I missed something?* A spinster's single bed with a padded pink velvet headboard and a duvet cover with a repeating pattern of red roses. She looked at the wall adjoining Louise's father's room, considered both rooms and the study downstairs.

'Everything is here,' she said to herself.

She unfolded a set of aluminium steps, climbed it to get a view of the top of the wardrobe and saw nothing but a thick layer of dust. She stepped down, opened the wardrobe. Skirts, blouses, cardigans, a jacket and three coats. Shoes along the bottom. Shoes to the left for autumn and winter. Shoes to the right for spring and summer.

There was a smell in the air of a manufactured fragrance, a perfume that Clay hadn't come across since her childhood in St Michael's Catholic Home for Children in Edge Hill. Mrs Tripp, the home's manager, used to wear enough of it to repel insects.

She focused on the walnut dressing table with its triptych of mirrors. On a china tray there was an assortment of jewellery – gold brooches, a pearl necklace and earrings. Between the teeth of her brush, dozens of white hairs were trapped, knotted around each other in tufts.

There were two drawers and two doors in the dressing table. She opened the left-hand door and found a black leather Bible. She flicked through it carefully and, finding nothing wedged between its pages, put it back. Behind the right-hand door, nothing. Clay opened the top drawer and found three rows of neatly folded knickers. She lifted each row, feeling the fabric carefully, but there was nothing concealed. The back of the drawer was clear. In the bottom drawer, grey tights were set out in tightly sealed balls, next to a section of plain white bras. She lifted the bras out, then the tights. Nothing hidden in her most private of places.

Louise Lawson, thought Clay, wouldn't have to face that further trauma that victims of violent crime and their loved ones often had to endure. The exposition of their secret lives. The surface of the room told Clay that if Louise Lawson did have any secrets, they existed only in her heart and mind.

On the dressing table, a box of pills. 'Lyrica. L Lawson.' She glanced at the manufacturer's information sheet inside the box. Miss Lawson's epilepsy tablets.

Clay looked at the china jewellery tray, moved it with her thumb and revealed a piece of pink paper. She unfolded it. It was a photocopied flyer.

```
Open Day and Summer Fair
     The Sanctuary
     Croxteth Road
Saturday 9th June 2018
```

'Bill?'

'Yeah?' His voice filtered through from Leonard Lawson's room next door.

'Come and have a look at this!'

'What have you got?' he asked.

'So far, the only possible link to other people in her life. The Sanctuary? Can you find out what it is?'

11

4.00 am

Watching Louise Lawson drifting through the margins of consciousness, Riley felt like an astronaut travelling deeper into space, not sure if she would ever return to the noise and bustle of earth.

On her phone, she looked for the umpteenth time at the dominant image she had pulled up for *The Tower of Babel*. It was a painting by an old master called Pieter Bruegel, but she could see nothing in it that would make an elderly man want it on his bedroom wall or prompt the person who killed him to take it away as a trophy.

She regretted her inability to ever get past the cafe on the ground floor of the Walker Art Gallery and her consequent lamentable knowledge of art.

She focused. An old painting of a conical brown tower that was incomplete at the top, a work in progress. Black rectangles, windows into a void, were arranged around the tower's walls. The foot of the tower was surrounded by scorched brown earth and its unfinished summit poked through the clouds.

Riley gave Louise's hand a firm touch and the old lady opened her eyes.

'Louise, you're going to have to help me here.'

Her head turned towards Riley, her breathing slow and deep, her eyes closing and opening.

'I'm going to show you a picture of *The Tower of Babel*.' She turned her camera so that Louise could see. 'Was this the picture on your father's bedroom wall?'

'Yes.'

'Thank you, Louise,' said Riley. 'He must have liked this painting a lot, your father?' Silence. 'To have it on his bedroom wall?'

Louise settled back on the pillow, fresh tears rolling down her face.

Riley considered the one picture on her own bedroom wall. Emily, her niece and goddaughter, aged five. Smiling, milk teeth missing, her first school photograph. Riley's soft spot, her pride and joy, as she couldn't have children of her own.

'Why was the picture so important to your father?'

Louise replied, but Riley needed confirmation.

'I'm sorry, Louise, could you repeat that?'

'It was a non-discussable matter.' Her voice croaked with emotion.

'He refused to discuss why a painting, *The Tower of Babel*, was so important to him?'

She closed her eyes, nodded.

'Were there other non-discussable matters?'

'Yes. Stop. Please stop. My head is splitting. I might have another turn...'

'Louise, I apologise. I'll be quiet now. I promise. Silence.'

Riley walked to the door, stepped into the empty corridor and dialled Clay's number.

Clay connected.

'Eve.'

'How is Louise Lawson?'

'Really, really delicate. Eggshells. I managed to get it out of her. The picture on her father's wall is Pieter Bruegel's *Tower of Babel*.'

'That figures,' replied Clay. 'Leonard Lawson was an academic, an art historian. I'm in his study now.'

'An art historian who refused to discuss with his daughter why that painting meant so much to him. Along with other topics as yet to be identified. I'm sorry, but he sounds like a crank to me.'

12

4.03 am

Leonard Lawson's study was full of damp and the walls were lined, floor to ceiling, with over a thousand books.

'I reckon Leonard Lawson probably retired around thirty years ago, in the 1980s, before computers were compulsory.' The typewriter keys were grimed with dirt and Clay guessed that Mr Lawson had done a lot of writing in his time.

On the desk surface there was a small bowl of dusty paper-clips, a block of white writing paper and one small wooden picture frame. Flicking on the 1960s anglepoise desk light, she picked up the black-and-white photograph. Two young men, dressed in gowns and mortar boards, smiled broadly in the sunshine on their graduation day. Clay timelined it: late 1940s or early 1950s. The place, from the background, Cambridge or Oxford. In all probability it was Leonard Lawson with a university friend. As she placed the photo back down on the desk, she wondered, *Did Lawson think more of the young man in the picture than he did of his own daughter?* She looked around. It was the only picture in the room. *Or was it just a totem of a simpler, happier time in his life?*

She took several snaps of it with her iPhone.

DS Stone brought over an armful of large books, selected from the brimming shelves. 'Eight so far, all by Leonard Lawson,' he said, placing them on the desk.

The book on the top of the pile showed a painting of Jesus Christ in a blue heaven, surrounded by angels and disciples and looking down over a dark, violent pandemonium that Clay assumed was earth. The title, along the top of the picture, read: 'Hieronymus Bosch: Divine Visions'; along the bottom: 'Leonard Lawson'.

'Anything on Pieter Bruegel?' she asked as she lifted the book from the stack and sat down in Leonard Lawson's seat, taking in the room from his point of view. All kinds of books with the names of artists on their fat spines, but the only picture in the room was the photo on the desk.

'Yes,' said Stone, retrieving a volume from the middle of the heap. In between the words 'Bruegel' and 'Leonard Lawson', the cover showed a small army of skeletons reaping havoc on the human beings they had hunted down. She looked at the title of the picture: 'The Triumph of Death'. The image caused Clay a strange sensation, a cold spot on the crown of her head that spread across her scalp.

She opened the book. There was no author photograph on the rear dust jacket for her to check against the picture on the desk, but there was a brief biography. She read out loud: *'Professor Lawson was born in Liverpool in 1921. After serving in North Africa during World War Two, he was educated at King's College, Cambridge, 1946 to 1949. In 1955, he was appointed professor at the University of Liverpool.'*

Stone had the Bruegel book open. 'Word for word, the same biography.'

'Have a look for anything he's written on *The Tower of Babel*. He refused to discuss the painting with his daughter, but he couldn't very well do that with his readers.' She stood up. 'Have a seat, Karl.'

As Stone sat down to read, Clay knelt at the side of the chair. It contained two drawers: a small one at the top and a deeper one beneath. As she opened the top drawer, the light fell on her blue latex glove, giving her hand the strange glow of an alien claw.

'Yes!' she exclaimed, pulling out a black leather book, its

cover embossed with gold letters: 'Address Book'. She placed it on the desk and pulled at the bottom drawer, but that didn't shift. She tugged again, then saw a keyhole near the top. Looking for the key, she ran her fingers across the underside of the desk. Nothing stuck there. She scanned the desktop, then lifted the heavy Imperial typewriter.

There was no sign of a key to whatever it was that mattered enough to Leonard Lawson for him to lock it away.

On the desk, Stone had the book open at a spread showing a colour plate of *The Tower of Babel* and a column of small type alongside it. He looked up as Clay reached across to take a paperclip from the bowl.

'I was put on a disciplinary, years back, for popping a lock at a scene.'

'I remember. Guy leading the case, DCI George Watson? Dickhead.' Clay handed him the paperclip. 'We all know you're a born scallywag. If it's at a murder scene and it's worth locking away, it's worth looking at.'

She opened the address book at the 'A' page. There were no entries.

She turned to the 'B' page and found that empty of names too. 'C'. Blank. 'D'. Blank.

Heart sinking, she continued leafing through it while Stone fashioned the paperclip into a makeshift drawer key.

She flicked through to 'Z'. There wasn't a single entry.

Stone kissed the tip of the paperclip.

Clay felt the victim's isolation in a visceral lurch. The memory of long stretches of her own loneliness, as a child, as a young woman, came back to haunt her.

'He's gone from being a very important man to being completely forgotten. But not by the people who slaughtered him...'

As Stone showed her the paperclip key, the sound of voices and footsteps came through the front door. She recognised the intonation as Michael Harper's, trusted assistant of the pathologist Dr Lamb.

'I'll leave you to it, Karl – the APTs are here. I've got to deal with Leonard Lawson's body.'

As she headed for the stairs, she called, 'DC Price!'

'Yeah!' He was in the front living room.

'I need your body upstairs.'

He laughed as he followed.

'In your wildest dreams, fathead!' called Clay. 'And in my worst nightmare.'

13

4.15 am

'Brace yourselves,' said Clay to Harper and his colleague as they followed her into Leonard Lawson's bedroom. The two anatomical pathology technicians were silent, except for one sharp intake of breath and an almost inaudible muttering that could have been prayer but was probably blasphemy.

She watched the APTs look in disbelief at the body. Harper, fat and round; his colleague, thin. Laurel and Hardy in a horror movie. Clay followed their bewildered gaze. The sight of the old man's suspended body sent a fresh tremor of shock through her. She remembered Thomas's comment about the answer-machine message from another old man and wondered who the old man was and what he had of hers from the past.

'What do you want us to do, DCI Clay?' asked Harper.

Clay stationed herself by the dressing table to get the best overall view of Leonard Lawson's body. She looked at the APTs and said, 'Follow my instructions closely.'

She weighed up the situation. 'Price and Mason, either side of the pole, top and bottom.'

They moved quickly into position.

'Grip the top of the pole,' she said, ignoring the scratching of stirred memory beneath her scalp. *Not now.* 'Slide your fingers under the bottom. Thank you.' She fell silent, waited until she could see confidence in their eyes.

'Slowly, lift...'

Almost in slow motion, the officers lifted the pole from the surfaces supporting it, the old man's body swaying as they did so. Clay noticed there was something odd about the old man's torso, as if something was missing. The weight of his body shifted on the pole and for a few moments he swung from side to side like a piece of meat on a hook.

No man, no matter what he has or hasn't done, thought Clay, *deserves this indignity.* Hendricks's theory – that they were sending him to hell – made increasing sense.

Clay looked at Harper and his colleague. 'As quickly as you can, I want an unzipped body bag on the floor in the space to where I direct Mason and Price. Take two of our evidence bags and a pair of cutters from your kit box.' As they did this, Clay said to Mason, 'Terry, the APTs are going to cut and bag the sections of spear sticking out of Mr Lawson's body. They're going to make those cuts over the body bag so that Mr Lawson can go straight into the vinyl.'

Harper laid a silver body bag on the old carpet and unzipped it.

'Bill, you and me will hold the bag open, top and bottom end.'

They knelt down as Mason and Price guided the suspended body into place.

'Cut the top of the spear!'

Harper cut and the section of spear fell into the bag his colleague held beneath it.

'The bottom section, please.'

Snap. It landed with a rustle of paper.

'Lower the body to the bag.'

Mason and Price negotiated Leonard Lawson's back, head and bottom into the bag.

'Harper, I want you and your colleague to untie the knots that are securing Mr Lawson to the pole. As one of you unties, I'd like the other to guide his hands and arms, legs and feet into the bag. Any questions?'

'I understand.'

She looked across the length of the body bag and asked Hendricks, still kneeling at the bottom end, 'Did you find out about The Sanctuary?'

'Googled it. It's a residential home for adults with severe learning difficulties. It's private and, looking at their website, everything's pretty high-spec. The people who live there are pushed to fulfil their potential, so they don't just sit around watching TV all day. Guess what? It's five minutes away.'

Harper manoeuvred Leonard Lawson's untied hands and arms into the confines of the bag.

'Thank you, Harper,' said Clay. 'Go on, Bill.'

'It's art therapy, music therapy, sports, drama, trips out, here, there and everywhere.'

The APTs took one leg each and tucked them into the bottom end of the bag. Mason and Price lifted the pole away.

Standing up, Clay looked around the room and said, 'Thank you.'

She picked up an evidence bag and placed the strobe light into it. 'I've had an idea, Bill, about the strobe light. It wasn't put there just to disorientate whoever found the old man, it was a grim joke, a window into the killer's view of life and death. I wonder if he *knew* that Louise Lawson is epileptic? Trigger the witness – the daughter – into a fit. What a punch line!'

For a moment, Clay imagined she was dead centre of the picture on the cover of Leonard Lawson's Hieronymus Bosch book. She listened to the fractured birdsong in the dark, early hours, a blackbird disorientated by electric streetlights, and considered what Hendricks had said to her about The Sanctuary.

'Bill, if The Sanctuary is a residential facility, they'll have to have someone on duty through the night. There'll be someone there now who may well know Louise Lawson. We'll go there directly after the post-mortem.'

Clay watched the technicians carry Leonard Lawson from his bedroom. She wondered to herself if the section of the shaft that remained inside his body had pierced his heart, sealing his fate like some comic-book vampire and wiping him forever from the face of the earth.

14

4.25 am

'Eve!' Stone's voice came from Leonard Lawson's study. 'Can you come down a minute?'

Clay descended the stairs to where Stone was standing, in the doorway to the study. He held a thick wad of yellowing A4 paper. She approached him, nodded at the paper and dropped her voice. 'From?'

'The desk drawer.'

She smiled. 'Good. I like it.'

He turned the collection of papers so that Clay could see the top sheet.

```
Psamtik I
664-610 BC
The Quest for the World's Proto-Language
by
Leonard Lawson
```

'There are a load of photographs in the drawer that belong to this manuscript,' said Stone. 'I've googled it and been on a trawl through Amazon and AbeBooks. There's no match for a book of this title at all. I can only suggest it was unpublished or it was published under a different title.'

Clay took the manuscript from Stone and examined it.

The pages were dog-eared, from which she inferred that the book had been handled regularly over the years. She sat at Leonard Lawson's desk and, turning over the top page, imagined him sitting in the same place and reading the text.

'Did you look for the key?'

'All over the study, but I couldn't find it.'

'So he really cared about the manuscript. Enough to hide the key.'

She looked at the second page, words from a former world, formed of letters from the metal stamp of an Imperial typewriter on an inky ribbon, letters with blurred edges.

```
ISNSSN
For DN
Now and for always
```

'The dedication – *For DN, Now and for always* – is the same as in all his published works,' said Stone. 'But this manuscript has got this *ISNSSN* tag. It figures that the most important person in Leonard Lawson's life was a DN, not an LL for his daughter. Not DL, who could've been his missus. Unless DN was his common-law wife, but I doubt it, not in those days.' Stone looked around the room. 'Interesting life, right. Dreadful conclusion.'

Clay looked at the contents page.

```
Part One: The Ancient World
Part Two: The Modern World
```

'As soon as we have a chance to catch our breaths, I want you and Bill Hendricks to get your heads together on this.' She handed the manuscript to Stone. 'You read "The Ancient World", he can read "The Modern World", or vice versa.'

She reached into the open drawer, took out a collection of photographs, prints and postcards and started flicking through them. A stone tablet decorated with elegant Egyptian hieroglyphics and with a pharaoh in attendance, holding what looked like a lamp in his hand. She turned it over and read the neat handwriting: *Psamtik I making an offering to Ra-Horakhty.*

A warmth illuminated the darkness inside Clay and her instincts twitched. She stayed exactly where she was, but a piece of her mind went travelling through time and space and the room seemed to fade away. Outside, the wind that smothered the house seemed to roar suddenly as her sense of hearing sharpened. Leonard Lawson's manuscript was alive with something hidden and dreadful and dangerous.

'What are we on to?' Stone's voice dragged her back into the moment.

She looked at him in questioning silence.

'You just said, *We're on to something with this…*'

She looked at the next picture. A drawing of a man swathed in rags and carrying two bundles on his back. 'I want you and Bill to see if there's anything in the manuscript, anything he's written, that could have incurred the wrath that we saw staged in the bedroom.' Aware of the need to get to the mortuary for the post-mortem, she checked with Stone as she headed for the door, 'Anything else?'

He held up a piece of paper. 'I found this in the drawer.' He read, '709 6010.'

'Admiral Street police station?'

'PC Stephen Rimmer. It's handwritten contact details.'

'Get on to him immediately!' She glanced at the front door.

'I already have done. He's on his way over now.'

15

5.00 am

Leonard Lawson. 71.3 kg. 168 cm. Eye colour blue. Hair colour grey, balding. Caucasian. Male. 90+ years.

In the long, narrow rectangle that was Autopsy Suite 1 of the mortuary behind the Royal Liverpool University Hospital, Clay watched the APTs lift Leonard Lawson's body from the body bag on to the rubber board on which the post-mortem would be conducted.

She looked at Hendricks and followed his gaze to the centre of Leonard Lawson's rib cage. Blood-stained wooden circles plugged his body back and front. This detail, the sawn-off ends of the spear that had impaled him, gave the old man's body an unreal quality, emphasised by the fact that his eyes were now shut and his face was neutral.

'Eve, we must stop meeting like this.' The voice of the pathologist, Dr Mary Lamb, came from behind her. 'And at these ungodly hours.' She was close to retirement age and looked a decade older, but she walked past Clay with a gait that was sprightly.

Clay watched Dr Lamb's reaction as she made an initial visual assessment of Leonard Lawson's corpse. Her expression gave nothing away, but she said, 'I spoke with DS Stone on the telephone and he furnished the details of the scene of the crime.'

Over the light blue autopsy suite smock and trousers, Clay tied the straps of a green plastic apron tightly behind her back.

'In thirty-five years,' continued Dr Lamb, washing her hands at the sink, 'I've never known the like.' She turned to her APTs. 'Get some pictures of him, please.'

Michael Harper, the senior APT, pointed a digital camera at Leonard Lawson and took the first of multiple images.

Clay made eye contact with Dr Lamb. The pathologist smiled.

'However, I did see you in Liverpool One with your little boy, Eve. You were lifting him on to a bouncy castle. The man you were with, with the sky-blue eyes?'

'My husband, Thomas. You should have come and said hello, Dr Lamb.'

'I was going to... and then I thought, no. The only places we ever meet are here or in the Crown Court. You looked so happy. I didn't want to drag this side of your life into your personal space.'

Dr Lamb dried her hands with the same slow, precise movements Clay had seen her use in dozens of post-mortems. 'What's your little boy called, Eve?'

'Philip. Little but getting bigger and mouthier by the day.'

The smile dissolved from Dr Lamb's eyes and Clay steeled herself, forced herself back into professional mode, pushing all thoughts of Thomas and Philip away.

'Turn him on to his side, please,' Dr Lamb said to her APTs.

Harper placed the camera near Leonard Lawson's feet and, with his colleague, turned the old man's body on to his side. Dr Lamb moved from one side of the table to the next and back, inspecting the entry and exit points of the spear. She stopped, her expression reflective.

'We're going to have to remove the foreign object from the gentleman's body before we do anything else.' She scrutinised the site of the exit wound. 'Which will involve removing his heart. Judging by the entry and exit points of the spear, whoever's done this has gone directly through his heart.' She sighed. 'He's got a rare congenital abnormality of the rib cage. Poland Syndrome. The absence of a pectoral muscle causes the ribs to bend out of shape. It's probably how the spear came clean through.

Was he born like that, thought Clay, *born to die and end up like this?*

'I'm sorry, Professor Lawson,' said Dr Lamb, pointing the tip of her scalpel at his sternum. 'But we're going to have to pull what remains of you to pieces.'

60

16

5.20 am

At the window of Louise Lawson's hospital room, Riley pressed record on her phone. Outside, the snow had stopped falling. The city skyline was capped white and the sky and river were suffused with an amber glow. It was as if all sound and motion had been muffled.

She stirred herself, spoke into her phone and was grateful for the Sunday School she'd been forced to attend as a child.

'Back in the day, there was one language and a common speech. Humans understood each other perfectly. They decided to build a tower that could reach up to heaven. The Lord came down, saw that mankind was getting on just great and that nothing was impossible for it. So he scattered the people, stopped the building of the Tower of Babel and made the common language incomprehensible. Hence the six and a half thousand languages we have on earth today.'

Riley turned. Louise was watching her.

'People blame God for everything,' said Louise.

Riley walked towards her. 'I don't,' she replied. 'I'm a police officer. I've seen some dreadful things. I don't blame God. I blame people.'

'There's a reason why God created so many languages for the people of the earth. Mankind was proud and God had to show the people of the earth that they couldn't build a tower to reach into heaven and become like God themselves. It was God's role to build a bridge to the earth in the form of Jesus Christ, God becoming man and not the other way round.'

'I'd never thought of it that way,' said Riley. 'But God's ways are mysterious.' She sat on the edge of the bed. The gentle light of the arc lamp in the corner gave Louise a soft radiance. 'To understand, as you clearly do, is good. But God's deepest motives are his alone to know.'

She watched a barrier come down inside Louise Lawson. 'That's exactly what I think.'

Riley took Louise's hands in hers. 'Mind you,' she said, 'my sister's a French teacher. God's many languages keep her and many others in a job.' As her attempt to introduce a note of lightness into the room died a death, it occurred to Riley that Louise no longer knew how to smile.

'Louise, I've got a problem and I need your help.' Their eyes locked and Riley waited until the invisible bubble sealed itself around the two of them, blocking out everything else.

'I know you don't want to talk about the dreadful things that have happened, and I can understand that perfectly, but the longer it takes for you to tell us what you know, the harder it will be for us to catch whoever's responsible. And I'm very sorry and sad to say this, but if he's done this once, he'll want to do it again. Murder is like alcohol, cigarettes and other drugs. It's highly addictive. I would be very grateful, Louise, if you would talk to me and my boss, DCI Eve Clay. I know she'll want to be there when you speak about what's happened.'

Louise was quiet for what felt like a long time. She closed her eyes and Riley watched her lips moving, deduced that she was praying to God for guidance. Then she opened her eyes and said, 'I don't want anyone else to die. I don't want anyone else to go through this suffering. Call DCI Eve Clay. I'll try my best to talk.'

17

5.20 am

Dr Lamb made an incision through Leonard Lawson's skin from his sternum straight down to his pubic bone.

'The probable cause of death is the head injury. I suspect the killer smashed the victim's skull to disable him, so he could get on with the business of playing God with what remained.' She looked directly at Clay for a moment and said, 'I will of course give you a firmer conclusion once we've removed the top of his skull and explored the impact the bone fragments and splintering had on his brain.'

She looked down again. Her hand skipped deftly back to the top of the initial incision and with two swift, clean cuts she turned the straight line into a Y, the top points turning out to his shoulder joints.

'Harper!'

That was all the instruction Harper needed. He handed Dr Lamb a cutter that Clay thought looked like it could be useful to prune back garden trees. Then, with two hands, he peeled back the withered skin of the old man's chest to reveal the front of his asymmetrical rib cage and intestines.

With the rib cutter, Dr Lamb made incisions at either side of Leonard Lawson's chest cavity. The sound of ribs snapping died fast in the flat acoustics of the autopsy suite, but the noise echoed as it entered Clay's head.

'Look,' said Dr Lamb, catching Clay's eye. 'The spear's gone in through his shoulder, diagonally through his heart, avoiding collision with his abnormal rib cage, and out through his back. Whoever's done this was deadly accurate.'

Did they know you well enough, Clay wondered, *to know of your condition?*

Dr Lamb turned to her ATPs. 'OK, one either side, please.'

Harper stayed where he was and his colleague moved to the other side of the table. The APTs looked at each other and, on a silent count of three, lifted the front of Leonard Lawson's rib cage away from his body.

His pierced heart, with a length of spear poking out of it, made the skin on the back of Clay's hands itch.

'Let's clear the decks and give us room to free his heart!' said Dr Lamb.

Hendricks chuckled. All activity in the autopsy suite came to a standstill and everyone's eyes turned to him. In the silence that followed, he explained. 'That sounded like the opening line from a pretty corny love song.'

As Dr Lamb and her APTs returned to work, Clay smiled at Hendricks.

With a pair of large shears, Dr Lamb cut the attachment tissues of the intestines and, without pause, Harper and his colleague lifted the digestive system from Leonard Lawson's body and placed it on a nearby aluminium trolley.

Harper removed his hands from the old man's upper digestive tract and frowned.

'What is it, Harper?' asked Dr Lamb.

He stuck his hands back underneath the intestines and said, 'Yes. There's something hard in there.'

Clay clenched her jaw. This observation of Harper's felt like a massive distraction when there wasn't a moment to spare. She was desperate to get the heart removed from the spear so she could inspect the central shaft of the weapon.

'Harper, we'll find out what he had for his last supper later.

I'm sure DCI Clay is eager to retrieve the foreign item from the victim's heart.'

Harper, whose new beard did little to disguise his fat baby face, blushed and Clay said, 'But thank you, Harper, for your keen sense of detail.'

'Time to separate his heart from his lungs,' said Dr Lamb. She stuck a finger through the transverse sinus and with her right hand divided the aorta and main pulmonary artery. With two more incisions, his heart was isolated from the other organs.

The top and lower end of the spear were clearly visible under the overhead fluorescent light. Dr Lamb nodded. Harper and his colleague reached inside and carefully lifted the impaled heart into the air.

'Lower. Lower. Lower. Just there.'

Dr Lamb pulled a retractable metal tape measure from an open tool box to her left and, releasing the measure, placed it close to and in line with the section of spear. She pressed record on her dictaphone and said, 'Section of spear inside Leonard Lawson's body, twenty-one centimetres in length.'

Then she picked up a clean scalpel. 'I'll release the heart from the spear.' She squeezed the muscle with the fingers and thumb of her left hand and sank the scalpel into the space she had created. She made a steady slice and the heart was open but still hanging on to the shaft.

Clay's phone rang out. In the quiet of the autopsy suite, it sounded impossibly loud. On the display, she saw 'Riley'.

'What's happening, Gina?' she asked, still watching Dr Lamb.

'Louise Lawson. She's ready to talk. We're on the eighth floor.'

Dr Lamb placed the heart in a silver tray.

'I'm round the corner at the mortuary. I'll be there in a couple of minutes.'

As she closed down the call, Clay watched a trickle of blood seep from the heart into the silver tray. She pulled off the plastic apron, took off her blue smock and felt her pulse quickening. By the time she was on the stairs leading down to the ground floor

of the mortuary, she felt a rush of nervous energy at the prospect
of opening the doors that only Louise Lawson had the key to.

In the hours before dawn, the temperature had dipped a
further three degrees below zero, but as Clay raced from the
mortuary to the hospital, she felt feverish with the compulsion
to know.

18

5.33 am

When she arrived at Louise Lawson's ward, Clay paused in the doorway and saw Riley on the edge of the bed, dabbing the old woman's face with a wet flannel. She noted the tenderness in Riley as she looked at Louise Lawson, her tough façade completely gone. She stepped out of sight and knocked on the door.

'Hi, Gina!'

Riley's back straightened and her expression returned to one of concerned neutrality.

Clay pulled up a chair and smiled at the elderly lady.

'Is this...?' Louise looked at Riley.

'DCI Eve Clay,' confirmed Riley.

'How are you, Louise?' asked Clay. Riley pressed record on her phone.

'I'm exhausted.'

'I'm sorry about your father. He was a very distinguished and intelligent man. You must be very proud of him, Louise.'

She closed her eyes and sighed.

Clay tried to take her to a good place. 'All those books about art, ancient civilisations, old masters... I imagine when you were a small girl, Louise, your father must have taken you to many galleries and exhibitions.'

Louise was silent, seemingly remembering the past. Then she spoke. 'During school and university holidays, he took me to art galleries in all the big cities of England. And Europe. The Musée d'Orsay, the Academy of Fine Arts in Vienna. He loved religious art in particular, though I'm sorry to say he wasn't a religious man.' A look of profound sadness swept across her face.

Clay understood that what had happened to her father was looming large in her head. 'We have something in common, Louise.'

Louise didn't respond, but the lines on her brow creased enough for Clay to know she had hooked her interest. 'The woman who raised me until I was six was a Roman Catholic nun. She loved art, particularly religious art, and she showed me all kind of pictures in colourful books. We lived near the city centre and we were always in and out of the Walker Art Gallery.'

Louise looked away, picked up the cup of water, drank, then placed it back down as if it was a poisoned chalice.

'Thank you for agreeing to speak,' said Clay.

'Where is my father's body?'

'It's being examined, and then it will be prepared for the chapel of rest.'

'He'd just turned ninety-seven. He wanted to reach a hundred. But it wasn't to be, was it?'

'Your father...' Clay dangled the unfinished question in the air and Louise returned her full attention. 'Did he have a healthy lifestyle?'

'To live so long?' She nodded. 'Oh yes! He walked for miles every single day, up until last Thursday.' She looked into space. 'Around and around Sefton Park. Thinking his thoughts. Dreaming his dreams.'

'He was a creature of habit, your father?'

'Yes.'

'And you say he walked for miles every single day up until last Thursday?'

'He didn't seem himself on Thursday. On Friday he said his legs were sore. I asked him to go to the medical centre and he refused. I knew not to make a fuss over it because fuss makes him agitated.'

There was an innocent kindliness about the woman that made Clay think she had been sheltered from the world.

As Clay counted silently to five, a series of snapshots developed in her mind, images that acted as stepping stones into Louise's life. At home, caring for her elderly but active father. Two old people who had probably lived together for well over half a century. A dutiful daughter with religious belief as possibly her only outlet. A life suddenly overturned by a violent crime that would rob her of the place she called home. But time was tight and the minutes were slipping by. She had to broach the unthinkable.

'I've been inside your house on Pelham Grove,' she said. Louise's body sank and her lips moved as she averted her eyes. 'I'm sorry, Louise,' said Clay, 'I'm afraid I didn't quite catch that.' She zoned in on Louise's mouth, tried desperately to lip-read, but the movements of the old woman's lips were so small and subtle that nothing was given away.

Louise was silent. Clay watched the tension in her face as she mustered the strength to speak. Then, 'I said, it is a house of horrors.'

Clay glanced over Louise's shoulder at Riley.

'Go on, Louise,' said Riley. 'Tell Eve what you mean by house of horrors.'

'If you've been in the house, then you will have seen something... Something...' Louise raised a hand to the top of her head. She pressed down on her scalp and took in a sharp breath of air. *'Even though... even though I walk through the valley of the shadow of death, I will fear no evil, for you are with me; your rod and your staff, they comfort me.* I still have a father, a heavenly father. I must remind myself not to be afraid.'

'Your courage is astonishing,' said Clay. A thought, like forked lightning, shot through her. She pictured her own birth mother, her identity a mystery, a woman she had never met but who was probably of a similar age to Louise Lawson. She imagined her own mother going through hell and the urge to cry was sharp and urgent, but she drowned it.

'Tell me about Leonard. Tell me about your earthly father.'

'My father taught me all about courage, how to be brave in the face of adversity.' Louise looked at Clay, her expression searching. 'Did you go into his bedroom?' she asked.

'Yes. Did you?'

'Why did God allow this to happen? People will say that. Imagine! As if we're all puppets and have no free will. God isn't responsible for what happened to my father.' The old woman hung on to Clay's gaze.

'Louise, we need to talk about this. We must talk about what happened. But I have to warn you, I'm going to have to ask you some difficult questions. I need to catch whoever's done this and I need to do it as quickly as I can.'

Clay looked at the clock on the wall. 'Louise, can you tell me anything about what happened yesterday in your house in Pelham Grove?'

'He didn't go walking in Sefton Park, so it wasn't quite a normal day, but it was a normal evening. My father followed his regular bedtime routine...'

19

5.33 am

'Any forensic evidence from the killer will have been as good as wiped away by contact with Mr Lawson's internal organs and bodily fluids,' said Dr Lamb, carrying the section of spear taken from inside the old man to the aluminium sink.

In Autopsy Suite 1, Hendricks stood at a short distance from Dr Lamb as she inspected the central shaft of the spear. He attempted to watch matters from the point of view of the person who had murdered the old man.

What remained of his body had been decimated.

Dr Lamb held the bloody shaft in the sink and turned on the tap. A trickle of water fell on to the wood and diluted blood drizzled into the sink. She moved the shaft slowly through the stream of water, turning it as she did so, and within a matter of thirty seconds, the water washing from the wood was clear.

'Harper,' she said, 'bring me a light.' She looked at Hendricks. 'I'll act as your second pair of eyes, shall I?'

She handed the shaft to her second APT.

Standing behind, and towering over, Dr Lamb, Hendricks watched as Harper stroked the wood with light, from top to bottom. The APT turned the shaft, made darker by the water, and Harper repeated his inspection. Vulture-like, Hendricks watched and hoped.

'Stop!' he said, seeing a dark scratch, a line on the surface of the wood, roughly in the centre. 'Please keep the light where it is, Harper, and can you turn the wood, please.'

The junior APT turned it and the line extended into a geometric shape of interconnecting lines carved into the curved surface of the wood.

'Hold it still, please,' said Hendricks.

The whole shape was there on the curve of the wooden shaft. Hendricks counted ten separate linked lines. There was a large, dominant shape made of four lines – a rectangle – and at its base a pair of straight joined lines with a triangle projecting from the central body, a shape that suggested movement; flight, even.

He took a series of photographs and inspected them. Of five shots, three were clear and, of the three, one was excellent.

As he took more pictures of the carvings, Hendricks became convinced that they weren't a random set of scratches. The precision of the geometric lines said it wasn't a mindless doodle, and their position on the spear indicated that they were meant to be left inside Leonard Lawson's body.

'Let me see the rest of the shaft, please,' he said.

Harper sent the light across each square centimetre of the shaft as the junior APT slowly turned the wood. There were no more lines.

Hendricks looked to Dr Lamb. 'What do you think?'

She took the wood. 'It's not uncommon to look at something and see different things in it. I look at this and see a word, or letters even, that have been pulled apart and reassembled into a shape.' Hendricks looked hard but couldn't get what Dr Lamb meant. 'What do you see?' she asked.

He tried to come up with a unifying image, a title that would describe the picture that was connecting with his mind.

'What do you want me to do with the wood?' asked Dr Lamb.

'When it's bone dry, put it in a plastic bag and bring it to DS Terry Mason at Pelham Grove please.'

In a split second, Hendricks's eyes somersaulted between Leonard Lawson's detached intestines, his carved heart in a bowl, the empty cavity of his torso and the separated rib cage. It was as if the old man's body had exploded. In a flush of inspiration, a cold certainty settled in his mind and he wanted to share it with Clay.

He sent Clay the three best images and a message: *Eve, the killer is a complete sadist and hated Leonard Lawson with a vengeance. This picture shows an encoded message on the section of shaft left inside LL's body.*

He turned to the action of the saw as Harper brought the spinning teeth down on the old man's skull. In the grinding of metal on bone, Hendricks imagined another sound caught within it: the hysterical laughter of the person who had reduced the old man from a human being with a long and distinguished past to a set of disconnected body parts in a pathologist's laboratory.

He looked again at the image on his phone and the carving on the wood.

'I know what the carving looks like to me, Dr Lamb,' he said. 'It looks like a dragonfly escaping captivity through an open window.'

Hendricks started composing another message to Clay.

20

5.44 am

'He'd had a bath by seven thirty and at eight o'clock he was in bed. At eight thirty it was lights off and time to sleep.'

Deep inside the hospital, someone laughed, a single voice projecting five braying blasts of mirth, and then there was silence.

'Did you see your father at all during that hour?'

Louise considered the question. 'Only at one point. At a quarter past eight. I went to say goodnight to him, just to check everything was in order.'

'So your father was fully independent in these matters?'

'He was a very fit man, in mind and body. He was ninety-seven, but he could outpace people half his age.'

'Did he say anything to you when you last spoke to him?' asked Clay.

'*I've checked the doors and windows. Double-check them yourself before you come up and don't go to bed too late.* He said the same thing every night for years and years. It's strange...'

Clay watched her face closely. She was drifting deeper inside herself and, Clay guessed, back in time.

'What's strange, Louise?'

'I'm thinking back to when I was a little girl and how everything changes, everything turns around and reverses.'

'In what way?'

Louise paused, seemed to be looking for the right words. 'When I was a little girl, when he used to come and wish me goodnight, I used to tell him to make sure all the doors and windows were locked. I've never really thought about how we changed places.'

'How long have you lived in your house, Louise?'

'I've always lived there. I was born in the house – literally, in my mother and father's bedroom.'

'Your mother?'

'Died when I was very young. I don't remember her.'

'Tell me what happened after you'd said goodnight to your father?'

'I came downstairs and I watched a nature programme. I fell asleep in the armchair and when I woke up there was an American film on. I was woken by the sound of guns, on the TV. I don't know what time it was, but it felt late, way past my usual bedtime of ten thirty, after the news. I stood up, but I stood up too quickly and I felt dizzy, so I sat down again and composed myself. I... I got up again, slowly, and turned off the TV and I was going to do as my father had told me, but when I stepped out of the living room and into the hall...'

She covered her face with her hands and Clay was afraid that Louise would clam up.

'Go on, Louise,' she encouraged. 'Go on!'

'The light, the light was pouring from upstairs. I thought at first it was a fire, but then... It's all my fault.'

'It's not your fault, Louise.'

Louise took a deep breath and hung on to it. She shut her eyes tightly and shook her head as she breathed out.

'And then?' Clay coaxed. 'Tell me what happened.'

Louise opened her eyes and looked at Clay. 'I went upstairs. I knew something was very, very wrong because the light was coming from my father's bedroom. It felt like nothing was still, that there was something terribly wrong. And I wondered if I was having one of my awful dreams. I have a lot of bad dreams.'

The wind moaned down at the river and pressed against the window of Louise's hospital room.

'But when I got to the top of the stairs, I knew. I knew I wasn't dreaming. Everything was wrong. I called out to him. *Father?* I held my hand up to my face to shield my eyes from the light. I sensed Father wasn't in his bed, even though I couldn't see. Do you understand?'

Clay understood perfectly. Instinct had woken her up two nights earlier when her son Philip was out of bed and on the landing at two in the morning.

'*Father?* But he didn't answer. The light flooding from his room, it was horrible, disorientating. I turned on the light switch on the upstairs landing, but it didn't do anything to help because the light... pulsing... from Father's room was... I pushed his bedroom door open a little and he wasn't in his bed. I stepped inside the room and... someone – he must have been standing by the wall behind the door – slammed the door shut, trapping me in the room. I looked – the light was unbearable, white light and black shadows. No! Where was my father? I couldn't believe it. But it was my father, naked, like a beast hanging from a pole with all that hideous light pouring over his body. My head felt empty, but my body was like stone.'

She held her hands to her face, pressing her fingers over her mouth.

'Did you see anyone in your father's room?'

'I felt him,' replied Louise. She touched the nape of her neck. 'Right here. I faced away from Father, the dreadful light was at my back, then it stopped and the room was plunged into darkness. Black. Deep, black darkness. That was when I felt his breath on me, on my neck, and his hands on my shoulders, pressing down on my shoulders. My legs were like water and all my strength had left me. He was in control of me. He laid me down on the floor. I thought I was going to die.'

Clay watched memory play out on Louise's face. 'Did he speak?'

'I heard a voice. *I am the Angel of Destruction and I am*

watching over you. The First Born has spared you. Death, who we serve, has shown you mercy.'

'What was the voice like?'

'Strange. He didn't sound like a man, but he didn't sound like a woman either. Like something in between.'

'It was completely dark?' asked Clay, a knife turning in her core. The proximity of Louise to the killers and the absence of light equated to the cruellest form of mockery.

'There was some light, leaking in through the bottom of the door into the hall, and streetlight coming in through a crack in the curtains. And my eyes – I suppose they were getting used to the dark. I don't know how long it all went on for because I lost all sense of time.'

'Could you see his face?'

'I could see shapes. He stood up. I think he was tall, but I was lying on the floor and he may have appeared taller than he was.'

'Did he walk near the curtains, near the light?'

'He stayed in the dark. He stood very still. In between me and Father. His back was turned to me, I think. He stood still for a long time. I think he was looking at Father through the darkness.'

Louise looked into the middle distance, but, to Clay, she didn't seem to be looking at anything in the hospital room. She was reliving the nightmare and converting it into stone-cold reality.

'He turned on that dreadful light again. And walked out of the room.'

'Did you see anyone else leave the room?' asked Clay.

'I think so.' Louise looked harrowed. 'When that dreadful light was back on and he walked out, I watched. And I don't know if it was a trick of the light, but I saw another man follow him out of the bedroom. The First Born and the Angel of Destruction? But they weren't angels. They were men. Just wicked, wicked men.'

Clay held on to both of Louise's hands. 'Louise, look at me.' When she made eye contact, Clay said, 'We're going to help you, Louise. Gina Riley will sit with you, talk to you, listen to you. But for now, I want to ask you about The Sanctuary…'

'The Sanctuary?'

'We found a leaflet in your bedroom for a summer fair there. Did you go to that fair?'

'Of course I did. I go there every single day. Sundays included.'

'You work there?'

'It's not work. It's my vocation.'

'The people there, they know you very well?'

'Of course, everyone knows me. And I know everyone. It's my home from home.'

'Louise?' said Riley.

'Yes?'

'When I asked you if you wanted anyone to support you, you said, *No one.* Couldn't someone from The Sanctuary have come to your side?'

'Oh, no! It's a home for disabled men. They couldn't come to me, not at this hour. Imagine! They'd all be asleep. Even Gideon who was on duty last night. How could I drag anyone from their beds to this? It's a nightmare. And it's my nightmare. But it's real, isn't it? And it's mine. You should never ask for help. It's a sign of weakness.'

'Louise,' said Clay, 'we all need help. You're going to *need* help now.'

'*Only accept help when it's willingly offered.* That's what Father taught me. And my father was right, don't you agree?'

21

5.50 am

'The old boy's been murdered?' PC Stephen Rimmer, six feet four, twenty stone and without a single hair on his head or face, looked genuinely upset. He looked around Leonard Lawson's study and pronounced, 'Bastard. How...?'

'Constable Rimmer,' said DS Stone. Keen to press on, he shook his head. 'One thing at a time, eh? So why does Leonard Lawson have your contact details in his desk?'

Stone showed him the piece of paper.

'I gave them to him last Thursday, didn't I? After the incident in Sefton Park. I was on a routine patrol round the park in the car, with Constable Tom Donovan. It was just an ordinary, quiet middle of the day and we were about to skid back to Admiral Street for a bite...'

'What happened?'

'There was a bit of a crowd forming over the road from the Alicia Hotel, so we pulled over and got out to take a look. As soon as we got out, we could hear different voices, all like raised and well pissed-off. *Leave him alone! Don't you talk to him like that, y'weirdo!* So we waded in and told everyone to shut up and calm down. And everyone did exactly that except for one person. This tall, strange-looking bloke starts jabbing his finger in the direction of Mr Lawson – I didn't know his name at this point, but I did know him by sight because he's always walking round the park – and going, like, *Sinner, repent! Repent of your sins, weep and beg forgiveness of the Lord or suffer the eternal pains of damnation.* It would have been laughable, but you could see Mr Lawson was really distressed. And the Bible-basher? His eyes were wild but he was as cold as ice. I told him to can it or face arrest for breaching the peace. He looked at me and said, *Do you know what I am?* Dead serious. Dead cold. Dead calm. He pointed at Mr Lawson and said, *Do you know what he's done?* Mr Lawson started walking away, but he was sweating, his breathing was all over the place and he looked like he was about to keel over, so Tom took him to the car and got him to sit in the back while I dealt with the religious nutcase.

'I asked who saw what and a couple of people said they'd seen the lot, so I told the rest of them to beat it. The Bible-basher clammed up, went off slowly into this trance-like state. According to the witnesses, he was standing on a sandstone plinth by the grass on the edge of the park, staring into space. Mr Lawson was walking in his direction. The witnesses were walking behind Mr Lawson. The Bible-basher sees Mr Lawson and bam! walks right up behind him, following him and whispering in his ear. Mr Lawson starts walking faster and faster, but so does the Bible-basher, and the whispering grows louder and he starts going on, all cold and calculating, about Mr Lawson's sinful ways. Starts calling him the Devil's child, at which point the witnesses start intervening, telling him to back off. Then Mr Lawson falls over, falls over his own feet, and that's when the crowd forms, apparently. People stop to help Mr Lawson up and the Bible-basher starts laughing at him, coldly laughing his head off and talking about the chamber of hell that Mr Lawson is going to go to. Really soon. His time is up. So we're getting into death threats now.'

'This piece of hell that's been reserved for Mr Lawson – tell me about it, Constable. What did the Bible-basher say?'

'He said, in front of everyone – and this is when the crowd

really turned against the nutter – he said that...' PC Rimmer took out his notebook, flicked to the relevant page and read: *'Just as you have condemned half to the silent void, you and your other half will be condemned to the eternal silence of hell.'*

'You took the Bible-basher's details?' 'I did, yes. Samuel Forster. Date of birth: 14th August 1984. Address: here we go, 201 Ullet Road. It all checked out. I sent him away with a stiff warning. Pull any more of this and it'd be the cells and the magistrate.'

'*Here we go*, 201 Ullet Road?'

'It's a home for recovering alcoholics. Only most aren't recovering...'

'Did you get a picture of him?'

'Tom did. He sent it to my phone.' PC Rimmer took out his phone and showed the screen to Stone.

A human face. Stone reeled off eleven digits. Rimmer keyed them into his phone and sent the image to Stone's phone.

The man faced the camera. His eyes were a piercing blue and his nose was large and hooked, giving him the look of an eagle. His mouth was big and fleshy and his chin was square and strong, but Stone kept looking back at his eyes. Intensely cold and blue, with a glint of poison in the dead black pupils.

'Give me your notebook, please,' he said.

Rimmer handed it over, open at the relevant page, and Stone took a picture of the words the constable had written down and dated as Thursday 13th December 2018, 11.54 am. He turned the page and took a picture of Forster's personal details.

As Stone handed back PC Rimmer's notebook, he noticed something melting behind the constable's bullish façade, and he suspected he was holding something back. 'What is it? Spit it out. It could be important.'

'I felt unclean when I was near him. And ever since last Thursday, I've felt like there's something under my skin. I never dream. But I have since Thursday – every night. About him.'

'It's an occupational hazard,' said Stone. 'We all come across it at some point.'

'*Come across it?*'

'Evil,' replied Stone, hurrying to the front door and wishing he could be in Ullet Road in the blink of an eye. 'Pure evil.'

22

6.01 am

In the multi-storey car park of the hospital, Clay paused at the driver's door of her car and, looking out at the lights of the city centre, felt the weight of her iPhone in her coat pocket. As she took it out, she drank in the ethereal patterns of light cast by the moon across the dark waters of the Mersey.

She looked at the display – 'Hendricks. 1 jpg.' – and opened the picture.

At first sight it looked like a leftover piece of wood, a dark offcut set against the aluminium background of the mortuary. Then her focus fell on to its dark markings. She read the attached message.

Eve, Dr Lamb thinks it's a scrambled word or letters. It gives me the impression of a slightly disfigured dragonfly escaping through an open window. What do you see?

Her scalp crawled as she looked at the primitive image that had been forced into the centre of Leonard Lawson's body, saw what Hendricks was getting at. She was certain it was no accident.

The snow started to fall again, floating past the white lights of the city. She imagined the lines carved on the spear falling past her face, driven by the wind and gravity, disguised as snow-flakes and hidden by snowflakes. And on this night of great savagery, she found a beauty in the light and dark that prompted her to do something that not another soul knew about. She prayed to the dead guardian of her childhood, Philomena, opening her heart and mind to release whatever came from them and receive whatever arrived in return.

I am still your child. Please help me. Help me see. Help me understand.

'What do you think of it?'

The voice, familiar but distorted as it echoed, came from the shadows of the empty car park and Clay nearly cried out. She turned and saw Hendricks walking towards her.

'I think you're a regular creeping Jesus!' She laughed, the goose bumps on her skin settling down, warm relief filling her where ice-cold shock had swamped her a moment earlier.

'I bet you say that to all the boys.'

'Only the ones who stalk me into car parks during the graveyard shift. Get in out of the cold. Jeepers creepers!'

Hendricks sat next to Clay in the front of her car and she flicked on the overhead light. 'I saw you coming in here,' he said. 'I was on my way over to the Royal from the mortuary.'

'Louise Lawson almost certainly saw two men leave her father's bedroom,' said Clay. Hendricks sank down a little in the passenger seat. 'They're passing themselves off as the First Born and the Angel of Destruction.'

She pulled up the picture of the engraved shaft and turned it to him.

'It's the best shot I took. You'll see, the markings are much clearer when you look at it with your own eyes under a good light,' said Hendricks. 'Ten lines: two approximately 3 centimetres long, two about 2 centimetres, and five about 1 centimetre.'

She looked at the simple pattern of lines. 'I like your dragonfly and window image. Any other markings on the shaft, Bill?' Hendricks shook his head. 'There's nothing coincidental in any of this,' she said.

'What's your view of it?' asked Hendricks.

'You're the one with the psychology doctorate.'

'And you've got witchy instincts.' He winced as soon as the words left his mouth. 'Sorry.'

'Accepted. I know what you mean, Bill.' She laughed. 'But let's talk about *your* childhood instead.' She held her phone up to the light, the sight of her wristwatch reminding her that, in that moment, two sadistic killers were out there. She had to get on. She had to find a handle on the picture she was looking at. She had to get to The Sanctuary to find out as much as she could as soon as she could.

'The killers are making a statement about Leonard Lawson,' she said, 'but they're also making a statement about themselves. Louise Lawson said the one who spoke referred to them as *the First Born* and *the Angel of Destruction*. They're setting themselves outside the range of what's normal, what's human. Above and beyond moral laws in the service of Death.'

She stared absently at the windscreen. 'They attacked the sum of what Leonard Lawson was as a man. And in vandalising his whole body, they've reduced him to something less than human. It's a complete attack, designed to roll on long past the old man's death.'

In the ensuing silence, Clay switched off the overhead light. As he opened the door to leave, Hendricks asked, 'What do you want me to do?'

'Read Leonard Lawson's manuscript, "Psamtik I". And try and come up with an angle on the symbol they left inside the old man's body.' She paused. 'I was going to say—'

Hendricks stood outside the car, hand on the door, eager to close it and move on. '... I don't think there are any precedents.' He telegraphed Clay's thought.

She pointed back and forth at her own head and then his. 'If I'm witchy, so are you, Bill. Think!' Her mind returned to Hendricks's initial response to the way Leonard Lawson's body had been staged. Medieval. Torture. Terror. What horror could have inspired such a set-up? Images from dozens of old paintings of hell and its torments flashed through her mind.

Hendricks shut the door.

As she reversed, words flowed through Clay's head as if a voice was whispering in her ear. *Back in the way back when, what did you do, Leonard Lawson, to incur such wrath?*

Just as she was about to call Stone to tell him to meet her outside The Sanctuary, his name appeared on the display and her phone rang out. She connected.

'Eve, I've spoken to PC Rimmer. We've got a prime suspect. I've called for back-up. I'm pulling up outside 201 Ullet Road. Meet me there!'

23

6.06 am

The bell was broken, so Stone banged on the black door with the brass 2 and 1 and a gap where the 0 should have been. Footsteps hurried to the door. A light went on.

Bangbangbang.

The door opened and a tall, muscle-bound man with a neatly cared-for mane of blonde hair stared at Stone with calm arrogance. He looked as if he was addicted to his own reflection, not alcohol. The name on his ID badge, hanging from a Gold's Gym vest, read 'Darren'.

Stone showed his warrant card and said, 'This is a murder case. Cooperate or deal with the consequences.'

Sirens were closing in and Darren flipped up a gear. 'OK, yeah, come in.'

'Don't close your front door for now,' said Stone. 'Others are to follow.' He shadowed Darren through the vestibule and into the hall. There was a smell of Thunderbird in the air. The reception desk had a large book and a pen attached to it by string. Above the desk was a huge analogue clock and a sign:

RULES OF THE HOUSE
NO ALCOHOL ON THE PREMISES
CURFEW 7 PM
THREE STRIKES AND YOU'RE OUT
WE HAVE A WAITING LIST

'Has everyone obeyed the curfew?' asked Stone as a police car screeched to a halt outside.

Darren nodded, pushed the signing-in book towards Stone, the day's date at the top of the page. Three columns: *Print. Sign. Time.* Stone surveyed them. Small islands of legibility looked utterly lonely in a sea of squiggles. Down the print column a single hand repeated different names.

'I can't see Samuel Forster's name here?'

'Here.' Darren took the book. 'Some of the guys have got the shakes,' he explained.

Two constables entered the hallway. 'What's going on?'

Stone flashed his warrant card.

'There he is!' He pointed to a line in the ledger. The print was a series of crooked vertical and horizontal lines.

'Take me to him.' Stone turned to the constables. 'One here, one with me.'

Up a flight of stairs, the smell of Thunderbird intensified. Stone sniffed.

'It's offa their breaths and it's offa their skins. No booze onna premises.'

'Has he acted any differently since last Thursday?' Stone asked as they hit the landing. There were many doors leading down a wide corridor. 'Which one?' He held his breath.

'On the end, right-hand side!'

Stone marched to the door, opened it and threw on the main light. Four beds, four men, all asleep. He pulled up the picture sent to his phone by PC Rimmer.

The first man to his left looked like an eighty-year-old dwarf, struggling for breath and on the point of death. The Chinese man in the bed next to him had his mouth and one eye wide open and the other shut. Stone turned to the bed facing and saw a white man with shredded dreadlocks and boils on his cheeks and forehead.

The last man lay perfectly still and hidden under the duvet. Stone lifted the cover back and looked at Darren, in the doorway, combing his hair with the fingers of one hand. 'This is Samuel Forster, right?'

'Sam, yes.'

Samuel Forster, black, twenty-three stone and wearing a string vest and baggy Y-fronts, pulled the duvet back over himself.

Stone showed Darren the picture of the man who had harassed Leonard Lawson in the park. 'Do you know him?'

Darren scrutinised the image with contempt. 'He doesn't live here. Never has and I've worked here three and a half years. I have no idea who he is.'

'I'll remind you, Darren, that this is a murder investigation.' Stone showed the picture once more. 'Does he live here and is he here right now?'

'You can go and wake up every last arsehole and have a look for yourself. Do I give one? I'm telling you straight. He doesn't live here. I don't know him from Adam.'

Deflated, Stone stepped into the snow and wind just as Eve Clay pulled up outside. He walked over to her car and the passenger door opened. He got in and showed her the picture of the eagle-like, cold-eyed man whose name he didn't know.

'This is the religious maniac who terrorised Leonard Lawson on Thursday and fobbed off PC Rimmer by passing himself off as an obese black British man called Samuel Forster.'

Clay was in first gear and away.

'Where are we going?' asked Stone.

'Not far. To The Sanctuary.' Her windscreen wipers were on top speed, but the snow was winning the race. 'Tell me everything that PC Rimmer told you. And send whatever you've got to my phone and to Bill Hendricks, Gina Riley and Barney Cole.'

24

6.21 am

Clay got out of her car outside The Sanctuary. In the stillness of pre-dawn, Sefton Park had the silent aura of a space where magic might be possible. She evaluated the building and one word sprang to mind: money.

Illuminated by the security light he had tripped, DS Karl Stone walked through the freshly fallen snow towards the imposing front door. He was dwarfed by the three-storey, double-fronted, Victorian mansion, its windows black and its front wreathed in shadows. Not a single light was on inside the house. He knocked on the door.

The sinisterness of the old building was diluted by a bright blue board near the front door bearing a rainbow and in white letters:

THE SANCTUARY
Caring ~ Creating ~ Challenging

Clay followed in Stone's tracks through the snow and paused at the blue board. A white dove sailed through the sky above the curve of bright colours.

PROPRIETORS: MRS DANIELLE MILLER & MR ADAM MILLER
CONTACT 0151 496 8437

Stone knocked again as Clay joined him on the middle stone step. A light came on behind the stained-glass arch above the door. Transparencies of childlike paintings of animals, trees and flowers had been stuck on to the glass panels to either side.

'Who is it?' A man's voice, a Welsh accent.

'Mr Adam Miller? Police.'

'I'm not Adam Miller. My name's Gideon Stephens, I'm—'

'Hey, Gideon! Police!' said Clay. 'Open up!'

A bolt was drawn, but when the door opened, the chain stayed on the latch. Dark-haired and pleasant-looking, Gideon peered through the gap. Clay showed her warrant card.

'Come in quietly, we don't want to wake anyone up.' From the other side of the door, Clay detected a tremor in his voice. He was in his late twenties and handsome enough to be on TV selling kitchen roll to bored housewives, she thought. But his face was knotted with a mixture of fatigue and anxiety, an expression she knew well from her own reflection in the mirror, and she felt sorry for him.

'What's this about?'

'We need your help. We'll tell you inside,' said Clay.

He smiled at her. *I know you, though we've never met.* She read the thought on his face, and there was a transparency about him that promised helpfulness.

As Stone closed the front door, Clay took in the spacious hallway, the framed, unsophisticated pictures on the wall to the left and right of Gideon's back.

A light came on at the top of the wide staircase, on the landing above, and a middle-aged woman in a silk dressing gown appeared.

'What's going on, Gideon?'

'It's the police, Danielle...'

'The police?'

'I haven't got a clue.' He turned to Clay as the woman hurriedly made her way down the stairs. 'Follow me.'

'Danielle Miller?' asked Clay. The woman's face creased with concern.

A man appeared at the top of the stairs behind her, knotting his dressing gown. He looked at Clay.

'Adam Miller?'

He nodded as he padded down the stairs after his wife. 'Yes,' he replied, eyeballing her. 'How could any of our residents be of interest to *you*?' His face was long and narrow and covered in a thick, dark stubble that ran round the back of his head and chin.

On the wall, in the middle of the hall, was a framed picture of two men standing on a boat. Clay did a double-take of Adam and the picture and guessed it was a much younger Adam with his father.

Danielle reached the bottom of the stairs and, stepping alongside Clay, pulled a face. 'We'll take you into the kitchen. Get the kettle on, Gid!'

'Does Gideon really need to be here?' asked Adam. 'He's an employee...' As he passed the framed picture, Clay saw how much he'd come to resemble his father.

Gideon threw on the kitchen light and Clay followed him in. 'I've come to see all three of you. You may all be able to help.' She glanced around the kitchen, at the top-of-the-range fixtures and fittings, all onyx work surfaces and polished chrome, and priced it at £40,000 plus, recalling a similar kitchen she'd seen in a recent issue of *Ideal Homes*.

Adam Miller indicated the long table at the centre of the room. 'Can I see your warrant card?'

'I've already seen it,' said Gideon. Clay caught the smile on Danielle's face.

'Well, I haven't!' insisted Adam.

Clay showed him and, as he over examined it, she made a snap judgment about the three of them. Pain-in-the-arse husband, wife-at-the-end-of-her-rope, flirty young man.

Stone sat next to Clay, across the table from Gideon, Danielle and Adam. He slid the leaflet from The Sanctuary's open day across the surface. As Adam took a pair of reading glasses from a case in his dressing-gown pocket, Danielle snatched up the leaflet away from him. On a grim night, the dynamic amused Clay.

'We had a great day,' said Danielle. 'The open day in June, Gid!'

'Everyone was in such a good mood,' replied Gideon. 'Nothing happened, nothing went wrong on open day, DCI Clay!'

'We're not here about events on the day itself,' said Stone. 'We found it in Louise Lawson's bedroom.'

Danielle looked up from the leaflet, the colour draining from her face, anxiety consuming her features. 'Don't tell me something bad has happened to her?'

'She's in the Royal at the moment,' Clay replied. 'She has a minor head injury from a fall she had on the street in the early hours of this morning.'

'Louise on the street at that hour?' Gideon's voice was full of doubt. 'She was... Why?'

'Let the police officer speak!' Adam said.

'She was escaping from the scene of a crime, in her home on Pelham Grove. Her father was murdered in his bedroom.'

'Oh God, no!' Danielle's face turned pale, her eyes filling with shock.

'How?' The boom in Adam's voice had dropped to a whisper.

'This is a brand-new and ongoing murder enquiry. We can't reveal any details. The reason we've called here is because the leaflet on the table before you is the one link we could find between Miss Lawson and the outside world. We need information and we need it fast.'

'Fire away,' said Danielle. She sat up in her chair, her hands folded on the table in front of her, and Clay did a quick appraisal. Well spoken, well preserved, a woman in her late fifties who, with a coat of make-up, could pass herself off as a forty-something; quite a looker in her youth. Clay turned to Adam and wondered what the attraction was. Although he was younger than his wife, looks-wise she was out of his league. She guessed it had something to do with her own first impression of the building they were in: money.

'We know Louise volunteers every day, including weekends,' said Clay. 'You must know her really well. Has she ever expressed any concerns about her father?'

'Can you be a little more precise?' asked Danielle.

'Did he have any enemies? Does Louise have any enemies?'

Stone caught Adam's eye and The Sanctuary's joint owner held his gaze. Stone guessed that he didn't like being questioned by a female police officer.

'There's this. Us. Our residents. And there's her father,' said Adam. 'That's her world, beginning, middle, end.'

'That's what you *think*, Adam,' said Danielle. She reproached him with her eyes and he paid her back with silent contempt. 'But you don't know. We don't *know* anything much about her life outside The Sanctuary.'

25

6.31 am

'I can't imagine Louise having any enemies,' said Danielle. 'She's the sweetest woman in the world. But when was sweetness a defence against the world?'

'How about her father?' asked Stone.

'She doesn't talk about him much,' said Adam.

'But you don't really talk to her much, do you, Adam?' said his wife.

'She talks to me about him,' said Gideon. 'He's a fit old man, a creature of habit. Was.' The information of Leonard Lawson's murder connected with Gideon and he looked down for a moment, then up again. 'I knew him...'

'Are you all right, Gid?' Danielle looked at him fondly, almost touched his hand.

'Yeah. Jeez, I'm sorry, folks, it's just... I've never known any-one who got murdered.'

'You knew him?' Clay almost sang the question. *You knew the people-swerving recluse?* she thought.

'Oh, yeah. I knew Leonard. When the weather's bad or... or it's dark, Louise can get a little nervous about going home round the park. If I've bicycled into work, I often walk her home, or if I'm in the car, I'll give her a lift.'

'Well, I do offer!' said Adam.

'Let him speak, Adam!' said Stone. *Shut up!*

'I always make sure she's over the door, and wait... used to wait for her father to answer my knock. The bell had been broken twenty years or more. *Thank you very much for escorting my daughter home and delivering her safely to me.* Every time, the exact same words. Every time, I'd reply, *You are more than welcome, sir!*'

Gideon turned his face away suddenly, as if he'd been slapped by an invisible hand. 'God in heaven, the poor old man.'

'All right, Gideon, take your time.'

Danielle stood up and walked to the sink. A tap gushed and a few moments later she returned with a glass of water. 'Take a few deep breaths,' she said, lifting a lock of hair from his eye. 'Have a drink. Compose yourself.'

Clay saw Adam look darkly at the show of tenderness.

'Poor Louise, she'll be devastated. She didn't say much about him. She's a modest woman, not given to boasting,' said Danielle. 'But her father was a high-achieving academic in his time.'

'Does Louise ever talk about her mother?' asked Clay.

'Only that her name was Denise and she had no memory of her.'

DN. Clay thought about the dedications in Leonard Lawson's books. *Denise Lawson? DL?*

'Anything else?' she said, looking at Gideon, Danielle and Adam. 'About her father?' Silence. 'Her home life?' Clay waited. 'Her past?'

'I'm sorry,' said Danielle. 'I've known her for years, but when you're faced with it, you only know so much about a person, what that person wants to reveal.'

'I understand,' replied Clay, veteran of thousands of interviews.

'I know what she's like here, but the very little I do know... I guess I've run out of ideas.'

'Anything? Anything else?' urged Clay. Danielle looked at Gideon and Adam.

'She's a devout Christian, goes to church most days,' said Adam. 'I see her in the Anglican Cathedral on a regular basis.'

'You're in the cathedral on a regular basis?' Clay asked, wondering why the detail surprised her.

'I'm a volunteer there. I'm an interpreter of the building. I'm a Christian.'

'Do you talk to her in the cathedral?' Clay asked, hopefully.

'No. I'm a very busy man. When I see her at the cathedral, I'm usually showing Japanese tourists around.' He glanced at Gideon. 'I work hard and there's always work to be done.'

'I'm a complete atheist,' said Danielle.

'That's irrelevant,' said Adam. 'We're not talking about you, Danielle.' The words skimmed like razor-sharp stones across icy water. 'But what is relevant is Louise and she has a series of mountainous problems ahead of her.' He pulled his dressing gown together at the throat and looked at Clay. 'Her home's a crime scene?'

'Yes.'

'In which case,' said Adam, 'she'll need somewhere to stay. She can stay here. My father always told me, give shelter to the needy.'

Clay drank in the mutual astonishment of Danielle and Gideon.

'I gather we're all she's got now,' he continued. 'She can come and stay here in our flat on the top floor.'

Danielle placed her hand on the back of his, smiled at him. He looked at her hand and she withdrew it.

'She's given us tens of thousands of pounds of unpaid labour over the years. It's the least we can do. I have nothing further to add.' Adam stood up. 'If she's here in the evenings, she can help with bathtimes and bedtimes.' He looked at Stone. 'May I go? I have a very busy day ahead.'

'Yes, you can go,' said Clay.

He walked towards the door. 'Being here, it'll keep her mind occupied.'

When he'd gone, Gideon looked at Danielle and said, 'OMG!'

'Tell her, tell her she can stay with us for as long as she likes,' Danielle said to Clay. 'Tell her we'd love her to stay.'

Clay stood up. 'We have to get going.' She handed her card

to Danielle. 'If you need to contact me about anything, please do so immediately.'

As she headed back to the front door, Clay took in the various artworks around the hallway and gathered that self-expression was highly valued at The Sanctuary. A horse with legs fatter than its body. A man sitting in front of a bank of fog. A house with massive black blobs for windows and a tiny yellow square for a door. A brown chimney that looked like it was falling apart.

Adam, twenty-something, smiling in the sunshine of an upmarket marina, his father's hand at the junction of his neck and shoulder.

At the front door, Clay turned to Danielle and Gideon. 'Thank you for your time.'

From upstairs, the creak of a foot on a loose floorboard. Clay paused, looked up, expecting to see Adam, and made out the shape of a man. He stepped from the shadows and stood in the soft light at the top of the stairs. His hair was dark, his eyes open but empty. Dressed in plain black pyjamas, he stared into space, his face childlike, handsome, his gaze almost Christ-like. It was hard to call, but Clay pinned him in his late thirties, even though his expression took years off him.

Gideon walked quickly up the stairs, two at a time. 'Abey!' he said, his tone reassuring.

'He sleepwalks. Every night. He comes to the same spot at the top of the stairs.' Danielle checked the clock on the wall. 'Six forty-five. Quarter to the hour every time. Different hour every time, but always quarter to.'

A wave of compassion flooded through Clay as the thought occurred to her: *Almost there, but always short of the complete lap of the clock.* She wondered where he'd be and what he'd be doing at that hour had he not had learning difficulties?

In Clay's eyes, gentleness lay around the man like an invisible veil.

He'd be with his children, getting them ready for school, preparing himself for another busy day.

'Come on, Abey.' Gideon laid his hands on Abey's shoulders, turned him around and gave him a gentle push between the shoulder blades.

'Louise says she doesn't have favourites,' said Danielle. 'But he's her favourite by far. He follows her round like a shadow,' she whispered. 'He's like the son she never had.' She opened the front door.

Stepping outside, Clay took out her iPhone and asked, 'Before I text DS Riley with your offer of accommodation, are you absolutely sure Louise can stay here?'

'In spite of his religious faith, my husband's not a naturally charitable man, DCI Clay. For him, The Sanctuary's a profit-making business. Adam came into a lot of money when his father died and he saw a gap at the high end of the care market for people with learning disabilities. I'm not going to veto an opportunity for him to do something for someone else just for the sake of it. It's a very pleasant surprise.'

'We all have depths,' said Clay. Some clear, some dark. 'Sometimes we surprise ourselves as much as we surprise those closest to us.'

'Bring her in later this morning.' Danielle smiled. 'We'll be happy to give her shelter.'

Riley stared out at the sky across the Mersey and made a decision about the Louis Vuitton bag and the Jimmy Choo shoes that she was watching on eBay. Either or? No. She was going to put high bids on both and snuff out the competition.

Louise woke from her fitful sleep and cleared her throat. 'Gina?'

Riley turned, walked over to the bed. 'How are you feeling?'

'How long was I asleep?'

'Half an hour...'

Louise touched the white plaster on her forehead. 'It must have been the bump to my head...' Riley leaned closer to her, watching her with an intensity that made the silence palpable.

'Do you want to tell me something, Louise?'

'I had the most bizarre dream. About my father's picture. About *The Tower of Babel*. I only share my dreams with those who are in them.'

'Was I in your dream?'

The buzz of an incoming text – 'Eve Clay' – split Riley down the middle. 'The Tower of Babel?' She kept the theme alive as she opened the text.

Adam and Danielle Miller, owners of The Sanctuary, have offered to have Louise stay with them for as long as she likes. Encourage her to say yes and to go there asap. It literally is her sanctuary.

'Tell me about your dream,' said Riley, holding Louise's gaze.

'The whole of the bedroom wall facing his bed was completely covered, from ceiling to floor, with *The Tower of Babel*. You were walking beside me. We were walking towards the Tower of Babel. I asked you what had happened. You said Bruegel had risen from the dead and painted a mural on the wallpaper to replace the picture that had been stolen from my father.'

A dreaminess settled on Louise's face as she seemed to turn over some details in her mind. Riley glanced down at the screen of her phone, closed the text and discreetly pressed record.

'What happened next, Louise, in your dream?'

'The whole room altered. It stopped being my father's bedroom with a painted Tower of Babel on the wall and became a three-dimensional version of the scene itself. We walked. The earth was scorched. We headed towards the entrance. And the noise. The closer we came, the louder it became. It was horrific. Thousands of voices clamouring inside the tower and pouring out like red-hot windstorms. You put your hands over my ears. Your face was pinched and your eyes were slits, your hair was streaming behind you and you moved your lips and it looked like you'd mouthed the words *Jesus wept*, and I screamed back at you, *That's a fact!*'

When Louise paused, Riley passed her a glass of water. As the old lady sipped delicately, Riley made a mental note never to underestimate the power of another human being's inner life.

'Go on,' she said, hooked.

'And as soon as I said *That's a fact!*, all the noise stopped. Silence slammed down from the sky. We were near the entrance and you said, *Can you hear that?* I said, *No*. You looked up. One voice, high up in the tower, whispered. You pointed. There were two boys—'

'Two boys?' Riley interrupted, thinking, *Two killers*.

'Yes, two boys... leaning out of the tower. Oh yes, I could hear it now, a noise like a house fly buzzing far away. One of the boys was whispering, but we couldn't hear a word. The whispering boy stopped making the noise and then he... stuck out his hand...' Louise extended her arm, turning it over so that her palm was uppermost and her fingers were parted. 'Like this.' She lifted her hand up slowly. 'We rose from the earth. Like the boy had the power to make us levitate, the power in his hand.'

Louise paused and stared straight at Riley, as if daring Riley to make light of what she was telling her. Was this significant? Riley wondered. More importantly, perhaps, did Louise think it significant? Or were these just the ramblings of an elderly brain coming out of mild concussion? Either way, it seemed she wasn't finished yet.

'We rose higher and higher and when we reached the hole in the Tower of Babel where the boys were, there was only one boy there. The silent one. The whisperer had gone and we could see why the silent boy was silent. Underneath his nose, his mouth was sealed up with a single piece of skin that covered the whole of the lower half of his face.' She reached out with both hands. 'He touched both of us on the centre of our foreheads and, slowly, down we went. And when my feet touched the ground, it was no longer like being inside the Bruegel painting of the Tower of Babel. You had gone and I was alone in my father's room, looking at the painting on the wall, the one that had been there for as long as I could remember. And I heard my father's voice, behind me. *Louise?* I turned. He wasn't there. Then I woke up. Here. With you. And you were looking out of the window.'

Morning had arrived and the blood-red sky unfolded into grey light.

'Bump to the head,' said Louise. She gave the slightest shrug of the shoulders. 'Fantastic dreams...'

'Did the boys have names?' asked Riley.

Louise shook her head.

'The boy with the skin covering his mouth – did you see any other features?'

'I've told you everything there was in the dream.'

The wind roared against the hospital windows.

'You told me your father refused to speak about why he loved that particular painting?'

Louise thought about the question and Riley knew she had an answer of sorts. But there was something in Louise's face that she couldn't read. In answering the question, would she somehow be betraying her father's memory? A confidence, maybe?

'Once. He had a fever once. I nursed him back to health. When his fever was high, he talked about the painting. He said, and I think he was quoting a writer, *Every word is like a stain on silence and nothingness*. That is the truth of the Tower of Babel. For a man who wrote so many words, in his day-to-day life my father was a man of very few words. He could sit in complete silence for hours on end, locked inside the ebb and flow of ideas inside his head. We had no music in the house. No record player. I was the only girl in my class who didn't own a record by the Beatles. We didn't get a television until 1980. And even then I could only watch it when Father had gone to bed.'

'He sounds like a strict father.'

She considered the observation. 'Times were different then.'

Riley looked at the curve of her forehead, wondered at the vivid image systems that existed inside her, born perhaps of the constant exposure to art in her childhood.

'You know you won't be able to go back to your house for a long time?'

'I understand. I'll go to the Travelodge on Aigburth Road.'

'There's no need for that. You've had an offer of a place to stay.'

Louise sat up. 'With whom?'

'The Millers. The Sanctuary. They seem very keen for you to stay. I would take up that offer if I was you. You'll be able to see all your friends.'

Riley watched the information percolate in the passing of a brief smile.

'I will. Yes, I will stay there. You're right. All my friends are there.'

'Who are your friends in The Sanctuary?'

Louise's face visibly brightened. 'Tom Thumb – that's not his real name, it's Tom Thomas, but he's only five foot tall. Oh...' Louise looked at Riley. 'Abey. He's a wonderful man. But don't tell anyone I said that. I wouldn't want to hurt the other men's feelings, and they do have feelings; deep, deep feelings.'

'Louise, how about DCI Clay and I take you there as soon as the doctor says you're free to go?'

She nodded slowly and, looking directly at Riley, said, 'People are so kind, aren't they?'

'Yes,' lied Riley. 'People are kind.'

Part Two
Sunrise

The Last Judgment
by Hieronymus Bosch (1482)

How they screamed for mercy that simply wasn't there.
The First Born measured the ten years of his life with a sadness that he sometimes felt would kill him. He knew he must fight the pain, because he was terrified of what would happen after he died.

A sudden gust of wind raised the curtain, and light came in from the streetlamps outside. The three panels covering the wall facing his bed were immediately lit up. On the left was the Garden of Eden, and on the right was Hell. But it was the middle panel that scared him the most. Up in a blue sky sat Christ the Judge, and below him were all the people who would go to hell when they died. Some of them were burning and some were speared on horrible sharp hooks. There were so many twisted bodies, writhing in the dark. Hardly any bodies were flying up to join the angels in the blue sky. 'No one knows the moment!' The voice intoned inside his head. 'The Last Judgment must come to all.' It echoed from the plates of his skull. 'The first thing you see in the morning and the last thing you see at night.'

The First Born scuttled beneath the blankets and was filled with a sensation that comforted him. He felt as if his whole body was shrinking to the size of a pea. And he told himself, pea-sized and hidden in the double-darkness of night and blankets, nothing could find him.

Except for sound. A mean and heavy wind pressed down on the slates of the house he had never stepped out from, in a place he had learned was called Croxteth Road. It seemed to him that the wind was wrapping around the walls, squeezing the sides of the house. Beneath the blankets, The First Born felt his chest tighten and his breath started to come in short gasps. He was sure these were the first steps on the road to death, and to the darkness that lay beyond.

The First Born threw the blankets from himself and looked at The Last Judgment, his body heaving with silent sobs.

A demon with the face of a boar, and with burning coals instead of a heart, stood underneath a cauldron packed with bodies, screaming for help but boiling forever. The voice echoed once more inside his head. 'This is the eternal fruits of sin, the final entrapment of humanity.'

The First Born closed his eyes but The Last Judgment was printed on his mind.

How they screamed for mercy that simply wasn't there.

27

8.23 am

Slender shafts of daylight arrived from east of the Mersey and the temperature on Pelham Grove dropped. Clay walked towards Leonard Lawson's house, glancing back at the slamming of car doors. Beyond the crime-scene tape, she saw a fat man hurrying under a streetlight.

She shivered as she stepped into her protective suit. Inside the house the air felt colder than on the street outside. Red-eyed and tired, DS Terry Mason stepped out of the kitchen.

'Have you found anything, Terry?' asked Clay.

'He had a daughter, I assume he had a wife. I presume she's the mother of his daughter. But there's no physical evidence whatsoever that he had a wife, not a single photograph, not a love letter, not a piece of jewellery. It's like she's been written out of history.' He handed Clay two old pages, one folded inside the other.

She opened them, separated them. Leonard Lawson's birth certificate and his daughter Louise's.

'Where did you find these, Terry?'

On the street outside, a pair of footsteps echoed as they hurried in the direction of the house.

'In a Queen Elizabeth coronation tin, in a drawer in the kitchen. The only other thing in the tin was Leonard Lawson's passport, which expired in 1974. That's the closest it gets here to a lifetime's memento.'

From the front door, she heard Michael Harper's voice. 'But I'm Dr Lamb's APT from the mortuary at the Royal.' There was excitement and urgency in his voice.

'I'm sorry,' replied the constable on the step. 'DCI Clay hasn't listed you to enter the scene.'

Harper's usually timid voice bordered on assertive. 'I'm to give this directly to DCI Clay and no one else.'

Clay opened the front door.

In front of the constable on the step, Harper stood shivering and Clay couldn't tell if it was from the cold or the excitement that was apparent on his baby face.

'What have you got for me, Harper?'

He held out his hand and gave her a small key in a plastic bag. 'I found it in Professor Lawson's upper digestive tract,' he said.

'Thank you, Harper.'

She headed directly to the study, took the key from the bag and showed it to Stone and Hendricks, who were at the desk reading the manuscript.

'He swallowed the key?' said Stone.

'Or was forced to swallow it.' She handed it to Stone. 'Check it fits the desk drawer.'

Stone closed the open drawer, slid the key into the lock and turned it. 'That's our baby.'

Hendricks picked up the second part of Leonard Lawson's 'Psamtik I' manuscript. 'You just got a heap more significant,' he said to the dog-eared pages, and smiled at Clay.

Leonard Lawson's book on Hieronymus Bosch lay open on the desk. On one page were the panels colour of a triptych *The Last Judgment*. On the page beside it were two grey panels, the images at the back of the closed triptych, two saints in black and white, their names beneath their images. St James, weary as he walked through the sinful earth. St Bavon dispensing alms to the poor in a room overlooking the city of Ghent.

Clay took up the framed photograph from Leonard Lawson's desk and said, 'LL and DN.' She looked at the black-and-white image of two young men on their graduation day, the only personal effect in Leonard Lawson's study, at the heart of his private space. She pictured them on a summer's day, sitting under the shade of a tree, a heart cut into the bark and their initials carved inside the heart, a dragonfly hovering above their heads, looking for a window in the warm air where there was none.

Her phone rang out. She looked at the display, picked up the call. 'Gina, what's happening?'

The body language between the two young graduates in the photo spoke of a close relationship. She turned on the desk lamp.

'She's all ready to leave, in a set of borrowed clothes.'

'Get a taxi to The Sanctuary and I'll meet you there. Anything to report?'

'She had a weird dream about the Tower of Babel. It was all pretty surreal, but beggars can't be choosers. There might be something in it.'

Clay moved the image under the bright light and there was something in the way both men smiled that put her in mind of a wedding portrait, shoulder touching shoulder, looking directly at the camera, smiling.

'If she's spilling her dreams to you, you're doing a massively good job of bonding.'

'She's keen to go to The Sanctuary. It's like a home from home for her. *All my friends are there. Tom and Abey.* They're disabled men who live there.'

'Did you tape it?'

'I certainly did. She's our eyewitness. I'm interested in every single word that comes out of her mouth. Even if I can't quite fathom exactly where she's coming from.'

'Well done, Gina. Keep her talking, keep pumping her. As soon as we've left her in The Sanctuary, I want you to go to the University of Liverpool, human resources. I want to know what they've got on Leonard Lawson.'

She closed the call down and called, 'Terry?'

'Yes?'

As Mason appeared in the doorway, Clay picked up the framed photograph of Leonard Lawson and his friend on their graduation day and showed it to him. 'If you're wondering where this went, I'm taking it away with me.'

She opened the brief author biography on the back panel of the dust jacket of one of Lawson's books. *Hiding, hiding, hiding*... The words shot through her head like rockets.

'Karl?'

'Yes?' Stone looked up reluctantly, engrossed in Leonard Lawson's manuscript.

'What did Lawson write about *The Tower of Babel* in his Bruegel book?'

'That the painting can mean very different things to different people and in different eras. When he painted it, Bruegel was issuing a warning about pride in the face of God. But in Lawson's interpretation, his own view of God comes out loud and clear. God is a spoiled and brutal child who cannot take any challenge from his creation. One language was all mankind needed to fly, but – I'll paraphrase – in destroying the Tower of Babel, God acted like a vile little boy pulling the wings off a dragonfly (in other words, mankind) and enjoying the twisting of the wingless body in the dirt. If Lawson believed in God, he hated him with a vengeance.'

Clay looked at the austere collection of letters in the book's dedication:

For DN
Now and for always

The itch beneath her scalp sharpened. She decided to show the photo to Louise and ask what she knew about DN, even though she guessed that Leonard Lawson, who had divulged nothing to his daughter about his wife – her mother – would also have kept totally silent about the other love of his life.

28

8.23 am

The last of the sunrise over the River Mersey filled the sky with shifting bands of red and amber light, making its surface shine crimson.

David Higson, manager of the municipal tip at Otterspool Promenade, stood with his back to the wall of a hut near the entrance to the site, watching the sky through the steam rising from the mug of tea on which he warmed his hands. The wind whipped off the Mersey and made his skin break out into goose bumps. A shiver ran through him.

'Excuse me!'

Someone spoke, but it seemed to come from far away, a ghost's voice drifting on the unforgiving wind. He sipped his tea and continued to enjoy the sky.

'I said, excuse me!' This time it was loud.

The sudden aggression in the man's voice forced Higson out of his reverie and face to face with a man wearing a plain blue baseball cap and a pair of Ray-Bans. The man looked down from the driver's seat of his white van, a crooked crease between his eyebrows.

'Yes?' asked Higson. The man turned his face and stared through the windscreen. 'We're not actually open yet.'

'I've got a freezer to get rid of.'

'But we're not open until nine o'clock. If I let you past me and you have an accident, Liverpool City Council won't be insured against your injury and there's a technical term for what I'd be.' He paused for effect. 'Fucked.'

The man continued staring ahead. Higson looked at the man's hands. His knuckles whitened as he gripped the steering wheel.

'So...' The man still didn't look at Higson. 'Come back later – is that what you're saying?' There was a tremor in his voice that lay on the thin line between crying and screaming.

The man's nostrils flared and Higson was suddenly aware of two things. All they had for company were seagulls and he had no idea what kind of weapon might lie beneath the man's seat. He glanced at his mug and cursed himself for having drunk the red-hot tea down to the dregs. In the event of needing to, he had nothing left to throw into the driver's face.

'I'm not saying that at all. But there is a magic word that gets all kinds of stuff done.'

The colour on the man's throat rose. 'Please,' he said.

'Reverse out and leave the freezer just outside the perimeter. I'll make sure it ends up in the home electricals graveyard. Just over there.'

With a sharp jolt, the man reversed the van outside the tip and Higson blew a low sigh of relief. He watched the man climb out of the van, noted his knee-length padded jacket, blue overall trousers and black Doc Marten boots. *One of our not-very-well-in-the-head brethren*, he thought.

The back doors opened and, within a few moments, the man had the small freezer, bound by duct tape, out of the van and on to the grass verge. Once he was back at the wheel and reversing away, Higson returned his attention to the sky. He listened as the van squealed away at unnecessary speed.

The energising reds, ambers and violets had settled into a palette of grey and white. He placed his cup inside the hut, turned the kettle on for a refill of tea and, with a trolley, went to do a chore for the man who had ruined the best of the day for him.

29

8.55 am

The sky over Sefton Park was marked by two fading red lines, crossing each other. Day marked the spot with an X where night had nurtured a barbaric murder. As Riley travelled with Louise Lawson around the park's never-ending curve, she looked out of the taxi window and saw a flying V of geese reflected on the surface of the lake.

'Are you OK, Louise?' she asked, painfully aware that they were getting closer to the scene of her father's murder and would have to pass the top of Lark Lane to get to The Sanctuary.

'It's a beautiful morning.'

'It is. Look at the trees,' said Riley, drawing her attention parkside, away from Lark Lane and Pelham Grove.

'Covered, aren't they? Layer on layer. Snow on snow. This is the day that the Lord has made. Do you know that hymn?'

'We should rejoice and give thanks in it.' Riley delivered the next line. 'Those joggers...' She pointed at them. 'So dedicated, out running even in this cold.'

'There's Gabriel,' said Louise. Riley followed Louise's eye line. A tall man in a threadbare black coat with his back turned to the road was walking down a path leading into the heart of Sefton Park. 'Gabriel? A friend of yours?'

Louise shook her head. 'Just a man in the park.'

Riley blew a silent sigh of relief. They had passed the

entrance to Lark Lane and Louise was still staring at the trees in the park.

Outside The Sanctuary, Riley paid the driver, then helped Louise from the back of the taxi and on to the treacherously icy pavement. Clay approached them, carrying two large bags.

'Good morning, DCI Clay,' said Louise.

'How are you?' asked Clay. Louise's eyes were black and puffy, the bang to her head working out across the contours of her face.

'I'm cold!'

Clay went ahead and rang the bell while Riley supported Louise on the approach to the front door. As they waited on the step, Clay cut to the chase.

'I've a few things to show you and I'd like to ask you some questions once we're inside and settled. Is that fine by you, Louise?'

Louise nodded, her face vacant.

The door opened slowly, like the person on the other side was playing a game. Clay began to get impatient but reminded herself that this was a home for men with learning difficulties.

A face appeared through the narrow gap, the eyes smiley. The man made a small sound in his throat, a sudden intake of breath, an expression of pure surprise and excitement. A glow of happiness shone in Louise's eyes.

It was Abey, the sleepwalker, now wide awake and in playful mood. Clay took him in with a glance, saw the friendship bracelet on his wrist, a match with the one Louise wore. In his hair, drops of melted snow glittered. His breath fell thick and fast. *An overexcited child in a man's body,* thought Clay.

'Oh my!' Louise looked behind herself, theatrically. 'Let me in, Abey! Let me in! Save me from the big bad wolf!' She worked hard to act normally, to play a game with him.

Abey's smile broadened. He opened the door wide and pointed past Louise.

'Don't scream out loud, Abey! He'll hear you and come running towards us.'

He opened his mouth and let out a silent scream, waving his hands and gesturing towards the park. Then he grabbed Louise's hand and pulled her across the threshold. He looked at Clay and, waving her indoors, said, 'Quick! Quick! He's behind you!'

Clay and Riley entered The Sanctuary. Abey shut the door. Louise and Abey let out a long, harmonised sigh, each of them wiping their brows; a well-rehearsed play ritual.

'Go away, Mr Wolf!' Louise's voice was deep. 'Leave us in peace. Go chase Red Riding Hood today!'

The kitchen was full of the sound of men's voices, excited and happy. *Snow*, thought Clay, *and men who viewed the world with the eyes of children.* Philip? She took out her mobile phone, looked at the time and, with a sinking heart, knew she was too late to call her son.

Abey threw out his arms like a child and swamped Louise in a man-sized hug that looked like it could suffocate her. 'Lou-Lou...' She wrapped her arms around him and patted him on the back.

Clay felt like she was invading a tender, private moment. But she had to watch. It was a vision of uncomplicated love and Clay was filled both with the sweetness of Abey giving Louise that gift in that moment and with a sourness that she couldn't do the same for her son.

From the kitchen doorway, Gideon said, 'Come on, Abey. Come to me. Lou-Lou's very busy today.' He waved Abey over with big, deliberate gestures.

A short, fat man with Down's syndrome, of indeterminate age and with short sandy hair and a wispy beard, wandered down the stairs sucking his thumb, then jumped from the fourth step.

Abey looked across at Gideon, unwrapped his arms from Louise's body and addressed the man. 'Tom Thumb!'

Tom held up his hand and Abey high-fived him as he followed Gideon's instruction.

'Abey good,' said Abey, patting his own chest in the same way that Philip did when he wanted to assert his identity.

'DCI Clay,' said Louise. 'I need to go to the bathroom before we begin our discussion.'

'Of course,' said Clay, watching Gideon escort Abey away.

Danielle Miller, dressed in a black Jaeger skirt and an elegant cream-coloured blouse, stepped out of the kitchen and towards Clay and Riley. Her make-up was subtle, took years off her.

'Danielle,' said Clay. 'How much of what is said does Abey understand?'

'About as much as your average four- or five-year-old would understand.'

Cognitively then, Clay thought, he was slightly ahead of her son.'

'Why do you ask, DCI Clay?'

Clay considered what she had seen, the way Louise had opened up emotionally in the presence of Abey, the way she had come alive. 'I'd like Abey to be present in the room when I talk to Louise.'

Danielle's face clouded. 'You're talking about murder? I don't know.'

'We'd place him out of hearing distance, but we'd like him in the room,' Riley chimed in.

'He's her favourite, we know this,' Clay said. 'And he's clearly a great comfort to her. I think it would be immensely helpful to Louise if he was there. It's the kind thing to do.'

'If she becomes upset, he'll become upset.'

'We want to conduct an exploratory conversation about her father,' said Clay. 'We know what she saw last night. We won't be going over that right now. If at any point she looks like she's going to become emotional, we'll cut the interview.'

'He's a sensitive man.' Danielle turned her attention away from Clay, focused on Riley.

'We're professionals, Mrs Miller. We conduct difficult and highly sensitive discussions with all manner of people nearly every day,' said Riley.

'You'd better conduct your interview in our apartment,' said Danielle. 'At least you'll be able to hear yourself think.'

As they followed up the stairs, Clay noted the bottom wiggle of a woman who clearly thought she was made of the world's finest chocolate. She looked at Riley, who puckered her lips and cupped her hands under her breasts.

'Gorgeous!' mouthed Clay.

Everything in the Millers' living room was perfect. Tan carpet, white walls and black leather furniture that looked as if it had been specifically designed for the place. It was set out at angles, giving the room a sense of space and, at the same time, intimacy.

On the wall were framed pictures. Adam Miller, in a black gown, on the steps of the Anglican Cathedral. A large oil painting of the Anglican Cathedral. Adam and Danielle on their wedding day with a man Clay recognised, from the portrait downstairs, as Adam's father.

In the corner, Riley was on her phone, listening and then talking, her face becoming animated as the conversation developed.

Standing between the plasma television on the wall and the bay window, Clay flicked through her notebook but watched from the corner of her eye.

As Clay had requested, Abey had been set up in the corner of the room with something to do. Waiting for Louise to arrive, Clay observed Danielle's manner with Abey. Clay and Riley exchanged a glance. She was genuinely kind and patient.

Riley took her iPhone away from her ear, closed the call down and headed towards Clay. 'I've had a hit with the Hart Building, Liverpool University's human resources centre,' she said. 'I called on the off chance at eight this morning and got someone called Justine Elgar. Leonard Lawson's records pre-date computers.

She's just called me back. She's dug up his paper records and I've asked her to make me a copy.'

'Did she know anything immediately?'

'She said, *Every Professor is big in his or her day, but when their day's done so are they!* She told me there'd be some record of him. There had to be.'

'Good work.' Instinct prompted Clay and she spoke with urgency. 'Go there now, Gina!'

'Sure!' As she left the room, Riley recalled that her car was round the corner where she'd parked it in the pit of night.

Abey looked closely at Danielle from his table in the corner. 'This is for colouring,' said Danielle.

Abey took a piece of shaped card from her. 'What this?'

'It's a picture of a bird's face, Abey. Don't disturb Lou-Lou. She has to talk to her visitor. Be good.'

'Abey good boy,' he replied.

Adam Miller poked his head into the room. 'Danielle, did you put my van keys into the kitchen sink?'

She answered with a silent look and he left as quickly as he had arrived.

The living room door opened. Turning, Clay watched Louise enter, her face washed, her hair combed.

Engrossed in colouring, Abey didn't seem to notice her as she passed him and sat on a leather armchair.

Clay positioned herself on the sofa, at an angle to Louise, and pressed record on her iPhone. 'Are you ready, Louise?'

The sound of Abey's pencil scratching back and forth across the card drifted from the corner of the room.

'Yes, I'm ready.'

'Your father was a highly intelligent man...'

In the corner, deep in his throat, Abey hummed a series of random notes, but Louise didn't seem to notice.

'Did you ever read your father's books?'

She shook her head. 'No.'

'I'd have thought, Louise, if it was my father and he'd

written a book, I'd have been really curious to know what he'd written about.'

'Well...'

Clay watched the shifting contours of her face. 'You can say anything you like,' she reassured her.

'With all due respect, DCI Clay, you never knew your father. You were abandoned as a baby. So you don't really know what you'd have done if your father had written a book.'

Although it was common knowledge, Clay was surprised that Louise had articulated the information so bluntly. 'How did you find that out?' she asked.

'When you captured the sisters who murdered their mother.'

The memory caused coldness and sadness to pass through Clay. 'Go on...'

'Gideon told me all about it. It's a dreadful thing for a child to kill a parent. And then I went into the Sefton Park on Aigburth Road and read about it in a *True Detective* magazine.'

'So you know all about my Satanic cult background as well?' Clay faced it head on.

'I don't blame you for that. It's no one's fault where they are born or the parents they are born to. The Lord won't judge you for other people's sins. Remember, Jesus died to save us all from our sins.'

Clay looked across the silent room. Abey stared down at the page, drew a circle over and over. For a moment, he looked at Clay, but it seemed to her he couldn't see her. He returned to colouring.

'Not everyone has the good fortune to be born to such an eminent father as yours, Louise. Two things I picked up on. Your doorbell was broken and was covered with two sticking plasters?'

'We never had callers to the house. Father didn't welcome company of any kind. Visitors or people selling things we didn't need.'

'But he liked your friend Gideon Stephens, didn't he?'

'He did. He would speak to Gideon because his manners were good and he looked after my safety. They would speak briefly, the same conversation: words of thanks, words of response.'

'No other visitors or friends?' Louise shook her head, looked away. 'Which brings me on to the next thing I picked up on. His address book. It was completely empty.'

'Like I said, he didn't welcome company.'

'Is it fair to say he prided himself on being self-contained?'

'That would be fair.'

'That's why he kept an address book. To remind himself that there were no addresses in it?' Clay pictured Leonard Lawson's life, the never-ending struggle for knowledge, the professional obligation to talk and write himself into the ground, and she understood a little of his eccentricity.

'But...' Clay leaned in a little closer to Louise. 'He did have relationships in his life. Historically. He must have done.'

'For me to be here? My mother? She died when I was a baby. She had cancer of the throat. He found it impossible to talk about her. He couldn't talk to me about it. I stopped asking questions about her when I was quite small because I knew I'd never get any answers.'

Clay produced a copy of *Hieronymus Bosch: Divine Visions* and placed it on the coffee table. From the same evidence bag she then pulled out the framed photograph from Leonard Lawson's desk.

'Louise, I need to find out as much about your father as I can because I believe that the person who killed him knew him. Do you know who the people in this graduation photograph are?'

'One of them is my father. I don't know who the other man is.' Clay heard a catch in Louise's voice. 'It was something he wouldn't talk about.'

'Which one is your father?'

Louise pointed at the taller of the two and Clay connected his youthful features with the face of the corpse.

She opened the dedication page of the Hieronymus Bosch and showed it to her.

For DN
Now and for always

'Your father never mentioned a university friend called David or Daniel or Douglas...?'

'I do not know the name of the other man in the picture. I'm sorry. But I do know who DN is because I worked it out for myself,' said Louise.

In the corner, Abey blew his cheeks out and neighed, his lips rattling in the air.

'It's Denise Nicholas. She's my mother and that was her maiden name.'

Denise Nicholas? thought Clay, a cloud parting. DN. The person to whom he dedicated every single book that he wrote for the rest of his long, lonely life. Idea after idea tripped inside Clay's head and the picture of the ice-cold, aloof father that was forming gave way to another version of the same man. Leonard Lawson's private self had a tragic door leading to his secret self. She needed more light. 'What kind of a father was he?'

'He was a good father. It was the 1950s, a different world to today. He was strict because he was a single man bringing up a daughter. He did as much for me as he could, which was almost everything.'

Respect crept into Clay's vision of Leonard Lawson. Devastated by the loss of his wife, he hadn't turned to drink. Instead, he had immersed himself in the academic study of art and in looking after his daughter, sealing off the loneliness with self-imposed solitude and silence.

'Your father walked in Sefton Park every day.'

'Yes, regular as clockwork.'

'Did he tell you about an incident in the park last Thursday?'

'No. But he was upset when I came home to make his meal. Did something bad happen to him?'

'We have a prime suspect for your father's murder,' said Clay.

Outside, snow started falling.

Louise sat forward. 'Tell me. Who is it? And what happened?'

31

9.23 am

There were two places Adam Miller could be himself.

In his shed at the bottom of the long, rectangular back garden of The Sanctuary, Adam Miller turned the handle of the vice on his workbench and sealed the wooden window frame in place. He picked up a planer, drew the blade across the edge of the wood and felt a surge of pride at the skill and strength with which he manipulated the tool in his hand.

Outside, he heard the sound of excited voices coming out of the house and into the garden. The pleasure evaporated and anger took its place. He looked out of the window and saw the source of the excitement. *Snow*. Fucking *snow*. It always turned the retards' lights on. Made them act different. Just recently, Abey had gone wandering off in it after he'd been told to shovel the snow off the gravel path at the front of The Sanctuary. They only noticed he'd disappeared when Danielle returned home, and then it had taken Adam three hours to find the wandering idiot.

Adam opened the door and looked out through the snow at Gideon and eleven of the residents. They were standing in a circle and following his lead, their faces turned to the sky, their eyes and mouths open, their arms reaching up, fingers splayed, welcoming the falling snow. The twelfth resident, Abey, wasn't there. Him again. Louise's little pet and the most irritating of the twelve.

'You're all snowmen!' called Gideon. 'Go and find your own space in the garden and become very still. Just like snowmen.' He clapped his hands together and started lunging playfully at the men.

What a life, thought Adam. *Playing music, playing games. You're men! You should be working! You're capable of digging, and carrying weights! If fucking donkeys can work, so can you!*

The circle disintegrated and the men scattered, some running, some hobbling, some dancing, some limping. Half the group found their space in the garden and fell still within moments; the other half needed Gideon's help to reach even a semblance of stillness. Some wobbled, some rocked back and forth, and some fidgeted, but it was the closest the group would come to being snowmen.

'Who is the stillest of them all?' Gideon asked. His eyes connected with Adam's. Of the other people in the garden, only Tom Thumb looked at Adam.

What are you looking at, dwarf? 'All right, Gid!' Adam said, with a smile. He beckoned him over to the shed.

'What is it, Adam?'

'What are you doing?'

'Working.'

Adam hated the way the snow melted on Gideon's hair. 'Working?' He laughed. 'Playing, surely?'

'I'm a play therapist. That's one of the jobs I do here. That's why you employ me, Adam.'

'Working?' Adam pointed at the window frame in the vice. 'You know that window that won't open in the bathroom, because the damp conditions have swollen the wood? I planed two mills off it, round about midnight. I had to bring it back and try again because it still won't fit and I reckon it needs another two. That's working. Fancy a swap?' He extended the planer to Gideon.

Gideon shook his head and turned away.

'Oh for God's sake, Gid, I'm just having a laugh with you. Where's your sense of humour?'

Adam closed the door and took one of two keys from his pocket. He locked the shed on the inside and then, imagining Gid's face trapped in the vice, sliced the flesh of the wood and felt a rush of blood to his penis. He pictured Gideon's fat, over-sized penis wedged between the metal as he planed through the wood a second time. He heard Gideon's scream and watched the blood spray. It gave him an erection like iron.

That'll teach you to fuck my wife when I'm busy working!

He put the plane down and with his other key turned to the black box that he kept under the workbench. He pulled it out and, kneeling next to it, caught the aroma of fresh rubber. His stomach churned and a tremor tripped through his nervous system. He laid his arms across the lid, pressed his face against the leather surface and pictured the things inside the box. His body was locked in the moment, but his mind flew to another place, not far from where he was.

In his mind he replayed the sequence. He took out the key he'd been given, the one for the front door. He stepped inside, quietly, so the other tenants wouldn't hear him. He came to the door of the flat and used the other key to open it.

It was dark as pitch. He could hear the drip of a tap and laboured breathing in a room deep inside. He moved into the second place where he could be himself, closed the door and walked in silence through the gloom towards the sound of breathing.

The room was alive with candlelight and shadows and the sound of the Pig breathing hard. He looked at the Pig. The Pig was naked except for the leather mask that covered its face; its torso was still tied to the ladder-back chair, just as he'd left it hours earlier. 'Let me in, Little Pig!' Adam stepped closer, banged his fist into the palm of his hand. 'Did you hear that, Little Pig!' There was a squeal from behind the mask. 'I'm coming to get you, Little Pig. I'm going to hurt you really, really badly, Little Pig.'

Outside, he heard Gideon coming towards the shed, calling, 'Tom Thumb, don't go near Adam's shed, you know the rules.'

And he was snapped back into the moment.

Work! Time to go back to work! '*Work! Work! Work! Work!*' He could hear his father's voice and he was on his feet without thinking. He looked up at the window. Outside, the snow was hurtling from the mute sky.

32

9.23 am

Danielle Miller stood at the window on the top floor of The Sanctuary, the house beneath her strangely silent for once. She focused her attention on Gideon, organising games down in the garden with the men in his care. A smile blossomed on her face at the way he slipped effortlessly into their collective mindset and played with the carelessness of a small child.

As she watched him weave between the human snowmen, Danielle felt a deeply buried longing for the love that was completely absent from her life. She fell to wishful thinking, closed her eyes and pictured the darkness of Gideon's hair, the warmth of his smile, the ever-present kindness in his eyes. She imagined his hands falling on her shoulders – the hands and arms that had picked her up by the waist and swung her round, circle after laughing circle, in the garden on the open day; she imagined the gentle weight of his fingertips pressing into the knots of tension.

'Do you love me, Gideon?'

'What is there not to love, Danielle?' The tactful answer he always supplied to the men of the house when they questioned his affections for them.

In her mind, she turned from the window and faced him. 'No, Gideon, do *you* love *me*?'

His hands slipped from her shoulders and down the length of each arm. Thrill after pleasure-packed thrill raced through her. She imagined him cupping his hands at the base of her back and pressing himself closer into her. She drank in his natural scent – sunshine and musk – and her head felt light, drunk on the chemicals pouring off him, silent messengers that told her it wasn't a case of *if* he loved her, it was a case of *how much*.

With a subtle gesture of her head, she offered him her lips and waited. She felt a pulse in the middle of her ribs – his heart beating into her body. She raised her hands and pressed them either side of his face, could feel the smile drifting into her palms. 'For God's sake, Gideon, kiss me!'

His lips descended on her mouth, a fragile and tender collision that ignited a fire at her core and a wetness between her legs. He slipped his tongue between her lips and, as the tip connected with hers, his left hand slid away from the base of her back, down the back of her thigh, inside her skirt and up to her waist.

His tongue drew a loving circle around hers and a profound sigh of pleasure mingled with the heat of her breath as his index finger slipped into her underwear and slid slowly down from her waist.

He pulled his head back and urged her, 'Look at me, Danielle!'

She opened her eyes and looked directly into his.

'I've loved you from the moment I met you. But you're a married woman and this is wrong.'

'I'll leave him. I love you so much, Gideon. Do you know how isolated I am? Do you know how lonely I've been? Lonely and unloved for years on end.'

His mouth pressed down on hers and she sobbed as his index finger glided inside her. His kiss was ambrosial, his touch like magic.

He drew his face away from hers.

'No. He's got all the money in the world. I live in a shared house and I'm on the minimum wage. I'd be reducing you to poverty. Remember how afraid of poverty you are. Remember the terrible things you saw poverty drive people to when you were a child.'

Where heat had raged, coldness now flooded in. The grey light of reality sharpened around her, and the phantom of Gideon, and the fantasy of their love, departed abruptly.

She opened her eyes and looked down at the garden again. Gideon was lying on the lawn, making a snow angel. With the back of her hand, she wiped away a film of tears. She laughed and sobbed in the same breath, pressed the heat of her cheek against the coldness of the glass and remembered again the weight of his muscular arms around her on that hot day in June when the public had been invited in to see the charade that her life truly was.

'Jesus, Gideon,' she whispered at the window.

In the garden below, he jumped up from the ground and chased after Tom Thumb.

'It's right under your nose, man. Can't you see it, sweetheart? Can't you see just how much I love and worship you?'

Silence.

'What are you rabbiting on about?' She froze at the sound of her husband's voice. 'What are you daydreaming about now?'

She couldn't turn to face him, couldn't bear to look at him.

'Oh, you know, the usual,' she replied. She hung on to her breath, tried to bury any display of emotion.

'And what might that be?'

'World peace and universal happiness and...'

'And?'

'A really nice black dress I saw on eBay.'

'Quit dreaming and get on with some work...'

His voice drifted away with him.

A really, really nice black dress, she thought. *The one I'll wear for your funeral.*

33

9.28 am

'What happened to my father in the park on Thursday?' asked Louise.

'Did your father ever mention people he walked past in the park?'

She shook her head. 'He was in a world of his own. I watched him once, without him knowing. I followed him for a little while. He didn't speak to anyone. I was in the park on another occasion with some of my friends from The Sanctuary. He saw me, made eye contact, but didn't speak. What happened on Thursday?'

'He was pursued, followed by a man who said unpleasant things to him. We're currently looking for that man so that we can arrest him and ask him questions to help us with our enquiries.'

'Where did this happen?'

'Near the Alicia Hotel.'

'And what did the man say?'

'He was whispering, so it's hard to say exactly,' lied Clay. 'But the point is, your father didn't want to communicate with this man and he didn't want this man following him. Other members of the public became aware of what was happening and intervened to defend your father. Fortunately, two police officers came upon the scene and were able to take charge of the situation.'

'Did this man touch my father or in any way physically hurt him?'

'No. No physical contact or violence happened.'

Louise processed the information. 'DCI Clay, I'd like to see my father's body, please.'

Clay recalled Leonard Lawson's dismantled torso – his rib cage in pieces, his heart torn apart to release the spear shaft that pierced it, his intestines piled on a metal trolley – and said, 'There's no hurry, is there, Louise?'

'Hope is eating me, DCI Clay. Here.' She touched her heart. 'I need to give up that hope.'

'What is that hope?' asked Clay.

From the table, Abey said, 'No, Ken. Ken naughty. Naughty Ken.'

'I need to give up the hope that he is still alive. That I'm not really locked in this waking nightmare. I keep expecting him to walk through the door and tell me to come on home because it's all been a horrible mistake.'

'Stop it, Ken!'

Louise glanced over at Abey. 'Ken is his imaginary friend,' she explained.

Clay chose her words with intense care. 'Your father won't walk through the door. He can't tell you to come home, because he's no longer with us. I've seen his body and he's being prepared as we speak for the dignity of the chapel of rest and the grace of a Christian funeral.'

'Chu-chu-chu-chu! Chu-chu-chu-chu!' Abey uttered a string of sounds with a regular rhythm and then, as if hit by a bolt of a happy memory, he started laughing. He looked at Clay with a vacancy in his eyes, his mouth wide open with laughter, a rope of saliva falling from the corner of his lower lip.

Louise looked to the sound and was on her feet and heading over to him with a lightness of movement that, in an instant, took twenty years off her.

As she reached Abey, she glanced back at Clay and said,

'He doesn't understand what's going on here. But sometimes he remembers things and he has no filter. He has good and bad memories.' She wiped his mouth, mopped up the spit that had fallen on his hands and sleeves. 'A good memory will make him laugh for no apparent reason, just as a bad one will make him cry. Memory for us is memory; for him it's as real as the moment he is living in.'

She placed her hands on Abey's shoulders and said, 'Abey, stand up for Lou-Lou!' He obeyed her immediately. She sucked in a stream of air and held it. He copied her. She breathed out slowly and he did the same.

'The trick is not to let him get too carried away laughing, because he'll literally make himself sick. And on the other side, if he gets too sad, he'll start hurting himself.'

Louise repeated the trick with the breathing and Clay was amazed at the way Abey calmed down so quickly. She decided she would try it at home with Philip when he was agitated.

Abey looked at Louise. 'Hug, Lou-Lou, hug!' She held out her arms and he sank into her embrace, pressing his face into her shoulder. He turned his head a little and looked at Clay. 'Who's that?' He offered Clay a fixed smile.

She waved back and said, 'Hello, Abey. I'm Louise's friend.'

'You Lou-Lou mummy?' asked Abey.

'No, I'm Louise's friend. I've come to help her.'

'When I little boy... I my help my daddy...'

'Do you want to sit with me?' asked Louise, pointing to the sofa. He nodded and, as he followed and sat next to Louise, she appeared to grow stronger.

Three floors down, Clay heard a chorus of voices, laughing as if they'd just heard the greatest gag on earth.

'That explains it,' said Louise, ideas connecting in her mind. 'He didn't go to the park for the last few days. He said it was the weather, which wasn't like him, but I thought maybe it was his age.'

Abey turned his head in Louise's direction but looked past

her and at the window. 'Snowing!' He clapped his hands three times and his gaze rose and fell, following the action of the falling snow.

'Was the man arrested?' asked Louise.

'No, but he was given a warning.'

'What do you know about the man who harassed my father?'

'Seems he was a regular feature in the park. I've actually got a picture of him.'

'I'd like to see,' said Louise.

Clay stopped recording. 'He's not a very pleasant-looking man.' She pulled up the picture and turned the screen towards Louise.

'Oh!'

'Louise?'

'I know him. Not to speak to. He's well known in the neighbourhood because he's an eccentric. People call him Bible Bob. It's not a name I like or would choose to use.'

'What's his real name, Louise?'

'When there are a lot of teenagers in a gang together, they laugh at him, but when I see them on their own or in twos and threes, they walk the other way.'

'Do you know his name?' Clay pressed.

'Someone told me his name's Gabriel Halifax... Or Huddersfield or Harrogate... Something like that. He's always in the park when I walk from home to here and back.'

Clay was on her feet. 'I have to go.'

As she left the room, Abey's voice followed her. 'You play in the snow?'

She made a call to the incident room at Trinity Road police station.

DC Barney Cole, the anchor, picked up. 'What's up, Eve?'

'I've got three possible names. I need you to look on the electoral register and the NHS database.'

'Fire away!'

34

9.28 am

Daylight seeped into Leonard Lawson's study and the long silence between Hendricks and Stone was broken when Hendricks turned over the last page of the second half of Leonard Lawson's manuscript and said, 'Done. Almost.'

'I want a black coffee and a Sausage McMuffin,' replied Stone, head in hands, the first part of the manuscript on the desk in front of him.

'Will you be eating in or taking out?'

'And I'll have a bowl of porridge for little Billy Hendricks.'

'Aw, thanks, Uncle Karl.'

Stone rubbed his eyes and looked down at the manuscript.

'So, Part One. Fire away, Karl?'

'Part One. The Ancient World p.4-210. Egypt. Six centuries before Jesus walked the earth, there's a king called Psamtik the First. He was a bit New Labour. Opened the country up to mass immigration.'

Hendricks laughed. 'Was he a warmonger as well?'

'He was constantly at war because there were armies at the borders and other psycho kings claiming a slice of the Egyptian pie. Psamtik figured that the country that possessed the *original* language, the *lingua mundi*, as it were, had the right to be called top dog. Language was the proof in the universal pudding, the gods' stamp of approval. So in between war after war after war, Psamtik conducted a crude experiment.'

Stone showed Hendricks a picture of a rugged man on a mountain with two bundles on his back. 'Two babies were taken from their mother at birth and given to this shepherd.' He pointed at the bundles. 'Baby one. Baby two. The shepherd's job was to say nothing, feed them goat's milk and listen out for whatever came from their mouths. Many months of silence later, one of the little ones pipes up with *Bekos*, the word for bread in Phrygian.'

'Phrygian?'

'An Indo-European language from Asia Minor. Now lost. Psamtik said, *OK, Phrygian is the proto-language. My dream of primal greatness is just that – a dream.*'

'So he handed his kingdom over to the Phrygians?' asked Hendricks.

'No, just found new enemies to go to war with,' replied Stone. 'Very New Labour.'

Hendricks looked through the pages of Part Two and separated them into two piles, one thick, one slender.

'Part Two takes place in California in the 1970s. It's about a girl called Genie who more or less crawls into the LA county welfare office one autumn day with her partially sighted and whacked-out mother. She was basically brought up in a home dominated by an abusive father who deprived Genie of language from birth.'

Hendricks showed Stone a small colour profile photograph of a thirteen-year-old girl, eyes downcast, skin like marble, dark hair snatched back in a short ponytail, finger and thumb linked in a noose, other fingers splayed.

'Genie. Kept in silence and deprived of social contact from birth. Her story was up against the trial of Charlie Manson for *merde du jour* in the LA papers for a week or so.'

Hendricks fell silent.

'And?' prompted Stone.

'And we have a gap in the manuscript.' Hendricks picked up the larger chunk. 'Genie's story, page 211 to 378.' He touched the smaller section. 'Pages 379 to 390: some very bizarre tributes to Psamtik, and to Genie's misunderstood and visionary father. The glorification of child abuse and the need to continue these linguistic experiments until the mystery of how language is acquired is resolved. It's not even Leonard Lawson's field of expertise. He was an art historian and scholar. Two things, Karl. Did he suffer some sort of mental breakdown? Or substance abuse?'

'And what about the missing pages?'

'Exactly. This is page 378. Check the final two paragraphs before the gap.'

Hendricks slid the page towards Stone. Outside, a bus roared on Aigburth Drive and life on earth rolled on.

> The motives of Genie's father remain unclear, but his method - although crude - was essentially correct. In this he was similar to Psamtik. For this experiment to succeed, a more academic model is needed, supported by the top universities of England and Wales. A unique opportunity arose for the English Experiment. But, in spite of the mesmeric intellect of the man leading the research,
> it was doomed because of the lack of academic infrastructure and the covert nature of the work. The supposed criminality of its content turned the golden vision into brass.
>
> Hypocrisy is the root of all evil. Our society aborts children in utero by the thousands each year, yet it is unthinkable to use twenty to fifty unwanted children for an essential experiment into the acquisition of language.

'So Leonard Lawson was basically either a cruel bastard or off his head. Maybe both,' concluded Hendricks.

'We need to dig into his medical records. Did he go gaga? Did he get a season ticket for Yates's Wine Lodge?' asked Stone. 'I've dipped into his other writing and there's nothing like this.' Stone shook his head. 'Twenty to fifty children brought up in silence with no sensory stimulation?'

'*The mesmeric intellect of the man leading the research*? It's like a line from a funeral elegy. It's—' Hendricks was silenced by a sudden, astonishing noise.

In the hall outside the study, the landline telephone rang out.

Hendricks and Stone stood up and headed towards it. The telephone, cream coloured and plastic, looked like it belonged in a junk-shop window. Hendricks picked up the receiver.

Silence. Hendricks listened hard, but there was no background noise. He waited, could hear no breathing or sign of life on the other end. Stone took out his phone, pressed record.

'DS Bill Hendricks. Can I help you?'

'Bill Hendricks?' The voice was androgynous, ageless and without a trace of accent. It caused a coldness to pass through him.

'Who is this?' asked Hendricks.

'Where are you?'

'Who are you?'

'I am the Angel of Destruction. With the First Born, I serve Death. There's a body in the garden. Whose body? Which garden?'

Hendricks looked at the French window. Outside was a small paved yard enclosed by three brick walls.

'Whose body? Which garden?' The voice dipped.

'Name the body. Name the garden.'

The line went dead and the room was completely silent.

Stone stopped recording and played the call back. Even though the hall was flat and rectangular, the voice on the line seemed to echo as if the space was full of invisible curves and crevices.

Hendricks's phone rang out. On the display: 'Clay'. He connected.

'Drop what you're doing,' said Clay. We've got a prime suspect and an address.'

He hurried to the front door.

'It's very near where you are now.'

On the street, he ran towards his car.

'Eve, we've just had a call directly to the Lawsons' landline. It was from the Angel of Destruction. Where are you?'

35

9.41 am

Four minutes. The time it took DC Cole to locate the only Gabriel Huddersfield in Liverpool on the electoral roll. It took Clay less than five to arrive at the front door of 777 Croxteth Road, a large Victorian family house divided into six self-contained flats.

The bell of Flat 5, 777 Croxteth Road didn't have a name next to it, just a small picture of an angel, sideways on, playing a slender reed and facing right, its wings dissolving into the blue-whiteness of the celestial sky. Clay recognised it as a supporting player to Jesus from a colour plate in one of Leonard Lawson's books.

She pointed at the image. 'Is this how he sees himself? Heaven's foot soldier? God's hitman? The Angel of Destruction?'

After the fourth unanswered attempt at that bell, Clay pressed the bell of Flat 1 – 'Sally' – and a woman's gravelly voice came through the intercom.

'Who is it?'

'Police! We aren't looking for you. Open up, please.'

'K!'

Clay looked up at the second-floor window and hoped Gabriel Huddersfield was sleeping the sleep of the righteous.

'Come on!' she said, irritated by the sloth-like lack of action behind the door. 'Come on! Come on!'

The door finally opened to reveal a painfully thin, purple- and grey-haired woman, who could have been in her thirties or possibly fifties, taking a puff on a hand-rolled cigarette. The smell of weed around her disappointed Clay. Not a reliable witness.

'Who are you after?' She blew a trio of smoke rings through her brown-stained fingers and teeth.

'Gabriel Huddersfield,' replied Clay. 'Move aside, please.'

'I don't think he's in,' she said, allowing Clay inside the wide, gloomy hallway.

Clay headed towards the stairs. 'If you know enough to know he's not in, do you know where he is?'

Sally thought about it as Clay ran up the stairs two at a time.

'There was a commotion in the night and then he was gone. That's all I know. He might've come back. I don't know.'

At the turn of the first floor, the darkness deepened and Clay noticed there wasn't a bulb in the ceiling light. An overwhelming smell of damp and the robotic beat of dance music followed her up as she continued to the top floor.

She slowed at the head of the stairs, looked right. Flat 6. And to the left saw Flat 5.

'Jesus!'

On the door of Flat 5 was painted a more complete version of the image on the bell outside. She processed some of the details as she approached the door. *In a cloud of light, Jesus sitting in glory. In heaven. His arms bent at the elbows, right hand pointing up to an unseen Father, left hand pointing down to Creation. Jesus the hinge between the two.* It was the upper part of the central panel of Hieronymus Bosch's triptych, *The Last Judgment.* She recognised it from one of the professor's books.

She knocked on the door and called, 'Gabriel Huddersfield! Police! Open up immediately!'

There was no reply, no sign of life on the other side. She pushed the door, but it remained shut. A rich, smoky smell oozed from Huddersfield's home. Incense.

Clay raised her arm, felt along the top of the door frame for a key but found only a damp, greasy surface.

'Is this what you're looking for?'

Clay turned towards the educated voice. In the doorway of Flat 6 stood a tall, middle-aged black man with a shock of white hair, holding a key in one hand. She showed him her warrant card but withdrew it when she saw the white cast to his eyes. A melancholic Labrador waited beside him. He smiled and tapped the floor with his white stick.

The witnesses were a semi-conscious stoner and a blind man. Bitterness ground its fist into the back of Clay's skull and she couldn't help feeling short-changed by Chance.

'Is Gabriel in trouble?' asked the neighbour. He handed her the key, his speech and manner respectful.

'I think so,' said Clay. 'My name's Detective Chief Inspector Eve Clay. Mr...?'

'Evergreen. Mr Elliot Evergreen. I hold the key for Gabriel.'

'He trusts you then?'

'Gabriel says he has no secrets. So a man with no secrets must have no problem allowing the Law inside his home. He went out last night at ten o'clock. He wasn't alone.'

'Thank you.' Clay took the key from Mr Evergreen. 'Was there trouble in the building last night? A commotion?'

'There's always trouble in the building. Commotion follows Gabriel like a pet dog. And when commotion sleeps, Gabriel is as silent as a shadow.'

'What kind of commotion, Mr Evergreen?'

'Gabriel has a regular visitor. I don't ask questions of him. But from what I can hear, he's the only person apart from me who goes over his threshold. Gabriel doesn't mind what his other friend *sees*. Gabriel's friend was angry, following him down the stairs, bullying him, I'd say.'

'Did you hear any words?'

'*You have to do it! Do as I say!* The rest...?' Mr Evergreen shrugged.

'Did he come back to his flat?'

'Briefly. I was listening to the radio. His door opened as the three o'clock news was finishing.' He stroked the dog's ears and Clay could feel the blood pumping inside her head. The blind witness was quickly turning out to be more valuable than seven fully sighted ones.

'He came back for a few minutes. He tried to do so discreetly, but I could tell. He couldn't open his front door, he was breathing like he'd just run a marathon and he was highly agitated. That's all I can tell you.'

'Thank you, Mr Evergreen.'

'You know where I am if you need me. I'm told that the eyes can play tricks. But I know that my ears can never deceive me. Give me your number. I will call you if I hear anything that might be useful to you.'

She reeled off eleven digits and he parroted them back to her. In placing Elliot Evergreen across the landing from Huddersfield, it seemed Chance had done her a favour.

Two floors down, she heard DS Bill Hendricks arrive. As he hurtled up the stairs, Clay stuck the key in the lock of Flat 5. She pushed the door open, calling, 'Gabriel Huddersfield! Police! We're coming in!'

36

9.41 am

Close to the top of Brownlow Hill, Riley stepped off the frozen street and through the doors of the grey-tiled Hart Building. She took in the blue shield of the university's crest, the three cormorants bearing leaves, and the motto '*Haec Otia Studia Fovent*'.

'Detective Sergeant Riley?'

In the reception area, Riley followed the voice and saw a very tall woman in her twenties wearing a University of Liverpool ID badge on a band round her neck. 'Justine Elgar?' she asked, and showed her warrant card. She'd been expecting a raven-haired siren from an old horror film but was faced instead with the blonde captain of the ladies' basketball team.

Justine nodded. 'Let's go to my office,' she said.

As she followed, Riley asked, '*Haec Otia Studia Fovent*? What does that translate to?'

'These days of peace foster learning. Peace? Here?' She laughed.

Justine's office, a cupboard that wanted to be a room, had a small window overlooking the elegant red-brick buildings across the road. She handed Riley a card file. 'I copied everything I could find.'

Riley opened the file. The papers were more yellow than white and the musty smell reminded her of her great-grandmother's parlour.

'I've put it together the way I found it. It's a jumble.'

'Did anything leap out at you, Justine?'

'He kept his head down for decades. There are no disciplinary proceedings, no letters of complaint, no departmental controversies going to mediation.'

Riley stopped at a page of University of Liverpool headed paper. Personnel department. It was a brief letter of thanks issued close to his retirement. 'That's quite an achievement,' she said, showing it to Justine.

'Yes. Professor Lawson started work here in 1956 and retired in 1986. He didn't miss a single lecture, seminar or meeting. That kind of dedication doesn't exist any more.'

Riley turned over a bundle of pages. P60s and wage slips gathered in a thick silver paperclip. Professor Lawson hadn't bothered to collect them and another strand formed in Riley's mind. Obsessed with work, head in the clouds.

'Did he have any enemies?' she asked, fishing wildly.

'No. He was a model employee.'

Riley turned the page and came to a letter in an envelope with an American frank and the words 'Harvard University' in the top left-hand corner. It was addressed to Professor L Lawson. She took out two pieces of paper, the top one with Harvard University's coat of arms at the top and dated June 1974. Riley read the letter and let out a long, thin whistle.

She focused on one paragraph.

```
The lecture tour we would like you
to undertake, sponsored by and on behalf
of Harvard University, would involve you
visiting twenty of the top universities
and colleges across the United States
of America. We would especially like you
to focus your lectures on two areas of
your expertise: Dutch art of the fifteenth
and sixteenth century, and Egyptian art
```

```
of antiquity. Your travel and living
costs would, of course, be covered
by Harvard University and we would pay
you $US 200,000 for your services.
The lectures would commence in
October 1976 and end in December 1976.
```

'A carbon copy of his response is on the next sheet,' said Justine. Riley turned to it. University of Liverpool headed notepaper.

```
Dear Professor Pink,

Thank you for your kind and generous
offer. I am sorry to say that I will be
unable to take you up on this as it would
involve taking my daughter out of school.
I also have teaching commitments here
in the University of Liverpool.

Yours faithfully,
```

Prof. Leonard Lawson
```
PROFESSOR LEONARD LAWSON
```

Riley felt electricity run through her nervous system as she did some sums. 'How much did Professor Lawson earn in the academic year 1976 to '77?'

Justine consulted the P60s in the original file. 'Before tax, £14,000.'

'And he turned down $200,000 for twenty lectures on subjects he was passionate about.'

'He could have taken leave of absence. Lots of English academics were on the gold rush to America in the 1970s. The universities there had obscene amounts of money and weren't afraid to spend it to entice the world's finest. If Professor Lawson had gone, he'd have been a star. And it could well have turned into a permanent move, on mega-money.'

Riley came to the last piece of paper, a cutting from *The Spectator*, a lengthy book review. *The Sacred Vow* by D.L. Noone. A picture of the cover showed a Carthusian monk in a hooded gown, kneeling in front of a vivid image of Christ crucified, the red of the wounds enhanced by the white of the monk's habit.

Riley scanned the review. Superlatives leapt from the page. *Brilliant. Ground-breaking. Imaginative. Mesmeric intellect. Inspirational.*

At the bottom of the review were the initials LL.

She showed it to Justine.

'Reads more like a love letter than a book review,' said Justine. 'Why's it in his file?'

'He's either disclosed it in the interests of transparency or someone's flagged it up as a little bit odd.'

Plates spun in Riley's mind. 'Why did he really stay in Liverpool?' She heard herself speak the thought out loud.

Justine shrugged and Riley double-checked the name on the book review. D.L. Noone. 'Did Noone work here at Liverpool at the time Professor Lawson was offered all that money?'

'I can find out,' replied Justine.

'Maybe Professor Lawson couldn't bear to leave that *mesmeric intellect* behind. Do me a favour, Justine. I desperately need to talk to anyone who knew or worked with Professor Lawson. Can you go through your records and find anyone still alive who fits that bill.'

Justine's face clouded and Riley read the weather forecast: *I'm busy and haven't I done enough for you already?*

'Justine, I really appreciate the time and effort you've put into helping me so far, but I'm going to jump off the bridge here with a piece of confidential information. Can you promise me, and it is a matter of life and death, that you can keep this to yourself?' She turned what was already public knowledge into the coordinates for the Holy Grail.

Justine nodded. 'God, yes, of course...' Her façade crumbled.

'Within the last twenty-four hours, Leonard Lawson was murdered in his bedroom. We think he knew his killer. Who worked with Professor Leonard Lawson in 1986?'

'I'll begin searching immediately.'

Riley stood up. 'Thank you.'

Outside the Hart Building the air was alive with particles of mist and mean needles of snow. Riley texted Clay and considered Leonard Lawson's response to Professor Pink and the unnecessary lie that he had committed to paper.

Eve, we need to talk about Leonard Lawson. Gina

37

9.42 am

The hiss and click of a needle hitting the inner edge of a vinyl record was the only sound inside Gabriel Huddersfield's flat. The corridor that divided the space was narrow, dark, the air infused with stale incense that stung the eyes.

Hiss. Click. Hiss. Click. Hiss. Click.

'He's not here,' said Clay to Hendricks, sensing the hollowness of an empty living space.

There were five doors. Two to the right, two to the left and one at the top of the corridor.

Clay opened the first door to the right. Boxes upon blue plastic boxes were stacked to the back wall and were three-quarters high to the ceiling.

Hendricks opened the door opposite. 'Same story,' he said. 'The room's not used as a room, just as storage space for boxes. So far, he's Mr Neat and Tidy, but I suspect he can't bear to throw anything away. He's an organised hoarder.'

Clay sniffed the air, caught the edge of something strong and oily under the stale incense. 'Paint?' she said. 'Do you get that?'

She tried the next door, found another neatly ordered collection of boxes and was hit with a much stronger aroma of paint. She turned on the ceiling light and saw art materials through the handle of a box at her eye level.

Hendricks opened the next door. A bathroom. 'Come look at this, Eve.'

Clay stood in the doorway and felt her breath evaporate.

Mirrors ran from floor to ceiling and all the way across the ceiling itself, rectangles and squares pieced together to create a reflective whole. The shower curtain was pulled all the way round and Clay's neck tingled when she saw the shape of a man standing behind the semi-transparent fabric. She edged closer. The form behind it was perfectly still.

She took a breath, waited for the dark shape to twitch and then explode into life, jumping at her, seizing her by the throat with hands and teeth.

Another step and the rattling of a pipe caused a light-headedness to transfer to goose bumps right across her skin.

Clay clasped the curtain and swished it back.

It was a life-sized male mannequin, dressed from head to ankle in leather and draped in chains. The head and face of the dummy were covered in a leather mask, with slits for dead eyes staring out into the void.

Although the bathroom was scrupulously clean – the mirrors and ceramics shone – a fat, black, sticky cockroach scuttled over to the mannequin's foot, antennae twitching.

Clay turned away and headed for the door, her reflection unavoidable in the mirrored walls, her features contorted in disgust.

'The cockroach in the bath's probably got friends and relatives in the kitchen. Which is what I guess the last room is.'

From behind the closed door the sound of the record-player needle repeatedly misfiring invaded the corridor like a curse. Hiss. Click. Hiss. Click. Hiss. Click. The smell of incense became more pungent.

Clay opened the door and was silent for a moment. She surveyed the space and its contents with the assurance of a hunter knowing that this was the empty lair of its prey. It wasn't a kitchen. There wasn't one. But she didn't have a word to name the function of the largely empty room.

'Bill, I want you to ask Karl Stone to look up Gabriel Huddersfield on the national police computer. Circulate the image we have of him to constabularies across the country and to all ports and airports. When we know what he's done in the past – and it's going to be violent crime – I want you to coordinate the manhunt, starting in and around Sefton Park. We need as many officers out there and looking for him as are available. Go now.'

As she stared into the room, Clay phoned Terry Mason. The more she saw, the more certain she was that Gabriel Huddersfield had killed Leonard Lawson. She had to catch him before he did it again.

'Terry, leave Pricey in place at Pelham Grove and draft in other Scientific Support officers to support you here. I need you at 777 Croxteth Road. This is our boy's bachelor pad.'

38

9.50 am

At Otterspool tip, David Higson watched a fat man in his fifties drive a blue Audi through the gates and pull up at the hut. His forehead sloped and fat hung from his cheeks like saddlebags. In the passenger seat, a pretty blonde girl in her early twenties stared straight ahead with the same pale blue eyes as the driver, lost in thought or ashamed to be seen in public at the tip with the man who was surely Daddy.

Mr Forehead and the Blonde Conundrum, Higson named them.

Higson glanced inside the back of the car and saw a small fridge that looked like it had come from a war zone. He pointed straight down the road that ran past the line of skips 1 to 12.

'Hurry up, Dad!'

As they drove towards the overturned shipping container in which broken and discarded electrical goods were laid to rest, Higson wondered how on earth such an ugly man could have fathered such an attractive young woman. He sat down on the deckchair in his hut and watched the back of the car as it slowed down in front of the electricals shed. Higson, who could see them through the convex mirror on the gatepost, knew what Mr Forehead was thinking as he leaned out of the open window and looked back at the empty space behind him. He assumed that he, his daughter and the car were all unseen.

I reckon they will, thought Higson, self-taught expert on human nature.

In the mirror, he watched as both front doors opened and Mr Forehead and the Blonde Conundrum got out of the car with sly swiftness.

Get on with it!

Blonde Conundrum double-checked behind her and got into the back seat. Meanwhile, Mr Forehead pulled out the old fridge, wobbled over to the electricals shed and plonked it down at the front. He looked left, right and backwards and then at the other abandoned fridges and freezers.

You're eyeing up that almost-new freezer, thought Higson. *The one Laughing Gas brought in before opening time this morning.*

Sure enough, Mr Forehead picked up the freezer and hurried back to the car. He placed it on the back seat next to the Blonde Conundrum, slammed the door shut and got into the driver's seat.

Higson stepped out of the hut and, pretending to throw the dregs of his tea on to the tarmac, took a brief look at the Audi. Through the rear windscreen he watched the Blonde Conundrum engrossed in the newly acquired freezer.

She's taking off the tape that kept the door shut, he thought, as Mr Forehead turned the corner at the top of the line of double-row skips and began to drive for the exit past skips 13 to 24.

The Audi picked up speed and a lone gull shrieked over and over. Then the tyres screeched and Mr Forehead pulled up in an emergency stop. A muted yell drifted from the exit side of the skips. The gull above cried even louder and others joined in, circling in the sky.

As if stirred from a dream, the heads of Higson's three colleagues appeared above the skips they were working in – Harry in green garden waste, Bezza in wood and Robbie in non-recyclables.

Two of the Audi's doors opened, half a moment apart, and a piercing scream cut through the air, a scream that travelled with the Blonde Conundrum as she panicked away from her father's car.

'Jesus, Kylie!'

Higson listened. Her screams followed her as she ran like fury towards the exit. The gulls picked up the note. As she took her screams to the bottom of Jericho Lane, the gulls replied with louder, stronger screeches, threatening to split the sky in two.

And then, as Higson took the shorter route through the entrance to the tip, another sound filled the air. The bass screaming of Mr Forehead.

Higson ran at speed as the freezing air came alive with the sounds of terror.

He turned the corner and saw Mr Forehead doubled-up at the back of his car, throwing up, eyes bulging, body shaking.

David Higson headed towards him and wondered what was in the freezer that Laughing Gas had left behind.

39

9.51 am

Hiss. Clay stood in the corner of the fifth room of Gabriel Huddersfield's flat. Click. The room was almost bare and the record on the turntable in the corner continued to connect with the pulsing needle. Click. Clay looked at the spinning LP. Hiss. Gabriel Huddersfield had been listening to Handel's *Messiah*. Click. And psyching himself up for murder.

She lifted the arm and turned off the power to the record player.

Two walls were empty. The third wall was dominated by a sculpture and on the fourth wall was a skilfully painted mural in three sections: a broad central image and two narrower images either side. Hieronymus Bosch's *The Last Judgment*. *What is it with this picture?* thought Clay. *Lawson writes books about it and Huddersfield likes it so much he has it on his bell, his front door and now in here as well!*

Her eyes wandered across Bosch's vision of earthly chaos: monsters going about their daily business of punishing human flesh, a disembodied head marching on its feet, a freakish figure riding bareback on a naked man towards a makeshift crucifixion on a tree. Each torment was a punishment for one of the seven deadly sins, and they were watched over by Jesus in radiance and his disciples in a sky-blue heaven.

She looked at the top of the left-hand panel, recognised

heaven overlooking the Garden of Eden at the dawn of creation. In heaven, God sat surrounded by a look of light as the
loyal angels cast out the rebel angels. In the Garden of Eden,
a narrative emerged. God fashioning Eve from Adam's rib; the
temptation at the Tree of Knowledge; Adam and Eve being
chased from the garden by an avenging angel.

Clay paid closer attention to the central panel. Beneath
heaven and Christ's feet, the dark earth churned, a living purga-
tory in which mythical beasts and demons stabbed, impaled and
tortured human beings, harrying them into eternal damnation.

She looked at the fires that raged in the city of hell at the
top of the right-hand panel. Beneath them was Satan in his
dark grotto, awaiting the latest sinners from earth, those who'd
already arrived thrashed and wailed above his head as they were
boiled in a pan.

In the middle of the room was a ladder-back chair and a gag
hanging limply off it. She looked at the floor, saw old blood-
splatter marks combined with fresher stains on the bare boards.
Underneath the seat was a whip curled up like a sleeping snake,
and a box of matches with an ashtray and a packet of cigarettes
on the seat. Clay shivered.

She turned to the sculpture, a life-sized statue of Jesus dying
on the cross, a spear sticking from his side. Clay pulled out her
phone and took a series of pictures of the spear. Electricity raced
across her scalp as she slipped on a pair of latex gloves, placed
both hands on the top of the shaft and gently tugged. The point
and head of the spear were loose in Christ's side.

Turning the spear, she felt the metal tip grate against the
fabric of the statue. Huddersfield had created a hole inside the
statue in which to embed the spear. Clay pulled as she turned
and the spear came clean away.

It was made from the same wood and was the same colour
as the spear on which Leonard Lawson had been impaled. The
metal tip was also roughly the same shape and size as on the
other spear.

Clay walked to the dim light at the window and turned the shaft in her hands.

In the same location as on the other shaft was the same engraved symbol: the dragonfly exiting the rectangular window.

As she looked at the hole in Christ's side, she felt a deep sense of inexplicable sadness and imagined there was someone else in the room with her.

You have no time for this. She heard her own voice shouting inside her, but another voice whispered behind her and, for a moment, it was to this that she paid heed.

'*We have all placed the spear in his side. We have all hammered the nails into his wrists.*'

She turned to Sister Philomena's kind and loving voice, but there was no one and nothing there, just a very well painted mural, a warning of the consequences of sin.

'What do you want us to do, Eve?' asked Mason.

'Once you've dusted and removed any prints or fibres we can connect to Leonard Lawson's bedroom, I suggest you empty the three storage rooms one room at a time. He's a hoarder, but he's meticulous. My hunch is the junk in each room is themed. Probably art, sex and religion.'

She showed Mason the spear, engraved with the same symbol that came to rest close to Leonard Lawson's heart, then dropped it into the evidence bag that he held open for her. 'That spear on its own is enough to bury Gabriel Huddersfield, but I need you to find out as much about him as you can from his possessions.'

She was drawn back to the central panel of *The Last Judgment*, and to its lower left-hand corner. A man with the head of a mythical beast – part bird, part platypus – and wearing white tights and a blue coat with tails, carried a stick on his shoulder. Tied to the stick by his hands and feet was a naked man; he was upside down and impaled on a spear that entered through his shoulder and emerged from his lower rib cage.

She took a photograph and sent it to Hendricks, Riley, Stone and, manning the fort at Trinity Road, Cole. Beneath the image she wrote a comment: *The inspiration behind the staging of Leonard Lawson's body.*

As soon as she'd sent it, her phone rang out. She connected as she walked.

'DCI Clay, it's Jessica from switchboard.'

'Go on, Jessica!'

'We've just had a call from the site manager at the tip on Otterspool Promenade. He's got a corpse turned up there.'

'Elderly and male, right?' said Clay.

'How did you know?'

Clay headed for the door, her head filling with the cold blue of Gabriel Huddersfield's eyes. As she hurried down the stairs, she imagined him in his bathroom, naked except for the leather mask that covered his head and face, listening to Handel and gazing at the cockroach on the back of his hand.

40

9.58 am

'Play?'

Louise Lawson was woken by the word. When she opened her eyes, she saw Abey standing over the bed on which she was sleeping. He smiled at her and she tried to smile back, but her head was banging and her throat and mouth were bone dry. She struggled as she sat up on the bed.

She focused on him. He was dressed in a replica blue Everton shirt and pale blue jeans. Each time she saw him, he looked more like a little boy than a man in his thirties.

Outside there were footsteps in the hall.

'Who's there?' she asked.

'Outside is Adam,' replied Abey. 'Listening. Keyhole? Happy, Lou-Lou?'

'I'm so happy to see you, Abey, but—'

'Is Lou-Lou sick?'

She watched his face. After a moment of deliberation, he held up one hand and then one finger, as if a good idea had arrived. He placed his hand behind her and pushed her forward gently, lifting the pillow and placing it at her back. He took a glass of water from the bedside table and handed it to her.

'Drink. Lou-Lou feel better.'

She sipped the water and Abey sat on the edge of the bed.

'But how did you get into their flat, Abey?'

He smiled, placed a conspiratorial hand to his mouth and whispered, 'The door open. I want see Lou-Lou.' He joined his hands together and looked to the ceiling. 'God looking after Lou-Lou now. Abey say prayer for Lou-Lou. Abey love Lou-Lou, God love Lou-Lou too...'

'I love you too, Abey. And so does God...'

She heard a sound outside, a footstep on a floorboard.

Abey's face lit up with the arrival of another good idea. Louise frowned, shook her index finger and pressed it to her lips. Softly, she shushed him. He copied her, action and sound.

'You're not supposed to be here,' she whispered. 'Their home is strictly out of bounds.'

'Louise?' Adam's voice crept into the room before he did. 'I thought I heard voices. I was wondering, do you want or need anything?'

'I'm fine, thank you.' She closed her eyes. 'I'm just going back to sleep...'

She opened her eyes. It seemed that Abey had dissolved into thin air.

In his left hand, Adam carried a large bunch of red roses. 'I bought these for you. I'm so sorry about your father.'

Louise looked directly at Adam and, on the edge of her field of vision, saw Abey standing in the corner of the room.

Adam placed the flowers on the bed and sat next to them. 'From me to you, Louise. You have my sympathy.'

'Thank you.' Louise closed her eyes again, hoped he'd just go away.

'Louise, I know that over the next few weeks and months you're going to have to face a lot of practical and emotional hurdles. I want you to know that I will be here for you, every step of the way. It was my idea that you came to stay with us here. Did you know that?'

'No. Thank you, Adam.' She looked at him.

'I'll do anything to help you, Louise.' He smiled, moved the flowers closer to her. 'Including helping you sell your house.'

'Sell my father's house? What do you mean?'

'Given what's happened, Louise, do you think you could ever live in that house again?'

She sat up a little straighter. 'Go on, Adam.'

'You know I'm a jack of all trades. When the time comes to sell your house, I can do it up for you, get you thousands more for it. How does that sound?'

'Go on.'

'Big old house? Big old furniture. Loads of your father's books. You know I do house clearances. Man in a white van, hee hee. I'll help you move into, say, a modern flat. Maybe supported accommodation with top-notch security so you can sleep safely in your bed at night.'

'I didn't know you cared about me that much, Adam!'

'My father always used to say, take best care of the ones that take best care of you. I don't talk to you much because I'm always working.'

'Yes, yes, you're always busy, aren't you, Adam?'

'Right now, you're going to the top of my priority list. Number one, Louise Lawson. Have a little think about what I've said and we'll talk later.'

Adam stood up, walked backwards to the door, his eyes fixed on Louise and with a smile on his face that made her go hot and cold. When he was gone, Abey stepped out of the corner.

She smiled at him. 'You're a funny bunny, Abey!'

Abey shook his head. 'Me no funny bunny!' He pointed at himself. 'He no see me. Me the invisible man...'

41

10.06 am

TIP CLOSED UNTIL FURTHER NOTICE

When Clay arrived at the municipal tip, the entrance and exit had already been sealed off and a young constable was redirecting traffic back up Jericho Lane to Aigburth Vale. The wind from the River Mersey lashed her back as she ducked under the tape. She heard a young woman crying inside the rectangular pale-brick office between the entrance and exit.

Four refuse workers in high-visibility jackets and hard hats watched Clay approach as if she was a phantom. She showed her warrant card to the group and asked, 'Who's in charge here?'

David Higson stepped forward and introduced himself. His skin was covered in a veil of sweat.

'Take me to the body, David,' said Clay. She followed him as he turned a corner towards an Audi, its doors wide open.

'Did you touch the body?'

'No.'

'What happened?'

'The owners of this car dumped an old fridge and then tried to *borrow* this practically brand-new freezer. A dad and his daughter.'

She put it together. 'They're in the office?'

Higson nodded. 'They certainly got more than they

163

bargained for. The daughter, Kylie, twisted her ankle at the bottom of Jericho Lane, trying to run away. Robbie carried her back here.'

As she came closer to the car, Clay caught sight of the compact freezer and pictured an old man's body bent and concertinaed to fit into the confined space. Leonard Lawson's staged corpse flashed through her consciousness like liquid light.

Higson pointed to the cold vomit near the car. 'Kylie's father's breakfast.'

On the back seat, a half-sized freezer was tilted at an angle, the door shut, the tape that had sealed it broken.

'Prepare yourself,' said Higson.

Clay slipped on a pair of latex gloves.

'Do you remember who brought it here?' asked Clay.

'Yes, a sly shit in a white van. Laughing Gas, I named him. Brought it here this morning before we opened so I couldn't let him on site.'

'Licence plate?'

'Sorry, didn't notice it.'

'But you've got CCTV?'

Higson was quiet for a moment. 'Oh, yes we do.'

'Can you describe him?'

Clay looked at the small white freezer, the unlikeliest coffin, then turned to the site manager.

'Yes, but... Long face. Plain blue baseball cap. Ray-Bans over the eyes.'

'You'd recognise him if you saw him again?'

'Yes. If he was wearing the same disguise.'

'Did he speak to you?'

'Very little. No accent. He said *excuse me*, but it sounded like *fuck off*, pardon my French.'

'French pardoned. How did he strike you?'

'He spooked me. He had an aura. *If I don't get what I want, I'll put you in hospital or worse.* I told him to leave it outside. I carried it in myself.'

On her iPhone, she pulled up the picture of Gabriel Hudders-field's face and asked, 'Could this be him?'

Higson looked at the photo. 'No, that's not him.'

Clay stooped, leaned into the car and looked at the graffiti of smears and grease marks on the surface of the freezer. She set her iPhone to camera.

She took the deepest breath and, slowly, opened the door of the freezer.

'OK!' she said to herself as she released her breath slowly, then inhaled again.

She counted three separate body parts she guessed were from the same victim and took a succession of pictures, of the three together and each of them separately.

The head was wrapped in a length of rough grey cloth; an old man's face poked out. The eyelids were stitched to the skin above the sockets to keep the eyes wide open. His eyes looked directly at Clay with a layer of surprise under the glaze of death. Underneath the head were two feet, one flat down on the bottom of the freezer, the other with its toes down but its heel raised against the freezer wall.

A long red feather and a short dark feather sat in a pool of pink water on the bottom of the freezer. The defrosted flesh was wilting, drips rippling the surface of the pool.

'It's him again,' Clay said. She turned to the site manager. 'David!' Higson dragged his gaze away from the sky and looked back down at Clay. 'Where's your nearest electrical socket?' She shut the back door, sat in the driver's seat.

'The office over there.'

Clay turned on the ignition and drove as close to the office door as possible. She carried the freezer, tilted at an angle, into the hut, and noticed that the head and feet didn't shift on the short journey from the Audi to the plug socket.

'Get it away from me!' the Blonde Conundrum screamed as she limped to the door, followed by her father.

Clay placed the freezer on a small wooden table and thrust

the plug into the socket. As a green light came on and the freezer whirred into life, she sighed and speed-dialled DS Karl Stone. After two rings, he picked up.

'What are you doing, Karl?'

'I'm in Leonard Lawson's study, on my laptop just looking up Gabriel Huddersfield on the national police computer—'

'Can I stop you there, please. I'm at the tip on Otterspool Promenade. We've got another victim, another old man. They've left the head and the feet inside a freezer. There's no body. But they've staged it like a sick joke. A human being with no body, just a head positioned on a pair of feet, walking. It's them, it's got to be.' Clay fell silent, weighed up the big picture. 'They've had these body parts for God knows how long, frozen to preserve them.'

'What do you want me to do?'

In spite of the cold, she felt her face flush, the onset of a rise in blood pressure. 'I want you to come here.' She looked into the dead man's eyes. *No peace for you*, she thought. *Eternal wakefulness, that's what they wished on you.* 'I want you to pull together everything we've got.' She looked at the CCTV camera pointing at the entrance and exit and smiled. 'Tell Barney Cole you'll email him the CCTV footage from the tip. We could have our white-van psycho within hours.'

Alone in the office, she looked at the four-screen colour monitor with its crystal-clear view of the front entrance and texted images of the head and feet in the freezer to Hendricks, Riley, Stone and Cole.

Just outside the office, the site manager's back was turned.

'Hey, David!' He didn't move a muscle. 'Mr Higson!' The sound of his sniffs and broken breathing worried her. He turned.

'I'm sorry.' His voice wobbled. 'I've got something to tell you.'

42

10.12 am

Five minutes on the telephone was all it took for DS Bill Hendricks to learn that Gabriel Huddersfield was not in the custody of any police station on Merseyside or in the care of any NHS facility.

And with Sefton Park crawling with police officers, Hendricks grew increasingly convinced that the one place Huddersfield wouldn't be was his regular haunt.

He pulled his car over and took out his phone. He called up the image of *The Last Judgment* that Huddersfield had painted on to the wall of his flat, and then the photo Clay had sent of the body parts in the freezer at the municipal tip.

He returned to the imitation of the Bosch painting and focused in on the images at the bottom of the central panel. He stopped at the naked man, suspended from a pole just as Leonard Lawson had been, and moved left a little. Beneath the suspended man's head a foot sat flat on the earth and behind this foot a disembodied head, eyes open, looked up at the suspended man's face; the head was wrapped in a grey blanket with feathers coming from the back and, underneath, a heel, half on, half off the ground.

Hendricks called Clay, but her line was busy. He texted her instead: *Eve, the body parts in the freezer correspond to another detail in Bosch's* The Last Judgment. *The head on the feet marching off to hell just behind the Leonard Lawson figure. Check it out. Bill*

As he typed, the strongest probability came into Hendricks's mind. He sent the text and fired his car into life.

Why? he wondered. *Why would Huddersfield and his accomplice kill like this?* The words 'religious conviction' flashed through his mind.

'They're convinced that they are right and that God's on their side.' He spoke to himself, felt an enlightened smile on his face. The smile disappeared as quickly as it had formed. *What did you do, Professor Lawson, to deserve this level of earthly punishment and eternal damnation?*

Religious conviction? Hendricks pulled away from the kerb.

If I was Gabriel Huddersfield, where would I go now?

Hendricks picked up speed as he followed the curve of Sefton Park and headed for the nearest exit leading to the edges of Liverpool city centre.

43

10.14 am

For once, The Sanctuary was completely quiet.

'Where been?' Abey's voice leaked from his room on to the landing, where Adam Miller was bleeding air from the radiators.

'I've been to the kitchen department of John Lewis to buy a fucking big knife to skin you alive, you fucking smiling cretin.' Adam Miller spoke quietly.

There was a pause.

'Ken, that you?'

Hot water seeped out of the radiator. Adam sealed off the valve. Danielle was out. Gideon was playing games downstairs with the quarter wits.

'That you, Ken?'

Once, Adam had heard Abey conduct a full-blown conversation with his imaginary friend. He pitched his voice up a few octaves into baby-speak, mimicking the voice he imagined filled Abey's head.

'Yeah, it's me. Ken.' He walked to Abey's door, looked through the crack and saw Abey sitting on the edge of his bed, back to the door, staring out of the window.

'What just say, Ken? No hear.'

'I said, don't move.' He pushed the door open a little wider, making the crack bigger and Abey fully visible. Abey's head turned slowly. 'Uh uh. No. Be a statue.'

Abey froze. 'Like that?'

'Just like that, Abey.'

'I hear you. Outside. Not inside. My head. Just for once.'

'That's right, Abey. I was tired of living inside your head, so now I've come to live in The Sanctuary. Won't that be fun?'

'Yes. But?'

'But what, Abey?'

'But... will others... hear you?'

'No. Only you, Abey.'

'You want... come in...?'

'Not now. Later maybe.'

'But?'

'But what, Abey?'

'But... will others see Ken?'

'Uh uh. No one can see Ken. I said, don't move.' Adam's nerves jangled and his heart picked up pace. 'Gotta be a good, good boy, Abey.'

'I be good.'

'Gotta do what Ken tells you.'

'Oh what Ken says, I do.'

'Stand up, Abey!' Abey stood up. 'Stand still. Don't turn around!' He stood perfectly still. 'What can you see, Abey?'

'Window.'

Pleasure and power dried Adam's mouth and his gut squirmed with pleasure.

'Walk to the window.' Abey walked to the window. 'Lick the glass, Abey!'

'Why, Ken?'

'No, Abey, never ask *why*. If you ask *why*... why... I'll have to hurt you.'

'No ask why! Abey no ask why!'

'Lick the fucking window, Abey!' Abey pressed his face to the glass and licked the window. 'You can stop now!' Abey stopped, pulled back from the glass. 'That was fun!' said Adam.

'Wasn't it?' Abey said nothing. 'Don't want to hurt you. That was fun. Wasn't it?'

'That was fun.'

'Ha ha ha, you're not laughing, Abey...'

'Ha ha ha, Abey laugh... Abey good boy... Do Ken say...'

'Sit down on the bed, Abey.' Abey sat back down. 'Put your hands on your head.' Abey placed one hand over the other on his skull. 'Hold your hands in the air. Higher, higher, higher... Keep it like that.'

Adam watched time passing with the second hand of his watch. After half a minute, Abey said, 'Ow, ow...'

'Is it hurting you, Abey?'

'Abey arms hurting, Ken. Be nice, Ken. Please. Sore now.'

Downstairs, a door opened and Gideon's voice drifted up the stairs.

'OK, you can put your arms down now, Abey.' Abey's arms dropped. 'Did that hurt?'

'Ouch!'

'That's nothing to what Ken can do to you. Ken could cut your arms off with the axe in Adam's shed. If you don't do what Ken says. Are you going to do exactly what Ken says?'

'Exactly what Ken says, I do.'

'Listen, Abey. You've got to keep a big secret. No tell anyone Ken has come to live in The Sanctuary. Ken is a secret. Say it. I promise...'

'I promise.'

'Listen. Always keep Ken a secret. If you tell anyone at all, Ken will come into your room and stop you breathing. You be as dead as the blackbird you buried in the garden.'

Gideon's voice came closer to the stairs.

'Hey, I've gotta go now. I gotta sharpen that axe in Adam's shed. Chop chop. Are you happy Ken's come to live in The Sanctuary?'

'Yes, Ken.'

Gideon climbed the stairs.

Moving along the landing to the next radiator to be bled, Adam, back turned to Abey's door, glanced over his shoulder at Gideon and said, 'What?'

44

10.18 am

'The site manager didn't turn the CCTV on until nine o'clock when the tip opened.' Stone listened to Clay's bad news and wanted to swear. 'I've sent some constables on a fishing expedition for CCTV footage from here up to Aigburth Vale and down Riverside Drive into the Albert Dock.'

Sitting on a plastic chair in the office of the municipal tip, Stone looked closely at the surface of the freezer. It was covered in black fingerprint dust. Scientific Support had already lifted all the full and partial prints. He opened the freezer door, looked inside, closed the door again and grimaced at Clay.

He stood up. 'Another old man. It figures.'

'Another old man?'

'The Gospel of Gabriel Huddersfield according to Saint Police National Computer and Blessed Fingerprint Database IDENT1.'

Stone moved a step back, held his hands against the radiator, gathered his thoughts.

'Huddersfield's one sick individual. Fourteen years old, he gets done for ABH. Sixteen years old, GBH. Twenty years old, manslaughter. The Crown Prosecution Service couldn't make murder stick, so he was tried for manslaughter and sentenced to ten years in Strangeways. I phoned them. They were helpful. He found Jesus in jail and went from being a prison warder's nightmare to being a model prisoner, taking his meds, reading the Bible, hanging round the chapel, praying for every-one 24/7 and writing long letters of apology to all his victims and their families. Then he started having visions and hearing voices, and gentle Jesus meek and mild morphs into this foul-tempered Old Testament prophet of doom and damnation. But he didn't do anything wrong other than shout at the walls of his cell. Aged twenty-four he was on the receiving end of a knife attack by another prisoner. He called the guy's wife the whore of Babylon. He was released on parole eight years ago after serving seven and a half years. He's now thirty-five going on thirty-six years old and since he was released from jail he's only been on warnings for obstructing the highway and being a pain in the arse in public places.'

'Psychiatric diagnosis?' asked Clay.

'Paranoid schizophrenia. Hold on to your hat and get this. Huddersfield's ABH victim when he was fourteen, Arthur Bailey, lived in the same street as Gabriel in Walton. Bailey was seventy-two years of age. GBH aged sixteen on Simon Taylor, a complete stranger to Gabriel, in the wrong place at the wrong time on Utting Avenue. How old was Mr Taylor, Eve?'

'Eighty-five...' She sighed.

'Hey, well done. He was actually eighty-six.'

'Was there any reason why he'd targeted these two old men?'

'No. In spite of his tender years and mounting mental-health issues, he was tighter than a sphinx's arsehole. The manslaugh-ter victim was a seventy-eight-year-old man. Gabe's got it in for old men in a major way.'

'Thank you, Karl, that's great work.'

'Get this. The print on the glass from the back door of Leonard Lawson's house is a match for Gabriel Huddersfield. Context and forensics, game, set and match.'

Clay's mind switched to the victim. Hungry to build a bridge between Lawson and Huddersfield, she asked, 'Did you and Bill manage to look at the manuscript?'

'Psamtik I. The manuscript itself is all about what's known as the Forbidden Experiment. Depriving children of language. Two examples, one ancient, one modern. But the thing that's maddening and the thing that's probably going to give us some daylight isn't there. There are twelve pages missing and they're referred to as the English Experiment. And it was those twelve pages I was looking for when you called me.'

'Did Lawson let anything personal slip in his writing?'

'Based on his unpublished manuscript, it seems he thought it was a good thing to condemn unwanted babies to silence and lasting unhappiness.'

'Did he?' She immediately pictured her son Philip sitting in a dark room having had no social contact, no love, no language, no touch, no light, no games, no fun, no hope. The light came on and his face twisted as an animalistic groan emerged from his mouth. He rocked back and forth...

She felt the first tug of tears. *Pull yourself together*, she commanded herself, in the same voice she used to remind herself that profound antagonism towards the victim was not helpful.

'Anything else on Leonard Lawson?'

'The English Experiment. Leonard was in awe of whoever ran it, if it was ever run. Reading between the lines, he had a crush on him. We need those pages, Eve. But Lawson's study... Book after book! An expression containing the words *sand* and *desert* springs to mind. I think Leonard Lawson was a bad guy.'

His features darkened and she sensed a switch flicking in his mind. 'What is it, Karl?'

'This is the phone call we got just as we finished reading the manuscript.' He took out his phone. 'Listen to this.' He pressed play on the recording of the call to Leonard Lawson's landline and when the caller hung up, Clay repeated, '*I am the Angel of Destruction. With the First Born, I serve Death. There's a body in the garden. Whose body? Which garden?*'

Mason and Price dug up the flags in Leonard Lawson's back yard and there was absolutely no sign of anything buried there.

A body. A garden. The words sounded over and over inside Clay's head. Specific words, in the voice of the Angel of Destruction, that mocked her as they filtered into her subconscious. Another set of wheels began to turn.

45

10.25 am

'Where are you, Bill?' asked Clay, shivering as she held her phone in one hand and a mug of tea in the other.

'Walking towards the Catholic Cathedral, looking for Huddersfield.'

She recalled the old cafe in the basement of the Catholic Cathedral in the early 1980s, the cheese sandwiches shared with Sister Philomena: white bread with a slab of butter on each slice and a thick layer of red cheese. *'Eve, you do know these are the sandwiches they have for lunch in heaven...'* The memory of Sister Philomena brought a smile to her face.

'Good thinking. Maybe Huddersfield's gone there on a guilt trip. Have you got the pictures I sent you of the victim's head and feet?'

'I'm looking at them right now. Did you get my text?'

'Yes,' replied Clay. 'The head-footer is the atrocity alongside the Leonard Lawson figure in Bosch's *The Last Judgment.*'

The old man's eyes stared at Hendricks as he wandered up the bone-white steps of the cathedral.

'We need to know who the victim is and where the rest of him is,' said Clay, gazing at the river. 'There haven't been any decapitations on Merseyside for years, never mind a decapitation with both feet taken for good measure.'

She recalled the old man's face and focused on the neatness

of the stitching that kept his eyelids attached to the line of his socket and his eyes wide open. She pictured the cleanliness of the kill in Leonard Lawson's bedroom and sensed Hendricks, benevolent but vulture-like, across the city, picking away quietly at the workings of her mind.

'Old men being targeted for murder by the same perpetrators: it's very rare, Eve, but not unheard of.' In reading her mind, Hendricks had scored a dead-centre bullseye.

'What the hell's going on, Bill?'

'Just that,' replied Hendricks. 'Hell. Discuss, Eve?'

Clay put two images together in her mind and let her thoughts unwind. 'Two victims. One starting point. A painting depicting the merry march to hell. Huddersfield and his accomplice believe they're sending their victims to eternal damnation.'

'What does Gabriel Huddersfield's private space say to you, Eve?'

She added up the religious imagery of Christ on the front door of his flat, a door that could be seen by anyone inside the building, and the things she'd seen in the lair of his secret self. The fetishist mask on the dummy in the bathroom and the progression of mankind from the Garden of Eden through the violence of the fallen world to the eternal sufferings of the damned. 'They're sending their victims to hell.'

'We've been hanging around together too long, Eve. I'm going into the cathedral,' said Hendricks, closing the call down

On the edge of Clay's vision, a small cargo ship glided slowly towards Garston Docks and she was filled with a sweet sadness. She remembered visiting Otterspool Promenade as a small girl with Sister Philomena and how they'd waved to the deck hands on the boats. It was a game she played with Philip on the same Cast Iron Shore. A wheel turned in her childhood memory.

As she got into her car, the ship on the water sailed closer to the dock and her head spun faster and faster.

46

10.35 am

As she buttered a slice of brown toast, Danielle Miller smiled at the racket coming from the table. She would never understand how a handful of men could make themselves so loud. They shouted and laughed across the table at each other. She looked around. Standing near the garden door, Abey was the odd one out. Quiet and distracted, he looked out of the window as Adam approached the house from his shed.

'Toast, Abey?' she asked.

'No thank you. Not hungry.'

Maybe, she thought, *he's picked up on Louise's upset.*

'That's a first,' said Gideon from the table. 'Are you OK, mate?'

'OK, mate,' replied Abey as the door opened and Adam entered the kitchen with his thermos flask.

'Tea,' said Adam, holding up his flask to Danielle.

'You'll have to boil a kettle,' she replied.

'What are you laughing at, Gid?' asked Adam.

'A face that Tom Thumb just pulled.'

'I hope you're not laughing at me.' Adam smiled.

Abey looked at Adam's back and then at the garden shed.

'Oh, for God's sake,' said Danielle. 'Drop it!'

Abey slipped out of the kitchen and started to walk down the line of footsteps that Adam had made in the freshly fallen snow.

He looked back. No one was coming.

His breath heaved from his body in vast plumes of vapour and his heart beat faster as he came closer to the shed.

A frightened bird flew from a shrub and a branch weighed down with snow dropped to the ground. Snowflakes landed on his soft eyelashes. He wiped his eyes.

He glanced over his shoulder. No one was behind him.

The shed door, normally locked, swung a little in the wind.

It was dark in the shed and the smell of Adam's body poured from it like darkness.

He looked at the door and back over his shoulder.

There was a light on in the shed. And the air tasted like the zoo.

He turned to walk back, then pivoted round again in the same moment.

His fingers fitted the edge of the open door.

Abey went into the shed.

47

10.41 am

As Clay was about to turn on to the roundabout at the bottom of Jericho Lane, heading away from the tip, DC Barney Cole approached in his Renault Picasso. She pulled up in the middle of the road, wound down her window.

'We'll have to stop meeting like this,' he said.

'What's the alternative? You're too cheap to buy me a coffee. Good news or bad on the CCTV?'

'Good and bad.'

'Start with the bad.'

'Looking to place Huddersfield and AN Other at Lark Lane, top end near Sefton Park, in and around the vicinity of Pelham Grove, in the two-hour window before the 999 call, we have three sources. The wine bar, the Mexican restaurant and an antique shop. They all have cameras pointing on to Lark Lane. I've been through six hours of footage and there was absolutely no one on there.'

'OK, how about the good news?'

DC Cole laughed. 'No, no, there's more bad.' He pointed in the general direction of the tip, formed a gun from his finger and mimed shooting himself in the head. He then pointed in the direction of Riverside Drive, the road that paralleled the course of the River Mersey into town. 'I got footage from two sources. The Festival Garden's front gate and the Britannia pub.

Both crystal-clear footage from between eight and nine o'clock
this morning. That's one way of getting away from the tip. There
were several vehicles but not a single white van. Even given the
number of white vans out there. Not this morning.'

'Dare I ask?' said Clay.

He held up a pen drive. 'Fulton Court, the apartment block
back there on Jericho Lane. It's got a CCTV camera on its front
gate. The lady from the block's management company assures
me that it's got a direct and clear view of any traffic leaving the
tip between eight and nine this morning. And that is the only
other way of getting away in a vehicle from the tip. I've only just
copied it.'

'Phone me as soon as you ID the vehicle!'

'I'll make two calls on two phones at the same time. You and
the DVLA in Swansea.'

'You know I love you, don't you, Barney.'

'That's why you put me on CCTV watch.'

'You're a sensitive soul. I'd rather you were watching cars
than looking at what turned up at the tip today.'

'I heard.' He smiled. 'Rufus and Chaka Khan.'

'Eh?'

'Ain't Nobody...'

She turned on her ignition. 'You're really quite a sick
individual.'

He waved the pen drive. 'A sickie with a stickie and a pair of
beady eyes.'

48

10.42 am

The shed door opened and Adam froze in the doorway. Abey stood in the centre of the shed facing him, silent.

'What are you doing in here?' asked Adam, his voice like barbed wire.

'Fresh air. The kitchen noisy. Head hurts.' Abey took a step backwards. 'Walk in garden. Door open. Come inside. Cold garden.'

A look of rage filled Adam's face, but almost immediately it was replaced by a look of amusement.

'OK, that's fine by me, Abey. But, really, you should never come into my shed on your own. Do you know why?'

'No.'

'First of all, it's my shed and you have no business being here. But I might as well give you directions to the Runcorn Bridge and expect you to understand that than elaborate about manners. So I'll tell you the other reason.' He indicated the walls, and the saws, hammers, planers, screwdrivers and pliers all neatly set out on their individual hangings. 'It's full of tools and tools can be very dangerous, particularly for a fully certified village idiot such as yourself, Abey. Tools. Dangerous. Dangerous. Tools.'

Adam poured himself a cup of tea from his thermos flask, saw Abey watching and asked, 'Would you like a cup of tea, Abey?'

'Yes, please.'

'Go to the kitchen, there's plenty tea there. What are you staring at?'

'No.' Abey shook his head sadly.

Adam sipped his tea and asked, 'I overheard you talking in your bedroom this morning. I was bleeding the radiators, working hard, to make sure you lot don't catch a chill. So, yeah, I heard you talking out loud. I heard you say *why*. Were you with someone?'

'No.'

'You can't be asking yourself why. I'll ask you again. Were you with someone?'

'No, not anyone. Talk.' Abey prodded himself in the chest. 'Me talk to me.'

'Are you sure you weren't with someone?'

'Sure.'

'On your dada's grave?'

'Dada's grave.'

'Goooooood boy! You know, I think you can be trusted, Abey.'

Adam's eyes danced to the door of the shed. He went over to it and sliced the inner bolt shut.

'All locked in, safe and sound and snug, Abey. You and me, boy!' Adam produced a small key from his pocket. 'You know, you're a good-looking fellah in a simple kind of way. I know a few people who'd love to make your acquaintance.'

He bent down, pulled a locked box from beneath his workbench and opened the padlock. He looked at Abey. 'It'd do you the world of good to get out of this place and meet new people. How does that sound?'

Abey said nothing.

'Would you like to meet new people?'

'No.'

'Abey?'

'No like strangers.'

'Abey?' He took a step towards Abey.

Abey looked over his shoulder. His back was against the back of the shed.

'They're nice guys, Abey. Would you like to meet them?'

'Yes.'

'That's exactly the right answer. And because you've given the right answer, I'm going to give you a little treat. Look at this.' Adam opened the box and reached inside. He took out the top object and showed it to Abey. A whip. Unwinding it, he held the handle firmly in his right hand and half-whipped the narrow space of the shed. 'Do you want to have a go?'

He placed the whip in Abey's right hand and the long, thin strip of leather dangled to the floor at his feet. 'It's all in the wrist and elbow. Have a go.'

Abey made the whip shake and dance around his leg.

'Hey, we're having fun, Abey. Maybe, Abey... Ha, maybe, Abey, we could spend more time together. Having fun. With the toys in my box.'

'That your toy box?'

'Oh, yeah, it's full of toys.'

'Me see.'

'Can you do as you're told?'

'Me can do told.'

'Can you keep your mouth shut and not tell?'

Abey closed his mouth tightly, placed both hands over his mouth.

'Listen, I'm going to have to ask you to leave, because some clever so-and-so up in the house will no doubt be wondering where you are. But before you go...' He put the whip back in the box and locked it. 'Who gets whipped?'

Abey dropped his hands. 'Horses. And Jesus.'

'And anyone who breathes a word about my toy box.' He pointed at Abey, who zipped his own lips with his fingers.

Adam unbolted the door and lifted a large silver axe from the wall. He picked up a block of wood from a plastic bin full of oddments of timber. The door of the shed gaped open. The garden was empty and snow fell like frozen tears.

'Do you know what this is? This is an *axe*. An *axe*! Have you ever heard the word *axe* before?'

'Yes. Axe.' Abey crossed his arms, held on tightly to his shoulders.

'This is what an axe can do.' Adam placed the block on the workbench and with an expert swing split the wood in two. He swung again and the wood flew off the bench. Taking the axe up high, he buried the sharpened blade in the work surface. 'Which is what I've been explaining to you, Abey, about being safe around dangerous tools. What have we been talking about?'

Arms still crossed, Abey pointed at the axe. 'Dangerous tool. Adam tell Abey... how be safe...'

'Go on, beat it back to the house now!' Adam held his finger to his lips and whispered, 'Ssshhh!'

When Abey was out in the snow, Adam closed the door and pulled the bolt over. He took out his mobile phone and connected to the one contact on it. AG.

'I want more, more of the same, Angel Gabriel.' He spoke to the ringing of the phone. The phone had one function. To manipulate Gabriel. It rang out. Gabriel wasn't picking up, was probably too weak to get out of bed.

Adam disconnected and placed the axe back on the wall.

When his phone rang out, a wave of shock hit him. Gabriel was under strict instructions never to ring him. He guessed at a cold call from some PPI repayment scammers but was shocked to see 'AG' on the display.

Adam connected and said, 'Do you realise you've just *disobeyed* me?' There was silence. 'Do you realise that actions have consequences?' Silence. It sounded like AG's place – the sour ambience, the hollow spaces. Coldness crept across Adam's skin as footsteps echoed in another room and men spoke in the background. 'Are you there?' Something was wrong. 'Talk to me.'

He disconnected, stared at the phone and wondered if Gabriel had visitors and if so, who they were. He unbolted the shed door and locked it on the outside. Looking up the garden, he felt the first wave of giddy panic crash inside him as a police siren sounded, passing the front of the house.

He had made a call and that call had been returned to the same place. His shed. Adam looked at the sky. Satellites. Calls could be pinned down to the shed.

In the distance he heard more sirens, but the loudest siren was inside his head.

49

10.46 am

As Clay walked into the main room of Huddersfield's flat in 777 Croxteth Road, she picked up the buzz of excitement in the air.

'I was just about to call you, Eve,' said Mason.

The floor was filling with three categories of Huddersfield's possessions.

Paints, canvases, brushes, modelling plaster, books, magazines, prints.

Statues of saints, crucifixes, Bibles, pictures of Jesus, pamphlets, books on spirituality.

Ropes, chains, knives, vibrators, magazines, whips, handcuffs, ankle shackles.

Art. Religion. Sex.

'Good God, you've been working hard,' said Clay.

Mason held out a small, cheap phone. 'Huddersfield's mobile.'

Clay walked over to him and squinted at the eleven digits on the display panel.

'I think the First Born called.' Mason smiled. 'I answered a call to Huddersfield's phone, I played the silent card, the caller hung up. But this number came on the display.'

'When did this happen?' asked Clay.

'A minute ago. We're already on to the service provider and should have a name and address within the next few minutes.'

'Did you call back?'

'I did.'

'And did the caller speak?'

'Yes. He said, *Do you realise you've just disobeyed me?* Then something about actions having consequences. I bet it's Huddersfield's sadomasochistic other half.'

'You have this taped?'

'Of course.'

'Hey, Terry!' A voice from another room called.

It felt as if the coldness of the entire house had manifested itself as an invisible finger that brushed the back of her neck. A name was coming and with that name an address, an identity...

A face framed in a white hood peered from the doorway. She watched the mouth picked out by a landing light, a mouth that seemed disembodied, and the effect was chilling.

'News from the service provider...' She watched vapour pour from the mouth. 'Their system's down. All the client data's locked up in a glitch.'

Clay felt it like a direct punch to her stomach and, for a moment, she feared she was going to throw up.

'Their engineers are working on it.'

Cold mist, abysmal news. *Was the First Born at work, using humans as toys and meddling with mankind's toys and gadgets?*

'They're going to phone us as soon as they've fixed their systems and can divvy us a name.'

'No!' Clay was surprised at the volume of her own voice and the way it seemed to fill the room. 'Don't wait for them to phone back. Phone them back every minute on a free line.' She headed for the front door. 'They'll fix the system and fail to call us back because there's been a change of shift and someone forgot to tell!' She stopped at the door, anger peaking. 'Terry, get the biggest pain in the arse you've got to get his or her teeth into their ankle!'

50

10.57 am

On Croxteth Road, in the thickening fog, Riley almost collided with Clay. iPhone in hand, Clay said, 'I was just about to call you.'

The disappointment Clay had just experienced lifted when Riley said, 'Successful trip to the Hart Building. I'm waiting on Justine Elgar to come up with some people who knew Leonard Lawson back in the day.'

'Gina, walk with me to my car, please.'

As they walked, Clay realised she could barely feel her feet. The cold had numbed them. She blew into her hands and wished for spring.

'Leonard Lawson spent the best part of his life hiding something,' said Riley.

'Go on,' said Clay.

'His whole career at the University of Liverpool was marked by an almost supernatural blandness. Decades passed and he never missed a lecture, never missed a beat. Then, in the early eighties, he was offered megabucks to go Stateside and cough out twenty lectures. He turned it down with a, an excuse and b, a complete lie.'

'The excuse being?'

'Teaching commitments in Liverpool. He could have easily got out of them. And the unnecessary lie was that such a trip would involve him taking Louise out of school. I did the sums.

Louise was hitting thirty when he turned the gigs down. It was a *don't bother asking again* lie.'

They approached the constable manning the edge of the scene of crime. He looked cold and miserable. Clay met his eye. 'Thank you for keeping all those nosey bastards from getting under our feet.'

He laughed as they passed him. 'No problem, ma'am.'

'Don't be so old-fashioned, lad. What's your conclusion, Gina?' asked Clay.

'Two hundred thousand bucks for twenty lectures versus four-teen thousand pounds before tax for a whole year in Liverpool Uni tells me that he'd done something or had been involved in something that made him want to be like the Invisible Man. He'd have been the Led Zeppelin of the academic world.'

Clay opened her driver's door and Riley got into the passenger seat. Clay put the heater on and warm air danced around their feet. 'Any ideas?' she asked.

Riley opened Leonard Lawson's photocopied file and pulled out his book review from *The Spectator*. 'This is *really* odd.'

Clay turned on the overhead light and began to read. Three sentences in, she stopped, looked sideways at Riley. '*In this absolutely brilliant and ground-breaking study of the need to follow monastic principles of silence and meditation as a means of enhancing the quality of life, Professor Noone outlines how the systemised retention of language could eliminate crime, poverty and a whole range of social ills.*' She raised her head. '*Absolutely brilliant and ground-breaking?*' she queried.

'Read on. He's only warming up, Eve. This is the one and only time he stuck his head over the rampart in decades. Noone's proposition is that if a man can gain a profound understanding of how a child acquires language – how the blank canvas is filled – then he can control how people think en masse. Whoever controls language would have the tools to change the world and re-create it in his own image. It strikes me Professor Noone's book is a control freak's Bible.'

It took Clay two minutes to read the review and weigh it up. She sighed. *'Professor Noone is a mesmeric intellect and his inspirational ideas, if adhered to, would lay the foundation for a new world order that would foster the best qualities in human nature and make war, famine and disease a thing of the past.'* She looked at Riley. 'King-size Messianic Complex. Absolutely bloody barking mad. But who's the bigger head case?' In spite of the cold, Clay suddenly felt hot. 'Professor Noone?' Illumination was near and the light threatened to be blinding. 'Or Professor Lawson?'

Clay took out the framed photo from her bag. 'This was the only photograph in Lawson's house. This young man is Leonard Lawson and that young man is...' She checked the author's name on the review. D.L. Noone.

'What are you smiling at, Eve?'

'Every dedication in every book that Lawson published was to this man. I thought at one point they were to Denise Nicholas, the maiden name of Louise's mother.' Fireworks set off inside her head and a knot tightened in her stomach. 'Gina, google Professor DL Noone, please.'

As Riley pulled out her phone, Clay flipped over the framed photograph and released its back panel. She took the picture from the frame, saw that there was a line of neatly inked words on the back and held them up to the overhead light.

'The first page up is Wikipedia,' said Riley. 'Looks like meagre pickings.'

'In sepulchrum nos sequitur silentium nostrum.' Clay read the words as she showed them to Riley.

They both looked at the Wikipedia page for Professor D.L. Noone. There was a black-and-white close-up of his face. A striking, good-looking man with eyes that appeared jet-black and stared darkly at the viewer. He was the other man in the little portrait in Clay's hand.

Riley read: *'Professor Damien Noone was born in London in 1921. A conscientious objector, he served as a stretcher-bearer in the North African campaign during World War Two. He was educated at King's College, Cambridge, 1946 to 1949. In 1958, he was appointed Professor of Linguistics at Cambridge University.'*

Clay found an English to Latin translator on her phone, typed in the words *In sepulchrum nos sequitur silentium nostrum.* The *ISNSSN* on the dedication in the Psamtik manuscript.

The brief details of Leonard Lawson's biography flashed through her head. 'They met in North Africa during the war and went on to study at the same college in Cambridge.'

A cloud of thrushes swept across the sky.

'Do you have anything else?' she asked, clicking on translate.

'Just waiting on a call from Justine Elgar.'

'Look at this. Look what *In sepulchrum nos sequitur silentium nostrum* translates to in English.'

Riley read: '*Our silence follows us to the grave.*'

51

10.53 am

With a plainclothes constable stationed at the main entrance of the Metropolitan Catholic Cathedral and another at the exit in the basement, DS Bill Hendricks entered the building. He walked slowly around the curve of the circular interior, pausing in front of every one of the thirteen dedicated chapels, hoping Gabriel Huddersfield would be in there on his knees, looking for affirmation or forgiveness.

As he walked, Hendricks repeatedly glanced over his shoulder, distracted by a growing unease that someone or something was right behind him. But each time he turned, he was alone. He put the sensation down to the atmosphere in the cathedral.

Serene blue light from the stained glass of the huge central tower filled the interior and the place swam in competing silence and echoes. Hendricks completed his first circuit at the Amnesty International chapel, the place he had started, feeling as if he was going to explode with frustration.

He walked to the back row of benches near the main door, to watch the entrance, the feeling of being watched or followed coming back at him with increasing intensity. *This time*, he thought, *ignore it*.

The smell of candle wax and floor polish became infused with a floral note. He sniffed. Lavender. Softly, footsteps echoed towards him.

He watched the door.

'Can I help you?'

He turned towards the gentle, husky voice and saw an elderly priest.

The priest smiled at him. 'You seem as if you're looking for someone?'

Hendricks stood up, towered over the old man and offered him his seat.

The priest looked around at the dozens of empty benches. 'May I ask, who are you looking for?'

Hendricks smiled at the hand-rolled cigarette behind the priest's left ear. He took out his warrant card and showed it to him. 'My name's Detective Sergeant Bill Hendricks.'

'Ah, yes.'

'I'm with the Merseyside Constabulary.' He called up the picture gallery on his iPhone and showed him an image of Gabriel Huddersfield. 'This is the man I'm looking for.'

The priest looked at Hendricks and nodded. 'Oh dear. What's he been up to now?'

'You know him?'

'Yes.'

'A serious crime, Father.'

'Oh no.' His face filled with sadness. 'Gabriel's not very well. His mind is full of confusion.' Hendricks gazed into the priest's eyes, which seemed to draw down the cool blue light of the stained glass in the tower. 'He's a paranoid schizophrenic.'

'How do you know that, Father?'

'I was a doctor before I became a priest and I practised medicine as part of my priestly vocation before I was put out to grass.'

'How do you know Gabriel Huddersfield, Father?'

'You came here looking for him, didn't you, Bill? That was an astute move. He's a regular visitor here. As am I. We speak. He asks me questions. He is conflicted. Questions, questions, questions.'

'What sort of questions?'

'*What are the colour of Jesus's eyes? Where is the soul of Judas Iscariot? What will happen when Creation breaks and falls away?*'

'What do you tell him?'

'What would you say?'

'Brown. Hell. Global nuclear war.'

'Wrong on all counts.' The priest smiled and Hendricks found himself smiling with him. 'If he's committed a serious crime, it's my belief that his mental health will suffer a major downturn. This will make him quite easy to catch because of the delusional state, but the same delusional state will make the process of interviewing him about his crime difficult.'

'You seem very sure of yourself, Father.'

'*Seem.* The operative word.' Silence. 'Speak, Bill. What's on your mind?'

'Gabriel took part in a murder, eight to ten hours ago. Tell me what you think about his state of mind now.'

'If he's done something that wrong, he'll be especially vulnerable.' He touched his heart. 'Here. For all his confusion and his extremely strange questions and obsessions, Gabriel Huddersfield has got a very special gift.' He paused as a tourist passed close by their bench. 'He's got a conscience. And deep down, he's very afraid.'

'Of what?'

'Of going to hell when he dies. Which is why he constantly asks about historical figures. Like, *If there are many mansions in my Father's estate of heaven, how many different mansions are there in hell? Which part of hell does Adolf Hitler live in? Whereabouts in hell is the soul of Caiaphas?* He's a very talented artist. Did you know that?'

'Yes, I've seen his work.'

'Let me guess. A painting of hell?'

'One part of it. One part is of the earth, but that's not much different to hell. One part is paradise.'

The elderly priest looked at the confessional box a few

metres away. 'I have to go now. Discussing the sins of others has reminded me. It's time to confess my own.' He held out a hand and shook Hendricks's. His fingers were icy. The skin on his hands was like paper and thin blue veins ran like deltas into the rivers of his fingers. Although his touch was full of tenderness, Hendricks felt almost as if he'd been caressed by a ghost.

'I don't think you're capable of sin,' said Hendricks.

'Pardon?'

The priest smiled with his eyes and an inexplicable sadness coursed through Hendricks. 'Never mind,' he said. 'Never mind. Oh... if you can't find him here, have a walk down Hope Street and try looking for him in the Anglican.'

Hendricks stared after him as he walked towards the door of the confessional box. Then he turned and said, 'Give my love to Eve Clay.'

'You know Eve?'

'Tell Eve to come in and see me sometime, Bill. I'm proud of the way she turned out.'

It felt like the final seven grains of the sands of time were falling through the egg-timer. 'How do you know Eve, Father?'

'She's been in the *Liverpool Echo* more than once.' As he opened the door of the confessional box, his voice seemed to roll around the circumference of the cathedral.

'Father, what's your name?' But Hendricks's voice was lost in the gaping space, and the door of the confessional was shut.

In the light-soaked reception area at the main doors, Hendricks glanced back at the ethereal space and chided himself. *Since when did you believe in ghosts?* A trick of the light and the stillness of the place.

Hendricks watched his feet as he walked down the treacherously steep white steps to the pavement. At the bottom, he stared down the length of Hope Street, towards the Anglican Cathedral.

A woman trudged through the snow, leading a class of junior school children into his path. As he allowed them past,

Hendricks saw a man in a black coat crossing the junction of Hope Street and Mount Pleasant.

The man looked up at the blue glass tower of the cathedral and made the sign of the cross as he walked towards the steps.

Hendricks waited, double-checked the man's features as he looked directly at Hendricks.

The man stopped.

'Gabriel?' Hendricks stepped towards him. 'Gabriel Huddersfield?'

Huddersfield turned, ran into the road and back towards Hope Street.

52

11.03 am

A car swerved to avoid Huddersfield as he sprinted towards the Everyman Theatre and ploughed into the base of a traffic light. Hendricks watched as a stream of traffic screeched to a halt behind the lead car.

Huddersfield was across the centre of Mount Pleasant and Hendricks weaved through the frozen cars, avoiding the drivers as they jumped out of their vehicles and got directly in his way.

A double-decker bus steamed towards the junction with Hope Street. Hendricks looked at the bus, the black ice on the road and Huddersfield's departing figure. He ran into its path, heard the horn screaming at him and felt the disturbance of air as he avoided the vehicle and made it to the corner.

He scanned the length of Hope Street and clocked Huddersfield heading towards the huge black and gold Art Nouveau gates of the Philharmonic Pub. A column of traffic forced Huddersfield to pause. He looked back as Hendricks made a diagonal cut across the road towards him. Their eyes met.

Huddersfield streamed past the pub's decorative turrets and domes, turned the corner into Hardman Street and left Hendricks's sight.

The sounds around Hendricks lifted and all he could hear was the pulse of blood inside his head. He felt his body melting into the air and the weight of his legs vanish. He got closer and closer as Huddersfield headed down the hill then cut across the road, drawing angry blasts of car horns.

On either side of the pavement, pedestrians stopped to watch as Hendricks held up his hand to a line of oncoming traffic, raced to the middle of the road and was then penned back by a single-decker 86. He darted through its slipstream to the other side, ran into the gutter, where red grit had turned the ice to slush, and kept his eyes pinned on Huddersfield's back as he hit the corner of Pilgrim Street. Expecting him to turn the corner, Hendricks was surprised to see him cross the road towards St Luke's, the bombed-out church.

Without warning, Huddersfield stopped in the middle of Pilgrim Street and tried to turn. But a motorbike hit him. Bike and rider curved to the ground as Huddersfield's body flew into the air then slammed on to the tarmac.

As Hendricks closed in on him, Huddersfield got to his feet and hobbled down the side of the ruined church, past the black railings of its garden. An old man stopped and moved in his direction. 'Are you all right?'

'Police!' called Hendricks. 'Get away from him!'

Huddersfield pulled a knife. The old man backed off. Hendricks was ten paving stones away. Closer. He could see the cold cast of Huddersfield's eyes.

Hendricks felt his body rise as he leapt towards Huddersfield, feet first into his back. He connected, full on with both feet in the base of Huddersfield's spine, and Huddersfield crashed to the pavement. Hendricks landed half on the pavement and, adrenaline pumping, was on him, both hands pinning his chest, his knees on his hips.

Coldness poured off the pavement.

'You're under arrest, Gabriel.'

A ring of onlookers started to form. Hendricks kept one hand on Huddersfield and flashed his warrant card. 'Beat it right now!'

53

11.15 am

Driving to the Royal Liverpool Hospital to meet with Hendricks and Huddersfield in A&E, Clay slowed down at a red light. Her phone rang out, she connected, hit speakerphone and burned the light.

'I got your text,' said Stone. 'You want me to come to the Royal?'

'Yes,' she replied and then, remembering the victim's daughter, 'No. Go to The Sanctuary and tell Louise Lawson that we've got one of the men who killed her father. Confirm we're looking for his accomplice. See if you can press her for anything else.'

As Clay sped down Lodge Lane, she considered the explosive cocktail of mental illness, religious mania and sexual deviancy on which Gabriel Huddersfield was so extremely drunk and wondered how hard it would be to crack him open.

At the junction with Smithdown Road and Upper Parliament Street, her phone rang again. Excitement gripped her when she saw the name 'Cole' on the display.

'Barney! The white van, the CCTV from Fulwood Court?'

'The central stretch of Jericho Lane leading away from the tip was swamped in fog from the playing fields alongside the road. The driver was CCTV savvy and held his hand up to his face when he passed Fulwood Court and their camera. He needn't have bothered. The fog was so thick, I can only tell you that the van was a Mercedes-Benz, probably a Citan. And I could only pull two digits from the licence plate. K and C. The woman from the DVLA laughed at me, told me she wasn't capable of performing miracles. *Go find the rest of the numbers and letters, Plod, and maybe I can help you then.* Quote unquote. Bitch!'

Clay buried the crashing disappointment that Cole's news brought and tried to sound bright. 'Barney, stop feeling sorry for yourself and get to work on the symbol from the shaft of the spear. Unravel the dragonfly at the open window.'

54

11.15 am

In the communal kitchen of The Sanctuary, Abey sat alone at the table, a plate of toast and a milky cup of tea in front of him. Another plate of toast and another cup of tea sat on the table in the empty place opposite.

'So, where did you slip off to when everyone else was having their snack?' asked Gideon, loading the dishwasher.

'Eat up toast, Ken,' said Abey to the empty place. 'Drink tea, Ken. Hungry if don't, Ken.' With a delicate gesture, he pushed the plate and cup a little closer.

Gideon stopped what he was doing and, smiling, watched.

'Come on, Ken. Be good boy now and me tell Lou-Lou, Ken be good boy.' Abey nodded. He fell still and Gideon positioned himself so that he could see the expression on Abey's face. He appeared rapt, listening attentively, nodding and making affirmative noises with his mouth.

'No, Ken. Can't. Can't see. Can't see no Dada. Dada dead. Body bury, soul in heaven. With?' Pause. 'Jesus!'

Abey's head turned. His eyes tracked the space from the chair opposite to the door. 'Where going, Ken? Come back, Ken! Ken! No eat toast. No grow big strong like Abey.'

Gideon made his way to the seat opposite Abey and the skin on his arms puckered into goose bumps when Abey looked directly into his eyes and smiled.

'Can I sit there?' Abey nodded and Gideon sat in Ken's place. 'Oh, look!' said Gideon, indicating the tea and toast he had made earlier. 'You said Ken would eat and drink it if I made it.'

Abey took a few moments and responded. 'Ken naughty. No eat tea toast.' He pointed at his own empty plate. 'Me good. Me eat up and say thank you.'

'What's Ken like?' asked Gideon. Abey licked the tip of his finger and dragged it through the crumbs on his plate. 'Is he a good friend?' Abey stuck the finger in his mouth and Gideon, noticing the friendship bracelet on his wrist, wondered just how much Abey would ever understand of Louise's trauma.

'Ken mean to Abey this morning.' The door creaked open, but no one came in. 'Ssshhhh!' Abey placed his finger to his lips. 'Hello, Ken!' Abey lit up, tracked the phantom friend from the door to the chair opposite. Gideon watched Abey's eyes make the journey through thin air. 'Where been, Ken?' An imaginary step. 'Been good, Ken?' Closer came the illusion.

'Oh, I do beg your pardon, Ken,' said Gideon, standing up for Abey's imaginary friend. 'Your seat. Here, please...' He paused. 'Sit down, Ken. That's good, yes, just great.' Gideon pushed the empty chair into the table and smiled. Abey made a switch. The tea and toast was in his place, the empty plate and cup in Ken's place.

'Ken eaten up. Abey eat he toast now.'

The door opened and Adam walked in, a smile on his lips. Abey stood up quickly and, head down, walked past Adam and out of the room.

'What's wrong with you now, Adam?' asked Gideon. 'You look like you've lost three pints of blood.' Adam looked at Gideon with an intensity that stopped him in his tracks. 'You don't look yourself. I think I know what's troubling you.'

'Do you really?' Adam closed the kitchen door. 'Tell me, what's troubling me?'

'I'm worried about you, Adam.'

'What a coincidence.' Adam advanced towards Gideon. 'What's troubling me?'

'Danielle. She doesn't know, does she?'

'Doesn't know what?'

'777 Croxteth Road,' said Gideon.

The smile on Adam's face froze and the colour rose in his throat. He moved closer, his eyes not leaving Gideon's. 'Go on.'

'The longer it's been going on, the more careless you've become.'

'What are you talking about?'

'I'm talking about the purple-haired pot-head who screws you for weed money.'

Adam stopped. The tension in his body reached saturation point and he appeared to turn to stone on the spot. 'Don't even think about using that against me.'

'I wouldn't dream of it. But I'm confused, Adam. She's a bag of bones. I've been behind her in the checkout at Tesco on Aigburth Road and she stinks. What's her name? Sheila? Sally? Sandra?'

'How do you know about me and Sally?' There was a tone in his voice, a feline purring or a bomb about to go off.

'I've seen you letting yourself into the building with your own key.'

Adam smiled and the effect was unnerving. 'Go on, Gideon, keep that slanderous tongue wagging.'

'I don't get it. The attraction.' In little more than a whisper, Gideon asked, 'Is it the grubbiness of her?' Adam said nothing, but his eyes were dancing with a muddy light. 'You're married to Danielle. She's attractive, a lady, and you keep disappearing to that *woman*. I'm warning you, it's out on the neighbourhood tom-toms: you, a pillar of the Church of England, and the local skank.'

Adam laughed and was then suddenly silent. 'I've been visiting her because she wants me to pray with her. She's desperate to come off the drugs. We had a chance meeting in the same Tesco's where you made judgments about her because she lacks the basic skills to care for herself. You should listen to yourself. You've got a diseased mind, Gideon. Shame on you!'

The doorbell rang, three sharp blasts. The sound galvanised Adam and he was in the garden at speed. Gideon watched him and listened to Danielle's footfall as she headed to the front door.

You're a liar, Adam! The truth of this overwhelmed Gideon as he tracked Adam heading through the snow. The man was poisonous. *A dangerous liar and a total hypocrite.* Adam opened his shed door and, not for the first time, Gideon wondered what he did in there. Fear pricked Gideon's skin like hot pins. His heart beat faster at the coldness in Adam's eyes and an old-fashioned word came into his head. *Evil.*

He heard the front door open and Danielle's voice. 'Come in, Detective Sergeant Stone. It's a cold day. Let me fix you a hot drink.' They came into the kitchen.

Gideon walked but wanted to run. 'Would you like me to get Louise?'

'Yes, please,' said Stone, sitting at the table.

'You don't look well, Gid, are you OK?' asked Danielle.

'I think I'm catching a bug,' he said, leaving the room. *A nasty, violent bug.*

55

11.30 am

At the Royal Liverpool Hospital, in a windowless room near the A&E suite, Clay and Hendricks sat across a table from Gabriel Huddersfield.

Huddersfield looked back at Clay, staring through her as if she was a fleeting shadow. His top and lower lips were broken, crusts of blood rimmed his nostrils, a black eye was making its way out on his left side and to the right his whole cheek was deeply grazed. His clothes – black trousers, top and coat – looked as if he'd been living in them for weeks.

'Gabriel,' said Clay. 'DS Hendricks and I are making an audio recording of this interview. Do you understand that?'

Silence.

'You have the right to a solicitor and I'm going to offer it to you again. So far, your response has been silence. Gabriel, would you like the services of the duty solicitor?'

Silence.

'You know, Gabriel, you're lucky. You're lucky you have no broken bones.'

'That's not luck. My bones are filled with my spirit and my spirit, like my bones, is unbreakable.'

'Again, do you want a solicitor?'

Silence.

'Then we'll proceed with the interview. Who beat you up?'

For a moment he looked surprised by the question. Instead of looking through Clay, he focused on her.

She pointed at the purple bruising around his neck. 'I can see suction marks on your neck and the imprint of human teeth marks. Yet on the knuckles of your hand I see tattooed *JESUS DIE4U*. I suggest to you, Gabriel Huddersfield, that the person who inflicted these sexualised wounds on you was the same person who assisted you in the murder of Leonard Lawson in his bedroom in his house on Pelham Grove. Am I right?'

Silence. He tilted his head back, stared at the ceiling directly above him.

'Give me a name, Gabriel. Where were you between the hours of ten o'clock last night and two o'clock this morning?'

He scraped a crust of blood from his nose with a thumbnail, looked at it, ground it into dust between his thumb and finger on the table. 'How can I talk to you if you don't know what I am?'

'We've spoken on the phone, Gabriel, when I was in Leonard Lawson's house,' said Hendricks. 'Leonard Lawson's house. You've been there, haven't you?'

'Oh, but I do know what you are.' Clay considered his role in the sadomasochistic relationship. 'You're the Angel of Destruction. And your earthly lover, your partner, is the First Born.'

Gabriel looked beyond Clay at Hendricks and then back at Clay. 'How do you know what I am?'

'You're the killer of Leonard Lawson.'

'Indeed.'

'But this was not something you did on your own?'

'Indeed.'

'Give me the name of the First Born.' Hendricks leaned in a little closer.

'The First Born,' echoed Huddersfield.

'And his name is...?'

'Why should I need to know a name? *The First Born* is enough. The First Born raised me to be his angel.'

'What does the First Born look like?'

'The First Born looks like a man, it is a clever mask. I think you know the First Born. Why don't you ask him yourself?'

'How do I know him?' asked Clay.

'How do you think?'

'Tell me.'

'With your eyes and your ears.'

Clay looked at him and saw his eyes hardening and knew he was not going to give up the name of his brutal lover. 'Are you afraid of the First Born?' she asked. 'Are you frightened that the First Born will destroy you?'

Silence. His hands were pressed flat against the surface of the table, palms down, fingers splayed. Lips moving without sound. His head fell forward, he closed his eyes, raised his arms in the air in evangelical fervour, hands cupped to heaven.

'I know why you murdered Leonard Lawson, Gabriel.'

'You know nothing.' He looked at her through the trees of his raised arms, fingers spread like diseased branches.

'Just as he condemned one half to the silent void...'

Gabriel's arms fell suddenly, thumping on to the table with force.

'...Leonard Lawson and his other half are condemned...'

He banged his arms again. The pain made his hands shake and a look of ecstasy flashed through his cold eyes.

'...to the eternal silence of hell.'

His face twitched and Clay could almost see the adrenaline pumping round his body. A film of sweat glazed his face.

'You delivered him to that punishment, you and your partner.'

She could smell his blood and a hint of sweat beneath the metallic tang.

'With these hands.' He spoke with complete detachment as he lowered his fingers and, under the ceiling light, examined his clawed hands as if they were the crowning glory of some mythical beast. 'The deliverer's deliverers.' He spoke to his hands, kissed the tips of his own fingers.

Clay looked at him closely, analysed every detail and took

a picture with her mind's eye. 'Do you know who Leonard Lawson condemned to the silent void? Or were you just repeating what your partner told you?'

'Silence,' said Huddersfield.

'Do you know who Leonard Lawson's other half was?'

'Silence.'

'Do you know what the eternal silence of hell is like, that you have delivered Leonard Lawson to?'

Huddersfield covered his mouth with both hands.

'Any questions, DS Hendricks?'

'Yes. You mentioned a body and a garden in your phone call to Leonard Lawson's house. Whose body? Which garden?'

Huddersfield closed his eyes.

'What is the colour,' asked Hendricks, 'of Jesus Christ's eyes? They're not brown, are they, Gabriel?' Huddersfield opened his eyes. 'Unlike yours. And what about the end of the world? It won't be a global nuclear war. One moment it will be here and the next gone. In time for the Last Judgment. Speaking of which, Gabriel, which part of hell does Judas Iscariot live in? He isn't in hell. His soul is in heaven. I hope the same can be said of you one day, Gabriel. I do hope the First Born has his facts about the afterlife straight. I hope so, don't you? No more questions.'

Huddersfield clasped his hands together in front of him, looked straight ahead at Clay. She held his silence, stared deeper into his eyes and, in a double blink, saw the faintest sign of a crack within him.

'We know something about the history of your mental health,' said Hendricks. 'And we know what you're up to. That was a fine performance, Mr Huddersfield.'

'You're a policeman, not a psychiatrist. You know nothing.'

'I've got a PhD in forensic psychology. You had the presence of mind to run away from me when you thought I might be a police officer. Your notes are on the way over from Broadoak as we speak. I've booked in to see Mr Leavis, your consultant psychiatrist, to discuss your history.'

Huddersfield looked up at him.

'You're fit to stand trial, Mr Huddersfield, because you understand the nature of the crime you've committed and the charges that will be brought against you.'

'I have severe mental illness.'

'I've never seen such cold premeditation as in Leonard Lawson's killing,' said Clay. 'Your little act isn't going to win you a term in Broadmoor Hospital. You're going to end up on a Category A wing in Wakefield!'

'I'm not well!'

'You've got to understand,' said Hendricks. 'People have been trying to pull the wool over my eyes for many, many years. I can see right through you. And so will every psychiatrist the justice system can throw at you. If I was you, I'd cooperate with us.'

Huddersfield covered the lower half of his face with his fingers.

'When we spoke on the phone,' repeated Hendricks, 'you mentioned a body and a garden. Whose body? Which garden?'

Silence.

'That's fine,' said Clay. 'Shall we stop wasting our time, DS Hendricks?'

'The garden. Its name. It's on the back of the triptych.'

'Mind games,' said Clay, 'will get you nowhere. A garden? For dead people?' She smiled. A curtain parted behind her eyes.

'I'm sick, I tell you.'

'You're referring to a cemetery!'

His eyes dithered.

'A garden for dead people.'

'I'm sick. Sick, sick, sick, sick, sick, sick!'

56

11.35 am

Danielle Miller, early fifties but with the figure of a woman half her age and the indelible stamp of the pretty girl she had once been still visible in her face, turned and smiled. 'Milk and sugar?'

'Milk, no sugar, thank you.'

Sitting at the kitchen table in The Sanctuary, DS Karl Stone watched her pouring coffee and, for a moment, imagined what it would be like to be in a relationship with her. As she turned and brought the coffee over, he abandoned the pleasant but self-defeating daydream. She was way out of his league. Her husband had at some point in time presumably had looks and charm, and most certainly money.

As she put the cup of coffee down, the edge of her hand brushed his. The accidental touch filled him with a loneliness he only dwelt on in the privacy of his clean but rather unhomely flat. Eighteen months after his last disastrous date, he abandoned a solemn pledge he'd made to himself. *Internet dating,* he thought, *come back, all is forgiven.*

The door opened and Louise came in and sat down at the table. Danielle placed a cup of tea in front of her and put her hands on her shoulders. She looked at Stone. 'I'll leave you to it.'

Stone waited until Danielle had closed the door on her way out.

'Miss Lawson, of the two men involved in the murder of your

father, one of them is currently in our custody and on his way to Trinity Road police station. His name is Gabriel Huddersfield.'

The door to the garden opened and Adam entered.

A strange look crossed Louise's face. 'Can it really be Gabriel Huddersfield?'

'Gabriel Huddersfield?' Adam sounded perplexed. 'Who's he?' He closed the door, but the room was now full of cold air.

Stone looked at Louise, who said nothing for a few moments and then asked, 'Are you going to the cathedral, Adam?'

'I am.'

Stone checked his watch, then said quizzically, 'Carols, is it?'

'No. I'm an interpreter. At the Anglican Cathedral. I interpret the building for visitors.'

'Like a tourist guide?'

Adam Miller smiled coldly. Stone watched the way Louise tracked him as he crossed to the door into the hallway. The lines in her brow seemed to deepen with each step he took.

'I'll light a candle for your father,' Adam said. He closed the door and was gone.

'Miss Lawson, it *is* Gabriel Huddersfield. You know him?'

'I've spoken to him in Sefton Park. The first time we met, he was distressed, alone on a bench and in tears. I asked him what was wrong. He was full of fearful questions about God and the Devil. I calmed him down. It took hours. Ever since, whenever I pass him, he bows his head towards me, joins his hands and says, *Thank you, kind lady.*'

'I'm sorry to have had to reignite your grief,' Stone said. Her eyes remained on the door. 'Miss Lawson, have you remembered anything, anything at all that you've failed to mention to us so far?' He saw a flicker in her face as she reconnected with him.

She leaned across the table and laid her hands on the back of his hand. He placed his free hand over the coldness of hers and, as they sat in silence, she looked directly at Stone.

'You're a good man, Detective Sergeant Stone. I can tell. Your wife is a lucky woman.'

He didn't tell her the truth, that he had never been married and that it had been three years since his last brief relationship folded.

'You are giving me strength through your kindness. I didn't imagine it. It's like my memory is a locked room, but the door is opening and light is seeping in. Do you understand?'

'I understand, Miss Lawson. You've had a huge trauma. The mind shuts down to prevent the totality of what you know from overwhelming you.'

'I thought maybe I did imagine it, but I didn't. There was definitely another voice in my father's room. Long, breathy sounds. I remember two things. Something about a garden and a body, maybe? I'm convinced of that. Strange. And... *the triumph of death*. The voice definitely said the words, *This is... the triumph of death. You are the First Born and I am the Angel of Destruction and we serve Death. Death is our master.*'

Stone heard the voice on the telephone in Leonard Lawson's hall echoing inside his head and it sparked a sense of being on the edge of a personal revelation.

'Does that... Does that make any sense to you?'

'Oh yes, Miss Lawson, that makes a whole lot of sense.' He paused. 'Your father was a man of few spoken words.' She nodded. 'Can I ask why you had a telephone in your house?'

'We were both old. I have epilepsy. It was for medical emergencies.'

'Are you ex-directory?'

'No, our number is listed. But no one ever calls. Why should they? A spinster and her elderly father. No, it never rings.'

'You have friends, Miss Lawson. I've heard about Abey and how he follows you like a shadow. I've heard of his love for you.'

'The love he has for me comes from the simplicity of his heart and mind. I don't deceive myself, Detective Sergeant Stone. He is a child forever trapped in a man's body. But love is love and must never be chased away. If he wasn't disabled, he wouldn't give me a second glance.'

Stone was stumped. 'Adam?' She looked at the door again. 'I was there when he offered to shelter and support you.'

'He has his reasons. My best interests don't come into it.'

Stone sipped his coffee. Warm and aromatic. His senses strayed into Danielle Miller territory and he pulled himself back into the moment.

'I can't think of anything else for now,' said Louise, looking as if the weight of the universe was pressing down on her narrow shoulders. 'But if I do...'

Back on the pavement outside The Sanctuary, DS Stone typed the words *The Triumph of Death* into Google Images on his phone. Immediately, a gallery of pictures came up, all of them showing the same painting: an apocalyptic vision of the destruction of humanity by an army of skeletons. He tapped the first image and the screen filled with it. Along the top, the name *Pieter Bruegel* and the title *The Triumph of Death*.

Immediately, Stone noted similarities with *The Last Judgment*. Bruegel, like Bosch before him, had painted an apocalypse, a dark vision of human beings being hunted and tortured, not by monsters and demons as in *The Last Judgment*, but by sprightly skeletons. He imagined he saw many satisfied smiles in the jaws of their faces. Redness and darkness prevailed, with just enough patches of illumination to highlight the grim palette against which the terrors unfolded. As he drank in the detail, Stone felt that Bruegel had upped the level of horror. In *The Last Judgment*, the humans had been hunted by mythical beasts and demons. In *The Triumph of Death*, the terror had come much closer to home. The hunters had the form of human skeletons, people who had themselves faced the triumph of death and had come back to harvest the flesh of the next generation. Ancestors pitted against their descendants.

He mailed the image to Clay, Hendricks, Riley and Cole and followed it with a text: *Louise Lawson now recalls the killers – the First Born and the Angel of Destruction – talking of the Triumph of Death. Her memory is sharpening. She has much to tell us.*

57

12.20 pm

Over 300 feet up, on the roof of the Anglican Cathedral's Vestey Tower, the wind poured through the decorative stone arches of the parapet. Peter Westwood, stonemason, stood on a metal scaffold secured to the stonework by strong blue ropes, mortar board in one hand, pointing the sandstone at the top of one of the pinnacles and wincing at the cold. And although the panoramic view of Liverpool and the Wirral was veiled by shifting bands of fog, the stonemason was bewitched by memories of the River Mersey and the landscape around it.

'Watch out, Peter, we've got a visitor!'

Peter turned to the voice of Jim Bacon, the security guard on duty at the top of the bell tower. The security guard stood near the entrance to the roof space and made a slashing motion to his throat. Peter laughed and then narrowed his eyes at the north wind as a third party arrived on the roof.

'Hello!' Adam Miller stepped on to the roof, breathless from the climb up 108 steps that led to the roof space. He walked past the security guard as if he was invisible and marched towards the stonemason, who had his back turned and was busy pointing red mortar between the tight spaces in the stone.

'Hello, Peter!' Adam stood at the base of the scaffolding and looked up at the stonemason, who turned his head and looked down at the unwelcome returning visitor.

Tall and good-looking, gym physique evident in spite of the layers he was wearing, the young stonemason continued to work as Adam gazed in the direction of his feet and up the length of his body. 'Hello,' he replied, eyes fixed on the point of his trowel.

Adam placed both hands around the neck of a length of scaffolding and shook the metal tubing.

'Excuse me!' said the security guard, advancing. 'Please don't touch the scaffolding when the stonemason is standing on it doing his work.'

'I was just testing how safe it is.'

'It's a hundred per cent safe,' said the security guard. 'The stonemason *erected* it. He's a master craftsman. He knows what he's doing with his erections.'

Adam felt the accusation and mockery in the guard's words like knives in his eyes. He picked up a length of the blue rope that secured the scaffolding to the stonework. Metal and stone were welded with the glue of rope. 'I'm impressed with your knots!' he called up.

'I was a good boy scout.' Peter laughed.

Adam looked around, saw the hardboard on which the mortar was mixed and asked, 'Do you need me to mix up a batch of mortar? You're running a bit low.'

'No, thank you. It's a very precise mix I use.' Peter moved along the wooden platform.

'Adam?' said the security guard. 'It is Adam, isn't it? He's busy. He's 331 feet up at the top of the bell tower overlooking Liverpool. The weather's horrible and he needs to do his job as quickly as he can. I asked you nicely yesterday. Can you please leave him alone?'

Adam heard a sound in the sky. Something laughing at him? He looked up, but all he saw were dense clouds. He looked back at the security guard and asked, 'Are you working here all day?'

'All day, every day, until five o'clock today. Why?'

'Just asking,' replied Adam. 'Say!' he shouted up to the stonemason.

Peter stopped working and looked down at him. 'What?'

'Any chance you could show me how you mix your mortar? I'm in the building game. I'm a bit of a jack of all trades, but I'm always willing to learn from a master craftsman like yourself.'

'When I'm not busy!' Peter said. 'But at the minute I've got until one o'clock to finish pointing here and then I've got a list as long as my arm to do indoors.'

'You're a tourist guide, aren't you, Adam?' said the security guard.

'I'm an interpreter. I interpret the building. What of it?'

'Interpret this.' He gave a wide smile that went nowhere near his eyes.

Adam returned the smile and looked up at Peter, who had paused to watch.

'Stop bothering the stonemason.' The security guard leaned closer and whispered, 'Fuck off, faggot, he's not interested in you.'

'That was a rather foolish thing to say,' said Adam, the smile dissolving from his face. 'Up here all day in this weather? Isn't that punishment enough?'

'Are you threatening me?'

'No, I'm empathising with you. We're all good Christians round here, aren't we?'

'You might be. I'm just an employee of the diocese.'

Adam looked up at the stonemason and felt a clash of desire and humiliation. He walked away. 'I'll leave you to it.'

He said something else and the security guard asked, 'What was that?'

'It's as cold as the grave up here,' said Adam.

58

12.23 pm

Driving down Aigburth Road back to Trinity Road police station, Clay passed the top of Mersey Road, where she lived with her husband and child. She felt the pull of home as a physical twist deep in her core. She pulled over across the road from Liverpool Cricket Club and took her iPhone from her pocket.

The Triumph of Death, an image of the Bruegel painting, her temporary screensaver, peered up at her like a curse. She felt a wave of pity for the people being harvested by the skeletons and glanced briefly over her shoulder to check for her own stealthy monster, but there was nothing but oncoming traffic.

Three missed calls, all from her husband Thomas. She called him back.

'Thomas, pick up your phone! Pick up, pick up!' she said to the purring tone in her ear.

'Hello, stranger.' She could hear the smile on his face in the tone of his voice and this dampened the unease that had just gripped her.

'Thomas, love, is everything all right?'

She could hear the scraping heels and dull background rumble of the reception area of the medical practice where Thomas worked.

'Two things. I just called to reassure you. I spoke to the nursery manager. Philip's having a whale of a time. Ate every scrap of food they put before him and slept soundly during siesta. Just another day in nursery for him. How are things with you, Eve?'

'Mixed. We've got one perpetrator in custody and another maniac still out there.' She saw a marked police car looming in the wing mirror and watched it pass. Huddersfield stared out from the back seat and their eyes met. And the monster she'd just looked for was gone.

'What's the second thing?'

'Hang on a minute. I'm going into my room.'

His footsteps were swift and the background noise faded quickly. She recognised the squeak of the hinges and the soft thud of the door as he closed the door of his consulting room.

'Go on?' Clay's curiosity had been fired.

'I've just been handed an envelope from the lunchtime post. It's got your name on it, but, obviously, it's addressed to you here at the surgery. It's been posted in Liverpool...' There were three loud, sharp knocks at Thomas's door. *Ignore it, Thomas*, she urged. 'FAO Detective Chief Inspector Evette Clay,' Thomas read.

Evette?

Something delicate connected inside Eve. She was almost certain that something from her childhood was coming.

'The receptionist brought it in when I was between patients. I palmed my next patient off on Gary so I could talk to you. I tried you three times.'

'Thomas, open the letter, please.'

The knock on the door came again, this time louder and longer. Eve's heart sank as she heard him answer it. 'Not now, thank you. I'm not to be disturbed until I say I'm available!'

The world around Clay appeared to dissolve; the edges of her vision blurred and the traffic noise of the busy dual carriageway faded like the end of a song. All she heard was the ripping of an envelope and the action of her husband's fingers delving inside.

He was silent for what seemed like an eternity and then he said, 'Oh my goodness...'

'What is it, Thomas?'

'Are you there, Eve?'

And she realised that the question she'd thought she'd said out loud had been nothing more than the edge of a whisper. 'I'm listening to you, Thomas.' To the unique music of his voice.

'Two photographs, no covering letter. Let me double-check that.' The paper rustled. 'No covering letter.'

'Tell me.'

'There's an old black-and-white photograph...' He paused and she heard a crack in his voice. 'It's you and Philomena. You're probably four years old and you're wearing a dress with a pattern of dark marks around the neckline...'

'I remember the dress. It was my best frock, my Sunday best. There were cherries in the pattern. I was four. Tell me about Philomena.'

'She's sitting at a plain table. You're sitting on her knee. She has one hand on your head and the other on your heart. Both your hands are on her belly. She's looking directly at the camera and smiling. You're looking directly up at her. You're laughing.'

Clay's mind tripped through time and she was in the moment that the photograph was taken. Thomas's voice played like a soft soundtrack as her eyes closed and the memory unfurled like a clip from a film.

They were in the old cafeteria in the basement of the Catholic Cathedral. A man in a beige coat, the shoulders damp with freshly fallen rain, took a picture of them with a small black camera.

She wriggled on Philomena's knee.

'Why's he want to take a picture of us for?' asked Eve.

'Ah, humour the old fool,' replied Philomena softly from the corner of her mouth. Eve looked up at her face and laughed at the way she pulled a smiling Tweetie Pie expression, like their all-time favourite cartoon character.

'OK, all done,' said the photographer. 'Thanks.'

'Wait a minute,' said Philomena. 'You flashed your press pass at us like you were trying to bunk on the bus with an out-of-date ticket. Let's see...'

She held her hand out and the photographer placed his press pass on her palm. She pointed to the words and Eve recognised one word on sight but struggled to sound out the second word. '*Catholic Pic... Picty...*'

'*Catholic Pictorial*,' said Philomena, handing the press pass back. 'It's the diocesan newspaper.'

'The cathedral's cafe's doing really poor business...' The man spoke as if they were conspirators. 'The archbishop wants to drum up business, so we're running a feature on where all good Catholics should go for their lunch when they're out shopping.'

Eve looked round at the plain walls, the tiled floor, the rickety wooden tables and chairs, the counter with its cakes and buns and sandwiches, the steaming tea urn and the milkshake maker. It was her and Philomena's place and she couldn't understand why others wouldn't want to go there.

'We live in St Claire's, Edge Hill, you know it?' He nodded. 'Be sure to send us a copy from your darkroom.'

'Don't worry, Sister Philomena, I'm not going to get on the wrong side of you.'

When he was out of earshot, Eve asked, 'How come...?'

'How come what, Eve?'

'Wherever we go, people know who you are?'

She considered it for a moment. 'No, they *think* they *know* who I am, Eve.'

Eve sucked strawberry milkshake through a straw and wished the drink would last forever.

'Remember that talk we had about *seems* and *is*? And the *seems and is* game?'

'Let's play the *seems and is* game! Can I go first?'

Clay opened her eyes, the world came into focus and she heard Thomas's voice asking, 'Eve, are you all right?'

'I'm fine, just fine, thank you. Tell me about the second photograph, Thomas.'

Clay looked at the clock on the dashboard, worked out that Huddersfield would be arriving at Trinity Road police station, shifted into first gear and started off down Aigburth Road.

'The second picture is recent. It's a colour photograph of a very old man, a priest, standing on the steps of the Catholic Cathedral. He's got a kindly face. There's no one and nothing else in the picture, except... except he's got a burning cigarette in his right hand.'

'The sender?' Clay got up to 50 mph on St Mary's Road, felt compelled to get to Huddersfield in Interview Suite 1 and sweat him down fast. 'Have a look on the back of the pictures.'

'Aaaahhh. Sorry. There's nothing on the back of the picture of you and Sister Philomena, but there's a really spidery scrawl on the one of the old priest. And it says... *Come and see me here. God bless and keep you, Evette...* That's odd. *The Shrimp.*'

She knew who the pictures were from and the temptation to turn at the next junction and head straight for the Catholic Cathedral to find the old priest was intense. But duty kept her where she was and she knew she didn't have time for any diversions.

'Can you take pictures of both of them and send them to my phone?'

'That was to be my next trick.'

Tenderness and vulnerability consumed her. She was glad that there was no one else there in that moment.

'I recognise that silence,' said Thomas. 'Go on. Ask.'

'Shall we run away together, Thomas?'

'One day.'

'I'm a lucky woman to be so loved.'

'No luck involved. You deserve to be loved. Go crack that case.' He closed the call down.

He's right. Philomena's voice sounded inside her head and Clay wondered how on earth she had survived the twenty-two-year passage in her life, from her sixth year when Philomena had died to her twenty-eighth year when she met Thomas by chance in the stalls of the Liverpool Playhouse.

The opening night of Arthur Miller's *All My Sons*: 15th September 2006.

As she took her seat, number 34 in row C, she noticed the giant in B 34. The man next to her, in C 35, quashed her long-held conviction that there was no such thing as love at first sight with two simple actions and three words. He smiled at her, stood up and said, 'Let's swap places.' She extended her hand, thanked him and felt a jolt of sadness when he let go.

They hadn't so much fallen in love as hurtled into it, and the tenderness that the memory evoked inside her turned into a mournful wish: that Philip would never know the loneliness that she had taken as read until she met Thomas.

An incoming text arrived on her phone and a call came in. On the display: 'Mason'. She forced herself back into professional mode.

'We currently have the pleasure of Gabriel Huddersfield's company,' she said, not bothering with any preamble. 'How are things in his boudoir, Mason?'

'You'd better get over here, Eve, as soon as you can. There's something you've just got to see.'

60

12.30 pm

When DS Gina Riley returned to the incident room at Trinity Road police station, DC Barney Cole was hunched over his desk, engrossed, talking softly to himself and drawing short, sharp lines on a blank page with a pen and ruler. He appeared not to have heard her enter.

'You look like you're having fun,' she said.

'Hello, Gina,' he replied, without looking up.

'What are you up to, *Barns*?'

'It's bad enough being named after a cartoon character by my oh so ditzy mother – Barney Rubble, for God's sake! – without you abbreviating it and making me sound like a rent boy.'

Riley laughed. 'Thank your lucky stars she wasn't into Speedy Gonzales. Coffee, *Barns*? Black, three sugars?'

'Lovely. I'm trying to get the last living cells of my brain around the carving on the spear. The dragonfly exiting a window. I'm breaking it down and seeing if it's some sort of visual anagram.'

She flicked on the kettle and they looked at each other.

'Make it four sugars. I haven't eaten for hours.'

She looked at Leonard Lawson's books, spread across three desks and open at a variety of colour and black-and-white plates of great works of art.

'I don't like them,' said Riley. '*The Last Judgment*? Who'd want that on the wall? What's the point? Really, what's the point of them?'

'Most of these paintings are moral lectures designed to scare the shit out of the viewer so that they give time and money to the Church,' said Cole, continuing to draw straight lines on a piece of paper with a ruler and pen.

She placed the coffee down and laughed, 'You look like you're doing your homework.'

He looked up and smiled at her. 'I am, in a manner of speaking.' He held up the page and showed her straight vertical lines in three sets according to size.

There were two 3-centimetre lines, two 2-centimetre lines and five 1-centimetre lines.

She walked over and he handed her a picture he had printed off of the symbol engraved on the spear. On the white margin along the top, Riley read Hendricks's neat handwriting: *A dragonfly exiting a window.*

'I've been looking through Lawson's books for something to chime with the dragonfly image, something from a work of art. Nothing. I'm by no means certain, but my instincts whisper that it's a visual anagram of a word or letters. To me it even looks like a hieroglyphic.' He pointed at his feet and the bin overflowing with scrunched paper. 'I've tried all kinds of combinations.

It could just be a random squiggle on a bar of chocolate. Every letter of the alphabet can be made linear. Take C for example: C has a recognisable curve in it, but you can also make a C out of two or three straight lines if all the other letters are linear. So, at the moment, I'm thinking language.'

Riley's mobile rang out and she connected.

'Gina, where are you?' asked Clay.

'I'm in the incident room with Barney Cole.'

'I'm about to go in to interview Gabriel Huddersfield. I've had a call from Terry Mason. Something in Huddersfield's flat is making him *very* excited.'

Riley picked up her bag and coat. 'I'll get over there right now.'

'How's Barney getting on with the puzzle on the spear?'

'I'll hand you over, Eve.'

With Riley's phone at his ear, Cole took a photograph of the neatly set-out lines, deconstructed from the image on the spear. 'I'm sending you a picture, Eve. Is it language? Think language.'

'Stick with it, Barney. I like the way your mind's working.'

As Clay sat in Interview Suite 1, waiting for Huddersfield to be processed at the desk by Sergeant Harris, Cole's sets of lines arrived on her phone. She looked at them. The possibilities for rearranging them were endless.

Seems and is...

She scrolled backwards, pulled up a picture of where the symbol had been found, on the shaft inside Leonard Lawson's staged body, a three-dimensional sculpture in flesh and blood and bone. She closed her eyes and Lawson's body morphed into the naked figure being carried on a stick by the man with a platypus head in Bosch's *The Last Judgment*.

She studied the photo of the symbol itself. If it was a form of language, it had been deliberately buried in the depths of a macabre human sculpture. In her mind, language equated to knowledge, but the symbolic language on the spear was hidden and esoteric. Something stirred deep inside her brain and the symbol as scrambled language suddenly seemed like a strong possibility.

She heard three sets of footsteps, two of them familiar – Sergeant Harris and DS Hendricks. She homed in on the rhythm of the third.

Gabriel Huddersfield was coming.

61

12.35 pm

'Do you want legal representation, Gabriel?' Clay sat next to Hendricks across the table from Huddersfield.

He shook his head.

'What other name does the First Born go by?'

She could see a change in his state of mind since she'd last interviewed him in the Royal Liverpool Hospital. The theatrical lunacy was absent and there was a heat in the once cold blue eyes and a bead of sweat on his top lip. In patches, his shirt stuck to his body and the skin tones and body hairs were visible.

'Whenever you get a pair of people involved in a murder, Gabriel, there is always a leader and there is always a follower.'

He looked to the left of Clay's head.

'I know you're listening, Gabriel. I honestly believed that after DS Hendricks gave his informed assessment you'd stop playacting.'

'I've got a severe mental illness!'

'Every single human being on this planet can pretend to be something they are not, regardless of age, culture or mental state. Animals do it. Pretending is the thing we can all do when we need to. It's a survival technique. Look at me, Gabriel. Look at me! Your job isn't to convince me you're crazy at the moment. Your job... No, Gabriel, I'm not going to spoonfeed you. You tell me who the smart one is in this set-up.'

The only muscles Gabriel moved were in his eyes. He looked at Hendricks, long and hard. 'How do you know the colour of Jesus Christ's eyes? The end of the world?'

Hendricks didn't respond.

'Where the soul of Judas Iscariot can be found?'

'I understand you, Gabriel, let's put it that way. You've got a conscience of sorts and you also have a lot of fear inside you. Fear of ending up in the wrong place, both on this side of the life–death continuum and on the other. Prison and hell. Are you with me on that one?'

Huddersfield nodded.

'Let's go back to DCI Clay's idea, Gabriel.'

'Who's the one, Gabriel,' said Clay, 'who's going to serve the most time in the highest-category unit in the penal system?'

'The leader.'

'There's no way the instigator in this murder is ever going to get out of jail. Ever. The follower gets a life sentence with parole.'

'There was no way we could get caught. We were immune from the danger of being caught because we were serving God. The First Born convinced me.' Competing fears flashed across the surface of Huddersfield's face.

'Did you need a lot of convincing?'

'No.'

'What did the First Born tell you?' asked Clay.

'Serve God, stay free, go to heaven. Ignore God, suffer the perils of the earth and go to hell.'

'Seems and is, Gabriel.'

'What?'

'The First Born said this *is* the case and it *seems* the First Born was wrong. You didn't even last twelve hours before we pulled you in. The perils of the earth? You could have been killed running away from DS Hendricks and into that motorcycle. The First Born got it wrong. But you still thought you were safe at that point, that the arrest was a blip, that the First Born could save you because the First Born is infallible. I see now, I see. All that acting out in the Royal. You were amusing yourself at our expense, but that was foolishness. A big mistake, Gabriel. A big mistake.'

'When did the First Born make you his angel?' asked Hendricks.

'When his voice took residence inside my skull. His words went round inside me even when he wasn't there, especially when he wasn't there.'

'How long did it take him to brainwash you, Gabriel?' Clay watched as the silence unfolded and whatever strands of logic remained connected in his brain. The look on his face was excruciating. Clay went for him. 'What is the name of the person who brainwashed you, Gabriel?'

He looked at Hendricks. 'You seem right, but surely... Genesis... you're wrong.'

'Gabriel, in hell there are mansions. I believe this. Mansions where like attracts like. Just like prisons on earth. Murderers sleep next to murderers. Sex offenders with sex offenders. If the First Born is wrong about what happens on earth, then surely... surely... Where are you going when you die? Who or what are you spending eternity with?' asked Hendricks.

Huddersfield's mouth moved, but no sounds came out. His body shook and his eyes rolled.

'Gabriel, give us the name of the First Born.'

A noise like steam escaping from a crack in a pipe came from Huddersfield's mouth as his lips moved faster and faster. A body of noise weaved into the hissing and it sounded like two voices were coming from the same mouth, a pair of competing voices struggling to articulate the same word.

'Genesis?' Clay asked.

He fell silent.

'Genesis?' she repeated. 'Genesis?'

'Look at every single name you can find in the Book of Genesis and ask the question, *is this the one?*'

As Gabriel spoke, Clay wrote on a spiral-bound pad in front of her. She pushed the pad towards Hendricks and he read the words in silence: *The First Born shares his name with a character in Genesis.*

Hendricks took out his phone. 'Tell me about the body and the garden on the back of the triptych.'

Clay watched Gabriel's eyes, saw the ebb and flow of his thoughts, coming in closer and pulling away. He pressed his index finger to his broken lips.

'You spoke to me on the phone in Leonard Lawson's house, Gabriel,' said Hendricks. 'You've got a very unusual voice. It was *you* talking about a body and a garden. Whose body? Which garden?'

A remnant of the blistering strobe light in Leonard Lawson's bedroom danced behind Clay's eyes and, in the eruption of light, she pictured *The Last Judgment* painted on the wall of Gabriel Huddersfield's room. The darkness wiped his room away and when the light came again, she saw Leonard Lawson's bedroom, his impaled body, the bed, the dressing-table mirror, the clean rectangle and its missing *Tower of Babel*. Light, dark, light, dark. Huddersfield, Lawson, Huddersfield, Lawson.

She got up, opened the door and said, 'Sergeant Harris will take you back to your cell. It's on the back of the triptych, Gabriel. You told us so yourself, back in the Royal. The name of the garden.'

62

12.45 pm

'He's packed everything away so tightly,' said DS Mason to DS Riley as she entered Huddersfield's flat. Passing slowly by, he indicated the three rooms rammed with Huddersfield's possessions.

'I thought *I* was a hoarder,' said Riley. 'But he's obsessively tidy, I'll give him that.' At the bathroom door, she glanced at the mannequin dressed in leather and chains and felt as if she'd had pornography forced on her.

'Look at this,' said Mason, pushing open the door of the main room.

Riley looked at the statue of Jesus dying on the cross on one wall and the three-sectioned mural of paradise, the world and hell on the second wall. She was alarmed at the skilfulness of the two representations. The smell of oil paint and varnish percolated through the aroma of stale incense.

She stepped between the corners of Huddersfield's life. Art. Piles of dried-out rags and tubs of stagnant, oil-stained water; notebooks and sketchpads; bulging albums and dog-eared art books. Religion. Multiple Bibles, works of religious devotion, statues and crucifixes. Sex. A heap of pornographic magazines and sex toys.

'Gina, we found this,' said Mason. He handed her a framed print of Pieter Bruegel's *The Tower of Babel* and she wondered what the jury would talk about as they killed time in order to give the impression of having conducted a detailed debate as to the guilt of Gabriel Huddersfield.

Her iPhone rang out. On the display: 'Clay'. She connected and switched to speakerphone.

'Gina, are you there?'

'In the oh so charming apartment.'

'*Whose body? Whose garden?* Huddersfield said the name of the garden where the corpse is buried is on the back of the triptych.'

'I'm looking at the triptych right now.' Riley examined the wall, the paint that covered the plaster. Her eyes were drawn to the bottom left-hand corner and the figure that had inspired the staging of Leonard Lawson's body. Behind it was the head marching on disembodied feet and, underneath, just two tiny letters: G H. 'There's no paper on the wall that we can peel back to reveal the name of anything.'

'The exterior is the gable wall at the side of the house,' said Mason, chipping in to the conversation.

'What have you got for me, Terry?' asked Clay.

'It's in my hand,' said Riley. 'He found the framed picture of *The Tower of Babel* from Leonard Lawson's room,' said Riley.

Clay fell silent and then asked, 'What are the dimensions?'

'Fifty centimetres by thirty-five centimetres,' said Mason.

'Same dimensions as the print from Leonard Lawson's room. The clean space on his wall measured fifty centimetres by thirty-five centimetres.'

Riley looked at the image of the doomed tower and placed it in the context of the entire room: the world according to Gabriel Huddersfield's psychosis and the celestial forces that governed that chaos.

'Terry,' said Clay. 'I want you to throw a ladder up to the gable wall. Examine every single brick that corresponds to the top floor and the space where the mural sits on the inside wall. 'You're looking for writing, the name of a garden.'

Without a word, DS Mason headed out of the room, at speed.

'Anything else?' asked Clay.

Riley looked at the initials *GH*, the signature on the base of the triptych, and felt electricity pulse down her spine. An idea formed in the back of her mind and she gazed at the two letters.

'Are you there, Gina?'

'You know how Barney's thinking that the symbol on the spear is actually language, some sort of anagram... What was Leonard Lawson's body staged like?'

'Leonard Lawson's body was staged as a work of art...' Clay fell silent.

'Huddersfield signed off his copy of Hieronymus Bosch's work with his own initials, the cheeky bastard. I'm looking at his signature right now. I can feel the smile on your face coming through the silence. Go on! Call it, Eve.'

'It's their signatures. The dragonfly at the window is a visual anagram for the murderers' initials. Let me call Barney.'

63

12.59 pm

In the car park of the Anglican Cathedral, Adam Miller didn't notice the passage of time. He sat at the wheel of his white van, the radio mumbling away, and stared up at the bell tower, imagining the stonemason and the security guard ridiculing him.

As his heart raced faster and faster, the temperature of his anger alternated with every beat. Hot cold, hot cold, hot cold...

He glanced at the dashboard, saw it was a minute away from one o'clock, the time the stonemason would leave for another job.

Hot cold, hot cold, hot cold...

Adam looked to the very top of the bell tower, where the security guard would at some point be alone, and decided he would get out of his van and make the journey back up there.

Hot cold, hot cold, hot cold...

'So you'd talk to me like that, you fucking nonentity!'

Adam reached under his seat and felt the wooden handle of a hammer, pictured the terror on the security guard's face as the metal head came flying at the bridge of his nose.

Hot cold, hot hot, hot hotter...

'Fucking suck on that, you fucking motherfucking cunt!' he screamed at the windscreen and the top of the bell tower.

Hotter hotter, hotter hotter, hotter hotter...

Years of aimless talk with counsellors withered inside him and he was eighteen again, on fire, alive with rage.

Hotter hotter hotter hotter hotter hotter...

His early years passed through his mind; snapshots of faces blown on a remorseless wind. At sixteen, the stranger whose face he glassed on the street. Sixteen again, the terror in the eyes of the old drunk he battered to a lifeless pulp. Seventeen, the shock of the lad he knifed in the guts in a pub car park. Eighteen, the ageing rent boy whose fingers he broke with a hammer and whose agonised cries still echoed in his ears and sent waves of pleasure right through him.

'Fuck the consequences! I'll wait in the shadows and when you pass...' He gripped the handle of the hammer. 'Right into your fucking skull.'

Music came from the radio, the one o'clock Radio Merseyside news broadcast. He felt a cold wind on the nape of his neck and focused on the radio. He turned up the volume.

'Police have arrested and charged a man in connection with the murder of Leonard Lawson. They have named the man as thirty-eight-year-old Gabriel Huddersfield and are now seeking his accomplice. A spokesman...'

The fire that consumed Adam rushed to his gut and the rest of his body turned to ice.

'Fuck! Fuck! Fuck!'

Who picked up Angel Gabriel's phone?

The police.

Who called you back?

The police.

Who's got Angel Gabriel's phone?

The police.

Who can trace you?

The police.

He turned on the ignition and, tyres screaming against the red pavement, raced towards the exit barrier, the fire inside him rumbling hotter and hotter and hotter, ready to explode.

64

1.01 pm

DC Barney Cole looked down with frustration at the paper on his desk.

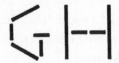

'Oh, Jesus!'

Cole looked across the incident room at Hendricks, who was hunched over a Bible and also brimming with frustration.

'What's the matter, mate? You can tell Barney!'

'The sheer number of names in the Book of Genesis. Gabriel Huddersfield dropped it that maybe his accomplice's name was buried in the opening book of the Old Testament. Dozens of them are way off the scale, because no one uses anything like them anymore, but it's still like he's sent us looking for a needle in a field full of haystacks.'

'Is he playing games with us?'

'I don't know. How's your afternoon, Barney?'

'Pretty shit afternoon following on from a similar morning.'

He showed Hendricks the GH. 'I can make a set of initials for Gabriel Huddersfield from the deconstructed symbol, but the trouble is, you can turn the lines into any letters you like if you try hard enough.' Cole smiled but, in Hendricks's mind, it only served to make his eyes look sad and tired. 'Maybe, Bill, they're leading us up a blind alley.'

Hendricks walked across the space to Cole and offered him the Bible. 'Swap?'

Cole took it. 'Halleluiah! Praise the Lord!'

65

1.15 pm

As a band of fog rolled in from Sefton Park, Adam Miller arrived from the Anglican Cathedral at the corner of Croxteth Road, doing 15 mph, his headlights fully on. All he could see was dense mist in the glare of his headlights, yellow light trapped in a thick cloud. *This could be the death of me*, he thought, pulling over and parking, two wheels on and two wheels off the pavement.

Voices drifted through the fog from the direction of 777 Croxteth Road, the only other place apart from his shed that he could be himself.

Cautiously, he turned the corner, recognising the streetlight that looked like a frozen giant set to pounce.

Fucking hell, fucking hell... If they (is it more than one or just one?) have picked up Gabriel's phone and the phone was inside Flat 5, what else have they found? Calm down. He took a set of deep breaths. *There are photographs in the flat, but my face is always covered. If someone's found them, how could they link them to me? It could be anyone. Anyone.*

The voices got louder the closer he came to 777. Across the road came the sound of a car revving up and heading away. Voices? Voices, three or four of them: a man, another man high up, his voice raised, sailing through the fog like something winged and lethal.

'Tell Gina Riley, it's impossible to see. I'm coming down the ladder...'

Oh, fuck's sake. Who's up a ladder? Why? Competing sounds, voices, engines. Someone came down a metal ladder, seemed to be sucked into the fog. An eerie silence froze Adam to the spot. And from the silence came a sound that sent bolts of terror up and down his nervous system.

He turned to the sound of his father's voice. '*You shouldn't have done what you did last night. You and your violent games. You shouldn't have done what you did to me! I was your father, but you put an end to that.*'

A darkness formed in the mist where the voice had come from, a darkness that came closer. '*What kind of a man are you, Adam? Killing? Killing your father for personal gain?*'

Adam wanted to turn and run as the darkness came closer and the breath from it drifted through the mist. But he couldn't move.

'*But you know best, don't you, Adam?*'

The darkness was upon him. '*Didn't I teach you the fear of God, boy? I've got a good mind to take your pants right down and spank you until you bleed.*' The darkness entered his body, paralysed and blinded him.

Memory possessed him and he was young and small again, listening to the creak of his bedroom door as it opened and closed, his father's footsteps coming deeper into the pitch-black darkness, the smell of cigarettes and tobacco, the meaty weight of his father's hand on his mouth, and the only sound that came from his father, night after night after night: 'Sssshhh!'

The darkness passed through his skin and bone, twisting his muscles and firing through his organs. Then it was gone.

The beam of a powerful spotlight – it seemed to hang in mid-air – pointed directly at 777, picking out the shape of the front door that seemed to be open.

Yes, people were moving around the building.

My secretions are all over the flat, thought Adam. He felt as if his feet were sinking into the fabric of the pavement, his ankles dissolving into the granite of the paving stones, his legs sucked down into the hardcore underneath.

My secretions are all over the flat. And all they'll need... My secretions are all over the flat.... is one... My secretions are all over the flat.... swab.

Sound returned in the form of a car's engine creeping up behind him.

He touched something wet and thin, taut and made of plastic. Something plastic. A continuous piece of rectangular tape.

The car pulled up behind him. He watched the shapes emerge from the car. They moved down the middle of the road, ducked beneath the tape in his hand, not noticing him.

'DS Karl Stone,' said one of the shapes.

'OK, sir,' replied a shape at the edge of the scene-of-crime tape.

Adam thought he was going to throw up, but then a stronger urge seized him. To turn and run. He turned, straight into a tall man with a broad body, a real physical presence. The fog danced around his face as Adam froze in front of him. Stray streetlight fell on to his face and Adam saw that the man was blind.

'I recognise your breathing, your heavy breathing and the catch at the back of your throat, when you're excited, when you're in Gabriel's flat hurting him. I live across the landing. When you go, I tend his wounds. I hear everything.'

'Move out the way,' said Adam, hearing only weakness and fear in his own voice.

'You move around me!' replied the man. Adam felt as if he'd turned to stone. 'I am told that the fog is blinding. Welcome to my world.'

'I don't know what you're talking about.'

'We've got the picture from Leonard Lawson's bedroom!' A voice, young, male and excited, piped up.

Lawson?

'*The Tower of Babel.* The trophy.'

'They won't be able to talk their way out of this.'

They? They... they... they... they... they...
Fear remained, gripped Adam, but evolved into a confused anger.

'Who are you?' asked Adam.

Two dogs barked at each other, their ferocity increasing with each in-breath.

'Who are you?' asked Adam.

'I am what you see before you. The police have Gabriel in custody.'

'Gabriel's crazy, Gabriel doesn't know what day of the week it is...'

Adam found himself walking around the blind man, his walk picking up into a trot. A siren nearly caused him to scream. He wanted to jump off the pavement and howl at the sky.

The place behind him, where he could be himself, had been opened up by the authorities. And there was a place he needed to go. The other place. The shed.

It felt like an hour passed in a handful of seconds as he struggled to press the right button to unlock his van. His face and hair were soaking with condensation. He turned on the ignition and drove quickly. A voice that sounded a lot like the blind man's but was inside him, asked, '*What day of the week is it?*'

Adam had no idea.

66

1.21 pm

Each time she turned to a new photograph of Gabriel Huddersfield submitting to yet another degradation, DS Gina Riley's heart dropped a little further. She counted. Nineteen. Gabriel chained to the sink, gagged and blindfolded. Twenty. Gabriel on all fours with multiple bleeding tracks where he'd been viciously scratched. Twenty-one. Gabriel inserting the handle of a whip up his own anus for the gratification of the person taking the picture. Twenty-two. She gasped, looked away and then back again. Gabriel with a large weight clamped to his penis.

She was on the verge of handing the task over to one of the Scientific Support officers because she knew that when she next tried to sleep, these pictures would play across the darkness of her mind's eye like a slideshow on PowerPoint.

Twenty-three. 'Jesus,' she whispered. Twenty-four. 'Je-sus.' Twenty-five. Silence. She froze, double-checked the image taken in the mirrored bathroom.

'You've tripped yourself up, Fuck Face!'

'You talking to me?' asked DS Terry Mason, passing her in Huddersfield's living room.

'My pet name for you, Terry, happens to be Cuddles, not Fuck Face.' She showed him the twenty-fifth picture.

'So that's the Grand Master of Agony and Ecstasy?'

He carried on and she moved to the window to milk the light

and analyse the image. She flicked forward through the pictures, but there was no other sign of him from the twenty-sixth to the fortieth image. She took out her phone and within three rings was talking to Clay.

'Eve, do you want the good news or the bad?'

'Bad, Gina.'

'In the one picture I've found of Huddersfield's beau, the elusive nasty is wearing a leather mask. It's taken in the bathroom with the mirrored walls. Gabriel's hanging by the wrists, chained from the shower head. There's a flash on it.' She peered at it again. 'His masked head's above the flash and his feet and legs are below it. Judging by his feet and legs, he's no spring chicken – late thirties, early forties. Oh God! Yack. Judging by the angle of his elbow jutting out from the side of the flash...'

'Yes, I get the idea, Gina. Masturbation, the sincerest form of flattery. Copy all the pictures to my phone, please. It's time to have another chat with Huddersfield. I'll print them off before I do so.'

'Asap.'

Within half a minute the image had been photographed and sent to Clay, Hendricks, Stone and Cole. Riley looked out at the dense fog, made out shapes, some still, some moving. The world around her assumed a silence, and then her phone rang. She looked at the display and felt a wave of nervous energy.

'Justine Elgar!' she said. 'How are things in the uni's human resources department?'

'I've got a name and address for you. Caitlin Braxton. Lives in the Albert Dock. She's just retired from the Fine Art faculty. She worked with Leonard Lawson for two years. Her career was starting as his was winding down.'

67

2.25 pm

In Interview Suite 1, Clay trudged through the photographs of Huddersfield and his partner and felt a profound dismay. As Sergeant Harris opened the door, she shuffled the ace in the deck to the top of the pack that she'd printed off from her phone.

'He continues to waive his right to legal representation,' said Harris as Huddersfield sat across the table from Clay. 'Do you want me to stay?'

'Yes, please.'

Clay held up the top photograph, showed the blank side to Huddersfield. She eyed him, held his gaze, said nothing as Sergeant Harris stood behind him.

'What are you looking at?' asked Huddersfield.

She smiled at him, turned her attention back to the picture, placed it face down on the table, out of his reach. Next she looked at the clamp attached to his penis and said, 'We couldn't find anything on the back of the triptych. We looked at the gable wall directly behind your mural of Hieronymus Bosch's *The Last Judgment*. We couldn't find any reference to a garden, therefore we can't find a body because we don't know which garden to dig in.'

'What are you looking at?'

She kept her eyes fixed on the photograph.

'You.'

'Me?' Silence. 'Show me?'

She looked over the top of the picture and into his eyes. 'You're not a bad person,' she said.

'What do you mean?'

'I mean, you're not a bad person.'

'When you say you're looking at *me*, what do you mean?'

She turned the picture round, heard Sergeant Harris take a sharp intake of breath, but kept her eyes fixed on Huddersfield.

'Have you been rooting through my things?' asked Huddersfield.

'You're not a bad person.'

'Are they all photographs of me?'

'You're not a bad person.'

'Can you show me another?'

She placed the penis-clamp picture face down and moved on to the image of him inserting the handle of a whip into his own anus.

'You're not a bad person.'

'Why do you keep saying that?'

'Because you're not a bad person.'

She placed that picture down on the desk and watched as Huddersfield's eyes moistened.

'Do you think I'm a sinner?'

'You're not a bad person.'

She turned the next picture round for him. He was chained to the sink, gagged and blindfolded.

'You're not a bad person, Gabriel, because this picture shows what someone else has done to you. This is a picture of someone else's sinfulness. This is a picture of you being blinded to the truth. This is a picture of you having your voice taken away from you. This is a picture of you being bound and shackled, having your body hijacked and kidnapped, made to do things that someone else wants. You're not a bad person, Gabriel. You're not a bad person.'

'Who is a bad person?'

'I can show you a bad person if you want.'

'Can you show me a bad person?'

'You can tell me the name of a bad person. At the moment, I've got people trying to work out what the lines on the shaft of the spear mean and sifting through the Book of Genesis for names. There are so many names in the Book of Genesis. You're not a bad person, Gabriel. You could put me straight. Like that.' She clicked her finger and thumb sharply and Huddersfield started as if a bomb had gone off. A single tear rolled down his cheek.

'Give me a name. You're not a bad person, Gabriel. I'd be very happy to stand up in a crowded courtroom, in front of the world's media, and make no mistake, Gabriel, of two things. This is going to go global. And you're not a bad person, Gabriel. You've been gagged and bound and chained like a slave.'

'Can you show me a bad person?'

'If you tell me their name.'

'How can I do that?' asked Gabriel.

'Speak.'

He placed his wrists together, his fists closed, face down on the desk. *JESUS DIE4U*. He closed his eyes and shut his mouth.

'Bound and gagged and chained,' said Clay, reaching across the table and placing her hands over his fists. 'Bound by the First Born.'

He opened his eyes, looked down at Clay's hands and closed his eyes again.

'I take the key and I turn it in the lock,' said Clay. She slipped her hands between his fists. 'Hear the click as the key unlocks the shackles that bind your hands.' Clay pushed his hands apart, lifted them. 'Delivered by the Law. Open your eyes.'

Huddersfield opened his eyes, tears streaming.

'Open your mouth.'

He opened his mouth, took in a huge breath of air.

'Speak. Look.'

She turned the picture of Huddersfield chained from the

shower head with his lover's reflection caught in the glass but distorted by the camera's flash.

'You're not a bad person, Gabriel.'

She handed him the picture.

He looked at it in intense silence, stroked the surface of his reflected lover and said, 'You lied to me, didn't you?'

'Yes,' said Clay. 'He lied to you.'

Huddersfield looked up at Clay. 'Do you want me to tell you the truth?'

'Yes, I want you to tell me the truth.'

'Leonard Lawson wasn't the first,' said Huddersfield. 'Abraham Evans, 112 Knowsley Road, Cressington Park, Liverpool 19. Abraham and his wife Mary.'

Clay was on her feet.

'Leave him with me,' said Sergeant Harris.

She opened the door and in the background heard a sound like an animal with its body crushed between the jaws of an iron trap.

In Interview Suite 1, Huddersfield howled.

68

2.47 pm

Adam Miller had difficulty breathing. As he flipped the bolt shut inside his shed, he found he had to think about drawing in air and pushing it out. The kernel of anguish that had ruptured inside his brain had swollen to the size of an orange and painkillers had done nothing to ease it.

Although he was quite alone in the shed, he began to feel that the knots in the wooden walls were eyes watching him. In the muddy light of the winter's afternoon, the shed, which had once felt like a barricade against the world outside, had turned on him.

He sat down on a three-legged stool and saw that the walls were littered with faces that he'd never seen before. A bearded profile of Christ peered sadly into the centre of the shed. A pair of eyes with a thin nose but no mouth or chin stared directly at him. A face distorted by weeping howled silently above his head.

He closed his eyes briefly, to shut them out, and felt violated. He tried to fight the light-headedness that had started as he drove away from the police and the ghost of his father and the blind man and the terror that 777 Croxteth Road had become, and the faces in the wood seemed to be moving.

He stood up and threw on a lamp, but the light did nothing to ease the gloom or stop the insane notion mushrooming in his mind. The walls of the shed, that had once been so wide and still, were growing narrow and moving in on him, threatening to bury him alive in a wooden box the size of a coffin.

The thump of a bird landing on the roof startled him and sent his heart racing, but the scream that was growing steadily inside him was gridlocked in the dryness of his mouth and throat.

I've gotta go, I've gotta go, I've gotta go, I've gotta go. Words like runaway trains thundered through his head and down his spine, causing needle-like pains in his extremities. *But where?*

A beam of hope. *I've got money*, he thought. *Lots of money. Savings no one else knows about, savings in all kinds of accounts, savings that will take me far away from here, for as long as I need. Forever, if necessary. To some country where life is cheap and I can live like a king.*

France. By midnight. South. Never stopping. The Mediterranean. A bribe. A boat. A short crossing. Africa. By midnight tomorrow.

He glanced at the walls. The faces that had haunted him had become still. Fear morphed into hatred. He looked around, bit his lower lip so hard that the taste of blood filled his mouth. Anger rocketed through him. He picked a spade from the wall and smashed it into Christ's profile. Into the weeping face above his head, he threw the sharp edge of the spade, into the eyes, blinding it.

A joyless smile was frozen on his face.

No time to lose.

He hung the spade back on the wall, dropped to his knees and placed his hands either side of the black box beneath his workbench. The familiar size and shape in his hands was a comfort, but he knew in his heart that, somewhere on the journey ahead, the box would have to be sacrificed. In the English Channel perhaps. A burial at sea for Adam Miller and the beginning of his new time on earth.

He pulled the box out and stood it up on its wheels, extended the handle and felt the weight of its contents. The whip, the knives, the sharp things, the things made of glass, the ropes and chains. The thought of them all sitting inside the darkness gave him a deep, dark thrill.

In his new world, he would be an oligarch and the possibilities would be endless.

The light inside the shed seemed to alter and his eyes were drawn to the small window. Gideon Stephens's face and head filled the small frame. Gideon looked at Adam, impassive, unblinking. And Adam wondered how long the little bastard had been standing there, peering in, spying on his privacy. The happy notes that his future life had sounded crashed into discord. Anger ran through his veins at the invasion by the smirking man-child.

Breathing was hard work again. So he held his breath and looked directly back at Gideon, into his eyes. He sent two fingers of thought through the glass and into Gideon's eyes, each finger gouging the fleshy bulbs from their sockets, leaving him hollow-eyed and repulsive.

'Hello, Gideon.' He breathed out, surprised at the depth and strength in his voice and the veil of charm. 'Can I help you?'

Gideon said nothing, shook his head.

'How long have you been standing there, Gideon?'

'Not long, a few moments.'

'Why are you standing there, Gideon?'

'I was worried about you.'

'Were you? Why?'

'You don't seem yourself. You almost ran through the house. You look sick.'

'I can assure you, Gideon, that I am, very much indeed, myself.'

Mist hovered above Gideon's head. It reminded Adam of a painting of Christ being baptised in the River Jordan by John the Baptist, with the Holy Spirit sitting above his skull in the form of a dove. 'Why do things like that never happen to me?' he said.

'Things like what?'

'Nothing,' he replied, consumed with resentment. 'Just thinking out loud.' He propped the black box against the workbench, drank in the neat rows of tools around the walls and wished them all a silent farewell. 'Say, Gideon, you've never been inside my shed before, have you?'

'Abey has.'

'I left the door unlocked. Careless. Would you like to come inside?'

'OK.' Gideon moved away from the window.

As he unbolted the door, Adam counted Gideon's footsteps crunching in the snow. He opened up and smiled. 'Come in!'

Gideon stepped inside and Adam pulled the door shut into the snugness of the frame.

'You didn't throw Abey out on his ear. He was in here for a good few minutes.' Gideon looked around at the precise display of tools on the wall. 'What were you talking about?'

'Health and safety,' replied Adam instantly. 'I was explaining to Abey that sheds were nice places, but...' He took the spade from the wall again. 'That they could also be extremely dangerous places. This spade, for instance.'

'You've been up to something, Adam!'

Adam took a sudden and heavy swipe at Gideon's head, the edge of the spade connecting with the centre of his forehead. As Gideon blinked and gasped and staggered, a thick black line of blood formed on his forehead and he dropped to his knees. He looked at Adam, full of astonishment and confusion as the light in his eyes petered out.

Adam flipped the spade so that the flat of the blade was fully available and smashed it into Gideon's face, sending him on to his back and into the back of the shed. The swollen orange inside his head was shrivelling. He stamped on Gideon's groin three times and placed the blood-stained spade back where it belonged on the wall.

'That's what you get for being a nosey parker!'

69

2.47 pm

Stone was waiting outside Abraham Evans's house, 112 Knowsley Road, shivering in the cold.

'What have we got on Abraham Evans?' asked Clay, hurrying from her car to his front door.

'Born in 1930,' said Stone. 'He lives here with his wife Mary.'

Eighty-eight years of age, thought Clay. *Another of Huddersfield's elderly victims.*

112 Knowsley Road was a small detached mansion with enough space in the front garden to build half a dozen big houses.

Clay anticipated the imminent non-reaction when she rang the doorbell. *The dead don't answer doors*, she thought, her finger pressed down on the bell, Stone and Hendricks at her back.

She eyed the Victorian wrought-iron gate at the side of the house and ran towards it, figuring that she could climb over it if necessary. The wind throbbed at the side of the house and the gate yielded easily to her touch.

She walked into the wind trapped between the tall red-brick wall that fenced off the property and the sheer face of the side of the house. She pictured her first impression of Leonard Lawson's corpse and the strength needed to stage it.

The wind whipped around her head, slashing her ears with wild noise. Dread washed through her as she stepped around the corner to the back of the house. It was completely concealed from outside eyes.

'Let me go in first!' said Hendricks behind her, following.

At Pelham Grove, they had left the front door of Leonard Lawson's house open as they left. Clay stopped, eyed the back door as she slipped on a pair of latex gloves. It was made of panes of frosted glass and the section nearest the handle was scored around the edges. *Huddersfield and S&M Buddy: home visits are us*, she thought.

The smell of death rushed from the house as she turned the handle and opened the back door.

She covered her mouth and nose with her left hand. Entering the house, she turned to Hendricks. 'We've already seen Abraham Evans. His head. His feet.'

The smell grew denser with each step further in. Sickness danced in Hendricks's eyes.

'Wait here, Bill. I'll call you when I need you.'

70

2.49 pm

As Clay stepped into the long, narrow kitchen, she pressed her hand against her nose and mouth and knitted the muscles at her core against the stench. A broken fluorescent light cast patterns into the space and filled her mind with the scene in Leonard Lawson's bedroom. She looked around. Terracotta quarry tiles, white units from the 1970s, mouldy bread and a putrid slice of bacon on a surface to her left – a breakfast that never happened, a pan on the hob that was never quite fried.

But the worst of the smell didn't come from the kitchen. It was drifting on stale air from deeper inside the house.

As she followed her nose, the first bead of sweat bobbed on the nape of her neck. An emerald light on the edge of her vision drew her gaze to the whirring of an old-fashioned white chest freezer near the kitchen door.

She lifted the collar of her coat to buffer her nose and mouth. Eyes closed, mind focused on the darkness within her head, she took a foul breath of air and hung on to it. Opening her eyes wide, she opened the kitchen door and flicked on a wall light.

'Jesus!'

The main wall leading to the front door, parallel to the staircase to her right, was covered with a pattern of arterial blood spray. She counted four fountain arcs of blood with individual stains in the pattern. Four, the number of times the victim's heart beat as it pumped blood from the severed artery.

She turned her eyes from the wall and followed the diagonal line of the banister from the top of the stairs. Halfway down, something came into the line of her vision and she knew it was naked and that the flesh was rotten.

Clay took a step forward. Between her feet and the wooden flooring, she felt the multiple popping of dozens of small, living creatures for which, in the moments that it took for her to cross to the bottom of the stairs, her memory refused to supply a name.

Male or female, it was almost impossible to tell from the back, but judging from the size of what remained, it was an elderly female tied to a length of wood similar to the spear that had impaled Leonard Lawson's body. This pole was angled against the banister post at the bottom of the stairs

'Mary!' Clay spoke her name out loud as she stepped in front of her. 'Mary Evans!'

Her hands were tied behind her at the base of her spine. Her head was forced down to her left shoulder by the cord that secured her to the pole and post, wrapping round her throat diagonally, winding round the back of her body and then diagonally again across her right hip, her vagina and round the back of her left thigh.

Clay's mind was filled with images from Hieronymus Bosch's *The Last Judgment*. She zoomed in on the painting's central panel, saw the suspended figure that had inspired the staging of Leonard Lawson's body and moved directly back through the chaos, in line with it. She passed the monster riding a naked man on all fours and arrived at a figure bound to a pole propped between the flat roof of a house and the earth below. Mary Evans's body had been arranged to replicate that figure – another direct copy of one of the damned souls in *The Last Judgment*.

She looked at the decay of Mary's flesh and estimated that Mrs Evans had been dead for a fortnight, longer perhaps. The smell hit Clay afresh and she bit down on the urge to vomit.

As she shifted her weight, she felt something pop near the tip of her left toes. A maggot – that was the word for the writhing pockets of life that littered the floor.

Clay turned and looked back at the blood on the walls. She guessed that no one could have heard the screams, the road being so far from the house, across the huge garden. She knew whom the arterial blood spray had come from. Abraham Evans. She wondered if they had cut his throat before they chopped his head off, or if they'd gone through the artery when removing his head from his body.

She was back at the Otterspool tip, looking inside the freezer at the head and feet of Abraham Evans. The head and feet that marched behind the suspended man in *The Last Judgment*. Leonard, Mary and Abraham, suspended, tied-up, decapitated.

She walked back into the kitchen, certain now of what she would find in the whirring chest freezer. Its green light stood out like an alien eye beneath the random fluorescence falling from the ceiling.

She touched the handle to raise the lid, gripped it and heard Hendricks's voice outside the house. 'Eve, are you all right?'

She lifted the lid. A naked body, bent into three and frozen solid. Blood frozen to the walls of the freezer, from the wounds where his feet and head had once been.

Bent into three. Folded over.

In her mind's eye, Clay folded over the outer panels of *The Last Judgment* triptych, closed it, and saw, in grey, the images from Lawson's book: St James and St Bavon, the figures on the back of the panels.

She walked towards the back door, each step faster than the last.

The back of the triptych? Whose body? Which garden?

It's on the back of the triptych.

71

3.05 pm

From the top-floor kitchen window of Caitlin Braxton's apartment in the Albert Dock, Riley looked out at the Liverpool skyline: the Anglican Cathedral and its bell tower, reaching up into the heavy sky, the Radio City Tower, the Catholic Cathedral and, closer at hand, the Liver Building next to the Cunard Building.

'Here's your drink, Detective Sergeant Riley.' Caitlin Braxton, still attractive even though her hair was now a white mane, held out a mug of hot chocolate. Riley took it gratefully. 'Professor Lawson was a strange man,' said Miss Braxton. 'Sit down. Please.'

Riley took a seat at the plain wooden table. 'How was he strange?' she asked, the ever-spinning plates in her head revving up.

'He was notoriously silent. But he took a shine to me back in 1984. Not in an inappropriate way – though many others tried.' She laughed and Riley liked her, felt she was a reliable witness. 'I was the most junior lecturer in his department. He was the professor. God Almighty at the end of his career. One day in October, after I'd only just started working there – a Wednesday – he summoned me to his study.'

'Wednesday? That's specific.'

'It was the first of many Wednesday afternoons spent alone with him. And it was always Wednesday. First time, I was terrified. It was like being summoned to the head teacher's office.' A dimness rolled around the brightness of her blue eyes, as the past unfolded inside her head.

In another room, a clock ticked and Riley pushed. 'What happened?'

'He told me to sit down. He indicated an armchair facing away from his desk, giving me a view over Abercromby Square. The neat garden in the first flush of autumn, fenced in by jet-black railings. At first the silence seemed to last for hours. When the fear I'd walked in with had dissolved enough, I asked, *Is there anything in particular you wish to talk to me about?* He replied, *What is love?* I thought about it and said, *When the happiness of another person matters more than your happiness and the happiness of anyone else in the world.* He told me he agreed. He agreed! With me! You could never be *relaxed* around Professor Lawson, but I came as close as I think was possible. He thanked me for coming to his study and told me to come at the same time next week. I didn't look back at him as I walked to the door. I figured if he wanted me facing away from him and out of the window while I was with him, he didn't want me to look at him when I was leaving. I stopped at the door and said, *Professor Lawson, I swear on the lives of all those I love and hold dear, I will never breathe a word about what passes between us in this room.*

'*I know you won't.* I could almost sense a smile on his face in the way he said those words. Then he said, *We'll talk about love again at some other time, when we know each other better.* The next Wednesday, I knocked on the door and when he told me to come in, I walked straight to the chair in the window overlooking Abercromby Square. I didn't look at him ever, in all those Wednesday afternoons. Each week, the format was the same. A long silence and then a question for me. *What is the truth? Is it possible to be truly happy? What is great art? Why are people afraid of silence? Why should we speak?* Each week. He said very little; questions mainly. I grew more talkative as time progressed. And then the final Wednesday came. He said, *We'll end where we began. What is love?* In May, I gave him the same answer as I gave in October. And then the most incredible thing happened. He spoke for the rest of the afternoon. About love. About the love of his life.'

Caitlin clammed up and Riley could see the conflict in her face.

'I understand that you swore not to reveal the content of those afternoons and you've skilfully managed to skim over the detail while still giving me enough information to make me feel I was there in that study all those years ago. I'm a police officer, Caitlin. Information, however implausible it may seem, can be the difference between life and death. Professor Lawson's already dead. As are others. There's a very dangerous man out there. Help me. What did Professor Lawson say to you?'

72

3.07 pm

In the hall of 112 Knowsley Road, Stone tasted sick in his mouth and the back of his throat as he watched two Scientific Support officers, whom he knew by sight but not by name, take photographs of Mrs Evans's body. Skin hung from muscle like wet dishcloths, the keynote image from a living nightmare.

Pulling the fabric of the hood of his protective suit tighter around his face, Stone turned away and walked towards the front door, past the blood-splattered walls, and considered what he had seen in the freezer at the Otterspool tip.

'Ah, Christ!' Michael Harper's voice cut through the stench, the air that was almost impossible to breathe.

Stone turned to him. 'The remains in the freezer are one thing, but this...'

'We'll just have to take her down quick and get her as fast as we can to Dr Lamb. Call Dr Lamb as soon as we're in the van and warn her.' Harper's natural shyness was forgotten in the demands of the moment. 'This is far worse than we were told to expect. Are you done?'

'We're almost done,' said the Scientific Support officer.

There were pieces of paper and a landline telephone on a table near the door. Stone walked towards them. He picked up the papers and started sifting through them.

An A4 leaflet from a nursery advertising Christmas trees for sale.

A colour advert for a firm installing stair lifts.

A white sheet: *Handyman in a White Van.* Words around a logo portraying just that. Beneath them, a list of diverse household and transport services offered. The name and mobile number of the handyman were in bold print at the bottom of the page: *Adam Miller: 07714936634.*

Stone frowned. Adam Miller? The co-owner of The Sanctuary, the place where Louise Lawson volunteered every day. A link formed in his mind. Adam. Louise. Leonard. Abraham. Mary. Adam's name was in Genesis. He looked again at the words on the leaflet and was drawn to two: White Van? *Just how many men in white vans are there in Liverpool?* Stone asked himself. *But only one visited the Otterspool Tip to dispose of a freezer containing Abraham Evans's head and feet.*

He focused on the Scientific Support officer. 'Can you come and bag this flyer?'

Stone headed into the kitchen and out into the fresh, bitterly cold air of Knowsley Road.

One man. One van. One tip. One freezer. One head. One pair of feet.

Stone needed to talk to Adam Miller.

73

3.07 pm

Riley stood up and walked over to the window again, her back turned to Caitlin. Seagulls wheeled in the sky over the Albert Dock.

She pressed record on her iPhone.

'The love of Leonard Lawson's life was another academic, Damien Noone. Leonard was from a comfortable but lower-middle-class background. Damien was from a moneyed family. They met during World War Two while they were in North Africa. As you can imagine, it wasn't the best time or place for two young homosexual men to fall in love. But they managed to begin their relationship and no one ever found them out. Leonard was never big on detail, it was all dot to dot, but he said it was in Africa that Damien told him about his interest in the acquisition and non-acquisition of language and how the whole of his life's work would be to study this. Leonard told me about Psamtik I's experiment with the two newborns... I was horrified that anyone could even entertain such a thought.'

Caitlin fell silent. Riley feared she was losing the will to carry on, so she stepped in. 'Yes, I know what you mean. I know about that experiment. How could such a thing possibly happen? The whole thing smacks of an academic pipe dream, two young men giddy with furtive sex in the middle of a war zone. Either or both of them could have been killed at any moment. To have replicated the experiment in England after the war would have been criminal folly. Keep talking, please, Caitlin.'

'They came back. Damien studied linguistics, Leonard studied art history. Damien was marked down for all kinds of future greatness; Leonard was due a little but not so much. They managed to continue their love affair by putting on a show of public disdain for each other. The same tactic that had worked for them in Africa. He told me that the secrecy between them, that bond, was the extra layer of glue that raised their love to an unimaginably strong level. It was them against the unsuspecting world. All talk of resurrecting the experiment drifted away as they were forced to address the day-to-day demands of their studies. This, Leonard told me, was the happiest time of his life. Realistically, he didn't approve of the experiment. It was wild talk, Damien's pet dream. Months passed, they graduated and gained teaching posts. Damien came into a huge trust fund. Life was good.'

'And the experiment?' Riley interjected, keen to cut to the chase.

'Nothing, until one day, out of the blue, Damien casually announced they would be going to London for the day. He wouldn't tell Leonard why, just told him it was part mystery tour and part test of his love. They arrived in London and travelled by cab to Whitechapel, to a set of rooms above a chemist's shop. Damien explained that he had taken a lease out on the property for the next year. He asked Leonard what the definition of love was. Leonard told him, *Love is when the lover puts the beloved before himself.* There was a knock at the door. Damien told Leonard to open it, saying, *Remember what you've just said.* A man entered with two young women. The man was Dr Roger Pattison, only he wasn't a doctor, not any more; he'd been struck off the medical register for a string of offences. He was a back-street abortionist, whom Damien had recruited to his cause. The women were poor pregnant girls with no means of support. They were at almost identical stages of their pregnancies. Eight weeks. Pattison had put a deal to the women. Instead of terminating their pregnancies, they could go through with them, deliver their babies and pick up £5,000 each, on condition they walked out and abandoned their children immediately. The deal specified that they were to live together with Pattison in the Whitechapel rooms in complete silence during the last days of their pregnancies. Once they had gone, they were never to return.

'The women agreed. Damien told Leonard that he wanted him to leave his teaching post and accompany him and the babies to a remote house. Leonard would be the shepherd, but Damien was going to put a twist in Psamtik's method. Leonard could speak continuously to one child, while the other would be subjected to total silence and sensory deprivation. Damien's part in it would be to record everything on spool-to-spool tapes, take photographs and make notes.'

In the sky over Liverpool, Riley saw a waxing gibbous moon. She wondered about the missing pages in Leonard Lawson's Psamtik manuscript and asked herself how Lawson could have written about the English Experiment, even twelve pages, if his relationship with Noone had ended and he had taken no part in it.

'The detail stopped there. Leonard stood his ground and said no. Damien ended the relationship, told him he would never see him again. Leonard moved back to Liverpool, did his best to get on with normal life, with a wife and child as a disguise. That's as far as he went.'

'Thank you, Caitlin. Do you have anything else to add?'

'No. That's all I know.'

'I can't begin to tell you how helpful you've been. Did he mention that he'd reconnected with Damien Noone at any point?'

Caitlin shook her head.

Or if there was another attempt at the English Experiment? thought Riley.

74

3.09 pm

At the cells in Trinity Road police station, Clay looked through the observation hole and saw Huddersfield standing in the middle of the space staring at the door, waiting.

With his right hand raised, he made a gesture – come in – and she knew that he was waiting for her.

Sergeant Harris unlocked the door and stayed in the frame as Clay went inside. Huddersfield held her gaze. She was within touching distance, and she could smell the bloody musk of his body.

'Close the door,' she said.

'The Holy Spirit will come upon you, and the power of the Most High will overshadow you. Look for first things first.'

'First things first?' echoed Clay. 'Give me a name.'

'Look for first things first.'

She knew in her heart that she had reached a dead end where once she had opened a door. But there was something else she needed to know.

'First things first, Gabriel?' Silence. 'We searched the outside wall behind the triptych painted on the wall in your flat. We found nothing.'

'First things first, most highly favoured lady. Who were the saints on the back of the triptych?'

She saw the two saints in shades of grey and events spun

backwards in her mind at blinding speed. Hours condensed into seconds and dragged her through the places she had been and the people she had seen since the call to her home in the early hours of the morning. And when she arrived at the front door of Leonard Lawson's house, the rewind suddenly stopped.

'First things first,' said Huddersfield. 'Always. Which triptych haven't you looked at?'

She walked up the stairs towards the disorientating pattern of the strobe light, entered Leonard Lawson's bedroom and looked inside.

'Open the door, Sergeant Harris!'

Gabriel Huddersfield smiled.

'First things first.'

His words followed her as she hurried to the nearest exit of Trinity Road police station and to Leonard Lawson's house beyond that.

75

3.10 pm

And I'm telling you now, when the police, the police, the police come calling, I won't be here... You've done it now... And they will come calling. I'll be gone, gone, long gone... You've done it now... When the police come calling, and I'm telling you now... The voice inside his head was his but not his, as familiar as it was strange, sometimes laced with the absolute depth of his father's disappointment and then himself as a child, cowed and baby-like. The words kept repeating like a stuck record.

Adam Miller pushed the black box into the back of his van with a growing feeling that he was being watched. He looked around at The Sanctuary, to which he would never return, and to the park beyond. There were people passing, but no one seemed to be looking at him.

He patted his coat and the pockets that lined it. His passport. His wallet.

He opened the briefcase in the back of his van and rifled through its contents. Bank books. TSB. Halifax. Money that the bitch Danielle knew nothing of. Santander. HSBC. Money that would save his skin. ISAs. Lloyd's. Money that would soothe his mind as soon as he got to where he was going. The Wesleyan. Barclays. Money that made money. National Savings and Investments. Money that he'd worked hard for and was all his, his and his alone.

'All there! All there! All there!'

The words in his head piped through his mouth, so he clamped his lips and, in his head, repeated a cliché that Louise The Mug Who Worked For Nothing Lawson often told the retards when they were acting up. *Silence is golden.*

And the effect was bizarre. As the words crept through the wetness of his brain, he heard her saying them as if she was on his shoulder.

He turned.

In the empty space he'd clocked moments earlier, Louise was there.

'Silence is golden.' She repeated the phrase, her eyes locked into his, and from behind her, like some animated shadow, Abey stepped to her side, his lopsided smile accompanied by a drizzle of spit on his square-jawed chin.

Instinctively, Adam reached his hand to his lower face, felt the narrowness of his lips, the receding dimples of his chin and heard himself gasp.

'Golden, golden, golden,' said Abey, and Adam wanted to raise the fists that were bunched at his sides and pummel the little bastard into an inhuman pulp.

'As God is your judge?' Louise's words caused the skin on his spine to pucker and a bead of sweat to slalom through the goose bumps on his back.

'As God is my judge, what?' he replied.

'Yes, Adam, as God is the judge of all, you being one of God's creations.'

He threw the case of clothes he'd hurriedly packed into the back of his van.

'Would you like to talk about my father?' asked Louise.

'I'm very sorry about what happened to your father.'

'I was thinking about boxing up his possessions, clearing the house of all that's in it. I was thinking about your little chat...'

He glanced at his watch. 'In time. Now isn't the time.'

She kept her eyes on him, her gaze deep and steady.

'I'm very busy at the moment. I've got work to do.' It felt like an invisible hand had seized his throat, choking the words into a killer silence.

'Ken say.' Abey pointed at him. 'Naughty.'

'Ken?' He frowned. 'Oh yes, Ken. No.' He slipped into the voice he'd adopted for the first time that morning. 'Adam's not naughty.'

'Stop it, Adam!'

He was surprised at the steel in Louise's voice. He turned away from them and headed for the driver's door.

'Where are you going, Adam?'

He had never heard anything remotely like anger in Louise's voice and the effect was vivid. He laughed. '*Where are you going, Adam?*' He mocked her.

'I've just realised something,' said Louise. 'Ten minutes ago, I was in the kitchen, looking out into the garden. I was watching. I watched you come out of the shed. I watched you lock the shed. I watched you walk through the garden and back to the house. Carrying your black box. It was when I was watching you walk that I remembered.'

'You remembered what?'

'It was the way you walked that triggered something very clear in my memory.'

'I'm going!' He opened the driver's door.

'I watched you walk out of my father's room in the early hours of this morning. You were with Gabriel Huddersfield in my father's room. You didn't speak, he did. But I watched you walk out of the room. You killed my father and strung him up like a beast. You. You and Gabriel Huddersfield. Gabriel Huddersfield pretending to be the Angel of Destruction. And you. You. Pretending to be the First Born. Making yourself out to be something bigger and more powerful than you could ever be.'

'Dead. Dada dead. My dada dead.'

'No!'

'Don't even try to deny it!'

271

A jogger thundered past them.

'Calm down, Louise,' said Adam.

'Don't patronise me. I will not be silenced. Not any more.' The anger in her voice had turned into outrage and her eyes shone.

'All right, Louise.' He walked to the passenger door and opened it. 'You've had a traumatic experience. You think I'm responsible for your father's death.'

'You are responsible! I was there! I saw you!'

'Get in the van, Louise. I'll take you to Trinity Road police station. I'll come in with you and you can tell the desk sergeant all about your suspicions about me. Then he can get that Clay woman to come and interview me. I can't say fairer than that.'

Louise said and did nothing.

'I'm being reasonable here in the face of some very serious allegations.' He moved quickly, opened the passenger door.

She linked hands with Abey.

'Get in the van, Louise. Tell the police what you've told me.'

She stood her ground. 'Murderer!'

He slapped her face hard, grabbed Abey and bundled him into the passenger seat. 'Fucking get into the van or I swear to God I'll kill your retarded pet.'

He drew a knife from his pocket, grabbed her arm, hustled her into the seat next to Abey and slammed the passenger door shut.

In the driver's seat, he pulled away and headed towards Croxteth Gate.

'Trinity Road's in the opposite direction,' said Louise.

He picked up speed to 45 mph.

'I said—'

'I heard you,' said Adam, reaching under his seat. 'I'm in the driver's seat. And I'm telling you, we're going on an errand. I owe a man something and it's payback time. Then I'll take you to Trinity Road. I'm the driver and what I say goes. I don't want to hear another word from either of you.'

Beneath the seat, he felt the shaft of a hammer, touched the sharpened point of a screwdriver next to it and, concealing it with his hand, buried the screwdriver inside his coat pocket.

'Who do you need to pay back so urgently at such a time?'

The words hit Adam hard. Like the voice of a stranger had melted into a sentence. He looked at Louise, bewildered, wondering if his mind was bending to a point where it would break so badly that it would never be mended again.

'*Who do you need to pay back so urgently at such a time?*' said Louise, but it sounded like her voice was masked.

Adam wanted to scream because his senses were warping and the walls inside him that separated what was real and what wasn't had suddenly collapsed.

'Who do you need to pay back so urgently at such a time?' asked Louise. On the third time of asking, her voice sounded like her own.

He heard the words, recognised the speaker, but wondered if his sense of hearing was warped by stress.

Pay back, thought Adam. *Someone who deserves everything that's coming to him.*

76

3.25 pm

Outside Leonard Lawson's house, the itch beneath Clay's crown became almost unbearable. *Everything is here.* Her own words, from the dead of night, followed her through the front door.

In the downstairs hallway, the nearest human being to Clay was the constable on the doorstep, guarding the scene of the crime. As she hit the stairs, it felt like he was already thousands of miles away.

She looked at the landline telephone and recalled Huddersfield's words to Hendricks and Stone. *'There's a body in the garden.'*

She hurried up to Leonard Lawson's bedroom with one specific goal and Huddersfield's words like a gang of demons at her back. *First things first.* The dressing table. The triptych of glass in which she'd first seen the old man's naked limbs, suspended from the ground as if by some magical force. But as she arrived at the top of the stairs, her attention was diverted to Louise Lawson's room, the door wide open.

The cross-stitch on the wall facing her bed.

Silence is Golden

She felt a drum beat at the centre of her being, a faint tap that increased in volume and speed with each new beat and a child's singsong voice echoed inside that beat as she walked into Leonard Lawson's bedroom.

'Silence is golden! Silence is golden! Silence is golden...'

The dressing table and the wardrobe were the only items still left in the professor's room. She turned on the light to dispel the gathering gloom and the room came alive with dust motes. She slipped on a pair of latex gloves and took the torch from her pocket.

The wooden body of the dressing table was covered in dark dust and there were rectangular strips where the dust had been lifted to salvage finger- and palm-prints.

Clay flicked on her torch and crouched in the alcove to face the back of the triptych of mirrors. The space was cramped and dark.

Starting at the back of the widest, central, mirror, she combed the black wood from the top, left to right, saw the grain of the wood beneath the dark surface, noted the odd little scratch as she dropped the light down and went back right to left.

'You're missing the obvious,' she said out loud. *'First things first.'*

She reached the centre of the mirror's back and hope collapsed. Left to right, another blank line. Right to left. She was close to the bottom and still nothing had been revealed. By the time she reached the bottom, she cursed Gabriel Huddersfield for playing games with her and herself even more for falling for it.

She stood up, made her way to the front of the mirrors. Carefully she unfolded the wings and exposed their backs.

Then she beamed in on the back of the right-hand mirror, using the same top-to-bottom, left-to-right and then reverse system. On the second right-to-left trawl, she paused suddenly, felt her stomach flip. In tiny letters carved on the surface of the wood:

St Bavon

St Bavon? She juggled the letters in her head as she carried on combing the wood, but there was nothing else; every other strip to the bottom drew a blank. There was no garden she knew of named after a saint she had never heard of and it seemed an unlikely anagram.

She turned to the back of the left-hand mirror, playing with the letters s t b a v o n and walking into mental walls as she reached the middle of the panel.

She carried on. One more chance, one more slow sweep from right to left. Closer to the middle than the right, she felt how intensely cold she was and saw her breath frosted on the light.

s

es

mes

ames

James

t James

St James

Whose garden? The Garden of St James. Whose body? The other half.

She took her iPhone out and was on her way to the top of the stairs when she turned back and went into Louise's bedroom. She got through to Hendricks as she reached the wall opposite Louise's bed.

'The garden on the back of the triptych. It's the Garden of St James, the cemetery at the back of the Anglican Cathedral.'

She took the 'Silence is Golden' cross-stitch from the wall.

'I'll ring round the troops,' said Hendricks.

Clay was on the stairs.

'Bring Huddersfield with you.' Huddersfield's words to Leonard Lawson, in Sefton Park just days before he was murdered, formed in Clay's mind. 'And as much back-up as is humanly possible.' At the bottom of the stairs, she said, 'It's a huge place. Looking for a body in there is going to be like looking for a rain-drop in an ocean.'

On the way to her car, Clay looked at the cross-stitch.

Silence is Golden

She had a question she wanted to ask Louise Lawson about silence, but first of all she had a body to find.

In the Garden of St James.

Whose body?

The other half? But the other half of who or what?

'The half Leonard Lawson condemned to the silent void!' Huddersfield's accusation poured from her mouth in a cloud of mist as she sprinted towards her car.

77

3.25 pm

Outside The Sanctuary, Stone heard footsteps crunching up the path behind him. 'Detective Sergeant Stone?' Danielle Miller's voice followed.

Stone banged on the front door for the fourth time, but there was no sign of life behind it. He turned round.

'What's the matter?' she asked as she unlocked the door and stepped into a strangely silent hall. Danielle looked at Stone, her face darkening. 'Hello!' she called. 'Where are you all?' She looked unnerved by the silence.

'Do you know where your husband is?' asked Stone.

'He's on duty at the Anglican Cathedral, guiding visitors.'

'The number?'

She rattled off seven digits and Stone dialled the cathedral on his phone.

'Anglican Cathedral. How can I help you?' A woman's voice.

'Is Adam Miller there?'

'Adam Miller?' She called into the office. A muffled voice responded. 'He showed up but left just before one. Most unlike him.'

He closed the call down, headed into the kitchen, where the back door was wide open. Shivering and wet, Tom Thumb sat at the kitchen table. He pointed at the back door.

'Where is everyone, Tom?' asked Danielle.

He thought about it for a few moments, looked in the direction of the front door. He drew a large circle in the air.

'Everyone,' said Danielle.

With his index and middle fingers, he mimed *walking*.

'Everyone's walked out.'

He nodded his head.

'They've *all* gone out?' asked Danielle, panic in her voice. 'Except you?'

'Phone your husband on his mobile, ask him where he is.' One man. One van. 'Don't tell him I'm involved,' said Stone.

She pulled out her phone and called Adam.

'What's going on?' asked Stone.

'It's gone to answer phone.'

'Don't leave a message. Hang up.'

'Tom, Gideon wouldn't leave you in on your own.'

'Tom?' said Stone. 'Where is Adam?' Tom turned, pointed away from the house and mimed rotating a steering wheel. 'Who did he go with?' Tom used the index finger of his right hand to point at the tip of his little finger, left hand.'

'He's signing the letter A,' said Danielle. 'A? A? Abey?' Tom nodded, kept his palm open and dragged his index finger across the middle, signing the letter L. 'Louise?' He nodded again.

'Gideon? Where's Gideon?' Danielle's voice rose with each syllable.

Tom pointed to the garden and made adjoining diagonal lines with his hands.

'The shed?' asked Danielle. Tom turned his face away, his bottom lip jutting out.

Stone walked out of the kitchen and headed for the shed at the bottom of the garden. Halfway there, he saw a spot of blood on the snow and felt his mind race faster.

The shed door was locked and he caught the aroma of a butcher's window.

'Gideon?' He heard Danielle's voice as he made his way down the side of the shed, but it sounded ghostly.

He looked through the window at the side of the shed.

Gideon's face, eyes wide open, the shock of violent death upon him. He felt Danielle's presence behind him. 'Go back!' The wound on his face was vivid and blood pooled around his head.

'Gideon?'

'I'm sorry. He's dead,' said Stone.

Her eyes swam with horror and sadness.

'I'm sorry,' he repeated.

She swayed on the spot and he held up her weight with both hands on her arms. Danielle looked at the shed and then down at the blood on the snow.

Her scream seemed to reach the leaden sky above them and when she stopped screaming, she shouted, 'I hate him! I hate him! I hate him! Gideon was...' She made for the shed, but Stone held her back. 'He was... Gideon... was the only nice thing in my life and he had to take that away from me.'

She fell into hopeless tears as Stone held on to her.

'I hope he dies,' she screamed. 'I hope he dies in agony and goes to hell!'

78

3.37 pm

Adam Miller snatched the ticket from the barrier at the front entrance of the Anglican Cathedral. The barrier rose and as he drove around the corner in the direction of the car park, Louise asked, 'Why are we going here, Adam?'

In the corner of the van, Abey whimpered.

'Tell him he'd better not start crying.'

'If he's afraid, he'll cry.'

'Get a grip of him, Louise.'

'Why are we coming here, to the Anglican?'

Driving at 10 mph, Adam looked straight ahead. 'You're to come inside the cathedral with me. Are you listening?'

Louise looked through the windscreen at the cathedral's sandstone bell tower. The Vestey Tower. It blocked out the sky, looming over them like a frozen giant.

'Are you listening?' he asked as the van flopped over a speed bump.

Abey started to cry. Adam took the sharpened screwdriver from his pocket and rolled it back and forth between the fingers and thumb of his left hand. His eyes met Louise's.

'Are you listening to me?'

'I'm very afraid of you,' replied Louise, quietly. The tremor in her voice was like balm to him. 'I'm listening to you. We'll do whatever you say. Of course we will.'

'You're to come in with me. To the cathedral. You walk in front of me and you don't say a word. If anyone happens to speak to you, you smile, but you keep your mouths shut, dead shut, tight shut.'

'Why don't you leave us in the van? Then you won't have to worry about us embarrassing you by speaking.'

'If I leave you in the van, as soon as my back's turned you'll be out and telling the first policeman you see that I killed your father. That's quite an allegation you're making, Louise. So I want to be there when you make it. Do you understand?'

'As God is my judge, we'd sit in the car and wait for you.'

'You think I'm a murderer. Why should I trust you?' He steered round the corner and down the ramp leading into the main car park. 'I didn't kill your father. Next you'll be telling me I killed my father!'

'Did you kill your father?' asked Louise.

He was silent. 'Don't be ridiculous.'

'Let Abey out of the van. Please, Adam.'

'Abey out! Abey out!'

'Speak to him and calm him down and then we'll go inside. The sooner we do that, the sooner we go to the police. I'll park as close to the front as I can, that way we can be as quick as possible.'

'Abey?' Louise turned his face towards hers. She leaned in to him, pressed her lips close to his ear and whispered.

'What are you saying to him?'

She continued whispering and with each in-breath he became a little calmer. 'I'm telling Abey where we're going. And, Abey, when we go inside, we must be very, very quiet. No crying. We have to go where Adam tells us and do what Adam says. And if you're very good, we can light a candle.'

'For Dada?'

'For Dada.'

No longer crying, Abey pointed at her.

'Yes, for my father too.' She took a tissue from her pocket, wiped his face clean. 'In the cathedral, no sad faces allowed.'

As Adam reversed into a parking space close to the main entrance, wind curled around the walls of the cathedral. 'Listen to that,' he said, with a note of tenderness that was shocking to his own ears. 'It's as if the Lord's voice has carried down from heaven. 'It's all right. Everything's all right.' He felt the screwdriver in his pocket. 'Everything will be all right. We're going to settle a score, we're going to light candles and then we're going to say our prayers because we're all good Christians around here, aren't we?'

The wind changed direction sharply. And within its powerful shift, there was a sound like someone crying inconsolable tears.

'Can you hear that?' asked Adam.

Just behind the wind, and just out of earshot, was another sound.

Sirens.

Adam placed his left hand in the air in evangelical prayer. He looked at the bell tower and the heat of humiliation flooded through him as the security guard's mocking voice echoed inside his head. '*Stop bothering the stonemason. Fuck off, faggot, he's not interested in you.*'

'How like that other tower, Babel,' said Louise. She looked up at the sheer face of the bell tower ornamented with elegant gothic arches. It seemed to support the weight of the sky.

'Get out. It's payback time,' said Adam.

Part Three
Sunset

The Triumph of Death
by Pieter Bruegel the Elder (1562)

Nothing could escape Death.
The First Born had known this for as long as he could remember. He had first learned this fact from a picture in a book. As he closed his eyes, in the darkness of his bedroom, the picture came alive inside his head. An army of skeletons, some of them dragging carts piled high with skulls, some of them riding horses carrying curved weapons to knock down the living. He tried to shut out the voice that followed him every single day.

'Look at the picture and know the truth,' commanded the voice. 'Death has servants and here are just some of them. Look at them and tell me what you see!'

The First Born closed his eyes tight and did not answer. The voice grew angry. 'Speak or else!'

He heard his own voice whispering into the dark. 'I see Death's servants. I see skeletons. I see people, terrified, they cannot escape...' His voice wobbled, and he tried his best not to cry. 'Far away, fires rage in the mountains. There are no leaves on the trees. There are no fish in the lake. The boats are burning in the harbour. I see the Triumph of Death.'

The First Born's mind stumbled and remained on one detail. A brick bridge with an arch. A man in a green coat, red hose and black shoes trying to escape from the water. A skeleton on the bridge pushing him back down, pressing on his right shoulder. A skeleton in the water beneath him, dragging down the man's right leg. Another man already drowned, face down in the water, his body upside down against the bridge. The skeletons smiling. The man in green and red would be next.

The First Born could hear his own blood thrumming in his ears and understood perfectly what the voice told him.

Man's suffering and death on this earth were the just deserts of sin. But what came afterwards made these agonies seem like nothing.

Man. Sin. Death. Damnation.

All had been made perfectly clear to the First Born.

Especially this.

Nothing could escape Death.

79

3.53 pm

As Clay drove down Catharine Street towards the Anglican Cathedral, she picked up a call from DS Stone.

'Eve, I think I've got a name for the First Born. Adam Miller. It looks like he's killed Gideon Stephens. He's done a runner and taken Louise Lawson and Abey with him. I found a flyer with his name and contact details at the Knowsley Road murder scene. Man with a white van? In my head, I'm linking it to the white van that dropped the freezer off at the Otterspool tip.'

'Gideon Stephens dead?'

'I've seen his corpse in Miller's garden shed. Smacked with a spade.'

'Let's run with your idea. Miller's the First Born.'

As she burned a red light and turned on to Upper Duke Street, the sobbing behind Stone's voice intensified.

'Where are you, Karl?'

'I'm in The Sanctuary with Danielle Miller.'

'Where's he likely to go?' asked Clay out loud. 'The Anglican Cathedral?'

'He was supposed to be there. I've checked. He walked out around one o'clock. What do you want me to do, Eve?'

'I want you to bring Danielle Miller to the Anglican Cathedral. We've got a hotspot. Whose body? Which garden? It's in the Garden of St James. Meet me there, Karl. Put me on to Danielle.'

Stone passed his phone over.

'Danielle, take a deep breath and listen to me. Is there anywhere other than the cathedral that your husband might go?'

'No. Not that I know of.'

'DS Stone's going to bring you down to the Anglican Cathedral, Danielle. We'll need any information and documentation you have on Abey, Louise or your husband. You're going to have to tell us everything you know.' She paused. 'The truth, Danielle. Is your husband a violent man?'

'Yes. Yes he is.'

80

3.56 pm

Clay's phone rang out again as she was walking across Upper Duke Street. She stopped to avoid a collision with a motorbike, then hurried to the other side against a wave of horn-blaring motorists. On the pavement, she connected to the unidentified caller and glanced at the Constables' Lodge in front of the Anglican Cathedral precinct. At its gate stood two officers, unaware of the bomb that was about to go off on their sleepy patch.

'DCI Clay?' A man, his voice dense with anxiety. 'It's Alan Ferry, Anglican Cathedral, head verger.'

'Thank you for calling me back. I need you to clear the cathedral of all visitors and personnel. I want all vehicles off the car park as I'm sealing off the entire perimeter of the precinct, including the Garden of St James.'

'That could take some time.'

'Get your constables, your clergy, your staff and volunteers together, get everyone on board, Mr Ferry. Officers are on their way right now to help you.' She heard the echo of feet.

'They're here already. What's happening, DCI Clay?'

'It's a murder investigation. Where are you assembling, Mr Ferry?'

'In the nave, near the west door.'

'Have you seen Adam Miller within the last hour?'

'No. I saw him at lunchtime, but he left.'

'If you see or hear from him, call me immediately. Does he have a friend?'

'Not really. He's not one of our more popular volunteers.'

'Does he worship in a parish church?'

'He worships here. He volunteers here. He doesn't like parish politics.'

'Does he go anywhere socially, any favourite place he's mentioned?'

'He keeps himself to himself. Is he in trouble?'

'Yes, Mr Ferry, he's in trouble. Please listen. If he shows up, don't approach him. There are enough police officers around to deal with him. You must clear your building as quickly as possible. Do you have a mobile phone number for Adam Miller?'

'It's on my phone... hang on.'

Clay felt the passing seconds like drips of cold water on the centre of her forehead. The verger finally read out a number, which she keyed into her phone, then tried to ring. The phone was off.

When she reached the top of the stone corridor leading down into the Garden of St James, Clay took a roll of scene-of-crime tape out of her bag. In her bag, Louise Lawson's cross-stitch tugged sharply at her need to know, but she pressed down the urge to look at it more closely and sealed off the main entrance into the graveyard.

'DCI Clay?' A voice found her out. She turned, saw two police constables advancing.

'Go to the outer gate, main entrance,' she instructed them. 'As uniformed officers arrive, you're to direct half to go inside the cathedral and assist the head verger, Alan Ferry, in evacuating the building. The other half are to come down to the Garden of St James to assist me with the search for a body.'

A police motorcyclist at the head of a convoy pulled up near the Oratory and the vehicles behind slowed and stopped.

'Come on, come on, come on...' Clay's breath was white as

the huge up-lighters came on, illuminating the exterior of the Anglican Cathedral.

Hendricks stepped out from his car and, in the next moment, Gabriel Huddersfield was on the pavement, handcuffed and in a borrowed coat that was three sizes too big for him. Hendricks grabbed Huddersfield's elbow. 'Walk with me, Gabriel.'

Clay touched the top of a gravestone inlaid into the wall of the corridor and felt the utter coldness of death, certain that the First Born now had a human name and a face. Adam Miller.

As Hendricks delivered Huddersfield to Clay, Huddersfield asked, 'How long do I have to stay here for?'

'Until I say it's time for you to leave,' replied Clay. 'First things first, Gabriel. The first man. The first name in the Book of Genesis. Adam. This is the name of the First Born, your lover, your savage, the man you have taken life with?'

'First things first,' replied Huddersfield. 'You found it then? The garden?'

'I've found the garden. But in the garden there are thousands of bodies. I'm looking for the one that you and Adam Miller buried.'

'Adam Miller?'

'The body? Where is it?'

'In the garden.'

'You wish to serve and please the Lord and save your soul. Because one day you will die and you will be summoned for the Last Judgment.'

Inspiration sparked deep inside her. She glanced at Hendricks. 'Follow us, Bill.' They walked deeper into the stone passage.

'But I have served the Lord,' said Huddersfield.

He was holding back, but she could sense him unravelling before her. Everything she knew about him, everything she had heard and seen, the chaos that was Gabriel Huddersfield, made perfect sense.

'And so have I,' said Clay. She hung on to the silence, walked deeper into the darkness of the stone passage.

'What do you mean?' he asked, catching up with her. He overtook Clay, walked in front of her. 'What do you mean, *And so have I*?' He turned, walked backwards, drilled his gaze into hers. 'I said, *But I have served the Lord*. And you said, *And so have I*. What do you mean?'

'Pray in silence,' said Clay. 'The best prayers are silent. The greatest form of prayer is to answer in silence the questions that need to be asked.'

She felt like she was being swallowed by darkness, but the conflict that danced across his wounded face kept her moving.

'What questions? What prayers?'

'I will ask aloud. You will answer in silence.'

She walked him to the bottom of the passage, the edge of the graveyard. It was quiet and the day was closing down at the edge of the Garden of St James. Gravestones were scattered within the natural stone boundaries of the garden, bodies buried under the snow, marked by nineteenth-century marble angels and sealed in beneath headstones carved with the briefest of biographies.

'In silence, Gabriel. Did the First Born deceive you?'

A blackbird flew quickly overhead as its mate called from the trees overlooking the dead.

'What is hell like? In silence, Gabriel,' said Clay. She waited, sensed the wheels of his mind turning in the mounting tension of his face. His eye movements slowed, processing fear. 'Can you be spared from hell, Gabriel? Angels have fallen in the past. Have you fallen? Do you know? Is there doubt? Can fallen angels be saved? And what is more loathsome in the eyes of the Lord? Sexual perversion? Or murder?'

The wind around their ears whistled and at their feet it moaned.

'Listen. Can you hear that? Do you know what the sound is? It's a requiem for a fallen angel.'

Tears filled his eyes and he looked utterly lost.

He opened his mouth to speak. 'Silence!' she ordered. She waited. 'I have stood in the darkness...'

In the span of a single moment, she was six years old again, standing in the chapel of St Claire's, looking at her protector Sister Philomena lying dead in her coffin. The spark of love that had always illuminated her had gone out, leaving only a cold, waxy approximation of her once lovely face.

'And I have walked untouched through fire to do battle with the Evil One.'

Forward in time, to nine years ago. Alone in a burning building, she faced Adrian White, Satanic prophet and serial killer, across a wall of fire. Death was almost certain.

'Do you know who I mean?'

'The Baptist!'

'Can you be spared the torments of hell, Gabriel?'

She took his left hand in her right, felt the profound coldness of his fingers and the wetness of his palms and knew she was touching terror.

'First things first. Redeem yourself. First things first. Show us where you buried the body. Show us where the other half is. Take Bill Hendricks to the body.' She leaned in to Hendricks. 'I've got to find Adam Miller.'

Tears streamed down his face.

'I will.'

81

4.01 pm

Close to the top of the Vestey Tower, a pair of lift doors opened. A sign on the wall, blood-red writing on a white background, read: 'Level 10: The Bell Chamber'. Artificial light leaked in through narrow windows.

'Where going?' asked Abey as Adam steered him and Louise out of the lift and into the narrow sandstone corridor. Adam pushed them forwards. Shadows wreathed the high walls above their heads.

The approaching footfall and echoing gabble of foreign voices forced a sickly smile on to Adam's face. As a group of Japanese tourists turned the corner and headed in their direction, he whispered to Louise, 'Just keep walking and shut up.'

'Hush now, Abey!' said Louise.

He slid a finger across his tightly shut lips.

'Lift?' asked one of the Japanese women.

'Oh, just keep going that way,' replied Adam, smiling broadly. 'Do you like the sound of bells, Louise?'

'You're hurting my arm, Adam. There's no need to hold on to me. I'm not capable of running away. I don't want to make you angry.'

'You already have done. Accusing me of involvement in your father's murder. You made a mistake, didn't you? Saying I was in your father's room last night. I'm not a murderer.'

He stopped dead in his tracks, sniffed the dampness in the air leaking in through the masonry, the coldness that radiated from the stone.

'I wasn't in your father's room with Gabriel Huddersfield. You're confused. You're upset. And you're wrong. Say it. Say of yourself, *I was wrong.* Say it. Go on. *I was wrong.* Say it.'

'I can't say that, Adam. Because I did see you in my father's room.' His grip tightened and she sobbed with the sudden hike in pain. 'I've got brittle bones, you're going to break my arm.'

He let go of both of their arms and placed his hands in the centre of their spines.

A set of stone stairs leading up to another level loomed. Two diagonal walls ran towards each other, defining the tight rectangle of a stone platform, a space to view the interior of the bell chamber.

'Do you like the sound of bells, Louise?'

'Yes, I like the sound of bells,' she replied.

'My father used to say that every time you hear a bell ring, an angel has won its wings.'

Adam pushed them to the low stone wall and metal fence overlooking the bell chamber. Thirteen huge upturned bells sat in the middle of the space. In the middle, a concrete structure housed the largest of the bells, 15 tonnes, Great George. Mist drifted in through slats in the carved arches in the wall and was picked up by the bright overhead lights.

'Yes,' said Louise. 'I saw that film too. *It's a Wonderful Life.* Clarence the aspiring angel says it: *Every time a bell rings, an angel gets its wings.*'

'My father had more wisdom in his little finger than the whole of every film ever made in Hollywood put together. He didn't need to steal other people's lines and pass them off as his own.'

Louise looked into his eyes, saw a chink of light. 'What would your father say to you, in his wisdom, Adam, if he was here now?'

A brief but undeniable look of shame passed over his face. 'Stop talking to me about my father!'

He stood behind Louise, breathing on her, eyeing the steep drop to the concrete floor where the bells were housed, sizing up the lethally sharp edges of the huge triangular panels that divided each bell from its neighbour.

Louise turned. 'I felt the same breath on my neck last night,' she said. 'If you throw me over the railing on to the bells...' Several voices and numerous pairs of feet came thundering down from the rooftop at speed, descending the 108 steps of the winding stone staircase to the bell chamber platform. '...people will know.'

A child's voice echoed into and around the bell chamber. 'Hello-lo-lo-lo...'

They were getting closer now, the people coming down the staircase.

'You're coming with me.' Adam grabbed Louise and Abey by the arms and marched them towards the voices.

As they turned the corner and advanced into the oncoming human wave, a solitary hand pressed against Adam's chest. 'We're being evacuated, mate. You can't go up there,' said the tourist.

'She's left her handbag up on the roof,' replied Adam. 'Is the security guard still up there?'

'Oh yeah.'

Adam stood back, let the people through. When a gap emerged, he pressed on towards the stone staircase. 'Faster, walk faster!'

A man's voice swirling around the roof of the bell tower. One man. One voice. The security guard.

The steps to the top were edged in white paint. Four steps. A corner. More steps. Another corner. Adam stuck his hand in his coat pocket and felt the reassuring grip of his screwdriver.

Turn. Up. Run.

It would only take a matter of minutes.

Turn. Up. Run.

The last steep set of steps, the open doorway to the roof of the tower.

Night was falling. From the ground, diagonal beams of broad yellow light lit up the tower's exterior.

'Go ahead of me!' With Louise first and Abey in front of him, Adam started the final climb, the screwdriver between his fingers.

Up. Walk.

He would be the only one to leave the bell tower alive.

82

4.09 pm

As he followed Gabriel Huddersfield into the graveyard, Hendricks flicked on his torch.

'You mentioned *the other half* in connection with the body we're looking for now,' said Hendricks. 'The other half of what exactly?'

'The silenced half. The starved piece.'

'*Starved piece*? Starved of what?' He looked at the back of Huddersfield's head, the casing of a damaged brain, and wondered if he was floating into oblivion.

'How do you know Adam Miller?'

'This place.' Huddersfield turned off the path and on to the snow-blocked expanse of grass at the centre of the graveyard.

'This place? As in, you know him from the Anglican Cathedral?'

'He works as an interpreter here. I've been a visitor for years. I come here and the Catholic Cathedral. I like them both. I used to see him watching me, staring at me every time I came in to pray. I'd sit on the back pew, looking at the stained glass over the altar.' He stopped and stared blankly ahead, lost somewhere in his head.

'Go on.'

'The first time I saw him was three years ago. I saw him watching me. I watched him walk away when he saw I'd seen him watching me. I came next day. I brought a small mirror. I hid it in my hand.'

He held up his hand, stared into his palm and a pair of tears rolled down his face.

'I sat in the same place. I looked in the mirror and he was watching me. I came every day... Sometimes he was here, sometimes not. I looked in the mirror. Every time, he came a step closer. I stopped looking in the mirror.'

He closed his hand, raised it to his mouth and bit down hard on the flesh beneath his little finger.

'Stop that!' said Hendricks.

He released his hand.

'Keep talking.'

'I... I could hear him breathing behind me. I was in the same place and so was he. I was at one end, he was at the other. I stopped looking with my eyes. I started feeling him... closer and closer along the pew... The heat from his body next to mine. I opened my eyes but did not look at him. I stood up and walked ten paces towards the door. He told me, *Walk*. I walked and he followed me, always ten paces behind me, all the way from this place to Sefton Park. I walked to 777 Croxteth Road, the place I have lived since a kind lady helped me. I opened the front door and left it open. I walked up the stairs and the front door closed. I walked up the stairs and he followed me. I opened my door and left it open. I walked into my living room and I heard my door close. I had never known such agony, such raw agony.'

Silence. Then a tiny voice, a raised voice from high above. Hendricks's eyes were automatically drawn to the top of the Vestey Tower.

Gabriel Huddersfield stopped. 'I am here.'

To Hendricks, surrounded by a circle of trees, it felt like they were in the middle of nowhere, a good place to get rid of a dead body. He shone his torch on to the ground. The snow was thick and there was no apparent sign of a grave.

'I am standing on it.'

'Step aside,' said Hendricks, slipping a pair of latex gloves on to his hands. He crouched, removed a layer of snow and felt the grassy, moss-riddled earth. With the tips of his fingers he stroked the ground, trying to tease out some sign of disturbance. His fingers fell still as he reached a small gap, a straight line. He shone his torch on to it and carried on, following the light with his fingers. The line stopped abruptly, changed direction to make a corner.

He got out his phone. 'Terry? We've got a square. Thirty centimetres each side, right angles at the corners.'

He banged the centre of the square and the ground outside it. It all felt solid, but there was something extremely hard beneath the square. It's a grave, he thought. But not a hastily dug grave, a bin in the earth to dispose of human evidence. He could sense precision and attention in its construction.

Seagulls tricked by the cathedral's huge up-lights screamed as they scattered in and out of the growing darkness.

He looked again at the square. It had been set out with care. More than that: it had been executed with love.

83

4.14 pm

As Adam Miller stepped off the last stair and out on to the roof of the Vestey Tower, snow started falling, its flakes like broken stars caught in the vivid lights beaming up from the floor.

He paused and watched.

The security guard was there, his back turned. Louise and Abey were advancing towards him as he gathered his things from the hut at the centre of the roof space. *He won't be able to protect you*, thought Adam. He imagined them as a trio of figures eternally trapped in a snow scene held on the flat of his hand, the hand that was about to deal with all of them.

He looked around the roof, at the rectangular structure of scaffolding posts in the centre of the space and the narrow ropes that hung from it, stretching out across the floor around the security guard's hutch.

Abey turned, looked at Adam, pointed and said, 'Bad man!'

The guard looked over his shoulder. 'What are you doing here, Adam?' he asked.

Louise stopped, turned towards Adam, and he didn't know if she was smiling or about to scream.

'I'm just a silly old woman...' She shivered with cold. 'Getting the wrong end of the stick, mistaking this upstanding Christian gentleman for a murderer. Silly me. Silly old woman.'

'What's going on?' asked the guard.

Adam walked towards the three of them.

Abey picked up a thread of rope from the floor, whipped the falling snow and freezing cold air. 'Bad man! Bad man! Bad man!' His chest began to heave and a rope of mucus hung from his nose.

The security guard pointed at the door and the steps leading back down to the bell chamber. 'Get inside now, the three of you! We've had an order to evacuate. I don't know what the hell's going on here, but I do know we need to get out of here and down to the ground floor. Now!'

'You want us to just get off the roof,' said Adam, 'and walk down the stairs and get in the lifts and walk out on to the ground floor?'

'The police are here. The building and grounds are crawling with coppers,' said the guard.

'Why?'

'There's something going on in the graveyard.'

'And you want me to walk into that?' said Adam, standing just an arm's length from the guard.

'Hey, what is the matter with you?' The guard's face fell. His authority dissolved into anxiety. 'You don't look right.'

'How did the police know we were here?' asked Adam. On the ground below, sirens swarmed from many directions. He pointed at Louise. 'You're a fucking liar!' He pointed at Abey. 'You're a fucking cretin!' He came right up to the guard. 'And you're fucking dead!'

The security guard's walkie-talkie fizzed with static. 'What's happening, Jim?' As he raised it to his face to respond, Adam snatched it from him and threw it over the side of the tower.

The guard walked backwards, his hands raised in front of him. As Adam closed in, the guard glanced back, saw Abey crying and Louise shaking, the two of them wrapped in an embrace. 'You don't look well, Adam. You don't look yourself,' he said.

'*Stop bothering the stonemason?*' said Adam. 'What did you tell me to do? And what did you call me?'

'I didn't mean to offend you...'

'Oh yes! *Fuck off, faggot...*'

'I was only doing my job.' The guard's back was against the masonry. 'You... G-give the screwdriver to me,' he said.

'As you wish,' replied Adam. He raised his arm and his hand lunged forwards, the tip of the screwdriver cleanly piercing the centre of the guard's left eye.

The guard staggered a few paces, reached up and folded a fist around the handle as he dropped to his knees. His hand fell away and his body collapsed.

Adam grabbed a length of rope from the scaffolding, looked up at Louise and Abey, and started tying the guard's feet together at the ankles. 'Don't move a muscle, either of you!' he barked.

Louise stood behind Abey, her hands covering his eyes.

With a few deft moves, Adam tightened the rope at the guard's ankles. He lifted the other end of the rope and looped it through one of the parapet's decorative arches. He looked back at Abey and Louise. They were stock still.

'You think the police are going to come storming through that door, don't you?' said Adam, securing the knot. 'Nah! I'm in fucking charge here.' He plucked the screwdriver from the guard's eye and lifted the man's body from the ground. 'If they come through that door, you're both dead. And here's a fucking warning from me to all of you!'

He levered the guard's body on to the top of the parapet wall and pushed it off the edge. His body slammed against the cold sandstone and the crack of bone filled the air.

'Interpret this, faggot!'

84

4.14 pm

Clay watched someone from the Constables' Lodge approaching the gathering of police officers in the nave of the Anglican Cathedral, saw the anxiety in his face and asked, 'What's the matter?'

'We've lost radio contact with the security guard on the roof of the Vestey Tower. And there are reports from people coming down from the roof that there are still people up there. A man. An old woman. A man with learning difficulties.'

Clay was flooded with a wave of nausea that turned her skin hot and her blood cold.

She took out her phone, saw Stone entering the cathedral with Danielle Miller. She tried Adam Miller's number. It was still off. She turned to a WPC and pointed out Danielle Miller. 'Hang on to that woman! Karl, quickly, come with me...'

Stone and Clay ran down the corridor at the side of the nave and across the vast space towards the lifts.

Clay felt another wave of nausea wash through her. 'We need the hostage negotiator and firearms here as soon as possible, Karl.'

She pictured what lay beyond the lift doors: the journey to the top of the 300-foot-high bell tower. A lift to the fourth floor. A series of narrow stone corridors. Another lift to the tenth floor. More narrow stone corridors. One hundred and eight stone steps, winding higher and higher, past the bells, round corner after rising corner. The final steep staircase up to the rooftop.

She remembered how Liverpool looked from the top of the tower and the breathtaking descent from its summit to the ground below.

85

4.19 pm

In the space of a minute and a half, DS Terry Mason and Sergeant Paul Price, Scientific Support, had cut a clean square in the topsoil of the Garden of St James and lifted a piece of turf from the ground.

'It's like a piece in a jigsaw puzzle,' said Mason as he laid the turf down on a section of plastic sheeting. In the glow of the arc lamp illuminating the dig, his face was drawn and tired and Hendricks heard his stomach rumble.

'What did you have for lunch, Terry?' asked Hendricks.

'An hour's sleep. These double shifts are killing me.'

Metal clanked against concrete as the edge of Price's shovel hit the exposed space beneath. 'It's a small paving stone.'

Mason reached into his bag and pulled out a crowbar. He dug it into the space Price had made, repeatedly pulled the handle towards himself and began prising up the stone.

Price took one corner of the stone and Mason the other. With a silent count of three, they lifted it away.

The scene of Christ's resurrection flashed through Hendricks's mind. The large stone that blocked the space inside a cave suddenly rolled back by some invisible force. An angel of the Lord sitting on the tombstone, *his appearance like lightning and his clothes as white as snow.* A breath of life easing out of the darkness of the cave.

Hendricks looked into the hole in the ground, saw a crumpled black plastic bag, its folds made silver in the overhead light. He knelt at the edge of the small grave and lifted the bag with both hands, conscious of the sound of bone against bone.

The air was alive with the smell of soil as he placed the bin bag on the snow and untied the single knot that sealed its contents.

'It's the other half,' said Hendricks, picking out Huddersfield. 'But who is it, Gabriel?' He opened the bag, looked inside, saw the hollow features of a human skull, the skeleton beneath in dozens of pieces. 'Who is it, Gabriel?'

'Here's your answer,' he replied.

Silence.

'Who did you bury in the ground?' Hendricks handed the bag to Mason and walked towards Huddersfield, his figure ghostly and still.

'Are you listening?'

'Bring him towards me,' Hendricks shouted, his heart pounding.

With a uniformed officer on each side, Huddersfield walked through the snow into the brightness of the arc light, his battered face coming clearer with each step.

They stood within touching distance.

'I'm listening,' said Hendricks. 'Whose bones are behind me?'

Huddersfield cupped a hand to his ear and zipped his lips with a finger.

Silence sat between them like a frozen stream.

'The silent one?' said Hendricks. 'The other half?' Huddersfield smiled. 'The silent other half. Tell me the truth, Gabriel. Whose bones are these?' Hendricks waited. 'They've been buried with care, with love, even.'

'The First Born had a brother. The First Born loved his brother very much. So much so that the First Born put his loved one out of the misery that had been inflicted on him. This is all I know. That is all she would tell me.'

'She...?'

'The one who tends the flock, the keeper of the keys, the one who gave me shelter.'

Hendricks took out his phone and called Clay. 'We've found the bones of a body. I think it might be Adam Miller's brother. We need to know: did he have a brother?'

86

4.21 pm

At the door of the ground-floor lift, Clay waited anxiously, watched DS Riley cross the space towards her. In her mind she walked into Louise Lawson's bedroom, saw the cross-stitch framed on the wall.

Silence is Golden

Beams of light flooded her and she was in the middle of Leonard Lawson's study, looking down at an empty space in the unlocked drawer and the manuscript on the surface of the desk with the missing pages.

'What do you want me to do, Eve?'

'The sergeant running the log at the door of the cathedral is holding my bag. Louise Lawson's "Silence is Golden" cross-stitch is in it. Ask him for my bag. Take it somewhere quiet and pull that cross-stitch to pieces, Gina.'

As Riley turned to follow her instructions, Clay's phone rang. She looked at the digits on the display and connected immediately.

The wind sobbed.

'Adam? Speak to me,' she said. 'Adam, are you there?'

'It's me, Louise Lawson.'

Clay's spike of relief was immediately doused with anxiety. She jabbed at the call-button for the ground-floor lift.

'What's happening, Louise?'

'Tell her!' She heard Adam's voice roar in the background, felt her stomach somersault.

'I'm to tell you... he's killed one man already and he's going to kill me and Abey next. Unless. You.' Her voice was cracked. She dropped the volume. 'Please come and save us.'

'Speak up! Speak up or I'll finish him off now.'

'He's tied my feet together. He's tying Abey's. It's what he did to the other poor man. He's finished tying Abey's feet.' In the background, Clay heard Abey's yells on the cold wind. Confusion and fear.

'Give me the phone!' A moment later. 'DCI Clay? Listen. What time is it?'

'Twenty-one minutes past four.'

'You've ten minutes, until four thirty-one, to get up here. If you're not here, they're dead. The old woman and her little slooooow friend.'

'Ten minutes.' She masked her anxiety at the unreasonable demand. 'It takes at least seven with the two lifts and all those stairs. Seven minutes if I dash. I'm not even inside the lift yet.'

'Ten minutes. No excuses.'

The lift finally pinged its arrival. The door opened. She got in and pressed for the fourth floor. The crossing. Stone stepped in with her.

'You'd better get a move on, because if you're not here in the next nine minutes and forty seconds, I'm going to kill the pair of them, and then I'm going...' He stopped, and when he continued, he'd slowed down and become more focused. 'To stalk you down all those narrow corridors. Do you know the bell tower well?'

'You sound like you're enjoying yourself, Adam.'

'You're not going to make it in time, Clay. But guess what? When you do make your way up here, I'm coming to get you.'

87

4.22 pm

In the subterranean quiet of the Lady Chapel, DS Gina Riley sat on the back pew and looked down at the framed 'Silence is Golden' cross-stitch from Louise Lawson's bedroom. She was surprised at its weight. She admired the skill of the needlework and wondered why Clay had taken it from the old woman's wall and why she wanted her to pull it to pieces.

A text came in from Hendricks: *Round Robin. Danielle Miller is en route to us. Anyone who talks to her, question one: does Adam Miller have a brother?*

She turned over the sampler, examined the four edges and the brown tape that sealed the hardboard back to the frame, and dug her thumbnail into the top right-hand corner. As the seam came loose, she felt the tension of something long suppressed pushing against the weight that held it down.

A sheaf of white paper had been packed tightly between the cross-stitch and the hardboard back. She lifted the back away.

Blank A4 paper.

She scooped out the sheets, estimated there were about ten pages and, turning them over, felt a shiver run from the roots of her hair to the tips of her toes. The pages were old but perfectly white, and the print on them was not the clean, black product of a modern printer but the uneven, inky dots made by an old-fashioned manual typewriter.

Riley inhaled sharply and looked at the title.

The English Experiment

A small colour photograph of two naked newborn baby boys slipped to the stone floor. She picked it up and, for a moment, wondered about the children she would never have, imagined for the millionth time what it would be like to go through the agonies of labour and have *her* baby placed on her breast. It had taken years of frustration and four failed attempts at IVF to begin the long route to acceptance.

She began to read the truth that Lawson had tried to hide.

> It began as a dream in a desert in North Africa
> during World War Two, a dream that came to life
> in London in the 1950s, the shared idealistic
> vision of two young men with a hunger for
> forbidden knowledge, a dream that was nurtured
> over the next twenty-five years and finally
> came to fruition in the summer of 1980
> and ended in 1993.

Riley felt a sudden dip in the temperature of the Lady Chapel and a mounting sickness inside her. She turned her head to the Noble Women Windows on the staircase, stained-glass images of Elizabeth Fry, Christina Rossetti, Kitty Wilkinson and Catherine Gladstone and whispered a plea.

'Come on, girls. Give me the strength to carry on.'

> The premise was simple enough and came from
> antiquity. Psamtik I took two newborn children
> and subjected them to a shared upbringing of
> complete silence, with a view to seeing which
> language they spoke instinctively, a search
> for the world's proto-language.

In the early 1950s, Damien Noone, the leading
linguist of his generation, had the time and
resources to replicate Psamtik's experiment
and adapt it to his own specific ends.
Two expectant mothers were recruited to deliver
two genetically different children in exchange
for a very generous amount of money.

Conducting the experiment alone proved too
much for Damien Noone. Finding himself locked
alone in a set of rooms with two babies, he
effectively became their twenty-four-hour
carer. The silent regime he sustained alone
for two months, and the demands of meeting the
infants' physical needs, led to a deterioration
in Noone's physical and mental health.

Nine weeks into the experiment, Noone took
the brave decision to smoother both children.
He travelled to the Isle of Man with both
bodies concealed in his luggage and buried
them in a cave. To this day, their bodies have
never been discovered.

Riley paused, bit down on the sorrow that caused tears to
form in her eyes and the anger that made her want to find
Noone and kick him to death. She took a breath and continued reading.

For many years Noone abandoned his dream
because the experiment was one he could not
perform alone. But as time passed, his desire
to try again increased. After his retirement
in the early 1970s, Noone decided to contact his
former friend and colleague Professor Leonard

Lawson, to seek the assistance Lawson had
so unwisely declined to lend to the 1950s
English Experiment.

With Lawson's assistance and the support
of a compliant young female, Noone started
preparing the English Experiment.

This time, preparation was key.

This time, the emphasis of the experiment
was different. Noone took two genetically
related babies and separated them with a view
to comparing and contrasting the effects of
language deprivation on one of two identical
twins. One was to be given the full stimuli
afforded a normal baby and the other was to be
locked in silence, with no toys, no colours, no
touch, no love, in complete isolation from birth.
The building blocks of humanity. Cain and Abel.

Lawson, an art historian, agreed and
supplied the compliant female assistant,
on one condition.

No wonder... thought Riley. *No wonder you write about yourself in the third person. Bastard.*

The child who was given stimuli but otherwise
cut off from the distractions of the modern
world would be subjected to another experiment.
He would be exposed, continually and without
remission, to the works of two specifically
related artists from a different historical era.
Hieronymus Bosch and Pieter Bruegel,

both Dutch. Bosch, born circa 1450 and died 1516,
and Bruegel, born circa 1525 and died 1569.

The English Experiment was the marriage of two
brilliant minds and two spectacular concepts.

She flicked through the pages and words leapt up at her. *Birth...
healthy... silent attic... mural... Last Judgment... Shepherd...
tape recording... darkness... Bosch... Noone... normal...
death... silent half... end...* She felt sick to the core.

Riley looked up and felt as if the ceiling of the Lady Chapel
had descended to within inches of her head. There were pages
more to read, but her brain was filling with fast-setting concrete.

In her mind, she travelled back to the ward in the Royal
Liverpool University Hospital where she had watched over
Louise and listened to the vivid details of her dream about the
Tower of Babel. Two boys, high up in the Tower of Babel. One
with a voice, one with a caul of skin condemning him to silence.

She turned the cross-stitch over, looked at the message that
Louise had so lovingly embroidered and wondered at the true
value of gold. She phoned Hendricks. When he connected, she
could hear he was outdoors. 'Where are you, Bill?'

'Coming inside with Terry Mason and the skeleton. He's going
to get the bones ready in the education room. Dr Lamb's on her
way over. What's happening?'

'I've got the missing twelve pages from Leonard Lawson's
book. The English Experiment.'

He was quiet for a few moments. 'And?'

'I've only dipped into it, but it's looking bleak. I think Lawson
and his pal Noone have tried to pull off something as cruel as any
of the quacks that floated round the Nazi concentration camps—'

'Bill!' A voice in the background called out with urgency,
interrupting their conversation. And again: 'Bill!' Riley could
hear it coming closer to Hendricks. Then, chillingly: 'Get into
the cathedral quick. Eve wants you to take charge on the ground.'

Needles of cold pricked the nape of Riley's neck. She heard Hendricks running.

'Gina, I've got to go!'

She closed the call down and picked up the papers again. Her head was occupied with just one question. *Louise Lawson, just what do you know about the past? And will you live to tell the tale?*

88

4.25 pm

Clay pressed to open the lift doors on the fourth floor of the bell tower. The damp sandstone of the massive, cold walls felt like pepper in her nostrils.

'We know he *was* on the roof,' whispered Clay hurrying along the central section of the tight corridor towards the lift that would take them up to the tenth floor. 'But what's to say he's not now waiting for us round the next corner?'

The corner ahead disappeared into darkness.

She lightened her footfall, tried to pad along more quietly. She held out her hands, turned her head to Stone and read the fear in his eyes. 'Stay back!' she hissed.

Something tightened at the core. *Move. Now.*

She veered as far from the corner as she could, to the right-hand wall, turned the corner.

A cusp of darkness under an overhead light, silence and an empty space.

Her phone rang out and she gasped. She beckoned Stone forward and connected.

'The clock's ticking, bitch. Where are you?'

She carried on at speed to the second lift.

'We've got your friend in our custody, Adam. Gabriel Huddersfield.'

'What are you talking about?' he snapped.

'You don't sound yourself, Adam. Is it the cold that's mak-ing your voice shake or the completely impossible corner you've painted yourself into?'

At the second lift door, she jabbed the call-button.

'Babble, babble, babble...'

'Speaking of which...' The lift arrived, the doors opened. 'Just why did you and Huddersfield take Leonard Lawson's pic-ture of *The Tower of Babel*?'

As she and Stone stepped into the lift, the image of two bodies being buried alive in the same coffin crossed her mind. Her stomach lurched as the lift ascended.

'Genesis 11:7: *Come, let us go down and confuse their lan-guage so they will not understand each other. He stole language first. Babble, babble, babble. Genesis 11:9: That is why it was called Babel – because there the Lord confused the language of the whole world. He played God. We showed him what God thought of that, what God thought of him.*'

She listened to the wind whipping around the parapet of the Vestey Tower.

'Are you still there?' The lift doors slid open and a broken fluorescent light made a pattern of darkness that threw her for a moment into the strobe-lit horror of Leonard Lawson's bedroom.

'Where are you, Clay?'

'On the tenth floor.' She picked up her pace, blinked hard to blot out the projection of Lawson's body, upside down and strung up like a hunted beast, seeping from her memory into her vision.

'Well that's just not good enough.'

'God was a petulant child then!' The words escaped her, had no identifiable beginning, no filter. She filtered the next word. Shit. He laughed and she hated the sound. 'But this is the mod-ern world...'

'Big mouth, big mistake!' He disconnected.

She ran along the gallery, past the huge chamber whose bells sat silently in the mist drifting through the slatted windows.

She reached the bottom of the staircase to the roof. A hundred and eight steps to go. She began the ascent. Her footsteps echoed and mingled with Stone's.

'I've never been here before,' said Stone at her back. 'What can I expect?'

'A spiral,' said Clay. 'Small sets of three or four steps, then a turn. More steps. Turn.' *And Miller ready to pounce at every one of them.*

'Let me go ahead of you,' said Stone.

She saw her coffin being lowered into the ground, Philip holding Thomas's hand and not understanding that she wasn't coming back. She travelled through time, saw Philip as a seven-year-old at the dinner table with Thomas and his shiny new stepmother, heard him ask, 'What was Mum like, Dad?'

Go! Away! Now!

'Cover my back,' she replied, turning the corner to the next set of steps. Nothing. She turned. 'What was that?' Deeper into the bell tower, below them, she heard a noise, a whistling sound drifting further away, and what sounded like a human voice, muffled but urgent. Clay looked at the stone platform ahead, then down at the curve of concrete masking the long line of steps below them.

Forwards and up? The noise could have come from outside... Backwards and down? The wind whistled, bringing a human voice on its tide. She looked up again and made an instant judgment call. Certain danger lay ahead. Possible danger lay behind them.

'I heard it too,' said Stone, turning away, knowing what Clay wanted him to do. 'I'll follow it. Be careful, Eve.'

A platform. Eight steps. Turn. Seven steps. Turn. Her mouth dried. Moving, moving, moving. She breathed in the mist around her, but it didn't touch her parched tongue. Stone stairs blurred into each other as she felt the burn in her thighs and calves.

The final set of stairs lay ahead, the angle steeper than the others, fifteen, twenty steps from the door at the top. Night and snow drifted past the open door leading out on to the roof.

She took a deep breath. Her clothes were drenched in sweat, but the spinning in her head had stopped.

'I'm here!' she shouted as she attacked the final steps. 'Less than ten minutes.' Silence. Wind and snow greeted her as she neared the top.

She arrived at the doorway on to the roof and looked around, 360 degrees.

It was positioned in the middle of the scaffolding in the centre of the roof space.

She walked into the light.

Oh no! she thought. *No, no, no, no, no...*

89

4.29 pm

Each step felt more perilous than the last. As Stone descended the stone stairs of the tower, reversing the route he had just done with Clay, he reminded himself that Adam Miller was alone and that there were two of them. He told himself his was the easier path, but that did nothing to dent the mounting dread inside him.

Stone listened. There was no other sound in the bell tower apart from his breathing and the padding of his feet.

He turned a corner into a blanket of shadow and felt his heart leap when the silence was broken by the screech of a seagull outside the bell tower.

He stopped and listened again. Silence.

The broken light danced before his eyes.

He could see the entrance to the lift space on the tenth floor.

There was no one there. *Turn. False alarm. Go and help Clay. Hurry.*

He walked into the patterns of light and dark, kept his eyes fixed on the doorway to the lift. He had to be absolutely sure there was no one behind that final corner.

Near the corner, in a flood of darkness, he stepped quickly and felt something soft underfoot. It moved under his weight. He lifted his foot and looked down. It was shrouded in shadows.

Stone took out his torch and flicked its light into the gloom at his feet. At first he thought it was a dead animal. He squinted, crouched down on to his heels and looked more closely.

A small pool of slimy red liquid oozed from the place where it had been cut. He followed the curve to its red tip, made out the pattern of dots that covered the surface and the grey fur at the flat end.

He heard the sound of a single out-breath behind him and, in the same moment, the impact of a heavy item against the back of his skull.

He dropped his torch as darkness descended. Before the cry in his throat was released, Stone fell into an unconscious heap next to the thing that had caught his attention and distracted him from the menace in the shadows at his back.

He lay perfectly still, a trickle of blood pouring from his ear in the direction of a severed human tongue.

90

4.33 pm

As she walked to the scaffolding at the centre of the roof space, Clay saw the knot on the masonry first, then the other end of the rope and the body dangling from it, swinging upside down in the twilight from the parapet of the Vestey Tower.

A second body was laid out on its back, naked, feet together, knees together, arms outstretched and pointing away from the head as if beseeching heaven, a friendship bracelet around the wrist, genitals shrivelled and pitiful in the freezing air.

She looked at the neatly folded clothes set to his right and recognised them immediately as Abey's. The jeans he'd worn earlier that day when she'd interviewed Louise in the Millers' living room. The black trainers and white socks. The replica Everton top.

Too much blood, Clay thought, *near the head and face.* She found she couldn't look directly at him, his face, his eyes.

From the feet to his head, look at him, Eve, look at him! she commanded herself.

She started with his feet, dialled Stone, knew his phone would silently vibrate wherever he was. The ankles were slightly parted, his feet flat down on the roof. The phone rang twice, three times, four. His knees were together and bent. His back was flat and his arms were wide: a crucifixion without a cross or nails, on the ground. Another torturous detail lifted from the central panel of Bosch's *The Last Judgment.*

The phone rang out and Clay felt increasingly nauseous as intuition told her something had happened to Karl Stone to stop him picking up her call.

Stone's voice on his answer-phone message. 'You've reached DS Karl Stone...' The wind picked up and the slender comfort of his voice was lost. She looked around and knew she was all alone on the roof.

His stomach. His chest. The redness around his neck, on the ground around his face and head.

'Jesus!' Shock hit her and she hit back by pressing the soles of her feet against the surface of the roof and forcing herself not to blink but to stare directly into the space around his face and skull and gaping mouth and process the information in front of her.

She disconnected the call to Stone. She looked away. She had to raise the flag.

She called Hendricks and he answered immediately.

'Miller's escaped with Louise Lawson as his hostage. He's murdered Abey. Something's happened to Karl Stone. He's not picking up.' She looked again at the body, the neatly stacked set of clothing. 'I need you here. Miller's got to be in the cathedral somewhere with Louise.'

The snow fell on to the corpse. She imagined her son Philip exposed to the same barbaric treatment and she felt a slashing pain down the centre of her body, as if her left side was about to separate from the right. She stood firm, watched her own breath rising through the snow and headed back towards the stairway.

Karl Stone. Find him. Right now.

'How did Miller kill him?' asked Hendricks.

'I'm not sure.' The image tumbled inside her skull, a picture she knew she would never forget. 'But he took a souvenir. He took away his tongue.' She was on the steps, hurrying back down, the wind whistling through the slatted windows and into the bell tower. 'And he took away his face and scalp.'

91

4.37 pm

On the back pew at the left side of the Lady Chapel, DS Riley looked again at the photograph of the two naked newborns, the twelve pages of the manuscript gripped tightly in her hands.

She heard footsteps coming down the steps to the chapel and a voice from the gallery above.

'DS Riley, Danielle Miller to see you.'

'Thank you, Constable,' she replied, without turning.

In the body of the cathedral above her head, Riley heard voices, the busy movement of bodies.

From the corner of her eye, she saw Danielle Miller sitting in the right-hand back pew. She listened to Danielle breathing, heard the tears in her throat. She stood up and crossed the chapel, sat in the row in front of Danielle.

'First off, Danielle, does your husband have a brother?'

'No.'

'No?' A shadow fell across Riley's mind and she wondered about the truth of Huddersfield's claims about the body in the garden.

'I'm certain. What's happening?'

'I've just had a phone call, Danielle. Your husband's still somewhere in the cathedral, probably in the bell tower.'

'Has he harmed anyone?'

Riley measured Danielle's emotional temperature and lied.

'I haven't heard the details. I need information and I haven't got time to play games.'

'I'll be absolutely truthful with you.'

Riley handed her the picture of the babies and the twelve pages from the back of Louise Lawson's cross-stitch.

Danielle looked at the babies and asked, 'Who are they?'

'I was hoping you could tell me,' replied Riley.

Danielle moved the picture into the light and looked closely. She sighed and said, 'Could one of them be Abey? They both have his eyes. I had no idea he was an identical twin though.'

As Riley tucked the twelve pages and the photograph back inside the 'Silence is Golden' sampler, she made a horrible connection between the picture of the babies and the pages she had just read.

Danielle indicated the needlework. 'Louise is very talented with a needle and thread. But why would she have this picture?'

Silence is golden, thought Riley, and suddenly understood the full horror of what Abey had been through. *The English Experiment. The story of the first thirteen years of Abey's life. He was an identical twin, brought up in cruel and bizarre circumstances.*

'How did Abey come into your care?' asked Riley.

Danielle reached into her bag and handed Riley an unmarked red card file. 'I was asked to bring this. DCI Clay said she wanted Abey's documents.' Riley's eyes drilled into her. 'Abey used to be in a residential facility on the other side of Sefton Park from us. Holland House. He was there from the age of eighteen, transferred over from children's services. He moved to The Sanctuary one year ago, when he was thirty-eight.'

'Holland House? I'm assuming it was a lot less high-end than The Sanctuary.'

'It's private, but it was pretty basic.'

'So where did the money come from to move Abey upmarket all of a sudden?'

'It's all in the red file: the lawyer's correspondence, the will.

He came into a huge trust fund last year. His father's been dead for years. He had no other family. The day after he came into money, he came to us.'

'Who brought him to you?'

'Louise Lawson. She met him when she was volunteering at Holland House, before she volunteered for us. She visited me in the months leading up to his money kicking in, arranged the move herself.'

'She had the authority to do that?' Inside her head, Riley felt the sun burning away clouds, and the shapes she perceived were worrying.

'She's his legal guardian.'

'Is she now!'

'Is there something wrong with that?'

Riley stood up, clutched the red file and the cross-stitch, attracted the attention of the uniformed officer up on the gallery. 'Constable, please stay here with Mrs Miller until I return.'

She stepped into the aisle and, opening Abey's red file, took out the top sheet, the personal information. She homed in on the top line, his name.

'Is this his name?' she asked.

'It's his full name. Abel Noone.'

'Is there a birth certificate in here?'

'There's nothing that pre-dates his admission to us except the legal papers.'

'Please stay right here, Danielle. I need to talk to you about your husband, but I need to talk with my colleagues before I go any further. Just one question before I go. Does your husband have a criminal record?'

'I'm very, very scared of my husband. No, he has no criminal record because he hasn't been caught.' Her frail composure collapsed and her sobs echoed around the arches of the Lady Chapel. 'He killed Gideon. Has he killed anyone else since?'

'No one. No one as far as I know,' replied Riley.

'I hate him. I absolutely hate him.'

'Why did you marry him, Danielle?'

'Where I grew up, there was a lot of grinding poverty. It terrified me, left a scar on the inside that still hasn't healed. Adam was charming at first and I ignored his angry outbursts. I thought I could tame him. I married him because he was wealthy and hard working with it. I married his money because I was terrified of being poor.'

'Stay here, Danielle,' said Riley, heading for the stairs up to the ground floor of the cathedral and nodding at the constable as she went.

Abey, thought Riley. *Abey Noone, surviving adoptive son of Professor Damien Noone.*

And, she wondered, if Abey was Abel, was the other half that Huddersfield talked about called Cain? Cain Noone. Did Abey know that Cain was dead?

As she arrived on the ground floor, she looked towards the main entrance of the cathedral and saw DS Terry Mason and his team heading in her direction.

In Mason's hand was a bin bag. She made the connection to the body in the garden outside and wondered if the bones belonged to Cain Noone or some other as yet unidentified victim of the English Experiment.

Their names chased each other round her head. Abel Noone. Cain Noone. Cain and Abel, Abel and Cain. Abel No one. Cain No one. No one. No one. No one. The person Louise had asked for when Riley had asked her if there was anyone she wanted when they were in the Royal Hospital.

No one.

92

4.37 pm

On the tenth floor of the bell tower, Clay felt as if her heart was about to stop beating. As she hurried towards the lift, Karl Stone's body lay motionless in a pool of blood. She slowed down.

'Karl!' she shouted. No sign of life.

Around the corner, the noise of the lift doors closing jolted her. They closed, but not all the way. They closed, jammed, and pulled open again.

Close, jam, open.

She knelt beside him, pulled down his chin and checked that his airway was clear. Clay listened to the thin rhythm of his breath and felt the faintest pulse in his wrist.

Close, jam, open.

His face looked haunted in the direct glare of his torch and she looked away as she called Hendricks on her phone. He connected.

Close, jam, open.

'Karl's been attacked.'

'Paramedics are in place, ground floor.'

Close, jam, open.

Clay placed her hands on Stone's shoulders, shook him gently. 'Alert them. Bell tower.' She cursed the wound that was making blood leak from his ear. 'Tenth floor. It's a head wound.'

Close, jam, open.

Clay sized up the scale of the problem. The endless stone staircases. The lifts. The maniac in the shadows in between.

'Is the firearms unit there yet?' she asked.

Close, jam, open.

'They're coming across to the lift, I can see them.'

'Where's Gina Riley?'

Close, jam, open.

Clay eyed the stray lump on the ground near Stone's head.

'Talking to Danielle Miller.'

Close, jam, open.

'Karl, listen to me, mate, we're going to have help with you as soon as...'

A freezing wind squeezed her face, her skull.

'Stay on the line, Bill!'

Close, jam, open.

She pictured Adam Miller standing in the lift just around the corner, one foot in the doorway causing the door to jam and open, over and over and over, his hand over Louise Lawson's mouth. She saw his face as he listened to her frantic conversation with Hendricks, the buzz of sadistic excitement in his piggy eyes.

Close, jam, open.

She stood up and made her way to the furthest point from the corner behind which the lift doors lay.

Close, jam, open.

Clay took a deep breath, prepared to fight whatever was beyond that corner.

Profound fear seized her, but the necessity to *get on* came in an adrenaline rush that forced her round the corner.

The lift doors opened on their own. Began closing. Jammed. They paused. They opened to their full extent.

There was no one there.

'What's happening, Eve?' Hendricks's voice on the end of the phone.

As the doors began closing again, Clay's eyes dipped to the

metal runner and saw a lump, dead centre at the entrance to the lift.

She stepped towards it. The doors closed on the lump, squeezing its soft, pliable mass, and she thought, *this is what it must be like in hell.*

Another piece of corrupted evidence, another piece of horror.

The crumpled facial skin took another compression from the base of the lift doors, giving it the look of an undiscovered species teeming with life. The doors opened out. The hair on the scalp was matted with blood, unrecognisable as anything human.

'Miller can't have taken Louise down by the lift,' said Clay, picking the skin from the runner. 'He's either still here on the tenth floor...'

She placed the skin on the cold stone floor.

'There's another way down,' said Hendricks.

Clay watched the skin unfold on to the flatness of the floor

'There's an internal staircase from the bell tower to the porch door at the front of the cathedral.'

She held the lift door with her foot, glanced at the corner beyond which Stone lay unconscious and vulnerable. 'Where's the door into it up here?'

'I don't know. You still want me in the bell tower?'

She worked it out. If he'd been quick, if he'd abandoned his hostage, Adam Miller could already be outside the cathedral and away.

'No. Try and intercept Miller, but you need to be armed.'

Time. More seconds lost on the ground floor. She wanted to scream.

'I'm sorry, Karl.' *I have no choice. Nothing is certain.*

If Miller was still in the tower, she wondered what macabre carnage he might weave from Karl Stone's vulnerable flesh.

She stepped inside the lift, pressed to go down, watched the doors slide closed and felt a sickening lurch as the lift descended and she left her friend and colleague behind.

93

4.40 pm

At the ground-floor lift, DS Bill Hendricks picked out the sergeant from the firearms unit in the gathering. The police medic was deep in conversation with two paramedics and the civilian hostage negotiator stood at a discreet distance from the group, talking on her mobile phone.

'Sergeant!' said Hendricks, taking the paperwork from him and pulling a pen from his own pocket. He signed the dotted lines and took the Glock 17 pistol and an extra cartridge of ammunition.

'Bill, what's happening?' Riley's voice behind him.

'Karl's taken a heavy hit, Eve's in the tower, there's a door by the porch at the front. I've got to go. There's a chance—'

Above the lift doors, the screen lit up and a downwards arrow announced the descent of the lift from the fourth floor to the ground.

'Back from the doors, everybody!'

The small space had evacuated by the time the indicator showed the lift had reached the third floor. As it hit the second, Riley was at the corner to the left of the lift doors and Hendricks was flat-backed against the wall to the right.

Riley took a Glock 17 from the arms sergeant and scribbled her name on the paperwork.

'First floor, Bill...' She peered from the corner. The descending arrow flashed and flashed. G. The lift stopped. 'The doors are about to open.'

Riley dropped to one knee and pointed her gun up. The doors opened. Hendricks stepped in front of them, gun pointing squarely at head height. At first, it was as if he'd seen a ghost.

The lift appeared to be completely empty.

He looked down.

In the left-hand corner, on the floor of the lift, Louise Lawson cowered, made herself as small as was humanly possible.

Hendricks lowered his weapon. 'All right, Miss Lawson, you're quite safe now.'

She looked out, at DS Gina Riley, as if she was peering through fog.

'Louise, it's me, Gina. Gina Riley. I went to the hospital with you last night.'

Hendricks's footsteps echoed as he hurtled towards the porch at the front of the cathedral.

Riley stepped into the lift, crouched to Louise's eye level. 'I want you to stand up. Are you ready?' She folded one hand around Louise's frozen left hand and another hand under her armpit. Slowly, she lifted Louise to her feet, felt the wetness that soaked her coat. 'Walk with me, Louise.' The lift door closed and Louise's eyes widened. 'It's all right, Louise.' Riley opened the doors again. 'You aren't going back up there. Walk with me.'

With her weight supported by Riley, Louise stepped out of the lift.

'Will you speak?' asked Riley.

In the lights of the cathedral, Louise's white hair glistened with silver dots of condensation as she shook her head. Her body shivered as Riley guided her to the nearest seat, in the back pew of the cathedral.

Riley sat herself down in the seat directly in front of Louise. 'Louise, please try and speak.'

She looked beyond Riley at the huge stained-glass windows above the main altar. 'I'll try.'

'Louise?' Her eyes drifted towards Riley's gaze. 'Every word is like a stain on silence and nothingness.'

'Pardon?' She exhaled the word.

'Your father quoted an Irish writer to you. You quoted your father to me. Silence. Nothingness. Only silence isn't nothing. It's precious. Like gold. How much work did you put into that beautiful cross-stitch?'

Louise turned her face away, looked up at the huge ceiling above her head. Riley said nothing, waited.

'Abey's dead,' said Louise. 'I'm numb. With horror. Horror after horror.'

'I'm sorry.'

'So am I. I loved him. And he loved me.'

'How long have you known Abey?'

'A few years.'

'Abey? Was that short for Abel?' Riley handed Louise a paper handkerchief. Louise's hands shook as she wiped her face and nose. 'Abel had a brother called Cain, didn't he?'

'Yes he did. In the Book of Genesis.'

'No, in your dream. The boy who spoke and the boy whose mouth was sealed by a layer of skin. Cain and Abel? Were they the two boys in your Tower of Babel dream?'

Louise looked at Riley. 'But that was just a dream.'

Riley nodded.

'I shouldn't have told you. You're a detective. I shouldn't have burdened you with my dream when all you seek is the truth. Dreams belong in the ether. The truth is all around, if you look in the right places.'

'Oh, I think we're looking in the right places, Louise.'

Riley's phone vibrated in her pocket. 'Excuse me, Louise.' She stepped out of earshot and connected. 'Eve, where are you?'

'Waiting for the lift. Are there armed officers there?'

'Yes.'

'I want them to accompany the paramedics collecting Karl, and the Scientific Support officers heading up to the roof.'

Riley heard the sound of the lift doors hissing open on the fourth floor. There's been a development,' she said. 'I've got Louise Lawson with me and Danielle Miller in the Lady Chapel.'

'What about Adam Miller?' asked Clay.

'Bill Hendricks is chasing him.'

The doors shut and the lift rumbled as it descended.

'The missing pages from Lawson's manuscript were in the back of Louise's cross-stitch,' said Riley. 'I've dipped in and it looks like Abey and his identical twin brother were the subjects of the English Experiment. Noone bought the babies, recruited Lawson and staged the experiment in Liverpool. Lawson was up to his eyes in it, trying his own aesthetic farce on the so-called *normal* one.'

Riley felt the depth of Clay's silence. She looked at the archway leading to the ground-floor lift. 'I'm twenty metres away when you hit the ground, Eve. Back pew. You need to read it. Am I adding two and two and making five?'

She watched the archway, heard a commotion near the porch of the cathedral.

'Wait there with Louise. Have you got the manuscript with you right now?'

She took the cross-stitch from her bag and the lift doors opened. 'Right here in my hand.'

Clay appeared in the archway. Riley held up her free hand.

'Why have you got my cross-stitch?' asked Louise, her voice filled with agitation.

Clay strode across the floor from the lift.

'That's my property, give it back to me. Please.' Louise rose from her seat.

'Louise, sit down!'

'Give me my cross-stitch.' She held out her hand. 'Do you know just how much of my life went into that?'

'Yes, I think I do know how much of your life went into that cross-stitch, Louise. And we need to talk. You. Me. And Eve Clay.'

94

4.43 pm

As Hendricks walked at speed away from the closed but unlocked door to the internal staircase, he heard voices cutting across each other. He picked up pace and sprinted towards the front entrance. From the body language of the officers in the vicinity, he sensed that Adam Miller had committed another act of violence as he'd made his escape. The crackle of walkie-talkies partially masked the noise of a paramedic vehicle in the distance.

At the swing doors of the porch, a burly PC swept past him, muttering, 'This is fucked, totally fucked.'

He saw a circular wall of Merseyside Constabulary high-visibility jackets, and a pair of paramedics pushing through the bodies.

A dark premonition flooded through Hendricks as he attached himself to the outside of the wall.

'Detective Sergeant Bill Hendricks, let me through.'

Without turning, without speaking, the bodies parted and Hendricks stood on the inside of the circle.

He looked down at the backs of two paramedics blocking his view of the body they were working on. The legs in the black trousers, and the black shoes, were still, helpless.

'He's dead,' said one of the paramedics, standing up.

The young constable's head hung at an impossible angle from his prone body. His left temple was red and swollen from what looked like a fierce boot to the artery. 'What was the lad's name?' Hendricks asked.

'Paul Jones. He's just passed out from the Training Academy on Mather Avenue. It was only his fourth day on the job,' said a voice, trembling with emotion. 'He was top of his class. An Oxford graduate.'

Hendricks noted that Constable Jones's cap and high-visibility jacket were missing, two items for which he had paid with his life.

He saw that the lad wasn't wearing a wedding ring and wondered who would tell the young man's mother and what she was doing right then, before the news came that would end her life as she knew it.

Hendricks went back inside and pictured Adam Miller walking out of the cathedral, past officer after officer, with the peak of the dead PC's cap half over his eyes and disguised by his high-visibility jacket.

The darkness receded and Hendricks gave in to a bitter hope. That the dead man was an orphan.

95

4.45 pm

As she stepped out of the lift at the ground floor, Clay could feel the blood pounding inside her head and swirling in her eardrums. She walked into the body of the cathedral and saw Riley and Louise in the middle of the huge space.

'He's escaped.' Hendricks's voice echoed. Clay turned to it, saw him striding over to her. 'He's killed a constable in the process. What do you want me to do, Eve?'

'I want you to help me lead the manhunt. We'll leave enough officers here to guard the entrances and exits. Go and take control of it, I'll join you in a minute.'

She looked around. The only civilians present were Louise and, in the Lady Chapel, Danielle Miller. Clay stopped a little short of Riley, weighed up the whole scene, settled her gaze on Louise. She took the cross-stitch from Riley, turned the writing towards Louise and lifted the back enough to see the hidden pages.

'Gina, take Louise and Danielle back to Trinity Road. Ask the custody medic to examine Miss Lawson.'

'Physically, I'm not harmed.' Clay watched Louise, tried to read her but saw only a blankness born of horror. 'Where is Adam Miller? He's escaped, hasn't he?'

'Yes,' said Clay. 'I'm afraid so.'

Riley showed the photograph of the two newborn baby

boys to Clay. 'From the back of Louise's cross-stitch. Silence is golden. Cain and Abel Noone.'

'Louise, which one's Abey?'

Louise wiped her eyes and said, 'Horror. I've seen such horror.'

Clay turned, called across as she headed back to the lift. 'I'll be back at Trinity Road as soon as I can. I just need to check the tower again.'

96

4.59 pm

The wind whipped a stray band of snow across the roof of the Vestey Tower as Clay walked across it towards the mutilated corpse. *Abey Noone. Abel Noone.* She looked again at the way the body was positioned and remembered the fish-headed demon in Bosch's *The Last Judgment*, preparing to mutilate its victim's face.

She looked at the pulp where there had once been a face, noted the bloody root of his severed tongue and the absence of scalp and hair on his head.

Clay thought about Adam Miller and how the other victims had been older men. So why murder Abey? It didn't fit the pattern, and nor did the killing of the security guard. Was it for sexual pleasure? After all, Miller took pleasure in systematically harming Huddersfield – perhaps this was no different. She guessed the scalping and removal of Abey's face had two dimensions: borrowing from Bosch, and giving him an erotic thrill. But she couldn't shake off the feeling that her ideas were round pegs and her mind a square hole.

'Jesus!' She pictured the scene and imagined Louise's terror. 'I'm sorry, Abey. I'm sorry I could scarcely bring myself to look at you earlier. The thing is, I have a son, you see. I have a son. His name is Philip. I'm sorry that you have suffered, Abey. I'm sorry for the sheer bad luck that you've had to endure.'

She listened to the wind, thin and lyrical as it whistled past her head.

She took out her phone and called DS Hendricks. Within one ring, he connected. 'Bill, you're going to have to lead the manhunt alone. I need to get back to Trinity Road.'

'Do you want me to return Huddersfield to the station?'

'I don't think we have any further use for him at the cathedral.'

'I'd like to speak to him before he goes back,' said Hendricks. 'We have to find out how he knew where those bones were buried.'

'Send him back when you've done with him.'

97

5.03 pm

In the education room of the Anglican Cathedral, the almost complete skeleton of a human being was laid out on a waxed cloth that covered a long desk.

Sergeant Price videoed as DS Terry Mason placed the last bone, the tip of the little finger of the right hand, in place.

A door slammed in a far-off place deep in the cathedral, emphasising the stillness and silence of the room.

Dr Lamb and her APT, Michael Harper, looked at each other and then with approval at Mason's handiwork.

'Absolutely nothing missing, nothing broken…' Mason eyed the skeleton and was filled with awe at the construction of the scaffolding of the human body.

Harper measured the neatly arranged skeleton from head to foot. 'Height, 152.5 centimetres.'

All eyes turned to Dr Lamb. 'It's a teenage boy. Look at the shape of the forehead and the narrowness of the pelvis. Average height for someone aged twelve to thirteen. No immediate cause of death evident based on the condition of the bones.' She pointed at the eye socket. 'In females this is rounded. In males it's rectangular and the nasal aperture is long and narrow. Classically male.' She lowered her face close to the skull, peered inside the mouth. 'No fillings or signs of tooth decay, which is one indicator that this was a well cared-for child.'

'A teenage boy?' said Mason. 'What about a short adult?'

'The skull,' replied Dr Lamb. 'The sutures, the gaps between the plates, are mainly open.' She drew her finger across a pair of fused plates at the front of the skull. 'This frontal suture closes fairly early on in life.'

Mason looked at the narrow gaps between the plates across the rest of the skull.

'They start closing over when a person is in their twenties.'

The education room was filled with a poignant silence and Mason, thirty years into the job and veteran of the worst that human beings could inflict on other human beings, felt a sadness for the lonely boy buried in a shallow grave and exhumed in a rising tide of chaos.

With his imagination, he furnished the boy's bones with flesh, gave him a face, eyes to see and a mouth to speak with. He dressed him in simple clothes and, silently, told him to *sit up from the table.*

'We know it won't be natural causes that claimed him,' said Dr Lamb. 'It could have been strangulation, a knife wound even. But the bones are perfect. Untouched.'

Stand up! Walk away! Live your life!

Mason watched him walk to the door, open it and leave without a backward glance.

'Terry, are you all right?' asked Price.

Mason looked down at the bones on the table and turned to Dr Lamb. 'We'll bag his bones and deliver them to the mortuary. Thank you for coming out so promptly. It's been a busy, demanding day for all of us, hasn't it?'

98

5.04 pm

As the last of the departing officers streamed out of the cathedral car park to the zones in the city centre and the suburbs
where they had been directed, Bill Hendricks suddenly felt small
and alone under the massive bulk of the Anglican Cathedral.

He phoned Sergeant Harris, the custody sergeant who had
accompanied Gabriel Huddersfield to the cathedral.

In one of the gardens of the modern houses to the west of the
cathedral, the wind played merry hell with a chime as it rolled
in from the River Mersey.

The ring tone sounded in Hendricks's ear.

There were only two other signs of human life in the car park.
The police van in which Gabriel Huddersfield was detained and
a white van that had been checked out as Adam Miller's vehicle.

'Sergeant Harris, I want to talk to Gabriel Huddersfield.'

'I can see you, DS Hendricks.'

Hendricks walked towards the white van and pictured Adam
Miller driving up to the gate of the Otterspool tip and dropping
off the freezer that morning. He looked through the windscreen
and saw only darkness within. The driver's door was locked.
He walked round, opened the back doors and shone a torch
around the interior. He opened the closest bag to him, saw the
bank books and a passport, and noted the black box, like a
makeshift coffin with a padlock to ensnare the spirit of the dead

things inside it. He recalled the scenes in Gabriel Huddersfield's flat and whispered, 'Fun and games, eh?'

The passenger door was open, a clear indicator that Miller had become careless and was falling apart under the pressure of his crimes. *I so want*, thought Hendricks, *to be in the interview suite with you and Eve Clay.*

He sat in one of the passenger seats, turned on the overhead light, opened the glove compartment and took out the only item in it. A leaflet from the Anglican Cathedral, the calling card of Adam Miller, a master of disguise hiding behind the vastness of the church.

Behind him, Sergeant Harris opened the back door of the police van and then the cage in which Huddersfield was contained. Through the rear-view mirror, Hendricks watched him march Huddersfield over to Miller's van.

'Get in, Gabriel. Sit down.'

Huddersfield, bound by handcuffs and in the early stages of extreme fatigue, slumped into the space next to Hendricks. Sergeant Harris closed the passenger door and Hendricks pressed record on his phone.

'Nice and cosy,' said Hendricks. 'Home from home for you.'

'How do you mean?' The wind picked up, lashing the empty space of the car park, causing the van to shake. The chime sounded louder.

'You must have travelled in this van with Adam Miller?'

After a long time, Huddersfield replied. 'No.'

'I want to establish some basic details, Gabriel. It's too late for lies. Tell me the truth. How did you and Adam Miller travel to Leonard Lawson's house?'

'We didn't.'

'Did you meet him there by pre-arrangement?'

'No.'

'Did he arrive first and let you in or vice versa?'

'No.'

'We will catch Adam Miller, Gabriel. He can't escape the

country because the ports and airports have all been put on red alert. His passport's in the back of the van. He has nothing but the clothes he stands up in and part of that belongs to a dead police officer. It's not a case of if he gets caught, it's a case of when, and that when's probably going to be within a matter of hours. You've got a chance to get ahead of him for once. Take it, Gabriel.'

Hendricks glanced at Miller's teeth marks in Huddersfield's neck. 'Look at me, Gabriel. Please,' he said with kindness.

Slowly, Huddersfield turned his head and engaged with Hendricks.

'Adam Miller's in a lot more trouble than you are. Please don't make your situation worse by defending him. If the roles were reversed, he'd be sending you down the river at the speed of light and begging for a plea bargain. What he's done to your body for his own gratification, he'd do to the whole of your being, including any hope you have for the future. And he'd do it without a second thought. Take off your chains. Help yourself. Stop being a perpetual victim.'

'How?'

'Tell me the truth. You're not the instigator in these crimes.'

'The First Born served Death and I served the First Born as the Angel of Destruction.'

All right, thought Hendricks. *If it's easier for you to talk in these terms.* 'How did the First Born communicate with you?'

'The First Born came to my room, followed me from the park, followed me up the stairs, came into my room and told me not to turn on the light.' Gabriel sighed, looked as if he was about to fall asleep. Hendricks looked out at the bell tower and guessed fatigue had made Huddersfield omit to say that he'd been tailed from the cathedral.

'It was dark. It was always dark when the First Born called to see me, to talk to me, to tell me about the wicked things that people did and how they needed punishment, and he left me an instruction to paint a vision of what would happen to these people when they came to their last judgment. The First Born showed me a picture in a book, but I knew the picture already because it was on the wall. The First Born was well pleased in me. The first task the First Born gave me was to paint over the vision, to bring the faded colours to life. And when I'd painted it, the First Born called in the dark, always the dark, and I was to stand outside when the First Born stood alone in the room and turned on the light and I listened as the First Born wept tears of joy and happiness. I heard the light turn off and the First Born commanded me to enter the dark room and I followed the First Born's voice to the centre of the room and the First Born pressed me down on to the floor and the First Born lay beside me, the lion and the lamb, and the First Born told me I was his angel and that we were to serve Death. And that is how it happened. And that is how it became. And that is how it is.'

'Did the First Born visit you often?'

'Often in the dark. Sometimes talking. Sometimes silent. Always lying together on the floor. Sometimes touching. Sometimes not.'

'How long ago did these visits begin?'

'I counted the days. 365.'

'You grew close to the First Born?'

'The First Born was preparing me to become the angel.' Huddersfield laid his hand on Hendricks's wrist, gripped the bone beneath his sleeve. 'Two weeks ago, the First Born tested me. We walked towards the river, to the big house where the old people lived. Abraham and his wife.' His grip grew tighter.

'Had they sinned like Leonard Lawson?' asked Hendricks.

'Everybody sins, but none like Leonard Lawson. No, it was simply their time and so we had to prepare them for the last judgment. He without a body, facing judgments as head and feet, she tied to the post and pole with diagonal bonds. It was simply a test of my faith.'

Huddersfield smiled.

'What's amusing you?'

349

'I loved every second of it, every moment inside every second.' The smile dissolved as quickly as it formed. 'Then I was confused. I asked the First Born what we would do with the body and the First Born said freeze it. I asked the First Born what we would do with the wife's body and the First Born said feed the maggots. I asked the First Born what we would do with the head and feet and the First Born said use them. The First Born would see to everything.'

Huddersfield's eyes misted over. 'When no one came knocking on my door, no police, I knew the First Born was true to the First Born's word. We were immune from the world in the service of Death and the working of the Lord's will. The First Born told me, find Leonard Lawson, let him know what fear is. Give him back what he gave to the other half. I obeyed. We lay in the dark and the First Born whispered, *Leonard Lawson, it is his time, he knows we are coming.*'

'Why did Adam Miller hate Leonard Lawson so much, Gabriel?'

Gabriel Huddersfield looked as if his mind had drifted away from his body. 'Did he? Are you sure of that?'

Hendricks paused. 'We know about your past, Gabriel. All those elderly men you attacked. But you weren't the leader here. Why did he target the elderly?'

'The First Born. He killed them. He hated the old. He hated what they reminded him of. He hated to think that there would be a time when his body was weak and limp and sagging. He hated his father and there was something about Leonard Lawson that reminded him of his poor dead daddy. But most of all, he just loved to inflict pain on others in as many different ways as he could. I've said all I'm going to say.'

'You've said enough for now, Gabriel. The First Born, Adam Miller, solicited your help in murdering three old people. One was a punishment killing, the others were a bloody dress rehearsal.'

Huddersfield's mouth closed and he took his hand away from

Hendricks's wrist. As Huddersfield looked away, Hendricks still felt the pressure of his fingers digging into his flesh.

He stopped recording, opened the passenger door and instructed Sergeant Harris to take Huddersfield to Trinity Road.

He phoned Clay. 'Where are you, Eve?'

'On my way back to the station.'

'Gabriel Huddersfield. Listen to this.' He pressed play. *'Nice and cosy.'* Hendricks disliked the sound of his recorded voice. *'Home from home for you.'*

99

6.28 pm

In the interview suite at Trinity Road police station, Riley looked at the clock on the wall and then at Louise, still and silent on the other side of the table.

'It's been nearly half an hour since DCI Clay took away the pages from the back of your cross-stitch. I've already read them and when she returns she'll have read them. I've asked you about them and you've stonewalled me. That makes this a one-sided conversation. When DCI Clay returns, this is going to become a formal police interview. You have the right to legal representation when that happens.'

Louise looked down at the palms of her upturned hands.

'Let me ask you again. What happened on the roof of the Vestey Tower?' Silence. 'Many, many times, Louise, when we interview criminals, they sit there and respond to every question we ask with *No comment*. If you choose to remain silent, we'll class it as a *No comment* interview. Nine out of ten *No comment* interviews result in the criminal being convicted and serving a custodial sentence. Innocent people who've found themselves mixed up in the horrible messes that we deal with... Innocent people cooperate with us, because they've either got nothing to hide or, if they do have something to hide, the circumstances surrounding that mean it's not their fault. They got sucked into other people's wrongdoing. Deeper and deeper, so they can't see a way out.'

Louise made eye contact with Riley for the first time since she'd entered the interview suite.

'I know you're scared, Louise, but—'

The door opened and Clay entered clutching the cross-stitch. She sat at the table next to Riley and said, 'We're making video and audio recordings of this interview, Louise. Do you understand that?'

'I'm not a fool.'

'Do you want the legal representation that you're entitled to?'

'No.'

'Then we'll proceed.'

Clay sent out a round-robin text: *DS Riley and I are in the interview suite with Louise Lawson. Please only contact in the case of an absolute emergency. Thank you. Eve*

She pressed the record button and formally opened the interview.

'I apologise for the length of time I kept you waiting, Louise, but I've had a lot of thinking and reading to do. And a call to make.'

Clay laid the sampler on the table, opened the back and took out the picture of the two newborn baby boys and the twelve pages.

'I'll start with the phone call I made, Louise,' she said. 'I telephoned the medical records department of the Royal Liverpool University Hospital and asked them to pull up two sets of records. Do you know whose notes I asked for, Louise?'

'I'm not psychic.'

'Your notes and your father's notes. You see, I went back to the first time I clapped eyes on you because I wanted to double-check everything. The first time I saw you, Louise, you were in the recovery position on the street, post-epileptic seizure.'

Clay waited, leaned forward and said softly, 'Louise, you've never been treated for epilepsy in your life. Your father has, but you haven't. The Lyrica tablets for L Lawson that you left on your dressing table were prescribed for your father, not you. Congratulations on a fine performance. Most people would have

353

broken their fall with their hands, but you did it with your head, which was most convincing. Most people sitting where you are would now go and tell me that it runs in the family and just because you haven't been diagnosed, you've had your moments and this being such a traumatic event and the strobe light being in play, you had your first fully blown fit… No, Louise, look at me, not the wall behind me… And it happened in the street in front of strangers, oh, the shame! Question: why did you fake the fit?'

Louise Lawson looked directly at Clay. 'Why are you asking me questions when you should be out there looking for Adam Miller?'

Clay turned to Riley.

'That sounded like *No comment* to me,' said Riley. 'A bit more confrontational perhaps, but *No comment* all the same.'

Clay picked up the pages of the manuscript. 'Did you fake the fit?'

'You're right. I have turns,' replied Louise. She looked at Clay again. 'But I've never been treated for them. Have you been treated medically for every symptom you've suffered?'

'You told my colleague Detective Sergeant Karl Stone that you had a telephone in your house because your father was old and you had epilepsy.'

'Did I?'

'Your friend has been brutally murdered and so has your father. Why are you playing games with us, Louise? What have you got to hide?'

'I… I don't understand what you mean?'

Clay spread the twelve pages from the cross-stitch across the table. 'This is your problem, isn't it, Louise? This sorry episode. Who concealed these pages into your "Silence is Golden" sampler?'

'My father.'

'We can't cross-reference that response because he's dead. How convenient. Let's try a different method. We'll proceed on the basis that, for once, you're telling the truth.'

'My father did conceal them. He took the sampler from my wall without my knowledge and he sealed the pages inside the back of my needlework.'

'Have you read the pages, Louise?'

She shook her head. 'Father wouldn't allow me to read anything he had written.'

'Why did your father conceal these twelve pages that he had written about the English Experiment?'

'Because he'd broken the law and didn't want to get caught.'

'If he had broken the law, why would he write about it and then conceal it?'

Louise sighed. Her shoulders hunched and her head dropped. 'My father was a mass of contradictions.'

'Louise, we're at a crossroads at the moment. You can tell me the whole story your way or I can tell you the whole story the way that I see it based on what your father wrote.' Clay pushed the pages on the desk towards Louise. 'Do you want to read it?'

Louise said something.

'I'm sorry, I didn't catch that, Louise.'

'I said, I don't have to. History is repeating itself. I'm being punished for my father's mistakes again. The reason I'm sitting here now.'

Louise raised her eyes, looked at Clay and Riley. And in spite of her age, Clay saw a small girl's expression in her face, lost and bewildered in a world that offered no sense.

'Louise, silence isn't golden. It's an iron yoke that has been placed around your shoulders. Talk to me.'

'I didn't want anything to do with the English Experiment!'

'In the twelve pages about the English Experiment, Louise, it mentions a Creator and a Shepherd. I believe the term *Shepherd* relates to the Psamtik experiment. Sixth century BC. The man who had control of the infants was a shepherd. I believe you were the Shepherd in the English Experiment that happened in the late twentieth century.'

'That's the way I read it too,' confirmed Riley. 'Louise, you were trying to tell me about the two little boys in your dream. You don't have to dress up the truth in dreams. Please, start at the beginning and tell us what happened.'

Clay watched a silent scream pass across Louise's face. The bleakness in her eyes was undeniable.

'One day in April 1973, there was a knock at the door. I thought I had imagined it, because no one ever called at our house. But then I heard the knock again, louder. I paused at the door of my father's study, listened to the horrible clack-clacking of his typewriter and asked, *Shall I answer the door?*

'He didn't reply. The caller knocked again, this time sounding angry and impatient. I was afraid.

'*Answer the bloody door, Louise. Can't you hear? I'm working.*'

Louise's eyes filled with tears.

'I walked to the door...'

100

6.37 pm

At the mortuary, DS Bill Hendricks stood next to Danielle Miller in the viewing gallery. The red velvet curtain in front of the glass window behind which Abey Noone's body would be shown for formal identification was closed and the red light above placed them in limbo. Michael Harper, Dr Lamb's APT, stood at the door, waiting.

'Abey Noone's body was mutilated. I haven't see him myself, Mrs Miller, but I believe that the skin from his face was removed along with his scalp.'

'Dr Lamb has covered his face and head with a cloth. She wants to know if you could confidently identify him from any unique markings from the neck down,' said Harper.

'Yes,' said Danielle. 'I had to bathe him once recently when he'd had a toileting accident. I would recognise his naked body.'

Harper left and as the door closed, Hendricks asked, 'Mrs Miller, was your husband ever violent towards you?'

'No. My husband was completely indifferent towards me. I was nothing to him, not even worthy of violence. I was a part of his mask of respectability. The wife of the upstanding pillar of the Church of England.'

'Why did you stay?'

'You know what he's capable of. He made it clear that if I were to leave, there'd be another accident. Just like the boating accident that killed his father. The father he loved and revered. Oh yes, Mr Hendricks. When his father died he came into all that money. That was the thing about my husband. He didn't deal in idle threats. His threats were real.'

'He murdered his father?'

'Cleverly. He was near enough for other people to see him jumping into the water to *save him*. But there was enough distance so that he could drown him and nearly drown himself in the process. *If I can do that to my father, Danielle, just think what I could do to you if you ever displease me.* What a hero. What a good son. What a tragic accident.' Her voice became angrier. 'Stick that in his face when you catch him. See how that rattles his cage. But me? Me? He'd only use violence against me as punishment. I wasn't worthy of it for any other reason. He didn't know. But I knew. Violence was his greatest pleasure, but only when he inflicted it on other men. He paid off a rent boy last year. He broke his jaw and burned him. It cost him £10,000. It nearly killed him, the miserly bastard.'

Hendricks pictured the bleak space of Gabriel Huddersfield's room, the wounds around his neck, the indentation of Adam Miller's teeth.

'He was a sexual sadist,' said Danielle. 'I had a key made for his shed. I knew what he had in that box of his. The pornographic pictures of men being humiliated and tortured. I knew where he disappeared to. Croxteth Road. My husband is a monster. A monster with a will of iron and a cruelty like no other. But that will crumbled today and cruelty took charge. Gideon.' She began to cry. 'Abey. The gentle ones savaged by the monster. I hate him. I hate him. I hate him!' she screamed at the curtain.

She took thick, heavy breaths, the surge of rage calming by small degrees as the red light went out and the green light came on.

'Are you ready?' Dr Lamb's voice piped through the speaker on the wall.

Danielle wiped her eyes and composed herself.

358

'If you're not up to this...'

'I'm up to it. Poor Abey. It's the least I can do after what that specimen did.'

Hendricks positioned himself behind her. 'We're ready,' he said.

The curtains parted. Danielle took a deep in-breath and gasped. On the table behind the glass lay the corpse, his face covered with a white cloth, his body dressed in a sky-blue coverall, the red, yellow and green friendship bracelet on his wrist.

Hendricks caught her as she slumped. Her eyes rolled and a noise like an animal caught in a vicious trap came from her throat.

'A... A... A... A... A....'

The tears of a woman exhausted by life.

Hendricks managed to manoeuvre her into a seat. He held on to her hands and listened and, for a moment, the noise sounded like hysterical laughter.

'Mrs Miller. Danielle. Take your time. When you're ready we'll try again.'

101

6.42 pm

After a silence that lasted minutes, Louise Lawson lifted her head and spoke.

'I opened the door and recognised Professor Noone immediately, an older version of the man with my father in the picture on his desk. He didn't ask if he could come in, he merely stepped past me as if I didn't exist and headed towards the sound of my father's typewriter. He opened the door and my father stopped typing. Professor Noone stepped into my father's study, closed the door. I stayed where I was outside the door, listening to the urgent whispering inside. It felt like only moments passed. But when the door opened, day had turned into night and the house was dark, silent.'

Her eyes clouded as painful memories played out inside her head.

'I lay in bed that night, unable to sleep, listening to the noise of their voices seeping through the wall. At dawn, I packed a bag, determined to leave but with no idea where I would go. As I reached the front door, my father said, *Stop! Where are you going? You have work to do.* It was the beginning of it all.

'My first task was to find a suitable property for Professor Noone. A detached house, close to my father's and hidden by large shrubs and trees at the front and back to secure privacy. A simple enough task, made easier by the fact that Professor Noone could pay for it outright. The deeds of the house were in my name to ensure Professor Noone's privacy. Over the years that followed, I acted as caretaker for the house, cleaning it, employing men to keep the gardens from running wild and fixing anything that needed repairing. I still had no idea what the purpose of this was. The next stages were not as straightforward. Time passed and nothing happened until one day, without warning, Professor Noone arrived at my father's house once more. This time he dismissed my father and lavished his attentions on me. My father's fury was barely concealed.'

The darkness that filled her face was pierced briefly by a smile, a smile that faded as quickly as it had bloomed.

'Professor Noone was a changed man. Damien. I was to call him Damien, there was no need now for formality. He took me out to a restaurant in town and I saw an altogether different man. He is the only man who ever did this. Caring, attentive, attractive in a dark way. He asked me what was the one thing I would like most in the world. I didn't tell the truth. The truth was a life of my own. I said, *A television set so I can watch medical documentaries.* He said, *I will order it and have it delivered to your house at the earliest convenience.* I said, *But my father...* To which he replied, *I'll deal with your father.*

'He was charming, witty and interested in me. He asked me what my dream was. I told him I would have loved to work in a caring profession. Nursing. He suggested that I would make an excellent midwife. I told him I couldn't go and train in a hospital because my father wouldn't allow it. My job was to care for him, not strangers. Damien told me that I was so intelligent that I didn't need to go and train as a nurse or a midwife, that I could and should teach myself. I was flattered. I was completely beguiled by him. No one had ever said such kind things to me. No one had ever paid me that much attention. By the end of the night, I wanted him to want me, I wanted him to take me away, but he didn't. He took me home and told me to go to the house I'd chosen for him and prepare it. I was head over heels in love with him at this point.'

Tears formed in her eyes and she wiped them away with the backs of her hands.

'He instructed me to open a bank account in my own name, against the wishes of my father. And from the start, every month he paid in £300 to cover the cost of my time in maintaining the house and studying.

'I was told to study at home the skills needed to be a midwife. I still had no idea what the purpose of this was, but I was happy to do something other than attend to the needs of my father. Damien sent me books through the post, all the latest books. A VHS machine arrived. Instructional videos for trainee midwives arrived. I read all the books, from cover to cover, watched the videos over and over. I befriended a neighbour who was pregnant and managed to be there at the birth, watching the midwife as she delivered the baby, asking question after question. I even assisted, and I cut the umbilical cord.'

She fell silent. Clay reeled her back in. 'Go on, Louise.'

'He telephoned me once a week, every week, and asked me questions about my studies. And every time he called, he left me with this message: one day, and he couldn't say when, a woman would come to live for a brief period at the house and I was to help her with all her needs. I was to prepare one room as a nursery for a child. And I was to prepare the attic space with nothing in it other than a cot and a changing mat.

'Years passed. Years. And nothing. Just cleaning and maintaining Damien's house. Learning. Every month a payment of £300 into my bank account. And every week, the phone call. The questions. The instructions. The promise of a woman who I must one day help.'

Clay heard the beginnings of anger creeping into Louise's voice.

'She arrived in 1980 without warning, nine months pregnant and unwilling to give me so much as her name. Damien turned up. Or rather Professor Noone. The cold fish had returned, the warm man who had been so interested in me was nowhere to be seen. My job was to care for the woman, but I was not to talk to her or speculate about his relationship with her. Talking was not allowed. I was to deliver the babies and await further instructions. On the day after she arrived, she gave birth to twin boys, within five minutes of each other. Professor Noone was there filming. He ordered that the mother was not to touch, look at or go near the babies. While I took the babies away to clean them, he gave their mother a document to sign, and an envelope. Then, raising her hands to the sides of her face like a blinkered horse, the woman walked past us, down the stairs and out of their lives. I fed both babies with formula milk and placed one in the bare attic, the other in the nicely appointed nursery.'

Louise's hands rose slowly to her mouth and Clay predicted that her statement was about to turn darker.

'When they were both asleep, Professor Noone summoned me to the kitchen. He offered me a glass of whisky to celebrate the successful births of the babies and the beginning of the English Experiment. Did I know how he'd recruited the woman? He'd paid a GP to inform him of any woman pregnant with twins who went in seeking an abortion. I told him I didn't understand. He poured himself another drink and told me that he and I were going to raise the boys and that my father was going to help by chronicling the experiment. *What experiment?* He explained that I was to be in overall charge of both boys. I was the Shepherd. My half of the experiment was to help him in the nursery with Cain, who was to have as normal an upbringing as possible. He would keep Abel separate. Abel would be deprived of many things in general but one thing in particular. Language. My father would help chart the progress of both children with a view to seeing if Abel could come up with a brand-new language or method of communication.

'I told him that I would not be taking part in anything so monstrous and that I would take both children immediately and make two journeys. One to deliver the boys into the care of social services, one to inform the police.'

She raised a hand and slammed it on the table.

'Suddenly, the secrecy and silence surrounding the scheme made perfect sense. He told me that it would be interesting to see how long a custodial sentence I would get. I told him I wouldn't be going to jail, that I hadn't done anything wrong, that I had known nothing of the vile project.'

'*Well... He smiled. I will never forget the way he smiled at me. Well, it will be your word against the word of your father and me. You've been involved from the word go. You purchased the house, on my behalf, in which the English Experiment was to be undertaken. You were given the house as a reward for your informed involvement. You employed people to maintain the property. You purchased books with my credit card and taught yourself to become a first-class midwife. That was your idea, remember. I have filmed evidence of the skill with which you performed this task. You have been paid handsomely month after month for your services. If you inform the police about me and your father, you may as well take your own life now. Because people will look at your father and me and think, men... cruel, callous men. But the same people will look at you and think, woman... how could she partake in and contribute to such an abomination against two babies? You will make Myra Hindley look like a saint. You will never get out of jail and if you do, you'll be murdered in broad daylight, a woman who went against the grain of nature.*'

Louise sagged, looked set to collapse. 'I was trapped,' she said. 'But one day, all that changed.'

'What changed, Louise?' asked Clay.

'Professor Noone thought he was God Almighty. And that was when the real God Almighty stepped in, just as he did all those years ago when mankind built the Tower of Babel. That's when he struck. It took time, but I had plenty of that. And I was there, not as Professor Noone's slave but as the handmaiden of the Lord.'

Clay's phone rang out. She looked at the display and felt the skin pucker on her neck. Riley glanced over her shoulder.

'Take the call,' said Riley. Clay was on her feet and heading for the door. 'You want me to carry on?' asked Riley.

'We must carry on. We must, we must,' said Louise.

'Yes, you must carry on,' said Clay, opening the door of the interview suite and stepping into the corridor. She closed the door and connected the call.

'DCI Clay?' A cultured, educated voice.

'Mr Evergreen?' Gabriel Huddersfield's blind neighbour.

'All the police officers have gone,' he said.

Clay headed at speed to the front door of Trinity Road police station.

'They closed the flat down with tape. I heard the last officer leaving. But there's someone inside Gabriel's flat now. I can hear him. It sounds like Adam Miller.'

102

7.17 pm

Clay paused at the bottom of the final set of stairs leading up to Gabriel Huddersfield's flat, felt the weight of a spanner in her coat pocket. She saw the moon through the skylight, picking out the landing in an ethereal glow. From the space above, she heard Elliot Evergreen whisper, 'DCI Clay?'

'Mr Evergreen, sssshhh.'

She walked up the last few stairs, ears straining to hear what might lie behind the door of Gabriel Huddersfield's flat. Silence. At the top, she took the door key from Elliot Evergreen. 'Go inside, close your door, stay inside.'

Outside, she heard cars arriving, engines turning off, the mounting back-up behind her that, once she was through the door, would be of no use. The sound made her intensely aware of how alone she really was. She felt an emptiness that she hadn't known since she was a small girl, when the truth had sunk in that she had no one in this world.

She listened, and for a brief second flew through time and space to her home in Mersey Road, watched Thomas giving Philip his dinner, both of them blissfully unaware of the danger she was in, both of them unable to see or sense the phantom of their wife and mother, desperate for what could be the final contact.

Back. Fast. Now.

Clay looked at the picture of Jesus on Huddersfield's door,

framed by the moonlight. She heard nothing behind it as she turned the key with infinite care.

The door opened without a sound. She stepped into the flat, left the front door open. A pipe gurgled. A tap spat out a stream of water. At the bathroom window the wind moaned. Every hair on her body stood up on end.

Clay turned on her torch, pointed it at the door ahead, at Huddersfield's chapel, art gallery and torture chamber. She passed the bathroom door. A board creaked beneath her foot and her heart banged. Her head spun as it danced with the memory of his atrocities. She listened through the rising tide of blood inside her skull. No sound of life behind the door, but she could sense a presence there, waiting, waiting for her.

Her hand pressed against the surface of the door. She gripped the spanner in her pocket, wondered what she would look like stripped naked and without a face or scalp. She looked down on herself from the ceiling of the mortuary, watched as Dr Lamb pulled what was left of her to pieces.

'*I did see you in Liverpool One with your little boy, Eve...*' Dr Lamb's words echoed on the wind outside the house. '*The man you were with, with the sky-blue eyes... I thought, no... You looked so happy...*'

And she hoped against hope that she was wrong. That Elliot Evergreen was mistaken. She opened the door slowly and she knew she was not alone. Clouds passed over the moon. Wisps of moonlight illuminated the figures at the top of the three panels of *The Last Judgment*. She saw Jesus in his heavenly glory. Beneath his feet was a bank of shadows. She stared into the darkness and made out the shape of a man.

He sat perfectly still, directly beneath Jesus, like the silhouette of a statue.

Clay grasped the handle of the spanner in her pocket.

She listened to the even sound of his breathing in the dark.

The smell of blood, semen and testosterone flooded her senses and she felt violated by the air she was forced to breathe.

The wind pressed hard on the roof and exterior walls.
Clay took a step inside and froze when she heard a voice.
'Stop!'
Was it Adam? She doubted her senses.
Freezing air rushed through the cracks in the old windows.
It gave her the coldest kiss as it streamed by. The front door
slammed shut.
'Alone at last, Eve!'
The floor beneath her turned to wax.

103

7.19 pm

Clouds sailed away from the moon and the room came alive with silver light. Something glinted in his hand, metal or glass.

Clay hung on to the silence as her eyes grew accustomed to the gloom. The details of what lay before her came clearer as the seconds ticked past.

She pressed record on her iPhone, placed it on the floor. His breath sounded like a primitive curse.

'Are you surrendering to me?' she asked with a hollow calmness. 'The building's surrounded. The street outside is crawling with police officers.' The silence was dense. 'You came back here? You killed a man to run away. So why have you come back?'

Her vision focused and, in the moonlight, the features of the room gained definition. He sat with his back to her, facing the wall. The sheen of his body told her he was not in his own skin. She narrowed her eyes and saw he was wearing the leather body suit. She heard a zip being undone, watched as he lifted the leather mask that covered his face and head.

He threw it backwards and it landed at her feet. It looked up at her, the hollow eyes sinister in their emptiness. An aroma of sweat, blood and tears wafted up from it.

'Masks. Do you ever wear masks, Eve?' Something fractured in his voice, made him sound unlike himself, and she wondered if this was Adam Miller's take on tender intimacy. 'The answer is yes, Eve. I've read about you. I've been fascinated by you for years. You wouldn't believe how pleased I was when you walked into The Sanctuary. Did I appear excited?'

'No, you appeared annoyed. Disturbed from your bed.'

'Masks, Eve. Masks. You wear masks, Eve. I know you do. You have to. You're wearing one now. I can see you through the shadows with the eyes in the back of my head.'

He laughed sourly, briefly, and fell silent.

'You can see me with the eyes in the back of your head. I can't see you. I don't want to talk to your back,' said Clay. 'Turn the chair round so that I can see you better and you can see me.'

He turned his hand and the silver blade in his grasp shone in the moonlight.

'Is that what you used to peel off Abey's face and scalp?'

'Poor Abey, he dead as doornail.' He slipped from one voice to another, Adam to Abey.

'Please don't mock him. Isn't it enough that you've killed him? Must you mock his speaking voice?'

'He's dead. Does it matter? If he was alive, would he understand?'

'Abey Noone was a human being and he had dignity and feelings and deserved to be respected for what he was.'

'What was he? I'd love to hear your take on poor little Abey.'

'He was born into a nightmare. He had a brother, an identical twin, and by no more than a flip of a coin he was placed in solitary confinement from the moment he was born, deprived of language by a father figure who had no mercy. You want to know my take on Abey Noone? He wasn't born disabled, his disabilities were inflicted on him by a man who had complete power over him.'

'Poor little Abel, Abel B Babel, that surely is bad luck. But what of his other, his brother, his twin pea in the pod?'

Clay froze, saw her breath in the moonlit air, felt her skin tingling. 'What do you know of his brother, Adam?'

'What do I know of his brother?' Something in his voice

shifted, became quite unlike either Adam or the mocking imitation of Abey.

'Tell me about his brother.' She heard the words leave her mouth and they sounded like they'd drifted in on some cursed wind.

'A telltale?' He sounded out the words. 'I used to hear the boy, Eve.' He raised an arm, pointed his finger up to the ceiling. 'Up in the attic.' Silence. 'Crying. I thought it was a cat trapped up there at first. I was told I was the only one.'

His voice was full of warmth and there was a music in there that compelled Clay to listen. He looked over his shoulder, his profile caught in a patch of light.

'Abey? Is that you?' She stepped forward, drawn to the voice like magic.

'Eve.'

'Adam?'

'I'm not Adam,' he replied in a clear voice, deep and mature. 'Don't!' he whispered. 'Eve, born in similar shadows to us, but different. Yes, different but the same. You don't have to come any closer. You are close to us already, Eve.'

'Abey? Abel Noone?' She remembered a trick from childhood, squeezed her toes to check if she was dreaming and found she was wide awake.

'No. Abel was my twin. I am Cain. Abel is dead. I am his other half and he is my other half. His were the bones in the Garden of St James. He was the silent one, I was the voice.'

He turned his head, his profile clear now. Clay felt as if a ghost had walked into her body, as if she had been cast out of her own flesh.

'Cain?'

'I've been dealing with unfinished business, Eve. Some things have gone well, others not. Do you understand?'

Events and images danced inside her head, the first bare bones of a story knitted together. She thought of the dead man on the roof of the Vestey Tower.

'What happened to Adam Miller?' she asked.

'He killed the security guard on the roof. And I killed him, took his face, his scalp. Took his clothes, left mine in exchange.

'This is the house in which you were born,' said Clay. She looked up to where he had pointed and imagined a cot, a changing mat and nothing else for the other half, the silent half. 'Where the English Experiment took place.'

She saw and heard the construct that was Abey, drawing pictures as she interviewed Louise in the Millers' living room, making the impulsive noises of a man with the mind of a four-year-old child. Cain Noone was a consummate actor.

'The First Born?' asked Clay.

'It's true I was the first born. But that's also a vehicle for an idea. An idea I sold to Gabriel Huddersfield and which he bought.'

Clay was filled with grim enlightenment. In her mind, everything crystallised. She had assumed that Gabriel Huddersfield had had one visitor, Adam Miller. But Cain Noone was the other. Cain, always masked as the First Born. Adam Miller, masked for sadomasochistic sex.

'I wanted to mark the end of Leonard Lawson's life with the same cruelty he'd brought to the start of mine and my brother's. I wanted vengeance for my other half and the miserable life he'd endured.'

He pointed at the figure in the corner of the central panel of the painting, the naked man suspended from a pole, carried on the shoulder of a human dressed in white and blue, his face covered by a mask, part bird, part platypus; man as monster. '*This is where you are now, Leonard*, I explained.' He pointed to the panel of hell. '*And this is where you are going for what you did to me and my brother.* I pretended, in his bedroom, that Huddersfield was my brother come back from the dead to take him over to the other side. The Angel of Destruction. You should have seen his tired old face, his eyes, his terror. It was sublime.' He raised the point of the dagger to his temple. 'I have a picture of it here. I wish you could see. I wish you'd been there to see, Eve.' He stood up. 'I did it for us. All of us. You, Eve. All the accidents of birth, those of us born into darkness.'

The knitting bones in her mind took on flesh, developed galloping feet. 'Gabriel Huddersfield and Adam Miller?'

'Oh, the things they did in the name of love, if love is the word for what bound them together. Gabriel and Adam, in this very room, my old bedroom.'

'Adam Miller was never involved in the murder of Leonard Lawson?' asked Clay. 'Or of Abraham and Mary Evans?' She saw him nod. 'Cain, how did Gabriel come to live here, where you used to live?'

'The Shepherd saw to that. She got to know him in the park. He told her about his past, his crimes against elderly men. He told her about his religious obsession. She showed him compassion and offered him shelter at no cost. He was grateful to her, wanted to please her. She gave him the paints and brushes when I told him to touch up the fading mural of *The Last Judgment*. I told him to learn that this was what happened to those who sinned, to learn it by heart, to know it with all of his head and heart and soul. But that there was a way to save himself, and that was to punish the wicked.

'The Shepherd told him that I was coming. The First Born. And when I came, I told him everything. From my first memory to the body in the Garden of St James. Who it was. Where to find him.'

'Tell me about Leonard Lawson?'

With his index finger, he drew an arc in the air across the span of *The Last Judgment*.

'Leonard Lawson. Every day. Bosch. Bruegel. Filling my head with other people's imaginary horrors and passing them off as the truth. Making me look at the pictures for hours and hours on end, beating me if I closed my eyes or looked away as he spoke about the images before me. *Disobey your teacher and this is where you'll end up, packed into a pan with all the other sinners and boiling forever in hell.* He gave me hell when

I was small and young. When he was old and weaker than me, I served it back to him.'

'As for Adam Miller, I can't tell you just what a bad man he was. The things he said and did in front of those who had no voice. My name is Cain, but I lived for one year as Abel. I lived as a disabled man for a whole year. It was a perfect mask: I saw everything, I heard everything.'

Slowly, he stood and turned towards her.

'Why did you come back here, to this room?'

'To lift the mask and tell the truth. You understand how things work in the dark, Eve. It's written on you, on your skin. I saw it when I stood on the landing of The Sanctuary early this morning, a sleepwalker watching you.' She saw his face, his whole face. 'We choose our masks. But no one chooses the where or when or who they are born to. I have worn the mask. But tonight the mask has to drop.'

'How did your brother die?'

'He was sick, so sick.' He faced her directly and it felt like the space between them was closing down, at the will of some invisible power. 'He couldn't stop crying. He was a pitiful thing. He babbled between his tears and he smeared his own filth across his face, making a soiled mask of what he was, of what he'd been turned into by the Creator. We were thirteen. The Creator was gone. I released Abel. I murdered my brother out of love.'

In the moonlight, his eyes shone with tears.

'I laid Abel's body in the attic until it was bones years later. When I left to wander, I placed his relics in the ground. I prepared his grave with love and when I left, I buried them and sealed the sacred space with a stone. I showed Gabriel Huddersfield where it was, so that he could show you. Will you make me a promise? Will you bury his bones in a good place?'

'It will be done with dignity and respect,' said Clay. She watched a tear fall from his face. 'Where have you been for all these years, Cain?'

'I have been a restless wanderer on the earth, in the Land

of Nod, east of Eden. I promised the Shepherd I would return. I returned.'

'What happened to Damien Noone? Who wore the mask – the Creator?'

'I was thirteen. The Shepherd went out with him one day, but he didn't return. This is why I came back. Also to tell you that my work is done. To tell you that the Shepherd is good. To tell you that I am tired of wandering. To tell you that I am tired of masks. To tell you that I mourn my brother. To tell you, Eve, who was born in hell, just as we were. To tell you that I want to join my brother in paradise.'

An intense grief consumed Clay, placed her at the centre of her own past and future. She balanced the pain of her own childhood against her fear for her son's future and imagined the torment that had driven Cain Noone to the spot on which he now stood, in a sordid room near the top of a perpetual house of horrors.

'Will you protect the Shepherd when I've gone?' asked Cain. 'I came back to tell, but I came back to ask this also.'

'Where are you going?'

'Back to the Land of Nod.'

'You don't have to go.'

'I've cast off my mask before you and I have settled the score. Listen!' he whispered. The window frame rattled. 'Look!' The waxing moon, more than half full but obscured by a band of darkness to the east. 'Words?' He touched his head. 'Are seeded here.' He touched his heart and lungs. 'And are given life here.' He touched his mouth. 'And are born from here. Listen, Eve! Look! No more words. No more masks.'

He opened his mouth wide.

'No!' called Clay. 'Don't do this. I can help you.'

'Can you turn back the hands of time? Can you undo the things that were done by others when you were no more than a little girl?'

'Ask me what I can do!' demanded Clay.

'What can you do?'

'I can take the knife away from you.'

'Then do so.'

He turned the point of the knife to his mouth. She stepped towards him, felt the walls and ceiling shrink in on her, pressing life out of her. Hopelessness.

She reached out her hand. 'Cain, please, I'm begging you.' She gripped the handle of the knife. 'Let go, Cain. Give it to me. If you really want to settle the score, settle it by living.'

'They took possession of our lives from even before we were born. We were nothing. They were little gods. Are you another god? Are you in possession of me now? At the bitter end? Do you have the power to sit above all this in the last judgment?'

'I only have the power to speak, to plead with you…'

Words piled up inside her, crashed into each other and forced her into a debilitating silence. She looked into his eyes and saw agony that could never be resolved.

'I made a vow.' She tightened her grip. 'Let me go, Eve. I made a vow in blood. Let me go and find my Abel. Let me go, Eve.'

She felt her hand falling back. 'Please, Cain, please…'

'I made a blood vow.'

He held her gaze. He thrust the blade hard and high into the roof of his mouth, hands tight around the shaft. He sank to his knees, released one hand and extended his arm towards Clay. His eyes closed and he twisted on to his back.

On her knees, she held on to his head, fixed her eyes on his. 'You're not alone,' said Clay. 'In the dark.'

She watched as the spark in his eyes went out and moonlight polished his forehead.

104

7.51 pm

'I wondered if you were ever going to pick up, Eve,' said DC Barney Cole. He sounded pleased with himself.

'I wondered the same,' replied Clay, as she turned on to St Mary's Road on the way back to Trinity Road police station.

'Are you OK, Eve?'

'Ask me at some point in the indefinite future, Barney.'

There was a throb in the centre of her head that threatened to explode into a full-scale migraine. Hands on the steering wheel, she could still feel the texture of Cain Noone's hair on her fingertips and the coldness of death as he'd lain in her arms.

In the silence that followed, she felt Cole's good mood deteriorate.

'What's happened, Eve?'

'Insane talk from the 1940s in a North African desert finally came to rest in the here and now.'

She pulled up at a red light, looked at the cranes of Garston Docks on the skyline and wished she wasn't there.

'What's happening, Barney?'

'Two pieces of news. Good or gooder?'

'The best you can possibly come up with.'

'Karl Stone's conscious. He's had a scan and there's no major damage. A burst blood vessel in his ear and a heavy dose of concussion.'

A layer of dead weight lifted from her.

'Get this. The symbol on the spear's shaft. I've think cracked it.'

'Go on.'

'I made a list of the names of all the relevant people, past and present, and crunched them down into their initials, name and surname. Using angular writing, no curves, the combining of the initials of two people resulted in only one possibility. It was a joint signature on a gruesome work of art.'

She pulled away as the light turned green, considered what Cole had said.

'Did you get LL and CN, Louise Lawson and Cain Noone?'

'How did you know?'

The lines forming in her mind distracted her from the sadness that threatened to overwhelm her. She glanced up at the waxing moon, at the shadow that masked its full face. 'Your four largest lines, two 3-centimetre lines and two 2-centimetre lines form LL, the initials of Louise Lawson,' said Cole.

'How do you get CN?' asked Clay

'The five 1-centimetre lines. two form an angular C and three form a standard N. Cain Noone.'

'Louise Lawson and Cain Noone locked in an eternal bond. They masked it well. They were stating the obvious and we were all blind to that. Thank you for seeing that, Barney. Send it to my phone.'

She closed the call down and within seconds heard the text arrive. She slowed down at a red light and opened it.

The taller letters of Louise Lawson's initials contrasted with the smaller initials of Cain Noone. In Clay's mind, the Letters LL and CN blurred into an image. A shepherd guiding her charge onwards and onwards...

105

8.04 pm

Clay looked through the observation hole of Cell 4 and watched Louise Lawson sitting perfectly still, spine straight, on the edge of the bed.

At Clay's back, Sergeant Harris said, 'She's been like this since I put her in the cell. She hasn't moved. She hasn't touched the food and drink we've provided for her.'

'And she hasn't spoken?'

'She talked to me when you left, Eve,' said Riley.

Clay let the down the eyehole cover and turned to Sergeant Harris. 'Open the door, please.'

Louise didn't react, didn't seem to see or hear as Clay and Riley entered the cell.

'Bring me a chair, please, Sergeant Harris,' said Clay.

'Louise?' said Riley. 'Do you want to tell DCI Clay what you told me or do you want me to tell her?'

Louise looked up at Clay. 'Has he gone, my stolen child?'

Riley sat down next to Louise.

'He loves you. He told me that,' replied Clay. 'Before he left.'

Harris placed a plain plastic seat behind Clay. She sat down and, at eye level with Louise, spoke softly. 'Please look at me. No more masks.'

Their eyes locked.

Riley spoke. 'When Cain and Abel were thirteen years of

age, Louise heard a sound that she hadn't heard before. She heard the sound of Professor Noone weeping. He was alone in the kitchen. Louise walked in and asked him...'

'*Why are you weeping?*' Louise took up the story. 'I knew the answer because I'd watched him day by day, as weeks turned into months and months into years. I watched the truth sink in. He resisted the truth with his whole being, but the truth was bigger than he was and stronger and better. At first he wouldn't speak, wouldn't take his hands away from his face. After many minutes, he told me to get away and, on a night of firsts, I did something I hadn't done before. I defied him. I said, *Make me. Make me go away.*

And I said, *You know, Damien, I don't want to bring you any more bad news at a time like this, when you have finally realised that the dream of your lifetime has been an unmitigated failure. But I don't want you living in ignorance either, because ignorance isn't bliss, Damien, ignorance is purely ignorance and who wants to live in the dark when the world is so full of light and colour? I watched the news on television, Damien, and a child has gone missing from the town of Douglas on the Isle of Man. They're looking in the place where you left the children you murdered, from the first English Experiment all those years ago. I wonder what would happen if... The largest search for a missing child in the island's history is underway... I wonder... I wonder...*'

Clay noted the steady motion of Louise's mouth as she spoke and the voice that poured from her was full of the strength and energy of a woman half her age.

'I left him in the darkness and left the darkness to do the rest of the work for me. When morning came, he hadn't slept at all. But he was his usual self, cold, distant, silent but anxious now, very, very anxious.

'In the morning, he told me that *we* were going to the Isle of Man. That *we* were going to reclaim the skeletons of the infants from the original English Experiment. That *we* were going to

bring them back and bury them in the wild seclusion of the garden of 777 Croxteth Road.

'My father was left in charge of the house and the boys and
by lunchtime Noone and I were on our way to the Isle of Man.
We walked for miles without a word and then he stopped. There
was nothing, no one in sight. It didn't look like a cave. It was
more of a crack in the grassy rock with a large stone covering it.'

Louise took a deep, slow breath.

'I found strength I never knew I had and I moved that stone
enough so I could squeeze inside, into the darkness. He followed
me in. *They're on a high ledge*, he said. *You'll have to climb up
to reach them*. Those were his last words. I hit him with that
same newfound strength. He dropped to the ground, unconscious, but he wasn't dead. He was breathing and had a pulse.
I left the cave, moved the stone back and packed the crack with
smaller stones, completely concealing the entrance. It was as
easy as drawing a curtain for me.'

There was a lightness about Louise, a dead weight rising from
her shoulders.

'When I came home, it was to a house in chaos. Cain had
rebelled against my father, had attacked him, sending him flee-
ing from the house. But not before my father had managed to
burn all the years of evidence. All that remained was a picture
of the boys when they were perfectly healthy babies. And two
teenage children, one of them damaged by design.

'That night, we all went to bed, Cain and Abel and I, but not
as normal. Cain insisted on sleeping with his brother in the big
double bed that their father had no further use for, in the room
next door to mine. I woke up in the early hours. I went next
door and Cain was standing over Abel, who was lying perfectly
still in the bed. Cain had a pillow in his hand. *I cannot bear his
suffering*. He lay down next to his dead brother. *I cannot bear
my own suffering*.

'I took Cain's hand. *Leave your brother for now. And leave
behind your thoughts of death. Come with me*. He lay in my

bed and we started talking. And talking. And talking. And I taught him what the world outside was like. And we talked. For hours and days and weeks and months until he finally said that he wanted to live. And that is exactly what happened. I explained what had happened. And I prepared him for the real world. I would follow him at a distance as he went into shops. I would travel on the bus in a different seat to him. I would watch him cross the road. For years. And years and year and years. I gave him the skills he needed to survive in the real world.

'One day, shortly after Cain had turned twenty, I returned to the house and he was gone. The only thing he left was a piece of paper on which he'd written a handful of words. *To my loving Shepherd. Do not come looking for your sheep, for your sheep is not lost but roaming. Do not leave your father. Guard the monster. I will return, I swear, and we will settle this score and silence that voice forever.* The only things he took with him were his brother's bones. After many, many years of waiting, I thought he has gone forever and would never return. But he did. Just over a year ago. The sheep returned to his Shepherd...'

Clay waited and saw light playing out in Louise's eyes.

'What happened?' asked Clay. 'In between Cain leaving and coming back?'

Louise fell silent. A shadow passed over her as memory possessed her. Se looked at Clay, took a deep breath.

'He's left you, hasn't he? These were the first words that poured from my father's mouth when he found me weeping in my room. He stood in the doorway of my bedroom with that horrible smile on his face. He saw I was broken. He saw I was weak. He saw the lost child in me returned and he seized on it like a wild beast on injured prey. *He's left you, hasn't he? Cain, your beloved friend, the son you never had.* In all the years I'd never seen him look as happy. *He left you because he didn't love you. He left you because he could never love you. He left you because you are beyond love. No one could love you. How absurd. You? To be loved?* He walked towards me. I was sitting

on my bed. I closed my eyes to try and block him out. *Open your eyes, you miserable specimen. Nobody could ever love you. Not me. Not your mother. Not Cain. You're worthless, Louise. A dried-up nonentity. Food, air and water are wasted on you. You're a parasite. Cain could see that because he was educated to understand such things, educated by me to know what was the truth of human nature. And he understood you, your insignificance, your weak intellect, the ugliness that surrounds you. You are mourning a man who despised you from the roots of his hair to the tips of his toes.* He opened my lips and pressed my tongue down hard to the base of my mouth with his fingers. He said, *Silence! We're going back to basics. We're going back to the good old days. Silence! Speak when you're spoken to. When I speak you listen. And when I tell you what to do, you do it with a glad heart because I am the only thing you have in this world and even though it's my misfortune to be your father, I am going to tolerate you and keep you where you belong, in your place. Do you know where your place is? On your knees before me in gratitude for the life I gave you. You will stay in your room until I tell you to leave. You will clean the house from top to bottom and cook my food to my satisfaction when I tell you. And if you even think of leaving I will know immediately what is going on in your mind because you are an open book to me, a dull and tiresome open book. If you even think of leaving I will expose all our secrets and you will become that worst of all possible things in other people's eyes. The woman capable of the most dreadful cruelty to innocent children. It was all your idea. You lulled me into The English Experiment. Didn't you? Didn't you?* he screamed in my face.

'*Yes, Father, I am the worst of all imaginable daughters. I am the most cruel and unnatural woman of all kinds.*

'*And don't you deserve to be punished for that?* He picked me up by the hair and marched me into his bedroom, made me sit on the bottom end of his bed and told me to look at the picture of the Tower of Babel. *Look at it! Look at it! Look at it and think about Damien Noone. What did you do to make him go away from me?*

'For the hundred thousandth time I told him, *One minute he was there, the next he was gone. As with all things, Father, here now, gone in the twinkling of an eye.*

'He stuck his hands either side of my face and shunted my head up. *Look at the Tower of Babel in complete silence. Stay there, stay right there and do not move, do not close your eyes, look, look at the picture and stay right where you are.* It was light when he closed the door on his way out. When he returned and opened the door it was dark, night. He didn't switch on the light, he just commanded me, *Go to your room. Go to bed. Do not leave the room until I tell you.* I walked through the darkness to the door. He blocked me. *Before you go to your room, tell me, what are you?*

'I replied, *I am nothing.*

'*Nothing?* He was in between amusement and anger. *Nothing?* He slapped my face. *Nothing?*

'My face was filled with fire and my eyes with tears. *I am less than nothing.*

'*Correct. You are less than nothing. Go!*

'Day in, day out. Week in, week out. Month in, month out, the same treatment, but I hung on to Cain's words. I would not leave my father alone. I would guard the monster because one day Cain would return and we would settle the score and silence that hideous voice forever. And as the years went by, Father grew slowly weaker, older, subject to all manner of infections and the sickness at the core of his being. His epileptic fits. It was a rare joy to behold him frothing at the mouth and twitching wildly when he was subject to a fit. One day he fell into a fit at the top of the stairs and fell all the way down and had to go to hospital. He was in for nearly two weeks. While he was in hospital, I went for a walk around the park, just like he did every day, just as he had forbidden me from doing. I walked and came to The Sanctuary and I saw the disabled men coming and going so

I knew where they lived. And I carried on walking and I found a man wandering. Tom Thumb. He was distressed and I said, *Do you want me to take you home?* He slipped his hand into mine and I walked with him back to The Sanctuary. I rang on the bell and Danielle answered the door. *I have brought him home to you.* She was grateful to me. She thanked me, said I was an angel and asked me in for tea.'

Tears rolled down her face.

'For the first time since Cain had left, I was valued, for the first time in years, I was shown kindness. It gave me a strength I hadn't known since the days that I spent with Cain. *Can I come and work here for a few days? I don't want money. I just want to help.* She accepted my offer immediately and the next few days, while Father was still in hospital, were so, so happy. I knew the day would come when he would return and I would have to stop seeing my friends – my friends – but I lived in those moments as if they were the last ones I would ever have.

'He came home, was bedbound with his injuries. A broken leg. Broken ribs. A damaged hip. I took him his lunch. It was almost at the time of day when I left the house for The Sanctuary. I stood in the doorway of his room with the tray in my hands and the words just came out. *I've got a job.*

'*Don't be absurd. Who'd employ a useless bitch like you?*

'*I'm going there right now.* I turned my back and walked away.

'*Bring me my food!*

'I turned. *I work in The Sanctuary. It's the home for...*

'*I know what it is, it's the asylum on the park, I walk past it several times a day, you idiot!*

'*I've been going there while you've been in hospital. They're expecting me. They know where I live. Wouldn't it be awful if they came to the door and asked where I was and why I wasn't in work and was I all right and I might just say,* No I'm not all right, not at all. My father keeps me as a prisoner in his house.

'Oh no, no, that is not right, that is against the law, *they may say.*

'*I have made friends, Father, and I have something to say to you. I am going to keep going to The Sanctuary every day for a few hours. I am going there now!*

'He was outraged but couldn't get out of bed to violate or control me. *If you want me to feed you tonight, Father, you will not tell me to not go there. I am going to go every day and you will not stop me. This is the only thing I ask. This is the only change I demand. When I am here, in your house, I will do exactly as you say when you say it, but I will go to The Sanctuary and you will not stop me. Do you want your lunch, Father?* I placed the tray on his lap and stood at the bottom of his bed. *I am too old to care if you expose me with your lies about that vile experiment. Do you want to eat tonight?*

'He couldn't look at me. He nodded. *I will beat you as soon as I am able.*

'*You have beaten me enough and often for years. That is no longer a punishment. That is a bad habit of yours. You cannot hurt me any more.*

'Bit by bit, day by day, his spirit weakened, and instead of terrorising me, he ignored me. I did everything for him, cooking, cleaning, caring for him. But he stopped ordering me into my room, stopped making me look at those revolting paintings, stopped his violence. Slowly, he gave up his campaign against me. And we lived in virtual silence and complete contempt.'

She smiled.

'And then Cain returned. And I was filled with the joy of a mother whose lost son had returned and the strength of a lion. Cain who loved me and was loved by me. Cain,' she whispered.

Louise looked at Clay. There was a deep silence before Louise asked, 'Did you find him, Cain Noone?'

'No. He found me,' replied Clay. 'He found me.'

'He's gone to join Abel, hasn't he? I was in the room with him when he was thirteen and I used words to stop him killing himself. What did you do, Eve?'

'I listened and he told me everything.'

'Did you let him go? Did you let him join his silent half, his other half?' Louise smiled and Clay was filled with the sadness of many lifetimes. The old woman looked deeply into Clay's eyes. 'I can see. It's marked you, Eve. You look different. The mark of Cain. He told you everything?'

'Yes, Louise, everything.'

'In which case, that is all.' A look of pure relief swept over Louise and she spoke softly. 'There is no more need for words.'

Epilogue

Friday, 21st December 2018

At the Nativity scene in the Catholic Cathedral, Eve Clay picked up her son Philip and watched his face closely as he looked at the plaster statues of Mary and Joseph with the infant Jesus. Blue light drifted down from the stained glass of the central tower.

'Mummy? Can I take the Baby Jesus home with me?' asked Philip.

Thomas laughed. 'Why do you want to do that?'

'I want a little brother.'

Thomas looked at Eve. 'Good idea, Philip!'

'We'll see,' replied Eve.

He wriggled in her arms. As she put him down, she looked across to the central altar under the glass tower. She reached inside her pocket and touched the edges of the photographs that had been sent to her care of Thomas's medical practice.

Close to the altar, she saw a lone figure with his back turned to her.

'Can we go to the café now? Mummy? Daddy?'

Eve felt the weight of Thomas's gaze falling on her. She looked at him, then back at the solitary man.

'We'll walk round the cathedral first,' said Thomas. 'Come on, Philip.'

She listened to their footsteps as they headed off and felt a strange mixture of loss and apprehension as she watched the still figure at the altar. She quashed the desire to turn away and instead walked down the aisle towards him, her eyes pinned on his back.

His hair was short and white. When she was five pews away, she was pulled up by the sight of a hand-rolled cigarette behind his ear.

'Hello, Eve.' He didn't turn, but she recognised his voice. 'We meet again after so many years.'

'Father Murphy?'

He looked back over his shoulder, a much older version of the tough priest she'd met more than three decades earlier in Mrs Tripp's office. He smiled at her and shifted up the pew a little.

'Mrs Tripp told me that she'd read an article in *Reader's Digest* about childhood psychiatric disorders. That's why she called me in to have a look at you.'

'You stood up for me, Father Murphy. I thank you for that.'

He took the cigarette from behind his ear, examined it. 'No matter.' He placed it back and said, 'I was impressed by you that day. You were quite a plucky girl. Who grew up to be a rather plucky woman. I confess, Eve, I've followed your progress with great interest.' He paused. 'You've seen a lot of it, so you must believe in it.'

'Evil?'

He nodded, drank her in with smiling eyes.

'Thank you for coming to see me today. I understand you've been rather busy.'

She showed him the photographs. 'No. Thank *you*. I can't tell you how much they mean to me.'

'I want to give you something that I hope will give you comfort as you continue to fight the forces of evil. Do you remember asking me if I knew Sister Philomena? And I told you truthfully that I hadn't met her. I was so sorry for the disappointment this caused you, so I took it upon myself in the 1980s to try and make amends. You remember Sister Veronica?'

'Of course.' A small young Irish nun with a huge smile; Sister

Philomena's deputy at St Claire's, the home Eve had grown up in until she was six. 'Within days of Sister Philomena's funeral, she was sent to Uganda to take charge of an orphanage there. Which is why she was never able to fulfil her promise to Philomena at her deathbed.'

Father Murphy reached inside his coat pocket and produced an envelope with Sister Veronica's handwriting across the front panel. Eve felt weightless as she recognised the writing, a direct physical link to her childhood, and saw the Ugandan stamp in the top right-hand corner.

'It's addressed to me, but the letter's really for you, Eve.'

He handed her the envelope and, for a moment, she felt paralysed.

'I wrote and asked Sister Veronica what happened, what was said at Sister Philomena's deathbed about *you*.'

Eve took the letter from inside the envelope and turned over the folds, her fingertips prickling, her heart pounding.

The letter was dated 6th January 1986.

Dear Father Murphy...

Eve heard her own voice as she read the letter silently, tripping up and skipping back over the three words of greeting, over and over. Silence. Eve forced herself on into the body of the letter and as soon as she read, Sister Veronica's voice took over. It was as if she was sitting next to her, whispering.

I was with Sister Philomena during the final hours of her life, praying with and for her. And though I rejoiced that my friend and mentor would soon be joining the saints in the joys of heaven, my heart was filled with sorrow as I knew these would be my last moments on earth with her and that we had a shared anxiety. What would happen to Evette Clay after Sister Philomena's death when, surely, St Claire's would be closed down for good.

Eve was thrown back into the chapel at St Claire's, looking at Philomena in her coffin and quietly begging the statue of Christ on the cross above them to open her eyes and let her lips smile just one last time.

> Right at the end, in the last few minutes, I can recall Sister Philomena's words perfectly on the subject of her beloved Eve and what she wanted me to do for her.
> She drifted in and out of wakefulness, but as soon as she became conscious, Philomena talked of nothing but Evette. She said, 'Wait until Eve is old enough to fully understand and, when she reaches this maturity, be sure to tell her this. Nothing in her life has been accidental. Her battles in this world are ones for which she has been chosen because of the strength of her spirit. The rewards she has come into on this earth, the love she has found and made, are her just deserts for the courage and selflessness that she displays as a matter of course.
> 'Wherever she has to go, whatever demons she has to confront – and they will be legion – she must know that I will be behind her every step of the way. When she feels most alone, at her most afraid, I will be praying for her and the ones she loves.
> 'Tell her this, for now and always. She was loved and valued to the heights of heaven, she is loved and valued to the heights of heaven and she will be loved and valued to the heights of heaven forever, if only by a poor soul such as me.'
> At this point, Sister Philomena died.

There were more words on the page, but Eve saw only marks on paper.

She looked up and realised that she was alone in the pew. Over her shoulder, she saw Thomas and Philip with Father Murphy, talking near the exit to the cathedral. Father Murphy held up an arm. Farewell. He walked away. As Eve stood up, Thomas came down the aisle towards her, Philip in his arms.

Many questions ran through her mind, but a single question
for Father Murphy dominated her thoughts.

She took Philip from Thomas, held on to him with all her
strength and felt Thomas's arms enfolding her.

'Why did he wait so long to show me the letter? He could
have found me sooner. What did he say?'

'He didn't say much,' said Thomas. 'He said, *Tell Eve I
was following the instructions that Philomena gave out as
she was dying. I was waiting for her to reach the point where
she fully understood.*'

A stream of blue light passed over them. Eve looked at her
husband and son, understanding completely Philomena's uncon-
ditional love for her. It allowed her to keep that love alive and
pass it on to Thomas and Philip. She held on to both of them,
seizing the moment of complete and selfless love, the treasures
of her heart and soul.

Acknowledgements

I'd like to thank Peter, Rosie and Jessica Buckman, Dr Steve Le Comber, Dr Catherine Molyneux, Jagjeeth Naik, Laura Palmer and all at Head of Zeus, Lucy Ridout, Linda and Eleanor Roberts, James Roberts, Frank and Ben Rooney, and Luke Sullivan.